GHOST OF A CHANCE

Jude Forrest

ISBN-13: 9798692300249
ISBN-10: 1477123456

Cover design by: @john_w_wood
Library of Congress Control Number: 2018675309
Printed in the United States of America

For John

GHOST OF A CHANCE

August 1993

This is not the kind of place Connor frequents. It looks unassuming from the outside: ye olde stonework and cursive promises. All-day breakfast on a Sunday and live music three nights a week. Tonight is late opening, disco night. Happy hour has done its worst and the place is in full swing. Before he even crosses the threshold Connor can sense the testosterone, hear the local boys building up to a rowdy night's machismo. He runs his fingers through his hair, roughs it up a bit, brushing out the spray, then passes his hand across his chin, glad he decided to skip the shave. He has dressed down for the occasion, but still he feels self-conscious. Wary. With luck he will pass off as shy. First time for everything.

The place is heaving. What takes him by surprise is the age range. Busty middle-aged women with too much on show cackling around the tables, their men sweating under leather jackets at the fruit machine or sending up smoke signals from a corner of the bar while the young folk hold the floor. The disco has not started yet. There is music but it cannot compete with the roar of voices. Laughter that rolls round the room like a Mexican wave. Small outbursts that come in gusts – just jokes or the acting out of a narrative but the suddenness of it, the aggression in it makes Connor's nerves tingle.

He makes his way to the bar, eyes scanning the groups of young men. By the look of some of them he guesses the landlord takes a flexible approach to the legal drinking age. Maybe that goes with the territory: the village vibe; the assorted clientele that make it feel like an auntie's wedding party or a works outing. The beautiful boy told him he was nineteen. Connor shakes off the whisper of a doubt.

There he is. A bit further along the bar, that sullen friend of his both hanging back and hanging on. The boy looks confident, waiting his turn to be served, keeping up a bullet-point conversation with his friend while he tries to catch the barmaid's eye, but Connor can see how his hand jiggles restlessly in his pocket, how he watches the other lads and the way they thrust their tenners forward in a bid to be served next. He is too polite or too unsure to do the same and Connor feels a welling of something tender inside him, something protective. Ironic, really.

He catches the boy's eye, fakes a double take with a point and a look of faint surprise. 'Buy you a drink?' he asks when he gets near enough to be heard. 'What are you both having?' If they think it's weird they are too keen to get free alcohol to worry about it.

'This your local?' he asks, while they wait for their pints.

'Yeah.'

'I haven't been here before. Usually go up town, you know, but I'm supposed to be meeting a mate who's back in town for a few days. He's staying with his mum.' Something in the boy's eyes: suspicion. Relief? He'd like to think there was a hint of disappointment. Perhaps the story was too much. A bit patronising, even.

But if I'd known you'd be here, I'd have come anyway.

The words won't get past his lips. Not here. You can't say that kind of thing to someone here. Well, he can't say that kind of thing. Those fat old blokes slavering over their drinks in the corner – they can say a lot worse to any of the girls in here who are half their age.

They chat for a while. God, he's lovely, Connor thinks. Got a bit of a Brett Anderson thing going on, but with shorter hair. He has the feeling the boy would be happy to talk longer, but his mate is restless, resentful of the intrusion. Connor hands them their pints.

'Have a good night,' he says with a smile. It lets them know he doesn't expect to be bought a drink in return, and they don't owe him company either. He's banking on the boy's politeness, his sense of fairness. Even if he doesn't have the courage to talk to Connor just because he likes him. And Connor is sure that he does.

He drifts towards a corner from where he can watch

the crowd inconspicuously, but in case anyone is looking he casts a glance now and then towards the door to make out he is waiting for someone. Checks his watch from time to time.

A couple of drunk girls titter their way towards him. He lets them flirt, humours them with smiles and it serves him well because it brings the boys back to him. They have had no luck on their own.

'Looks like I've been stood up,' he says, draining the last of his pint.

'Do you want another?' the beautiful boy asks. He turns to the girls. 'Can I get you ladies something?' He has grown more confident with the beer.

'I'll help you carry them,' Connor tells him, and they leave the boy's mate with the girls, his face a perfect blend of machismo and terror.

The lights change as they reach the bar, colours spinning over the dance floor, chinking off the optics and the mirror on the back wall. A shriek of delight goes up from a small crowd of women as the DJ gets going with Erasure's version of Take a Chance on Me and they rush onto the floor, all flap and noise, like seagulls on a spilt poke of chips. Connor can't help laughing and the boy laughs too. Their eyes meet fully and Connor is so entranced that he does not look away in time. He sees the alarm register on the boy's face and reaches out instinctively.

'It's ok.'

The boy flinches as Connor's hand touches his arm, flings it off as though he's been stung.

'Fuck off.'

The music is loud enough to drown out their words but the sudden movement attracts attention. A couple of blokes in the scrum at the bar turn to look at them. The boy is mortified. Connor holds his hands up in surrender and backs away. He can't risk a scene.

He pushes his way through the crowd and out the side door of the pub. Takes a deep breath and curses himself.

Half past nine and it's already nearly dark. The summer is drawing to a close. What a waste of a Friday night.

He could have been up town with the festival crowds, with people he could be himself with. What the hell was he thinking? He pulls a packet of cigarettes from his pocket. There's a collection of empty beer kegs by the hatch to the cellar. He folds his jacket over one and sits. It isn't even his case. Isn't even any case. He has no business poking around in it. Never mind letting his cock lead him astray. He lights up, leaning back against the wall. With the first hit of nicotine he begins to feel better. He hasn't wasted the night: it's still young. He blows smoke into the ultramarine sky. It won't take him more than forty minutes max to get into town.

The DJ is playing Haddaway now. By the end of the night it will be Whitney Houston and the voluptuous lovelies of Silverknowes and Davidson's Mains will be clamped onto their men, each trying to imagine he's Kevin Costner. In the meantime, the wet T-shirt competition.

Connor shrinks back into the shadows as the side door opens. He can't see who it is at first because they linger behind the door, then the beautiful boy steps out under the emergency exit light. He is looking the other way, up the side alley towards the main street, and he jumps when Connor speaks.

'Hiya.'

The boy turns, letting the door fall shut.

'Want one?' Connor waves his cigarette? 'Sorry about in there. Didn't mean to make you feel awkward.'

The boy hesitates. He's like a wild animal, Connor thinks. A deer. He's going to bolt in a minute.

But he doesn't. Instead he comes closer, takes the cigarette from Connor's fingers and puts it to his mouth. Takes a long draw on it. Connor feels the blood rushing to his groin. The boy offers him the cigarette back. His hand is shaking, but he doesn't take it away when Connor's fingers brush against his.

Moment of truth, Connor thinks. He stubs the cigarette out slowly, to give the boy a chance to change his mind. When he's still standing there after the last of the embers has died Connor looks at him steadily. He reaches out a

4

hand and brushes the boy's floppy fringe off his forehead. The boy tenses, but he doesn't run, and then Connor is up off the barrel, pushing him against the wall of the pub, his mouth on the boy's, his hands sliding deftly under his T-shirt. Under the nicotine and the beer the boy tastes of autumn: earth and oak and mild spice. He's hard too. Connor tugs his belt undone, flicks open the top button on his jeans. He slips his fingers beneath the boy's waistband, working them lower as he turns the boy to face the wall, pushing against him, his mouth on the boy's neck.

He is hardly aware of the footsteps until the boy twists under him. There is a burst of laughter and expletives behind them and the boy is frantic now, pushing Connor away.

'Oh no. Oh Jesus. Fuck. Get off me.'

There are two of them. Young lads by the sound of it. Standing at the entrance to the alleyway. Just shadows against the streetlight until one of them reels back laughing as the beautiful boy rushes past them and Connor glimpses the lad's face under the light of the pub sign.

Oh, no.

No.

He thinks he hears the lad say, 'Perfect,' and Connor feels a cold dread wash through him.

He's sizing up his options – can he get out round the back of the pub or is it a dead end? He's not much of a fighter – when something spooks the lads. There is a moment of confusion between them before they take off towards the bottom end of the high street. Connor understands why when he sees the blue light reflect off the window panes and the whitewashed brickwork of the shop across the road. He presses himself into the shadows. There's a solitary whoop of a siren, a warning, nothing more, and the panda car slides past the alleyway in lazy pursuit of the boys.

Connor barely registers relief before the panic returns. They recognised him. He sees the job, the future he's worked so hard for slipping away from him. Christ, he'll be lucky if he stays out of jail if they report him. He admits to himself what he has always really known, that the boy is not the age he claimed to be. He's barely eighteen. If that. And it wouldn't matter anyway. Nineteen, twenty, it's still illegal. Fuck.

He is shivering now; he has to move. He hesitates at the top of the lane, then chooses the direction the lads took. There is no sign of them but he spots the police car, paused at a junction further up Main Street. He turns off quickly, onto the road he knows will lead him to the main route back into the city centre, then ducks into the relative shelter of a bus stop.

He perches on the narrow bench fixed to the back of the shelter. Shifts his position. Stands again. He has to think. What to do. Maybe they didn't see him clearly. Not to identify anyway? Maybe it was just the boy. They know him too, after all. Connor could get lucky. Yes, it might be alright.

The minutes pass. The streets are quiet. Everyone around here with a pulse is in that pub. The rest at home with whatever passes for Friday night entertainment on the television these days. Connor drums his fingers against his thighs. Where is the fucking bus? It's too early in the evening for cabs to be dropping folk home out here, looking for a return fare, but he's desperate to get back into the city centre where he can blend in, be anonymous.

His ears strain to the sound of something approaching. Then his pulse quickens. It's the police car, the light off now, slowly taking the corner from the high street. Connor settles back on the bench as it comes towards him, quiets his restless feet, bows his head to look at his watch, then pat his pockets. Stop it! He's seen enough guilty people to know what he looks like.

It seems to take an age to pass. He senses, rather than sees, the heads turning to scrutinise him. Wills himself to keep still until they have reached the top of the road and the tip of the roof light has disappeared over the crest.

He waits again. The minutes pass.

Then suddenly he can stay still no longer. He pushes himself off the bench and sets off up the street at a pace. He can zigzag from here up to the big junction on the

Queensferry Road. There will be cabs passing there.

He walks fast, cursing himself, those lads, the law. Just cursing. But the police car passed him by, he thinks. And after all, those boys, they clearly have something to hide. They didn't want the cops to spot them. If they reported him they would have to admit to being there, and then they would have to own up to whatever else they had just been doing.

Yes, it might be alright. And if they did later make an accusation, it would be their word against his. The beautiful boy wasn't going to say anything and no-one else saw them. Who are people more likely to believe? Plus, he thinks, if it comes to it, he can explain how he has come to their attention and why he might have pissed them off. He's not really ready but if he has to he can give very good reasons for why they might want to get him into trouble and out of their hair.

Yes. Everything is going to be fine. He will go up town, just like any normal Friday night. Act as if nothing has happened.

He doesn't hear the footsteps. Not even as they hasten towards him. At the bend in the road he is so engrossed in his thoughts that he follows the hedge round before he realises he has strayed into a cul de sac. He turns abruptly and walks straight into the figure turning the corner behind him. He doesn't feel the knife go in – only the dull thud of impact as their bodies collide. He almost apologises. It's only when the knife twists that he realises what has happened. When it is retracted and thrust into him a second time. And when he sees the look of triumph and disgust on his assailant's face.

1
2019

Detective Sergeant Ellen Chisholm was having the kind of day she hated. Stuck in the office, she had a million and one things to do and not one of them a greater priority than the others. She began one task, her thoughts drifted towards another, she lost interest in both. And round it went. It wasn't that she longed for something to happen. She hadn't sunk that low yet. She just needed some focus. She looked over at her boss, Detective Inspector Dan Calder and instantly hated herself for it. Hated the fact that she couldn't expel the static from her own head, that she had, even momentarily, looked to an external source of authority to give her clarity of purpose. To tell her what to do. Not that Calder would have been much help, by the look of him. He was bent over a file on his desk, one hand holding the cover open, the other poised over the keyboard of his computer, but nothing was happening. He was miles away. Probably half way up some ruddy hill with nothing to aid his survival but a handful of twigs and a handkerchief. In other words, he was in exactly the same boat she was. Bored.

'Call for you, DS Chisholm.'

Had she been better occupied Ellen might have given James Barber a gentle brush off now, but today she was only too glad to find a different excuse for getting nothing done.

'Ellen, could we talk? Not on the phone. In person.' He upped the offer of a coffee with a chocolate brownie but even so, even in the mood she was in, Ellen wanted a little more to go on.

'It's about a murder. That's really all I want to say at this stage,' Barber told her.

She was interested now, but still she hesitated. Something in Barber's tone. His need to draw her out of the office. The implied urgency. It didn't feel right. It felt like a crazy person. It felt like being led astray. Like a trap. Ellen looked at the pile of nothing she had achieved so far that morning. Then at Detective Inspector Dan Calder. He was watching her now. Hopefully.

'Alright, then. Tell me where.'

*

'So he's something of a mentor?' Calder said as they got into the car.

'I only worked with him once.'

It had been her first taste of detective work, though. Her first murder. A mucky little killing over money owed, though they had not known that at first. Ellen had been drafted in to support a small, overstretched team. It hadn't taken them long to narrow down the suspects but faced with a blank refusal to co-operate from all involved it had taken them time and persistent, methodical policing-by-numbers to chip away until the truth emerged. Barber had been suited to the task and he had led by example. It was his own willingness to plough through minutiae that had kept the team focused. She remembered his unfailing politeness and courtesy, even in the face of a suspect who swore and spat at him, who folded his arms and hummed while spoken to, who drummed his hands on the table to drown out the questions being put to him.

'But you've kept in touch since then?'

'A bit.' She tried to think of when she had last seen or spoken to Barber. It had to be a good three years at least. Before Calder arrived anyway. Somebody's retirement do. Surely not Barber's own? She found she was looking forward to seeing him with a mixture of pleasure and guilt. She owed Jimmy Barber.

He had directed her to a small café in Blackhall, part of a short run of shops on the busy Queensferry Road. The place was quiet at this time on a weekday but all the same Barber had chosen a small table in a discreet corner. The tinkle of classical music from the speaker above his head and the traffic on the road outside gave them cover to talk easily.

'So, how have you been?' Ellen asked, while Calder ordered their coffees at the counter. Barber looked as composed as ever. He was a neat man with trimmed hair, white now, and dapper in a man-of-leisure kind of way, in a checked shirt and maroon pullover, a tweed jacket hanging over the back of his chair. He looked as though retirement suited him, Ellen thought: good colour in his cheeks, still fit, still curious. He didn't look as though he'd lost the plot. He looked – settled. She wondered whether he had already been there when he made the call to Ellen. Waiting, expectantly.

She saw that he was doing the same: assessing the changes time had wrought on her. Ellen had never been vain but it made her self-conscious. She was physically fit and to date she'd only found one strand of grey in her chestnut hair but she knew there were faint crows' feet at the corners of her eyes. She had tried using make-up to cover the dark patches underneath them but it only seemed to make them more obvious and she hated wearing foundation, not least because the woman at the counter in John Lewis had assumed she must want to cover her freckles. She made an effort to un-frown. She didn't want Barber to think she wasn't coping.

'I didn't expect you to bring back-up,' he said, jerking his head in Calder's direction.

She had been afraid that was what it would look like when Calder invited himself along. It didn't help that he carried himself like a bodyguard; under that tailored suit his joints just loose enough, muscles taut enough to spring into action. He had the haircut too – just a notch off a buzz cut. All he needed was the shades and that curly wire they always used in the films to tell you someone was CIA. There had been enough of the desperate puppy in his rust-brown eyes that she'd caved, though. That, and the power he had to delegate more paperwork. Anyway, she wasn't going to apologise to Barber. Wasn't going to make excuses.

'Murder, you said.'

'Slow day at the office?' A tiny smile lifted the corner of Barber's mouth, and she allowed herself one in return.

'All very mysterious,' Calder said, joining them at the table.

Barber took a moment to answer, sizing Calder up shrewdly before turning back to Ellen. 'I didn't want you to palm me off until you'd heard what I have to say.'

'Are we going to palm you off?' Ellen asked.

'Everyone else has,' Barber said.

'A murder you said. Why would people not take that seriously?'

Unless – no body? Or it hadn't happened yet? Surely their colleagues would only dismiss a man's claims of murder if it seemed that none had taken place.

'Does the name Connor Leask ring any bells?' Barber asked.

Ellen shook her head. She looked at Calder. He was frowning.

'I don't remember the details. He was a trainee procurator fiscal, is that right? Mugged. Battered?'

'Stabbed.'

'I was still at school. It was a long time ago.'

'Friday, the twentieth of August, 1993. We never caught the man responsible.'

We. Ellen's heart sank. 'It's a cold case.'

She saw Barber's eyes glaze faintly with disappointment.

'Why come to me?' she asked. 'Why not go to the cold case bods? Oh. You did.'

Barber looked away. 'You know how it goes. They want a reason, new evidence.'

'And you don't have any?' Calder said. 'Then we're even less likely to be able to help. We deal with fresh corpses.'

Ellen felt bad for that. It was unnecessary. Insensitive. Not just to Barber.

'One of the suspects tried to contact me two weeks ago.' He looked for the glimmer of interest or speculation in each of their eyes and got what he wanted. He leaned forward. 'Ronald Gilchrist. He was a person of interest along with two of his sons, Alistair and Malcolm. The message took a while to reach me. Eventually they passed it on to one of my old colleagues.' He turned to Ellen. 'Vihaan Shah? You'll remember him. Gilchrist said he wanted to talk to me.'

'About Connor Leask's murder?'

'I can't think why else. But I haven't managed to speak to him. He was admitted to hospital last week. I've tried to see him but his family won't let me.'

'Why's he in hospital?'

'Pancreatic cancer, they said.'

To her shame, Ellen was disappointed. 'Nothing suspicious then.'

'So, this is just about Leask,' Calder said.

'Not just Leask.' Barber twitched with annoyance. He hadn't liked Calder saying that. Hadn't liked Connor Leask being dismissed in that way. 'Why else would he try to contact me? And I only have their word for it that it's cancer and no other reason he's been rushed into hospital. It seems a bit of a coincidence.'

Calder sighed. Audibly. 'Not necessarily. Perhaps he wanted to make a deathbed confession? What do you want us to do about it?'

Barber turned back to Ellen. He was speaking fast now, trying to get it all out before they left. 'The thing is, I wondered whether you could make contact. Make it seem routine.'

She looked at him, incredulous. 'You are joking, aren't you?'

'No. No, I'm not. If you're right and he's dying, even of natural causes, then time is running out, don't you see? He wants to tell me something. Maybe he has evidence to give me. But I can't approach them again.'

Ellen swore inwardly. They were talking to a madman. The job had made him mad. She was annoyed with him, suddenly. She felt let down.

'He can't give you anything, Jimmy. You're retired. And I'm not Jessica bloody Fletcher. Do you have anything we could go on?' She knew he didn't. If he had, he'd have asked Vihaan Shah to look into it and Vihaan would have done it, too. She remembered him well: a shy, quietly spoken man with an exacting sense of justice. Unswervingly loyal to Barber.

She wished she hadn't brought DI Calder with her.

'I'm sorry, Jimmy.' She drained her mug and reached for her jacket, but she hesitated, watching the mask come down on Barber's face. As Calder got to his feet and went to the counter to pay for their coffees she leaned across and put her hand on Barber's arm.

'Really, Jimmy. I don't know how it must be to have this nagging at you, but I don't see how I can help. Try Cold Cases again. It might be enough that Gilchrist seems to be offering you something.'

'Well, thank you for your time. I'm sorry to have troubled you.' Barber was bitterly disappointed, Ellen could tell. She pulled on her jacket, then paused again. Behind the disappointment there was something else in Jimmy Barber's expression, something harder, hungrier.

'It's not just that they palmed you off, is it? You want to finish this yourself, don't you? What were you thinking? That we could work together, off the books?'

Barber did not reply.

'Don't do anything stupid,' Ellen said, and left.

*

'The one that got away,' Calder said as they pulled out into the traffic. 'Bit of a cliché, isn't it? When I leave, I tell you, I'm gone. That'll be that. No looking back. Clean break.'

Oddly enough, Ellen thought, she believed him. She imagined he could walk away tomorrow without so much as a backward glance. He would find something else to occupy his mind and his time, and he would not waste any of it picking over unsolved cases like Jimmy Barber. She wasn't sure she could say the same for herself. Despite everything there was something about Calder's attitude she found unsettling. She had reasons of her own for wanting to be able to draw a line under things sometimes, move on. Reasons to be glad when people left well alone. All the same, the fervent, almost childlike desire for justice still lurked within her and she couldn't imagine wilfully walking away from an unfinished case. Not without qualms, not without a lingering sense of disquiet.

'He was dogged, you know? Didn't give up on things. Didn't mind how long it took or how tedious it was.' She frowned, thinking about her last exchange with Barber. 'I don't understand why he came to me. He'd have wanted justice done but he played by the rules. He wasn't one of those territorial cops, chalking up results for his own glory.'

She wished she hadn't said what she had to Barber.

'Well, for some reason he was reluctant to go to Cold Cases,' Calder said. 'You realise he never actually said he'd contacted them? That all came from you. Maybe there's a reason he doesn't want the investigation itself looked into too closely?'

'No.' Ellen was adamant. 'Jimmy's a good guy. He always had – integrity, you know?'

She was sure of that. She had to be. Because it was more than an example Barber had set her. He had made the difference between her being here now and – she didn't like to think where. Firm, patient, down to earth, Barber had not only taken the time to give instruction and to encourage her development as a detective, he had made sure she sorted herself out.

It wasn't just that she had needed to learn to keep her own counsel, forgo that one last drink in the pub after work, share fewer details of the nights before and her opinions on everything. It ran deeper than that.

It came like a dressing down. Called into Barber's office, it felt at the time as though she was being disciplined. She had flushed with indignant fury, her whole body tensed, ready to put up a fight. She opened her mouth to argue but Barber got in before her. 'That,' he had said, pointing first at her clenched fists, then moving the accusatory finger up and down to take in all of her. 'That's what I'm talking about. That's what's going to get you into trouble.'

She knew he was right. It didn't make it any easier to take.

Barber had scribbled a name and phone number on a post-it note and handed it to her. 'It's not official,' he said. 'Not at this stage. Think of it as a preventative measure. But do it.'

He waited until the colour left her face and returned to her knuckles. Then he sent her back to her desk.

Be more Barber. When she finally accepted that he had been right, this had become her private mantra. Together with the techniques taught by the counsellor he had put her in touch with, it had kept her straight.

Calder was right, she supposed. Barber had been a kind of mentor to her. She suddenly realised how little and how poorly she had thanked him, how much she had taken for granted.

She had just given him the brush off.

'Why would he even come to me? Why would he want to look into it at all if he had something to hide?' she said.

'Fair point.'

There was something about Barber, though, she thought. It was not tangible enough to mention. Not – evidential. She tried to remember what it was. She knew that whilst he mucked in with them he didn't give much of himself away. He had always seemed reserved, held a bit of himself back. Not unlike Dan Calder, now she came to think of it. With Barber, though, there was something else. What was it that someone had said to her to make her think there was a reason he kept himself so guarded? A reason he seemed to understand her so well? The need to watch her back.

It wasn't worth giving any weight to it now, not unless she had something more concrete to go on.

'So you don't think there's anything in it?' she asked, as they climbed the stairs to the office.

Calder arched an eyebrow at her. 'I'm not even going there. And neither should you.'

'You remembered the case, though.'

'Vaguely. You know what it's like. It happened not far from school. It was a bit of drama, a murder in the neighbourhood. Perfect antidote to double maths.' He sank onto his chair and stared bleakly at the collection of sticky notes that had appeared on his desk in his absence.

She wanted to know more. When she first met Dan

Calder her heart had sunk. Another suit, and worse, an empty one. Or so it had seemed. Unlike some senior officers new to post he had made a small entrance. Where others slammed into the room and plastered their attitude and superiority over the walls, Calder had slipped in quietly, like water. Sometimes she'd forgotten he was in the room. Over time she had seen this work to his advantage. In the absence of anything else to go on, people – witnesses, suspects, superior officers – had a tendency to project onto him what they wanted or expected to see. Often that was a mistake.

It puzzled Ellen that Calder should conceal himself this way because one thing she understood was that he hated deception, loathed pretence, and gaslighting more than anything else. Then again, she had read once that the traits people despised in others were the same they disliked in themselves. Maybe Calder, too, had learnt to hold something back and he resented it. Learnt the hard way, perhaps. It happened rarely now that some ned in the cells would make something of his evenness of skin tone, those patient liquid brown eyes, but Ellen had been to school: she knew it didn't take much for someone to be marked out.

She wondered, and she watched. And in certain light and over time, bits of DI Dan Calder had begun to show through. The way he worried at the base of his skull when faced with a problem; the way his eyes sought the horizon or his fingers twitched with impatience when people talked about the weather as though it was news; his refusal to stand still on escalators versus his absolute stillness when he listened to liars. That momentary hesitation before entering an occupied room. Little by little, she thought, Calder was emerging.

Nowadays, she never forgot when he was in a room.

'So did you know these brothers? The Gilchrists. The ones Jimmy was talking about. Were you at school with them?'

'No. At least, the name doesn't ring a bell. They'd have been a few years older than me and they could have gone to any one of three different schools round there.'

She noticed he had avoided mention of which school he had gone to.

'I can't imagine you as a schoolboy.'

'I'd have been twelve, nearly thirteen then.'

'Even less as a teenager. Were you ever wild?'

'No. But I'm going to go mad if we don't get some of this paperwork shifted.'

Ellen sighed and turned to her computer. In the bottom right-hand corner of her screen she saw that she had another five hours to go before she could reasonably call it a day.

2

When I open my eyes I can see the branches of a tree spilt across the sky like black ink. It's at the wrong angle. Or I am. I don't know where I am.

Slowly I piece together the information my senses are feeding me. Cold air, my back hard against the ground. A soundtrack. At first I don't register it as music, as something separate from what I see and feel. Instead the rippling advance of the guitar is the sound of the thin gnarled fingers reaching across my field of vision; the voice that weaves through my consciousness is the sound of the pain in my limbs and at the back of my head. The echo of my waning body heat, my energy leaching into the soil. Fade out. The music is from the past, though for a moment I don't recognise that. For a moment my life folds over on itself and leaves me with no past, no future. There is only now. And a deep sorrow. Despair even. Fade out again. Then I am in the boys' room, though I know I should not be. It's their music. Malcolm's. Only I am not there and that was a lifetime ago. Stiffly, I feel over my front, find the wire and pull out the earbuds.

Above me a rush of wind sets the branches clacking together like skeleton bones. Other sounds filter in. A voice not so far away, calling to a dog. A car door shutting. Short scuffles in undergrowth somewhere to my left – a bird pulling away at the mulch to find grubs. These things, I recognise them for what they are, but what am I doing here? Where? My mind scans the different places I could be: gardens, parks, pathways in cities I have known. Until I find the right one: Bristol. Clifton Downs. I was running. This is where I am, I think. I am here. And I really feel it. That I am here, I mean. In a way that I have not felt truly present anywhere for a long time. I look at the tree above me. Sharp, clean black veins, perfectly still now.

Then I wonder how I came to be here and the presence of mind is gone. I reach into the past – how far I don't know. I was running. Then what? Did I slip? Possible. Have I been attacked? Possible also. My head hurts. I fumble at my pocket – my mobile phone still there. Of course. Stupid. That is where the music is coming from. Not mugged, then. But if I lie here much longer...

Someone is coming up on me fast. The pounding of feet beats an alarm on the tarmac and I feel it along the length of my spine. It sends shards of pain into my vibrating skull. Christ, my head hurts. I try to lift it, sit up.

'Hold on!' The feet come to a halt and a giant looms above me. 'Here, take it easy, let me help you.'

He is right over me then, sliding one arm under me, taking the base of my skull in his other hand. 'Nice and slow.'

He is close, too close, holding me against him. I want to push him away, keep checking my mobile, though it's not that I'm worried about. He levers me up slowly into a sitting position, holding my head as you would a baby's. I wonder, fleetingly, whether he's had practice.

A car passes, not slowing despite the drama we're enacting on the pavement. Its sudden coming sends a rush of fear through me and a slew of dirty water over my Samaritan.

'Jesus! Bastard.' The support is gone as his hand flies out and up, a finger held erect to the disappearing vehicle. My head lolls.

'Oops, sorry, my luvver.' He catches me again, clumsily. 'Lucky you didn't fall in front of that nutter. Wouldn't stand a chance.' Then, 'Can you stand?'

'I'm fine, honestly. Thanks.'

Shit. What's wrong with me? Why can I not hold my own head up? I want to shake him off and jog away as if nothing has happened. But I also want him just to lower me down again, let me curl up right here on the damp ground.

'You took quite a tumble.'

'Must've slipped.' I look at the pavement. The tarmac is black with the recent rain, but matt. No sheen. No leaves.

No cracks. Nothing to slide on, nothing to trip over. If I am looking to blame something, there is nothing there. But I keep looking. It's a distraction from the pain, from the embarrassment.

'I don't think so. I saw you. You just kind of ... went down. When you didn't get up again I thought: that's not good.'

I try not to cling so hard as he helps me to my feet. My limbs unfold awkwardly, painfully. My joints have set with the cold. As I rise the throbbing in my head gives way to a distant buzzing. I feel the heaviness in it drain away through my trunk, my limbs, down into my feet, anchoring my body to the ground while my head lists at the top, light and empty. I imagine it detaching itself completely and floating into the darkening sky, drifting up, up... Then I remember the tree. I see my head caught in its branches, stuck there like a child's lost balloon, for months, slowly deflating.

Am I going mad?

A wave of nausea hits me. Reflexing, I turn just in time and throw up into the bushes.

'Sorry. Sorry.'

'Take your time. Listen, I think we ought to get you to a hospital. Are you dizzy or anything? Can you see okay? How many fingers am I holding up?'

He puts up two fingers, then before I can answer he changes his mind, as though this is not enough of a test. Four. No, three.

'You're not a doctor.'

'No, my luvver. Builder. Used to lifting things. But that's where my expertise runs out.'

That 'my luvver' in its soft Bristolian burr makes me want to cry. I want to wrap myself up in it.

'How long was I out?'

'Not long. Seconds. Still, you went down pretty hard. You might be concussed.'

I want to go home. I want a hot shower, fresh clothes, something warm to drink. But when I think about the distance to my flat, about having to carry myself all that way back down the hill, having to cross the road between the traffic and negotiate the stragglers arranged around the bus stop and get my keys out and go up the steps and let myself in and get past Mike Downstairs's flat without having to tell him how many miles today and laugh when he pats his belly and tells me he'll join me one day, and then about having to undo my double-knotted trainers and take my clothes off and wash myself and dry myself and clothe myself, about having to fill the kettle and put a teabag in a mug and get the milk out of the fridge and put the teabag in the bin... It all seems such an enormous effort. Exhausting. So I let the builder guide me to his car and put me in the front seat. He has a dog in the back and that makes me feel better.

He talks in the car but I don't really hear what he says. Something about the day, the weather. When is it going to be spring? Where his wife wants to go on holiday, but where would they put the dog? Or is it the kids? I understand that he doesn't expect me to respond. He thinks there is something wrong with me so it's alright to just sit here silently. It feels quite nice to be looked after.

At the hospital he offers to wait but I tell him I'll be okay. I thank him. In the weeks to come, maudlin with the thought of his kindness, I will wish I had taken his address, a number. I don't even know his name. I will wish I could have thanked him better, bought him some chocolates or a bottle of something.

I sit in the waiting area looking at all the people with visible signs of injury and illness. I feel vaguely like a fraud, but it's warm in here, I get tea from a machine with the milk already in and the teabag on a string. And chocolate. I don't want to go back out into the cold. I really want to plug myself into my mobile, let music make something more of what is happening, but I am afraid I will miss my name being called. So I just sit there.

It's snowing when I go home. A late snow. The last snow. A sudden flurry swirling in the cab's headlights like the opening titles of the old Dr. Who. It won't lie.

3

It was late when Dan Calder got home. He had stopped to buy himself a couple of bottles of Black Gold and an oven-ready curry. He poured himself some beer and went to the window while the curry cooked. His top-floor East Parkside flat looked directly onto Salisbury Crags, tonight an irregular wall of black against the night sky. He slid open the floor-length window and leant on the railings, looking at the shape of the crags and Arthur's Seat beyond while he listened to the thrum of the city and tried to imagine what it would be like, the one without the other.

Talking to Ellen Chisholm about James Barber the other day had got him thinking not so much about retirement but about life outside the job. He meant what he had said about walking away when it was done. That wouldn't be a problem; Dan never got involved with anything he couldn't walk away from. But if he didn't lay some groundwork now, what would he do? He didn't want to be one of those coppers – one of those men – who were lost without their jobs. Work should be a part of life, not the whole of it, but he was letting the other bits slip. He tried to remember when he had last spent more than a couple of hours on a Sunday afternoon walking anywhere but the patch of land he was looking at now. It was time to put that to rights. He was due some holiday. Even this weekend he could contact his friend Gregor in Dundee; they might go up to Angus and do a bit of the Cateran trail or Glen Clova. He opened his laptop and pulled up the Walk Highlands website. As he ate his curry he clicked through various walks, read an article about Orkney in early spring, scrolled through a review of a new backpack. But he was only delaying the inevitable.

James Barber had piqued his curiosity. Perhaps it was a kind of nostalgia. If you could be nostagic for a time you would rather not revisit. Over the past week intermittent fragments had flitted through his mind: obscenities gouged into the surface of a desk; light playing on a girl's hair; trainers squeaking on vinyl flooring; the low stench of stale sweat and feet. Latent violence and anxiety. His own desperation to escape the monotony of the suburbs and the casual aggression of his peers.

Connor Leask.

He hadn't remembered the details but he remembered the impact the murder had had, the mood in the neighbourhood afterwards and the tension at school where the new term had just begun. Part excitement, part fear, and an undercurrent of violence, a kind of pent-up aggression coupled with defensiveness that seemed ready to burst out at any moment. He would need a psychologist to unpack all of that and he was not sure he would ever want to.

Unconsciously he put his hand to the base of his skull, his fingertips seeking out the small scar under the short hair there. Ellen had asked him whether he knew the brothers Barber had mentioned. He didn't. He was sure of that, because he would have known about it if one of his peers had been a person of interest in a murder enquiry. Any one of them would have boasted about being in the vicinity. Swaggered about the school, the big man who was out on the dangerous streets at night, amongst murderers and thugs. He would have tapped his nose knowingly and refused to answer questions he didn't know the answer to but wanted everyone to think he did. Even if he had been questioned. Especially if he had been questioned. That would have given him more kudos. He was a witness. He was important. Maybe he had even had a narrow escape from the same fate.

Maybe he had even done it.

For some, such bravado would have been forced, unnatural, but they would still have had to put on a show. It would have been the only way to deal with it.

Dan closed the laptop. He didn't want to go back there.

He opened it again. He tapped the name Connor Leask

into the search engine. A string of entries referenced the murder, mostly press from the time. Some restricted him to a summary paragraph unless he subscribed to the news website, others gave fuller accounts. Between them they confirmed what Barber had told them and what he vaguely remembered himself. That Leask had been stabbed to death on the night of Friday 20th August, 1993 in a quiet residential suburb of the city. That his killer or killers had never been found.

Leask had had a promising legal career ahead of him, one of only a few recent law graduates to be selected for the annual traineeship with the Crown Office and Procurator Fiscal Service. There was little mention of his work. Very quickly the press had begun to link the killing to Leask's sexuality. More than once Dan came across the phrase, 'random gay-bashing.' It seemed incredible now, when hate crime was one of Police Scotland's top priorities, to think that Leask's death could have been so easily dismissed. Dan had the feeling that had Connor Leask not been a trainee Procurator Fiscal, and had his murder happened half a mile to the north east, literally on the other side of the tracks – or the cycle path that had once been a railway at any rate – the press would have given a lot less time to the story than they did. As it was, after the first week or so of the investigation the articles petered out. There were one or two written in the intervening years, marking anniversaries, or mentioning Leask's murder in the context of others that remained unsolved, but it didn't take long before the items listed in the search became less relevant. Concerned with other Connors and other Leasks.

One thing Dan did find interesting was that when he added the word 'murder' to the search he found not only the same articles on Leask's own death, but a couple that at first seemed unrelated, until he read further into them and found mention of their being cases that Leask had worked on as part of his traineeship, or related to academic papers he had written. It seemed that Connor Leask had a taste for murder.

He could find only one picture of Connor Leask. A

graduation photograph. Leask in a kilt and mortarboard, proudly brandishing a scroll. Smiling brown eyes and sandy hair, he had a glow about him. Confidence. Leask was a man on his way to success. Dan vaguely recognised the photograph. It must have been in the papers and on the local TV news at the time. Most of what Dan had picked up would have come from his peers, though. Unreliable, to say the least. And easily misremembered. 'Jumped,' he thought they must have said. Leask had been 'jumped' on a quiet residential street in a part of the city Dan had known well at the time, having spent much of his youth riding his bike around the surrounding area, on the cycle paths that had once been railway lines that cut through the north and west of the city, or down to the shorefront between Cramond and Granton, past the old gasworks and the corporation housing that had stood in its shadows. He cycled everywhere until his early-teens when all that stopped abruptly. It must have been not long after Connor Leask's death. For a moment a memory threatened to stall him. That tick-ticking sound of the wheel still revolving... He pushed it away but his mind went to the bicycle frame he kept stashed in the cupboard in the spare bedroom; just the frame with one wheel still attached, no handlebars or saddle. He didn't cycle any more.

He went to Google maps. The satellite view of the area was like a biopsy of the city's suburbs. In the past it would have been farmland. Davidsons Mains still retained its village feel, with low stone cottages fringing the main street. To the west and south, linking the area to wealthy Barnton and Cramond, large stone mansions and mature trees, comfortable detached bungalows, a predominance of pampas grass and firebush; to the North and east the suburban sprawl of Silverknowes bled into Muirhouse and Pilton, stained grey harling and multiple occupancy. Bit by bit Dan zoomed in. Connor Leask had been killed in the margin, at a bend in a road where a small triangle of hedge and trees created a kind of cul de sac between bungalows. At the apex of the triangle a path led off the road and down onto the cycle track and beyond it onto a stretch of scrubby parkland backed onto by grim Drylaw tenements.

'What the hell was he doing there?' Dan murmured. It made little sense. One of the articles had said that Leask lived in a flat-share in the New Town. Miles away. This was nowhere near where he lived, where he worked or where he was likely to spend his time. In spite of himself, Dan felt the itch of curiosity. Was Connor with his killer when he went out that night? Had someone followed him? Or had he met someone along the way who, for one reason or another, attacked him? It seemed the investigation had concluded that the latter was most likely: a random encounter that ended in death. But something didn't sit right with Dan.

4

By the time we cross the border few people are talking. Their belongings have spilled and spread, empty sandwich packets and read newspapers on the tables, crumpled jumpers hanging over arm rests and knapsacks encroaching on the aisle, but the carriage's occupants have each retreated: into books, into earphones, into sleep. There is only the rocking, whooshing of the train and the thick quiet of fifty-odd bodies.

It's a dreich day, the clouds huddled conspiratorially around the hills. Against the dark green of the woodland on their lower slopes I can see that it's raining, but it must be coming from the west, hitting the other side of the carriage. I let my focus shift so I can study the shapes on the window made by my fellow travellers: the woman opposite with her head lolling, mouth open; her companion frowning furiously at a novel. I've been trying to see what she's reading but she is at great pains to conceal the cover and the spine. I draw my own conclusions. Across the aisle, where there should be a man I can see nothing but shadow. Negative space and reflections upon reflections. A sudden fear grips me and I turn to make sure he is flesh. He is. It's just that he's turned away, the dark of his hair and his jacket making a black mirror on my window. As I look he lifts his arm and puts a long finger to the glass, tracing the erratic movement of a raindrop. It's an action so childlike, so innocent that I'm embarrassed to be watching, as though I've intruded on a private moment.

I realise I must never really have liked this life much. I don't mean that I was depressed or suicidal, just that the real world never quite captured my interest or my imagination. I've been a lot of different places but most of the time I was somewhere else entirely: in my head, in my dreams, fantasies. Whilst my feet were on the ground, I moved through time and space. Plots were written and rewritten to suit my mood. Some have stayed the course; their protagonists naive, archetypal, timeless, they return to me like old friends, offering refuge when I need comfort. Others I've forgotten, discarded like old clothes.

I'm not deluded. I know where reality ends and fantasy begins. It's just that I often hankered for a bit more than was actually there. In my dreams the world appears brighter, sharper, full of portent. There's always the possibility of a mysterious stranger stepping out from the shadows into the light, phone conversations might be tapped, library books have coded messages slipped between the plastic covers, and the supermarket shop is so much less tedious when it is part of a covert operation. Right now, as the train's smooth passage is disrupted and it lapses into an older rhythm – clickety-clack, clickety-clack – I am on the Orient Express. No, I am packed into a crowded carriage, climbing a steep mountain pass towards a tea plantation in India. No, I am on a bullion train forging through the barren lands of the Wild West.

Is it childish? It's just ingrained. Fantasy is a filter that softens and enriches. It makes the meaningless significant, the mundane worthwhile, just as any object well-lit and viewed through a lens can be made remarkable, if not beautiful.

Or at least, it passes the time.

For a moment the train beats a rhythm like the opening salvo of drums and I am on the battlefield, expecting next the skirl of pipes. Then I'm thrown sideways as the train jolts over ill-fitting tracks and I'm back in this sombre carriage remembering why I'm going home.

I've never really minded how my dreams kept me. I neither noticed how they sustained me in times of need, nor did it trouble me that I put a filter on reality rather than face the world outside of my imagination for what it was.

Until now.

The hills fall away and we emerge into open land. The wind gusts, broadside, and I am outside, clinging, fingers tight, knuckles white, inching my way along the carriage roof.

*

As we enter the outskirts of Edinburgh I see a plane on its approach to the airport. It seems to hang motionless over Corstorphine Hill. Something to do with the curve of the track and our relative speeds and distances from the hill. I wonder briefly whether it might be Malcolm's plane, whether he is up there looking down at my train. But of course Malcolm has already arrived. They all have. I will be the last, as usual. The last in all things, but one.

There's a tight knot of panic in my gut, where breakfast and lunch should have been. Only now do I notice that I'm almost nauseous with hunger. Too late to do anything about it. I breathe carefully, just like the nurse showed me after my appendix operation when I was six: in through the nose, blowing out slowly through circled lips. It didn't work then. Ribena all over the white bedspread. What is the name of those ones with the fringes? I think of candleabras, candlesticks, candlemas.

As I walk down the platform at Waverley I scan ahead for Robert, peering at people who might be him but who are not. He must see me first because I feel the directness of his gaze before my eyes settle on him. He raises an arm in greeting and despite the tiredness and nausea my own face mirrors his smile.

I feed my ticket through the barrier gate and suddenly Robert is there. The force of his embrace knocks me off balance. He seems big, alive.

'I like this,' he says, ruffling my scarlet hair. 'Last time I saw you it was purple.'

'Get off,' I say. Then I see something behind his grin, something serious and expectant, and I realise that he's not just mucking about. He's trying to shake me out of myself. Trying to bring me into the here and now.

'There's no time to stop for a coffee, I'm afraid. Everyone's at the house. They're all waiting to see you.'

'It's ok. We can catch up later.' I cringe at the thought of making an entrance.

'No Bogus?'

'No.'

Angus was renamed by predictive text and never recovered his identity. I haven't told my family that he and I are no longer together.

'You look tired. Got your Charlie Brown eyes. Why didn't you fly?'

'Wanted to bring my soul with me.'

'What?'

'Nothing. Just something someone said once. This Finnish guy. Said we travel so far so fast now there's no time for our souls to catch up with us.'

'Oh, aye? Cute was he?'

I don't protest as Robert takes my bag off me and carries it to the car. Let him be big brother. It's taking more energy than I have to walk upright. I knead the flesh between my eye sockets and my ears. Come on, I tell myself. This is just the beginning.

'Is Fiona here?'

'Uh-huh.' Robert hesitates. 'Tina felt it wasn't the right time to meet you all. But she'd like to, sometime soon.'

'Of course. Yeah, I'm looking forward to meeting her.'

'Calum's here though. You won't recognise him. He's quite the little man now. I'm not sure Mum approves of us bringing him, but we reckon it's important – he needs the goodbye too. Al's the same with his.'

I don't reply. I don't know what to say. Already this is too much. Too much information, too many interactions, inter-relations, implications. Too much history, too much thin ice to tread. Too much future. Too much life.

I get into the passenger seat and buckle up while Rob puts my bag in the back. As we drive through the city I look out of the window at things changed and things stayed the same. Even in the dusk I can tell that the season is a couple of weeks behind Bristol. Trees still flecked with blossom, the new leaves small and acid green under the street lights. People hunched against the cold wind.

We turn down Howe Street and left into Stockbridge. The cobbles jar my bones and I grip the seat under my left leg so Rob will not see. Up past the old police headquarters and the new school and on towards Ferry Road.

'Dad would have had something to say about this route,' I say.

I expect Rob to smile, but he doesn't.

Oh, you went that way, did you? It was always the same. Whichever route you took, Dad knew a better one. You always made the wrong choice, or were unlucky. You were always left with the impression that you were still new to this, still a child trying to find your way in the world.

'I caught him out once,' I say. 'I think it might have been the first time you came home for a visit after you moved up north. Anyway, you were due to arrive that evening and I found him poring over the road atlas.'

'I knew he cheated,' Rob says, and I'm taken aback by the bitterness in his voice. We used to laugh at this.

Rob senses my surprise, and rallies. 'I wonder if he did the same to Malcolm? East-West approach today, I assume? So you flew in over the city? Did you circle wide over the Forth? Tsk.'

'He did actually.'

Rob laughs, but I'm not sure he means it. I thought you were supposed to be in denial or do bargaining or something before you got angry with the person who had died.

We lapse into silence. I understand better now, that need Dad had, to know how we got from one place to another, to be able to trace a pathway across the land, the sea, the sky. Not in a maudlin way, not to be clever or to make some grand metaphor like that Finnish bloke. (He was cute, but pretentious.) No, it is just that I find I like to know.

Robert is casting me sideways glances.

'Are you alright? You do look tired.'

'You look old.' I ruffle his receding hairline. Revenge for before.

'Seriously.'

'I'm OK.' I shrug.

He glances at me again, then sneaks a look in the rear view mirror at his own hairline. I smile and hunker down into my coat.

*

Where we lived as children used to feel more on the edge. The house itself is in a neat circular warren. Until Google maps I had never realised this. We made our own geography as children, and something was lost when I could place us within the concentric streets. There is still a field by the road that slopes down towards the esplanade on the firth but the suburb doesn't seem so much on the edge of things now. From the east new housing developments have advanced up the coastline towards the golf course. To the west Cramond too is expanding. And we are not children anymore: we can drive away or hail a taxi and be gone any time we like.

As we approach the front door I see a woman not much older than I am now, in pleated, belted trousers and a blouse buttoned to the neck, thick hair falling in a wave to her shoulders. Then the door opens for real and there is a small elderly woman standing there.

She steps out briskly to greet me, even manages a smile as she pulls me into a hug. It's still there as she puts me away from her again to look at me. Then time stops. For just a brief moment, but one that will last well beyond this day, her face crumples and grief shows itself for what it is: raw; desperate; terrified. I have never seen it before, not for real, and it's unlike anything else, unlike anything I might have imagined. It's terrible.

It's gone as quickly as it came. She sucks it back in with a huge gulp of air and swallows it down. 'Come away in, darling. Your brothers are here. And the children.'

And everyone will talk about how well she is coping, how strong she is, how dignified. But I will remember this small glimpse inside. It will linger in my mind as clear and sharp in every detail as if I were seeing it in person again. Since that fall on the Downs time has played tricks on me. Minutes can last for hours, days go by in a blink. But this moment will be stuck in slow motion action replay. I will have time, again and again to examine the pucker in her jaw, the light dusting of powder over the suddenly sagging skin, helpless pleading in watery eyes. This is what I will see when I wake at night gasping for breath. Because there is nothing there except the Loss.

I follow her into a house that is pregnant with the negative sound of people. In the sitting room they're arranged like statues. It's like an eclipse. Static human formations gathered under a blackened sun, a collective breath held as they wait to commemorate something they are each a little afraid of, in awe of. Death. I'm smitten suddenly by the same superstition. I find I don't know what to do next. Then I see Malcolm stepping lightly towards me. He wraps me in a big hug: 'Hello, Non.' He retreats from the intimacy with equal grace and takes his place again, outside the circle created by furniture, family and hearth, a silhouette against the street outside, beautiful in his pose, natural, apart.

Alistair, by contrast, commands the centre of the room, a finger wedged in the collar of his shirt. There is a tautness to his frame, sharpness in his features. Muscles accustomed to clenching and gritting hint at some latent fury. Already the air between these two is spiked with hostility. I feel the static charge that crackles between them – and it's not just coming off Al's jacket. (I must remember to say that to Robert later, I think.)

The women, the children, it's hard at first to recognise them, they're so solemn. It's only later that I will find the wit in Mel's eyes, Fiona's warmth. I know them now only by their arrangement in the room. It's funny how old-fashioned they are, how formal: the women and children seated, the men standing to attention. How unlike our lives this is, this death.

This is the first time the four of us have been in a room together for twenty-six years: Malcolm, Alistair, Robert and me.

There are too many people in the room. And one big hole where Dad is missing.

5

Ellen waited until Dan Calder had taken the first sip of his pint. 'There were three Gilchrist brothers,' she said. She caught the look he threw her but ploughed on regardless. 'The youngest was only eleven and at home in bed when Leask was killed, but the older two, Malcolm and Alistair were seventeen and sixteen and they were both out that night near where the murder took place.'

Their companion, DC Liam McGuire, looked from one to the other.

'Have you been talking to Barber again?'

'No.' She hesitated. 'I looked up the case.' She tossed back another handful of peanuts, avoiding Calder's stare. 'I did it in my own time.'

'Have I missed something?' Liam asked. DC McGuire was everything that Dan Calder was not. Disheveled in appearance, cheerfully unguarded of disposition and running to fat. He was everything Ellen wanted to be because he was entirely comfortable in his own skin and gave every appearance of being happy with his lot.

'Chisholm is pushing her luck,' Calder told Liam.

'My old boss came to us with a cold case the other day. There's probably nothing in it, but...'

'The one that got away,' Calder said to Liam pointedly.

Liam nodded, understanding. 'And you feel you owe it to him to look into it?'

'Maybe. I was a bit wet behind the ears when he first knew me. He was good for me.'

Dan grunted. 'He's not setting much of an example now.'

'He might be right, though. I read the transcripts of their interviews. Even on paper they come across as evasive.'

'Who doesn't?' Calder said. 'That's what happens to

people when they're being questioned by the police. Maybe they were just freaked out.'

'What's the case?' Liam asked.

'Guy called Connor Leask. 1993.'

Liam whistled softly.

'You know it?'

'My first year in training. He was a fiscal, Connor Leask, if I remember rightly.'

'Trainee,' Dan corrected him. 'He was being mentored by Lise Eklund.'

'Baroness? Senior Advocate Depute Lise Eklund?'

'That's right. What are you grinning at?'

A slow smile had spread across Ellen's face. 'I knew you wouldn't be able to resist looking into it.'

They filled Liam in on Barber's theory that Ronald Gilchrist had something to tell him about Connor Leask's death.

'Does he think these folk actually had something to do with the murder, though? Why would they even have had anything to do with Connor Leask?'

'I don't know.'

'You didn't ask him?'

'Don't.' Dan put up his hands.

'He said they lied,' Ellen said. 'I don't know what about, specifically, but one of them – Alistair – had been in trouble before.'

'What for?'

'Vandalism, offensive behaviour, theft.'

'It's a far cry from stabbing a stranger in the street.'

'Do you think that's what happened?' Ellen held Dan's gaze.

'No,' he said eventually.

Ellen hid a small triumphant smile behind her pint glass. Not well enough, judging by Calder's expression.

'What was Leask doing for the Fiscal?' Liam asked.

'From what I can gather,' Ellen said, 'He spent a lot of time re-interviewing witnesses, collating case material. Fairly routine stuff, but it might have brought him into contact with people who didn't appreciate his line of questioning.'

'You think his death might have been connected to his work?'

'I don't know, but I don't buy this "random gay-bashing" as the press called it then.' She looked at Calder.

'I have to agree.' He hesitated before continuing. 'When we met Barber the other week I had a vague recollection of the murder but I couldn't remember the details. I thought Leask had been beaten up. When Barber said he was stabbed, I just assumed I had remembered wrongly, but the more I read about it, the more I thought the way they described it in the press would skew anyone's understanding of what happened. He wasn't "bashed". He was stabbed. Cleanly and deliberately. And "random"? Yeah, I know that kind of thing happens. We all do. But it's up town on Lothian Road after someone's had a skinful. Or less than a mile to the north east of where Connor was found if someone takes exception to a stranger appearing on their turf. It might conceivably happen two hundred yards away, down on the cycle path late at night, just for the bloody hell of it. But up there, on that quiet road? I've asked myself whether I'm just looking at the past through a filter, but every which way I look at it I still don't buy it.'

'Are you saying they put that phrase out there deliberately?' Ellen asked.

'No-o. It's a possibility, though, isn't it? And if they did,' Dan went on, 'You have to wonder: was it a bit of tactical misdirection in order to help the investigation, aimed at getting the killer to slip up? Or did they do it to mislead everyone? To write it off?'

6

'They're burying Ronald Gilchrist tomorrow.'

Dan was just leaving the station when James Barber appeared at his shoulder. His voice was flat. If he resented Dan or DS Chisholm for the missed opportunity to hear what Gilchrist had to say, if he wanted to lay blame, there was no tell. That wasn't why he was here.

'Ronald Gilchrist died of pancreatic cancer,' he said, taking Barber by the elbow and steering him away from the station and further up the street. 'Nothing suspicious.'

It was cold outside, a sharp, clear, spring cold. Barber's words hung in a cloud between them. 'You looked into it.'

'You've got my sergeant to thank for that. She rates you highly.'

'But you don't want me leading her astray.' Barber looked back towards the station entrance, then nodded. 'Fair enough. No point undoing all the good again. She's worked hard to sort herself out.'

Dan hesitated. It was a necessary part of this job to listen to gossip. Share it. It was sometimes only through the scuttlebutt that you got what you needed, got where you wanted to be. And that was just in your career. That was before you even started to consider the cases. Nevertheless, as someone who had often been the subject of speculation while he was growing up he had a natural aversion to it; as much distaste for discussing other people behind their backs as he did for being talked about.

'She's doing fine. She's a very good detective.'

He wondered what Barber meant.

'Anyway, I did that much. I can't do more, I'm sorry.'

'He knew something.'

'He's dead.'

'They were all in the vicinity that night. Ronald Gilchrist. Malcolm and Alistair Gilchrist. Not one of them had a cast-iron alibi. Nothing that couldn't be overturned. And they lied.'

'Is it because he was gay?' Dan put the question gently. He had listened to a bit of gossip about Barber. 'Connor Leask. Is that why you feel you owe him this?'

'No, it's not because he was gay,' Barber hissed. For a moment Dan thought he would walk away. Or hit him. Then: 'It's because they thought that was good enough reason to sweep it under the carpet.'

'Who?'

'Starrett and Baird. And whoever told them to tell me to drop it. Whoever else it was pulling the strings. Someone got away with murder because the world thought it was just an unfortunate but inevitable fact of life that a young man was killed because of his sexuality. I had better things to spend my time on, they said. And I went along with it. We let him down.'

Dan felt a tension creep up his spine. Detective Chief Inspector Glen Starrett. Superintendent Hugh Baird. Legends.

He thought Barber was about to say something else. Could almost feel him weighing up the odds.

'Thanks anyway,' Barber said. After his outburst he sounded spent. Resigned.

Why would the Gilchrists have any reason to kill Connor Leask? Dan wanted to ask. How would they even have come into contact with him? He bit the questions back. It was twenty-six years ago. There was no fresh evidence. If Ronald Gilchrist had been about to confess he had taken it to his grave. He was hardly likely to have been about to betray one of his sons, was he? Starrett and Baird were long retired. He couldn't even remember whether they were still alive.

'Don't do anything stupid,' he called after Barber, echoing Ellen's earlier words. Less kindly this time.

7

I sit in the back of Alistair's car, my knees pressed awkwardly into the back of Mel's seat, with my resentful niece Kirsty in the middle and wee Sam in a booster seat on the other side of her. We follow the funeral car which in turn follows the hearse towards the crematorium. It's unbearably slow. In moments when there's a lull in the oncoming traffic I find myself twitching with the urge to overtake.

I lean my head back and let my eyes unfocus so that the small perforations in the fabric of the car ceiling dance three-dimensionally. Already the day has stretched out forever. I measure the patterns of sound from the passing cars. Watch how the light passes over the car ceiling. And suddenly I'm back in the hospital, where they made me lie on a tray and slid me into a machine that could see inside my brain.

The first time I didn't connect with what was happening at all. My soundtrack was one of transporters and shuttle craft. I was going into space. I was being put into suspended animation ahead of a long journey across light years into the future. They were going to make me bionic. I was any number of things in any number of other worlds and narratives but I was not there.

I lift my head again, painfully. On the pavement outside an old man has stopped to watch our approach. He pulls his cap from his head and stands respectfully to attention while the cortege passes.

*

I imagine a camera tracking across the front row: Malcolm, dignified, erect, barely breathing; Mum, both the grief and the false bravado now replaced by a faraway bafflement that will cocoon her for the rest of the day; Alistair next, looking uncomfortable; Robert with his head bowed and tilted to one side, a slight frown of concentration on his face, those same two lines Dad had pointing straight down his nose. And then me.

I stare at the coffin. I can't help it.

The minister puts aside his notes. 'Ronald was many different things to the people gathered here today: husband, father, colleague, neighbour, friend. I would like to ask you each now to take a minute to remember Ronald in your own way.'

The polished veneer, the flower arrangement on the top, it's like a piece of furniture. Furniture in someone else's house, not somewhere we would ever have lived. It says nothing about Dad. There is no clue to his presence. Can he really be in there?

I wonder how much of the minute there is left. I try to think something important, something that befits the occasion. This could have been the one thing we had in common. The one thing we might have shared. One hell of a father-daughter bonding trip. If I had known in time. If we had been the kind of family that told each other things.

We could have asked whether they did two-for-the-price-of-one.

The minister presses a discreet button and the coffin begins to slide through a small curtained hatch.

The second time they used a machine to look inside my head I couldn't shake my fear of radiation. I watched them scurry behind their screens, leaving me there like some lab experiment on a dish. I pictured them sitting safely at their control panel, setting their co-ordinates, increasing the levels of radiation a little bit and a little bit more. I could almost hear the rays passing over me; I pictured them in a sort of neon pink. Felt them filtering under my scalp, my skull; fingering their way across my cortex and along the occipital nerve, gently melting the backs of my eyeballs. I knew my fears were misplaced, that they were founded more in the science fiction of my childhood than the reality of what was happening, but they raised panic in my nerves, my muscles were stretched taught with helpless terror. Calming words were spoken at me from somewhere but they couldn't reassure me. It was only later that I realised none of it mattered anyway. The worst was already done.

The curtain closes behind the coffin. For a moment I see Dad inside the box, in tuxedo and black tie. Alive. Sean Connery as Bond. Fighting to escape as the flames shoot up around him. Then Robert tugs on my sleeve and I heave myself into a standing position to sing a final hymn.

*

Back at the house it's horrible. Fellow golfers, drinkers, friends and neighbours of Dad's, all trying to strike the right tone. Business associates – by which I probably mean freemasons. People who are all too alive still. Mr Scott, my old French teacher. (There ought to be a law preventing teachers and parents from socialising.) Lawrence Groat. Just looking at him makes my skin crawl. Muscle memory. I saw him looking at his watch during the service, too. Cretin. His son, Finlay, though. Blimey. All grown up and quite the charmer. He did a double-take when he saw me, too. At first I thought it was just my bright red hair, but if I didn't know better (we are at my father's funeral after all) I would say he was flirting with me when I passed round the sausage rolls. So perhaps not everyone is trying to strike the right tone. I find that I like him better for that.

Finlay and Al were thick as thieves as children. Well, they were thieves, if the local newsagent and the manager of the co-op were to be believed. And the police did believe them. So did Dad.

In the kitchen Mum is fretting because Alistair got everything ready and he hasn't used the right china. Malcolm hugs her gently.

'You're doing great, Mum. It's all a bit much isn't it?'

'I feel so silly,' she whispers urgently. 'I don't know who anybody is.'

'It's ok Mum. Look, they're all wearing black. And they're all being very serious. They don't look like themselves and they're not acting like themselves. They've all had a wash.'

She almost manages a smile. 'I don't know what to say to them.'

'You don't have to say anything, Mum.'

I mooch back into the living room, skirting the small groupings, lingering now and again to listen to a fraction of conversation without committing to any myself. I get away with a smile here, a murmur there. Somehow I am excused the role of host that each of my brothers plays. Maybe the hair is intimidating. Or maybe people still see me as the baby of the family. In recognition of this I slide onto the sofa next to Al's eldest, Josh. I have the impression that I quite like Josh though I can't remember why. We played a few games of Grand Theft Auto on the Xbox one Christmas: perhaps I like the way he steals a car. Right now, he sits burning a hole in the carpet through sheer willpower while his Dad talks about him over his head to complete strangers. I feel his pain: it really is none of their business what he does with his life and how he's going to do in his exams and who the hell are they anyway?

'Alright?' I say.

He grunts in response.

We sit in silence for a while. Eventually he says, 'I looked up your name.'

'Uh huh?' I think I know what's coming next.

'Norna is the Norse goddess of fate.'

'Yeah. Mum's – Gran's – family came from Orkney, remember.'

'You know you're also an IKEA cushion pad, right?'

There we have it. 'It has been pointed out to me.'

I've disappointed him. Stolen his thunder. 'Not just any cushion pad, though,' I say. 'I'm reversible.'

For some reason we both find this hilarious. Al and Malcolm are united for once in disapproval, but we find it impossible to stop giggling. It's only when it gets sore that we finally get it under control. And now I feel sick.

I slip quietly out of the room, exchanging a rueful glance with Robert in the hall. He's on one of his endless rounds of tea and sherries. His way of getting out of conversations is to say, 'Excuse me,' and waggle the teapot meaningfully. He has always envied me my cloak of invisibility, always had to work harder to find his peace.

Upstairs on the landing the air is still and cool, a relief. The weak afternoon light is throwing coloured panes across the floor from the window at the corner of the stairs. I pause for breath and for a moment I think I hear someone singing. Raindrops keep falling on my head.

Behind me now I hear the rasp and tumble of a Scalextric car running too fast off a bend, and then to the left the squall of a fight just as it turns physical. The rhythmic cant of worn out scoldings beat their wings on the still air and disappear.

I lean hard on the wall, forcing myself to breathe low and silent. What I think is the beginning to the opening theme tune of Taggart is only the squeal of the taps as Robert fills the kettle for another pot of tea.

There is movement to my right and I look up, half expecting to see the man in a brushed cotton shirt who has left a whiff of Imperial Leather in the air. But it's not him. Instead there is a buxom woman somewhere in her late sixties or early seventies. She has come out of my room. Not my room. Dad has been using it as an office-cum-storage space since I left home years ago.

'Oops. Caught in the act,' she says, with a naughty giggle. Then something passes across her face. Concern. 'Are you alright, dear?'

'I just needed a bit of quiet.'

'Of course. You're Norna, aren't you? You had better sit down. You look awful pale.'

I can't remember ever having met this woman before. She seems a bit racy to be a friend of Mum's. She's wearing black of course but there's a leopard print scarf knotted at her throat and her lips are a scandalous pink. I don't believe her lashes are real.

She guides me onto the chair at Dad's desk, which sits beneath the window where it always did when it was mine. I used to do my homework here. I spent a lot of time staring out of this window.

She is still talking. 'I went to the loo and then I couldn't help myself. Always had a fascination for other people's houses. This is so much nicer than mine. What lovely taste your mum has.'

'Really?' I've never thought about it before. 'It's certainly – coordinated.'

She laughs and her eyes twinkle.

'Are you a friend of Mum's? I'm sorry, I don't remember you.'

'Oh, you were just a wee thing last time we met, dear. I used to work for your Dad in the store. Well, in the back office, mainly. Just a couple of days a week, doing the books and such. My name's Margery.'

She sits with me for a while, then pats my arm and heads back downstairs. After she's gone I go through to the boys' room and sink onto Al's old bed. The aeroplane curtains and a few tenacious stickers still clinging to pieces of furniture are the only remnants of the past. Where there were posters on the wall they have left a chequered pattern of overlapping rectangles on the faded blue woodchip. I feel inside one of the side pockets of my bag and pull out a small bottle of pills, shake a couple onto my palm, then wait for enough saliva to wash them down. I don't have the energy to go through to the bathroom. When at last I can force them down, I curl onto my side on the bed and let the rumble of voices from downstairs blur into nothing.

*

Al and Malcolm are still in the sitting room when I go back downstairs. Their positions have changed, but they keep the same distance between them. Ghosts of their younger selves stalk the space between. Alistair's ghost, a sixteen-year-old taut with rage and frustration, circles the room in skinny black jeans and anarchist T-shirt, all dark glare and angles. Malcolm's ghost is translucent. He shimmers awkwardly at the corner of my eye. He has not yet learned the grace with which his adult self moves and speaks. He is uncomfortable in his first suit. Responsible, miserable and alienated already from his childhood and his home. He is not quite all there, as if he's already left though he is not gone.

I feel like that now.

Rob appears at my shoulder. 'Where have you been

hiding?' He's not annoyed, and somehow that makes me feel more guilty.

'Sorry. Can I do something?'

'If we can be subtle about it I was going to start clearing some things away.' He looks at Malcolm, then Alistair. 'They've been doing most of the hard work, to be honest. Let's hope they can just hold it together for another hour or so. Thank God Al has his own home to go to.'

'Where's Mum?'

'In the kitchen. She's ransacking the cupboards for paper doylies.'

'Seriously? What do we want doylies for?'

He makes a face and moves off to collect some empty plates and glasses. I go through to the kitchen to find Mum. She has decanted the contents of a kitchen cupboard onto the counter: old packets of half-used paper napkins, tupperware tubs and plastic tumblers from long-ago picnics. Now, the door to the garage stands open and she's at the bottom of the steps rummaging through a large plastic box by the light from the kitchen.

'Come on, Mum.' I step down into the garage and pull her gently away from the box.

'I should have thought – we could have used these,' she says, waving a pack of paper plates at me. 'I forgot they were here.'

So much for the wrong china.

If I had imagined grief before now, it was not like this. It was all weeping women and heart-aching and chest beating. Stop the clocks and all that stuff. It's nothing like that in here. Mum hasn't stopped. She's just been subtracted. She has become an incomplete version of herself. As though someone has downloaded only part of the programme. My eyes prick and I turn away quickly.

And that's when I see it. Him. That's when I see the man lying dead on our garage floor.

8

Their destination was in one of several concentric crescents in a development to the north of the city. When the call first came through it had sounded to Ellen like a domestic. There was no convincing herself of that now. She drowned out the alarm bells as she navigated the turns by humming internally the old Noel Harrison song, 'The Windmills of your Mind'. Like a circle in a spiral...

Calder was quiet in the car, too. Ellen was used to his silences, but there was something viscous about this one. She stole a glance at him as she parked up. 'Boss?' Once they got out of the car he would be Sir, but this was a signal that he could tell her something off the record. It was not the right time for 'Dan'.

Calder shook his head. 'I've got a bad feeling about this.'

The street was busy. The coroner's van, police and crime scene vehicles jostled for space with cars that were parked along the roadside. At the initial briefing they had been told there was a funeral reception taking place when the body was discovered.

'No shortage of witness statements, then.' Ellen had cringed at the tone in her own voice.

They walked the short distance up the road to a detached whitewashed house with a dormer window and red tiles on the roof. Ellen's eyes snagged on a ground floor window. Two men stood at the window. Alike, apart, both pairs of eyes trained on them, their faces expressionless.

Suited up, they followed the Crime Scene Supervisor through the house and into the garage via a door leading off the kitchen. Lights had been set up, a dot-to-dot of markers laid out on the concrete floor, the focal point of it all the body of a man. He did not look out of place in the setting. A pair of moleskin trousers and brogues, a jacket the kind she thought they advertised in Sunday supplements. White hair. He could have been the home-owner, rummaging for a screwdriver. In other circumstances it might have been a DIY accident or a heart-attack, a tragic but not inauspicious death in the suburbs. Except that even before she got close enough to see the head wound, the blood pooled on the floor and trickling into the cracks in the concrete, before she knelt beside him and saw the face half-concealed by his arm, Ellen knew she was looking at Jimmy Barber.

Something sharp like physical pain ran through her. Something hot like rage. She stood again, too quickly, and her vision flared and fizzed. She pressed her feet into the ground to steady herself, forced her hands not to ball into fists. When her sight returned she could not look at Calder.

Be more Barber.

The counsellor called it 'impulse control issues'. Ellen would have argued now that actually she had amazingly good impulse control. She had learnt to ground herself, trained the urge to lash out, until it was channelled into a set of small reflexes in her hands and feet. Toes pushing into the floor until the energy was spent. Hands drilled to spread like starfish: so much less threatening than a fist. Less likely to get her into trouble. If anyone noticed – and as far as she knew no-one had – these could be put it down to the cold or cramp. Muscle ache that came from either too long at a desk or a day spent on her feet. The result of crouching awkwardly beside a corpse. A tremor around her mouth was all that showed of the things she might say, but did not.

Ellen would argue that other people – not looking at anyone in particular – did not even seem to know they had impulses. Didn't seem to have them at all. They had no need for control. And yet she was acutely aware of the control she exerted. At this moment she wanted to punch Detective Inspector Dan Calder in the face. She wanted to scream at him and beat her fists on his chest.

She knew it wasn't his fault.

She breathed in slowly. Out slower.

'James Barber. Detective Inspector, retired.'

Jolyon Gray, the pathologist, was standing at her side,

not looking at her but attentive all the same. He seemed to pick up on the subtle shift between them. The way Detective Inspector Calder held back, deferred to the Detective Sergeant. When she turned to him, he didn't wait to be asked.

'Obviously I'll have conclusive facts for you later, but I suspect that in this case the manner of death is very much as it would appear.' He indicated the large spanner lying on the floor. It was about a foot in length, the head and shaft heavily coated in rust. Beside one of the markers, where there was a small dent in the concrete marked with rust, Ellen could see tiny flecks of blood. She pictured the spanner striking the floor. Heard the dull clatter. Had it come to rest before Barber had? She nodded to the crime scene officer waiting patiently beside her and he bent to collect the weapon.

'It's fairly recent,' Jolyon said. 'Though with the cold in here it's hard to be precise. Three to five hours, perhaps.'

That took in both the funeral reception and the period before that, when everyone was at the funeral itself and the house was left unattended.

'Thank you, Jolyon.'

His eyes slid towards her shoes – a brief nod – and away again.

'Right.' She looked up, but like Jolyon Gray she could not quite meet Dan's eyes. Close enough to register his comprehension. He stood aside to let her pass and followed her through to the kitchen.

Liam was waiting for them with a list of the people gathered in the other room. He handed it to Calder.

Calder scanned the list, then shook his head briefly. 'DS Chisholm is going to take the lead on this for now,' he told Liam, handing the list to Ellen. 'I think I'd better go and see Blackwood.'

'Right you are,' Liam said. DCI Hamish Blackwood was their boss. They were all aware of the compromising position they were in.

After he'd gone Ellen felt relieved. She didn't need to look at him now. She wasn't able to hit him. But she also felt bereft. Frightened. Not of being left in charge. Not of how she was going to manage. She could do this fine. But it felt as though something had broken. Something precious.

She turned back to Liam.

'Linda Gilchrist here is the home owner.' He indicated her name on the list. 'It was her husband Ronald's funeral today. Her sons: Malcolm; Alistair; Robert. Daughter: Norna. It was Norna found the body and called us. These here are Alistair's wife and children. Robert's ex and his son. The others are funeral guests. Former work associates, friends of the deceased. The reception was winding down. A lot of guests had gone by the time the body was discovered. These are the ones still here. The rest will need followed up.'

She stepped back inside the garage and looked round. The large up-and-over door at the vehicle entrance was undisturbed. The snib on the small side exit opposite the door into the house had been forced but until it had been thoroughly examined that meant nothing; it was easy enough to fake. Barber was lying near the far corner from where she stood, his face angled towards a repurposed chest of drawers against the wall. If he had been looking for something it was impossible to tell what or even where he had been looking. The racks of tools were neatly arranged, the drawers in the chest were firmly closed and trays and toolboxes on the work surfaces undisturbed. Though the garage was jam-packed with possessions, everything seemed in order. There were boxes stacked neatly on the floor, some labelled with the contents. Her eyes fell momentarily on a pile marked with the names of the family's grown-up children: Malcolm – uni; Alistair – keep. Elsewhere there were the remains of an earlier family life: children's bicycles; bright plastic skittles; footballs and tattered fishing nets on sticks. Overspill from the house, too: a nest of occasional tables; a magazine rack; a footstool, the upholstery faded and showing signs of damp. Against the wall nearest the door to the kitchen there was a large chest freezer. On instinct she lifted the lid.

'No bodies,' Liam said. 'I already checked.'

Ellen smiled and felt a tiny release of tension.

'Don't see the point in them myself,' she said. 'How do you ever find anything? Things could get lost down the bottom for years.'

'By that reasoning, you could say the same about your desk,' Liam said. 'Sarge.'

Ellen shot him a look of mock disapproval, but her shoulders went down a bit more.

'Mother's not in great shape to be interviewed,' Liam said. 'She was rummaging about in there.' He indicated a plastic box sitting just inside the garage which contained assorted tableware. 'She hadn't put the light on and she hadn't seen the body in the dark. It was only when Norna Gilchrist came looking for her mother that she spotted him. From that point on she says she and her brother Robert are the only people who came into the garage until the police arrived.'

Ellen looked at him.

'They say they just checked he was definitely dead. Claim they didn't disturb anything.'

'It took two of them?'

It hardly mattered. A great many other people could have entered the garage before that, Ellen thought. Most might have been a bit put out to find Barber snooping about on the day of a man's funeral, but there were two who had greater reason than most for feeling threatened and angry.

'I want to talk to Malcolm Gilchrist and Alistair Gilchrist,' she said.

9

They commandeered a small sunroom at the back of the house. The wicker seats were less formal than Ellen would have liked but they would do for now. While she waited she tried to quell the tingling in her nerves. It felt uncomfortably close to panic. Or the hysterical urge to laugh. Even before today she'd been feeling jittery. She had put it down to meeting Barber again. Like an adult child going home for Christmas and reverting to her teenage behaviour, she thought, seeing Barber again had rekindled something of the old Ellen. She had found herself struggling to hide her impatience, feeling cornered and wanting to lash out when someone stood too close behind her in the queue at the local coffee shop.

It might have been guilt at turning Barber down.

But she wasn't going to unravel. Not now.

All the work she'd put in back then, the things she'd done to channel the rage and the fear, she realised now that she'd become complacent, she'd let them slip. The exercise, the breathing. She had never had much time for the cognitive behavioural therapy. That just felt like spin and trying to override your intuition was just plain stupid. No, she wasn't doing that again but she should have kept up with some of the other stuff. Because right now she wanted to destroy whoever had done this to Jimmy Barber, and she needed to do things properly.

Liam brought Malcolm Gilchrist in first. He was strikingly handsome, elegant in an expensive suit, and there was a confidence and fluidity to his movement as he crossed the room and took a seat. Liam had told her he was a pilot and she could imagine him turning heads as he strode through the departure lounge with a coterie of cabin crew around him.

She introduced herself. 'May I call you Malcolm? It

would be easier, with so many Mr. Gilchrists.'

'Of course.'

'You've all been told about the discovery of a dead man in your garage.' She paused. Malcolm Gilchrist nodded, but he said nothing.

'He was murdered.'

Malcolm's lips parted in surprise. It looked genuine enough.

'Your brother and sister didn't give you any details of what they found?'

'No. Actually, they didn't tell us anything. It was only when the police arrived that we learned a man had died.'

Ellen frowned. 'Is that a little odd?'

'That they didn't tell us?' He thought for a moment. 'We would probably have wanted to see for ourselves.'

Did that make sense? Without siblings, Ellen had no frame of reference.

'I need to check whether anyone here had any connection to the dead man. Why he might have been here today. And of course, whether anyone here had any motive for killing him.'

'I can't believe… I mean, we've just buried my father. I only came home for the funeral yesterday.'

Ellen and Liam exchanged a glance.

'The dead man was a police officer. Retired. Former Detective Inspector James Barber.'

She saw his pupils contract. The colour drain from his face.

'You do know him, then?'

'No, I… Well, not know. I don't understand why… What was he doing here?'

'That's what we're trying to find out. How do you know him?'

The wicker creaked as Malcolm sat forward in his chair. For a moment she thought he was about to get up and leave but instead he hunched over his knees and his eyes fell sideways to the middle distance. They waited.

'Something happened a long time ago,' he said eventually. 'A man was killed near here and we were all interviewed about it. DS Barber – that was the name of one of the detectives. But I don't understand. It doesn't make any sense, him being here.'

Did he really not know that their father had tried to contact Barber? Ellen decided to hold on to that for the moment.

'Why were you interviewed?'

Malcolm shifted on the edge of his seat. His voice was dry when he spoke again. 'I was out with a friend, at the pub disco. They said he'd been there too. The man who was killed. They were asking people if they'd seen anything.' He swallowed, with difficulty.

Ellen looked at Malcolm steadily for a full minute. He was very white now, and trembling slightly.

'Can you give us an account of your movements since you arrived here yesterday.'

'Yes, of course.'

She could see that Malcolm's mind was still half in the past, but he recounted his actions since he touched down at Edinburgh Airport the previous day, and gave details of who had been in the house at various times since.

'Rob went to collect Fiona and Calum from their B&B this morning. They got back at about the same time as Alistair and co. arrived.'

'What time was that?'

'About quarter past ten, maybe? We were to be ready to leave for the funeral at half ten. That's when the car was coming. We had some coffee and waited.'

'And nothing seemed untoward?'

'No.'

'You didn't see anyone hanging around the neighbourhood? Any strange cars parked on the street?'

Malcolm shook his head. 'I wouldn't know which cars belonged here or not. But I didn't see anyone, no.'

'And no-one in the family was behaving strangely?'

He grimaced helplessly. 'We were about to go to my Dad's funeral so we weren't exactly behaving as we normally would. It was all a bit stiff and formal, but nothing like you mean.'

People always thought they knew what she meant, Ellen thought. She and her colleagues had to be so careful not to misinterpret what other people said, not to second guess or make assumptions, and yet the number of times people told her they knew what she was thinking...

Malcolm took them through the rest of the day's movements: the funeral car arriving, the wait at the crematorium, the ceremony and the line of people giving their condolences afterwards.

'Al came back to the house first to prepare for the guests.' He watched her write that down.

'None of you noticed that the side door to the garage had been forced?'

'No. Well, I didn't. No-one said anything.'

'Did anyone go into the garage that you know of?'

'I only found out Mum and Norna had gone in there when the police arrived and told us what had happened.'

'Alright, that'll be all just now. We'll need to speak to you again.'

'I'm due to fly out to Dubai tomorrow, from Heathrow.'

'Someone else will have to cover.'

He looked as though he was about to argue, then he nodded just once and rose. He left a lingering scent of something subtle but seductive as he left the room. But despite this and his movie star looks the impression he made was ephemeral. There was something missing from Malcolm Gilchrist, Ellen thought. Arrogance, certainly, but lacking that should only make him more attractive. Charisma, though. Character. Without those he was little more than an icon. There was an emptiness to him.

*

Alistair was a different man altogether. In contrast to his brother's sang-froid he gave off a nervous energy that filled the room. He had taken off his jacket and tie and loosened his collar but he still looked uncomfortable. He was not intimidated by them, though.

'How long will all this take? I'm worried about Mum.'

Ellen couldn't tell whether he was trying to rush her deliberately. She waited until he was seated, until he was still. 'We need to take some preliminary statements, then we can let you all go for now. Can your mother stay with you? I understand you live locally.'

'Yes, of course. I've already told her.'

She took a moment to consult her notes before looking up at him. He didn't have his brother's classic good looks. His face was too thin, the proportions of his features less regular, more angular, but he had a kind of bad-boy attraction. She felt guilty for thinking it, as though she was betraying James Barber somehow.

'The man who was murdered...' She watched as his eyes widened, his jaw slackened. 'Did you know him?'

He was all movement again. 'No. I mean, what? Murdered? Are you sure?' When she didn't answer: 'I don't know who it was so how can I tell whether I knew him? Wasn't it one of the guests, then?'

'We don't think so, no. As far as I understand it, he wouldn't have been very welcome here.'

Alistair frowned. 'Why? Who was he?'

She held eye contact before answering. 'Former Detective Inspector James Barber. I understand he questioned you as part of a murder investigation twenty-years ago.'

'What the fuck?' Alistair Gilchrist was on his feet. Liam rising to meet him.

'Could you sit down, please, Alistair.' Ellen waited until he had returned to the chair, where he perched on the edge, his knuckles white on the arms.

'This is messed up,' he said. 'The man was off his head, but... What the fuck?'

'Your brother told us you came back from the funeral earlier than the others.'

'Huh? Oh, that'll be right.' He scowled. 'Yes, I came back to get ready for the reception.'

'What time did you get here?'

'I don't know. About quarter past twelve, I think. I'm not sure exactly.' He picked restlessly at the wicker weave on the arm of the chair with his thumb nail.

'And you didn't notice that the side door to the garage had been forced?'

He shook his head.

'Did it look as though anyone had entered the house through the garage?'

He stilled for a moment, thinking, then shook his head again. 'I didn't notice anything out of place. It all looked pretty much how we left it.'

'Pretty much?'

He tutted. 'Exactly.'

'Why do you say James Barber was "off his head"?'

'The man was obsessed. It was bad enough then. He wouldn't let it go. It got so I thought he just wants to pin it on me. Just make a collar. He had no proof, nothing except the fact I was out that night and he didn't like the look of me. And then all these years later he comes back again. Bothering Mum about it when Dad's ill in hospital. Trying to get at him when he's lying there...' There was a catch in his throat. 'And now, when we're at his funeral...'

'Why do you think he might have been here?'

'How the hell should I know?'

'Could he have been looking for something?'

'More likely planting something,' Alistair spat.

Ellen felt the hairs on the back of her neck stand on end. She pushed the thought away but it didn't go easy. Why was Barber here? How could he have put himself in this position? It wasn't like him, not the man she knew, the man who had taught her, Find the truth, not the proof. This was rash, impulsive. He should have been more Barber.

'It was your father who tried to make contact with James Barber,' she said to Alistair. 'That was the only reason Barber had been trying to speak to him. He believed your father might have information about Connor Leask's murder that he wanted to share with him.'

Alistair stared at her, taking in the extent to which she already knew about the murder of Connor Leask and Barber's pursuit of the truth, taking in what she said about his father.

'That's bullshit.'

'Apparently not. It took a while for the message to reach Barber because, of course, he'd retired from the service. By the time it did your father was in hospital. And you wouldn't let Barber talk to him.'

Alistair's jaw clenched. She saw the muscles in his temples pulse.

'My father was dying.'

'And now James Barber is dead too. Murdered. In your garage. And I'm not going to let this investigation lapse. Not until I find out who killed him.'

10

It was a difficult briefing Dan led a couple of hours later. Blackwood had demanded that they document the contact they'd had with Barber and their subsequent actions but he had been happy for the case to rest with them – as long as they weren't constrained by Barber's theories.

'You have a slight head start in the sense that you know something about the victim and his state of mind in the weeks preceding his murder. But it's one angle and one angle only. No assumptions. Do the usual. Check his communications, movements. Go through his case history. Find out whether there's anyone else who might bear a grudge. Threats. Anyone he put away who has been recently released from prison. Find out if there were other old cases he was turning over. Check his personal life. Et cetera. Et cetera.'

All this as Blackwood pulled at his sideburns in time to the gentle tick-churr from the clock on his wall.

Already witness statements were piling up but they did little to help. There was no clear indication of who had or might have gone into the kitchen, the garage or garden during the funeral reception. The only clear consistency that seemed to have emerged so far was that no-one claimed to recognise Barber from either the funeral or the reception. The house-to-house was looking like it might be a bust. Besides the activity on the street that day, there had been family and friends coming and going over the preceding days, many of whom were infrequent visitors, and neighbours could no longer be sure what counted as unusual or not. More than one neighbour had commented on the fact that many of the visitors looked the same to them. They meant old. So far nothing stood out. It was going to take some painstaking work to comb through it all, looking for patterns, anomalies and inconsistencies.

Dan led with an emphasis on procedure, kept his voice neutral, but even before he'd made Barber's connection to the Gilchrists known the murmurs had started. He was one of their own after all. When Dan disclosed their recent contact with Barber and Barber's interest in the Gilchrists in relation to Connor Leask's murder he had to allow a full two minutes for the raking of memories, the speculation, questions and corrections, before he could bring the team back on track.

'It's one line of enquiry,' he said. 'It might be misleading. Bear in mind we still need confirmation that Barber was definitely killed there.' There was a low rumble of dissent. 'I know. It's hard to imagine someone being able to smuggle a body past thirty-odd funeral guests, however intent they were on their little triangle sandwiches. I'm just trying to stop us all from getting ahead of ourselves. Assuming he was killed where he was found, did he go there alone? Was he followed? Was he disturbed, or did he disturb someone else? And why was he there? Given the nature of Barber's previous interest in the Gilchrists, it seems possible he might have been trying to surveil Malcolm or Alistair Gilchrist.'

'Alistair Gilchrist pretty much accused Jimmy Barber of a personal vendetta,' Liam said.

'He admitted to knowing him, then?'

'Both of them did,' Ellen said. 'Alistair and Malcolm. Alistair said it was an obsession, that he thought Barber was determined to nail him at the time of Leask's murder and that he had been pestering his Dad on his deathbed. He claims not to know that it was their Dad who contacted Barber. Malcolm didn't seem to know there had been any contact at all recently, but we need to interview them both again.'

'What did you make of them?'

Ellen thought for a moment. 'I believe Alistair more than Malcolm. His reactions seemed more immediate. But I think they're both holding back.'

'Could be they just don't want to revisit events of twenty-six years ago.'

Ellen made a face. Dan shook his head. 'We can't make assumptions. Why kill a man then leave him in the garage for your mother or sister to find? How would they have had the time to fake a break-in, dispose of any evidence, get changed et cetera, without anyone noticing? We need to ask these questions.'

'But Ronald Gilchrist did try to contact Barber.'

'So Barber said.' He put up a hand to quiet Ellen's protest. 'Something to check. And if he did, why? He was hardly going to turn in one of his boys, was he? Perhaps he had other reasons for wanting to speak to Barber that had nothing to do with the Connor Leask case. Barber was a detective who was known to Gilchrist – perhaps his was simply the one name he remembered when something else came up?'

There was a sceptical silence.

'Plus, Ronald Gilchrist is dead. He couldn't talk to Barber anymore. So what was he hoping to gain by going to the house?'

'Barber never got to talk to Ronald Gilchrist,' Liam said, 'But we know he did speak briefly to Ronald's wife, Linda Gilchrist, and to Alistair. They turned him away from the hospital, but they must have exchanged words in the process.'

'Check with the hospital,' Dan told him. 'See if the staff remember anything that might be useful.'

'Maybe Barber wanted to speak to someone else?' Keisha Bell suggested. 'Another member of the family, or someone who would be at the funeral?'

Only recently out of uniform Keisha had a quiet determination, but Dan sometimes felt that her fear of appearing inexperienced or making mistakes meant that she held back too much. He was glad when she spoke up and did not want to discourage her.

'Why then? On the day of the funeral, I mean.'

'Maybe it was someone who would only be around then? Someone who isn't normally in Edinburgh. Or maybe he wanted to see who was at the funeral, to confirm that someone was a contact of Gilchrist's.'

'Surely it would be easier to see who was at the funeral by going to the crematorium, rather than creeping around the family's garage?' Ellen said.

'I'd like to confirm whether or not Barber had spoken to Cold Cases about the Connor Leask murder before he approached DS Chisholm,' Dan said. 'And if he did, whether he presented them with anything more substantial than he gave us. You know, he never actually said he thought the Gilchrists were responsible. Just that they had been persons of interest and that he thought Ronald knew something.'

Keisha nodded eagerly, scribbling furiously in her notebook.

'I've had a look at the original Connor Leask investigation file,' Ellen said. 'They did focus on the Gilchrists for a while. As Barber told us, they couldn't fully account for their whereabouts. Alistair was already known to the local police. Small stuff, kid stuff really, but he'd been reported that night already for vandalism and creating a disturbance in the area and the police had gone to the house looking for him. Seemingly Ronald had gone out looking for him after that, too, which is how he came to be out and about and unaccounted for. Alistair was alibied by his friend, Finlay Groat, but it wasn't exactly cast iron.'

'And Malcolm?'

'Apparently there was CCTV footage from the bar in the Mains Arms, that appeared to show him talking to Connor Leask less than an hour before he was killed, and he didn't mention it when first asked. Or, I hasten to add, when we interviewed him earlier today. Footage'll need to be digitised, of course.

'Beyond that, there was nothing concrete to tie any of them to Leask or his murder, but they were evasive, and at one point Ronald Gilchrist is noted as having said, "Leave the animals to the animals".'

There was a silence after that, each of them reflecting on the incidents where the violence of an act was offset by the callousness, disinterest or self-interest of those who witnessed it. They told themselves it was human. An instinct for self-preservation. But sometimes it stuck in the craw.

'You think Dad might have told his boys to say nothing, even if they'd seen something?' Liam said eventually. 'Then why would he try to reach Jimmy Barber all of a sudden, now? It's a funny thing to do if his boys are still the ones who would have to deal with it.'

Ellen shrugged.

'Where are we with preliminary forensics?' Dan asked.

'We'll need to wait for them to confirm whether there's any sign Barber went beyond the garage into the house itself,' Ellen said. 'So far, it looks like he didn't. It's possible his killer didn't either, that they both entered and left by the side door to the garage.'

'Alistair Gilchrist claimed that Barber could have been there to plant evidence,' Liam said.

'That's him getting his defence in early,' Ellen said, quickly.

Dan glanced at her. It was bad enough trying not to let the Connor Leask enquiry dominate this one, without having a sergeant blinkered by her loyalty to the dead man.

'We need to look at Barber's personal life, and whether there were any other cases or any old animosities that he had stirred up recently. Maybe the Leask enquiry wasn't the only one he was trying to rekindle. If we can eliminate all other possibilities and it looks like this really is connected to the Connor Leask case, then we can concentrate on that, but we'll look at it with fresh eyes, not with Barber's.'

He saw Keisha wince at that. She had said before that she had a vivid imagination, but he sometimes wondered whether her tendency to interpret words literally was more than that.

'Though I will admit,' Dan said. 'It's going to be very hard to get away from the fact that the man who seemed convinced these people knew something about Connor Leask's murder has just been found bludgeoned to death in their garage.'

I can't shake the feeling that I did something wrong.

I knew enough to get Mum out of the garage. Robert was just coming back into the kitchen. Of course he didn't believe me when I told him there was a dead man in our garage. I'm little Non. If we'd told the others they would each have had to check for themselves too. There is a pecking order. I watched as Rob tiptoed over to where the man was slumped on the concrete floor. From the kitchen I could only see the outline of the man's back, picked out in the light from the narrow windows along the top of the main garage door. It annoyed me that Rob didn't trust my judgment but in spite of myself I asked, 'Is he definitely dead?'

'Yes.'

Mum was standing at the sink, humming distractedly as she ran water. Soap suds were rising.

'Who is he?' I asked Rob. I don't remember seeing the man at the funeral, or at the house afterwards. He wasn't wearing black but not everyone was. My first instinct had been to think he was some old guy with dementia who thought it was his house.

But he was murdered.

'Do you recognise him?' I asked.

'I don't think so,' Rob said.

But Malcolm and Al know who he was. And I think Rob does too, because when he came back into the kitchen and pulled the door shut behind him, and when he handed me the phone before turning off the tap and ushering Mum towards the hall, he wasn't looking at me. He was very carefully not looking at me.

It's surreal. It doesn't make any sense and I feel detached from what's happening. Because how can this be happening? It's as though something has leaked from my imagination and taken solid form. I have no defence against that.

'Who was he?' I ask now.

We're in Al's back garden, the light from the kitchen illuminating the deck he built. Everyone else has gone to bed and it's cold, but I don't want to go inside yet.

'He was a policeman.'

Robert sits at the bottom of a plastic slide that has seen better days, rolling himself a joint. His ghost is here now too. He stares bleakly at the neglected sandpit, lifts the cracked cover to find sand overtaken by earth and weeds and cat-poo, and lets it drop again, disconsolate.

A policeman.

That female detective who seemed to be running the show, she drew my attention not just because she was in charge but because she seemed so real. So solid. Everything about her was an exercise in conformity and self-repression: the neat suit, hair tied back in a pony tail; dormant laughter lines around her mouth and eyes. Even her freckles were on a dimmer switch. She was dressed for her job not for herself, but despite her camouflage she made me feel as though I was the cipher. I realise now, that energy coming off her – it's because it was personal.

The real Rob lights up and takes a first satisfied draw, then lies back, wedging his shoulders awkwardly into the sides of the chute and gazes up at the blotted sky.

'Back home, you can see the stars, the milky way. It's amazing. The Northern Lights sometimes too. I never get tired of it.'

How can he be so calm?

'Why was he at Dad's funeral?'

'Let it go, Non, it's been a bastard of a day.'

He's not calm. I thought he was, but he isn't at all. He's angry.

I can't let any of it go.

Malcolm didn't even come into the house. He came half way up the path to say goodbye to Mum but that was it.

'We can easily make space,' Alistair said, though it sounded more like a challenge than an invitation.

'I think we've all had enough upheaval today,' Malcolm said. 'Anyway, the airline has these flats to be used.'

'But you'll come back tomorrow, won't you?' I asked.

'We could do something. Since we're all stuck here,' Rob said. 'Go for a walk. A drink.'

'That would be nice,' Malcolm said and Alistair's face twitched, a momentary snarl of scorn. It was barely noticeable but it was not lost on Malcolm. Why must Al do this? Was it the agreeable way Malcolm said it? Was it the platitude? Was it simply the use of the word 'nice'?

Rob and I said our goodbyes and went inside. I thought Al had followed and was locking up behind us, but when I went back into the hall to look for him I saw that he was still outside on the path with Malcolm. They were speaking quietly, urgently. I can't remember when I last saw them speak to each other alone or by choice, and I was surprised. This looked like something shared, but not. It looked like history. I moved to the door to listen.

'But I don't suppose you told them you went back to get your reading, did you?' Al said, jabbing a finger at Malcolm.

'I'm sure I can leave that to you,' Malcolm said. 'They might wonder why you're so desperate to implicate me, though.'

I felt the blood drain from my legs suddenly and grasped at the door. The boys turned.

'Norna? What's up?' Al asked, coming into the house.

'I came looking for you,' I said. The catch on the gate clicked. Malcolm had gone.

There is something going on that I am not part of. Something they all know about. And it has to do with a dead policeman in our garage.

She didn't interview me, that Detective Sergeant. Walked right past me on her way through to the summer room. She did give me the once-over: grey eyes, sharp, and her mouth set in a determined line. Even though I saw him first it was only a young DC who talked to me. All bright-eyed and bushy-tailed. We have to go and give proper statements tomorrow, but even so, the DS – Chisholm I think her name was – she made a point of speaking to Malcolm and Al. Why? She didn't look the type to follow some outdated sexist code of talking to the men of the household. Not that I'm saying women don't because sometimes they're even worse than men for that kind of thing. But not her, I don't think. It was something else. Something she knew and they knew and everybody bloody else seems to know. Except me.

The question is: do I want to?

I squeeze my bum onto the swing and begin to turn, twisting the ropes, the fibres squeaking against each other. When I can barely touch the ground with my feet, I reach out to grab the frame and pull myself round another time, and another, until I can wind myself up no further and the ropes are cutting uncomfortably into my thighs. Then I let go and the swing unscrews, jolting me round and round, the night-grey grass beneath my dangling feet blurring with the motion. The swing reaches the bottom and begins to wind up the other way, spinning back again a little less each time, before it finally comes to a halt.

That was a mistake.

I sit collapsed on the seat, my head hanging over the worn patch in the turf, waiting to be sick. I begin, cautiously, to do my nausea breathing. Eventually the queasiness subsides and I can raise my head.

'A minute we had to think about Dad and I couldn't even think of him for that long,' Robert says. 'Not properly, I mean, without my mind wandering.' He blows a stream of smoke slowly into the air above him and watches it disperse.

'Maybe it's because I don't really want to remember the last time I saw him, but it's hard to get it out of my head.'

Does he mean to make me feel guilty? Because I do. I wasn't there.

He tilts his head back to look at me. 'I wondered what you were all thinking. What were you thinking? Remembering?'

'Dunno. Nothing in particular. Holidays, Christmases, stuff like that,' I lie.

'Photographs.' He takes another long drag on his joint.

'What do you reckon the other two were thinking? I was trying to guess. I wondered if Al was remembering the skelps he used to get off Dad for all the trouble he got into. And if he was, what he thought of that now. Now he's turned into him.'

Robert's voice gets deeper and slower when he smokes, more monotonous. I guess that what he's saying seems significant enough to him that he doesn't need to enliven it. Somehow, the flat drone makes his words more terrible.

'And Malc? Prize-givings and graduations? You just can't tell with Malc can you? Maybe something before the rest of us were even born. Maybe that's when he was happy.'

'God, Rob. That's horrible.'

Robert twists round to look at me again. He sits up, shocked. I am crying, silently shuddering, my chin wobbling like a child's.

'Shit.' Robert chucks the remainder of his joint into the flower bed and scrambles to his knees. He ducks under the side support of the swing and kneels at my feet.

'God, I'm sorry, Non. I didn't mean anything by it.'

'What happened to us?'

'I just talk a load of crap, you know that. I should keep my mouth shut.'

'No, you're right, but it's terrible.'

'Jesus, I'm such a prick sometimes. Oh, come here, Nonny.'

He puts his arms round me and I rest my head on his shoulder. We stay like that for a while, Robert half kneeling, half standing, both of us rocking gently with the motion of the swing.

How ugly it is, grief. People say that you regret the things that were left unsaid. The thanks, they mean, the loving words. We allow ourselves to believe it is all about loss and love. But it carries with it years' worth of hard feeling. Jealousies, perceived injustices. Things that were said and done, they burn inside those who are left behind.

I let out a sob.

'Don't wipe your nose on my shirt,' Rob says.

12

James Barber's sister could not have been less like him. Where he was neat, Marion Carruthers had sprawled. Where his countenance had been shrewd and guarded, hers was open, her emotions close to the surface. Her attention and her speech were untidy too, full of half-sentences and distractions. Despite their differences, one thing was clear to Ellen: Marion had adored her brother.

'I was always afraid something like this would happen at his work. I was so relieved when he retired. Oh, look, he's still got that picture up. That's a long time ago: my three are all grown up now. Ah, and this is Richie.'

She picked up a framed photograph from a sideboard in Barber's living room and showed it to Ellen. It had been taken somewhere that was not Scotland. The other man in the photograph looked warm too and Ellen was glad.

'This was his partner?'

'For nearly ten years, yes. They didn't really settle down together until after Jimmy left the police, though. He was terribly affected when Richie died.'

'When was that?'

'Two years ago, now.'

'How did he die?'

'Crash on the A68. One of those sudden freezes, an articulated lorry went into him. It was terrible. There wasn't even anything for Jimmy to solve. It was just – bang. Awful.'

Ellen replaced the photograph carefully, but not before her fingers ran over the back of the frame and the catches. Just in case. Because already she was wondering.

'Did you know him?' Marion asked. 'Jimmy?'

Ellen met her eyes and was glad she could satisfy some of the need she saw there. 'Yes.'

Marion nodded. 'I'll be in the kitchen. I don't want anything left that's going to spoil.'

When she had gone, Ellen moved around the room, gently opening drawers and cupboard doors, gingerly feeling behind the books and objects on shelves, but with little expectation. They hadn't had cause enough to order a search of Barber's house, but even if they had, Ellen suspected they would find little here: the place was immaculate. That was what intrigued her.

They had spent the best part of the day questioning the two eldest Gilchrist brothers for a second time. Going over and over their movements on the day of the funeral and in the weeks preceding it; the contact they had had with James Barber now and twenty-six years before. She had learned little that wasn't already in the case file, or that she hadn't worked out the previous day. They didn't get on. Understatement. There were short periods when each of them could have entered the garage unobserved, indeed, when each of them was in the house alone. These periods were very short and left little room for a change of clothes or a change in demeanor. But they existed as possibilities.

Both brothers denied any involvement in the murder of Connor Leask. And she had to admit the old case file backed them up – after a while they had been dropped from the list of viable suspects.

Which begged the question: why was Barber so convinced that their father had information to give him? Why did he seem sure that they were involved?

Ellen moved on through the house and it was the same story: nothing out of place and nothing that looked as though it was a work in progress. Barber's house contained no notes, no computer, no hint of an investigation. Even in the spare room that Barber had clearly once used as an office, there was nothing on the walls, nothing on or in the desk to suggest he had been pursuing an enquiry.

Ellen thought about the man she had known and the man he had been the last time she saw him. There was suppressed anger there, regret, but nonetheless he was still contained, as meticulous as he ever had been. Despite a sense of urgency he held himself together. Above all, he had been certain. Convinced he was onto something.

She pulled out her phone and dialled. It took a while for Keisha to answer. Almost as long for Ellen to realise she would be off-duty by now.

'Boss?'

'Keisha, did you find out whether Barber had gone to Cold Cases with his suspicions about the Gilchrists?'

'Yeah. He didn't. Apparently he approached them a couple of times over the intervening years about reopening the Connor Leask enquiry, but he hadn't gone back to them after Ronald Gilchrist tried to get in touch.'

'Okay. Thanks.'

It wasn't a surprise. When Ellen had accessed the Connor Leask case file, no-one had been near it in years.

Ellen stared at the large blank wall in front of her. She went up to it, close, and ran her hands over the surface. A big blank wall like this in a room used as an office, it made a perfect incident board, and yet there was nothing here to suggest Barber had used it as such. She pulled open the desk drawers for a second time, then got down on her hands and knees and looked under the desk. The electrical socket was empty.

She pictured James Barber in the café where they had met. His jacket hung over the back of his chair, and – yes – a briefcase at his feet. It was missing. Barber's keys and wallet had been missing, too.

Ellen had always thought Barber was old school, but that might just have been because once upon a time she was new and he was old. Her feeling was that even the most intuitive software wasn't a match for a good old-fashioned incident board. But maybe it was Ellen who was old school. Barber could have carried his investigation around with him. All of it. Laptop and charger, print-outs and flash drives, all together in that briefcase. But why? When you had a wall like this. When you had a room like this. A house.

She took one last look around the bare office.

They were only at the beginning and already she couldn't help feeling that someone was one step ahead of them.

13

DS Chisholm had wanted to interview Vihaan Shah but Dan had pulled rank. Reminiscing about Barber with another former colleague would not do her or the investigation any good. She was still angry, and that wasn't like her. No banter, no quips. Even her Aberdonian accent seemed to have hardened. He was more concerned about what was happening inside. He didn't mind if she blamed him for not taking Barber seriously. Far better that than she blamed herself. An officer bent on self-recrimination was no good to him.

Shah led him into a cramped office and pushed aside a stack of files so Calder could put down the cup of coffee he had given him. Shah was a year or two off retirement. His hair was greying at the sides and the deep bags under his heavy-lidded dark eyes gave him a solemn air. He put Dan in mind of an ageing Basset Hound. He had not made any attempt at small talk, but Dan didn't think it was out of rudeness or resentment. Rather, he thought Shah didn't want to trivialise what they were meeting to talk about.

'Were you close to James Barber?' Dan asked, when they were settled. 'I know you worked together for a long time.'

'I did consider him a friend. We rubbed along alright. Kept up after he retired. I hadn't seen him for a couple of months, though, before all this reared its head again.'

'You were the one who got the message that Ronald Gilchrist wanted to see him?'

'Eventually, yes. I was the one who finally passed it on to Jimmy. Wish I hadn't, now.'

'You didn't speak to Ronald Gilchrist yourself?'

'I tried, but his wife said he'd taken ill.'

'In his original message, do you know whether Ronald Gilchrist mentioned the Connor Leask case specifically?'

Shah answered carefully. 'He had mentioned the case, apparently, but he didn't say specifically that that's what he wanted to talk to him about. It's possible it was just a way of locating Jimmy, or explaining how he knew him. It's why his message found its way to me, though. I'm the last serving officer who worked on the case.'

Shah's hesitance echoed Dan's own feelings. It was tempting to believe both Gilchrist's call and Barber's death were connected to the murder of Connor Leask, but they couldn't afford to make assumptions. 'Did Jimmy regularly look into his old cases? Did he ever ask you for access to other files?'

'Not after he retired. A couple of times when he was still on the job he would review stuff, but – hang on.' He began rummaging through his desk. 'There was one time, a couple of years ago. Not one of his own cases. I think he said it was personal. I seem to remember thinking he might have been doing a favour for a member of the family.'

He was flicking through an old notebook now. Vihaan Shah was clearly a man who kept precise records. From what Ellen had told him about Barber, Dan could see why they had been a good match.

'Here we go. Accidental death on a building site in 1992. Young lad by the name of Lee Quigley. Yeah, this wouldn't have been long after Richie, Jimmy's partner, died, so I suppose if the family had looked to him for help he would have had some empathy.'

Ellen had told Dan about Barber's partner's death. And what his sister had said about it: that there wasn't even anything for him to investigate. It made sense that he would have understood what other grieving relatives were going through, want to find answers for them.

All the same, an accidental death in 1992? A year before Connor Leask died?

'This recent interest in the Connor Leask enquiry, was it purely a reaction to Ronald Gilchrist's call, do you think?'

'I thought so. He hadn't mentioned it for years.'

'Would you mind telling me what you remember about it?'

Shah ballooned his cheeks and expelled the air. 'I'll do my best. If I'm honest, though, what I remember is mixed up with what Jimmy stirred up the other week. I don't know how reliable it is.'

'You don't think Barber was reliable?'

'I didn't say that.' Shah said. 'I just meant that I hadn't thought about it for a long time before Jimmy brought it up again.'

He gave Dan a recap, some of which he already knew, about Leask and his last known movements on the night he died.

'He was spotted by a patrol car at the bus stop on Corbiehill Road, but either he then decided to walk or he was fleeing someone. There were reports of a couple of eggings in the area that night. There was no evidence at the bus stop but one theory was that he'd moved off to get away from potential trouble.'

'So right away people began to link his death to the fact he was gay.'

'Like I say, it was one theory. The fact is, all we had were theories. There was so little concrete evidence. No murder weapon. No sightings after the bus stop. No threats. Work was going well. A bit of aggro with an ex-boyfriend but he had an alibi. Connor had a good life, nice flat, his career was taking off. During the week he socialised in fancy wine bars with his friends and law chums and he let off steam in the gay bars at the weekends. We couldn't find anything to suggest he'd made any dodgy contacts, or was involved in anything he shouldn't have been.'

'What about his job, though? That must have brought him into contact with some criminal cases.'

'He was a trainee. It was mostly grunt work. His main job seems to have been to prepare material for the Fiscal, to help her assess whether a case would go to trial, but he didn't interview suspects. Re-interviewing witnesses was about as thrilling as it got. Maybe not as thrilling as he would have liked, by all accounts.'

'What do you mean?'

'Well, he had a bit of a reputation for being a hotshot

and a man in a hurry. Anxious to climb the ladder fast and make a name for himself.'

'Why was Jimmy so convinced one of the Gilchrists was involved?'

Shah gave a baffled shrug. 'Back then? It was more a suspicion that one of them might have seen something and in the good old British tradition they didn't want to get involved. We put a bit of pressure on them to try and get them to open up. You know, the kind of thing. Leask's injuries were consistent with the murder weapon being a Stanley knife and the Gilchrists had access to several, what with Gilchrist owning a hardware shop...'

'But Stanley knives are common.'

'Exactly. If they did know something they didn't take the bait.'

'What about this CCTV footage of Malcolm Gilchrist and Connor Leask? We've sent it to be digitised but it might take a while.'

Shah tilted his head in acknowledgement. They both knew that some footage of two blokes in a bar twenty-six years ago was going to be low on the priority list for a unit that was already overworked. Though it might provide them some respite from the horrific material they were confronted with on a daily basis.

'We got very excited about the CCTV,' Shah said. 'It was still quite a new thing and there weren't many private businesses that had it but the pub landlord was a bit of a gadget nut. And pretty untrusting, it seems. The footage wasn't as useful as we hoped in the end because it turned out he wasn't that bothered about the punters. The camera was trained on the bar. He was trying to catch out any members of staff who helped themselves to a sneaky half pint, or decided they needed a few extra tips.'

'But you did get something.'

'We got Malcolm Gilchrist and half of Connor Leask waiting at the bar. If I remember rightly the body language suggested there might have been a bit of an altercation, but we're talking seconds here. Connor is only on screen for a minute or so. Malcolm gets his drinks. That's it.'

'But Malcolm didn't mention it when he was shown a picture of Connor and asked if he recognised him.'

'No, but a bloke next to you at a crowded bar compared to a nice picture of him posing for the camera? It was possible Malcolm just didn't recognise him at first. He was very nervous when we interviewed him. Teary. By all accounts he was a good boy, grade A student on his way to university, and this was his first brush with the law.'

'What about Alistair Gilchrist?'

'Ah, Che Gilchrist was a different matter. He was your typical teenage wannabe rebel. Spouting all this schoolboy Marxist/anarchist crap. We were organs of the state. I was nothing but a token gesture. He was a victim of prejudice and oppression. Yada, yada. He and his mate had already been reported that night for mucking about in the car park of the Safeway store. No doubt leaving trolleys in the shrubberies of nearby gardens was striking a blow against the capitalist regime.'

Dan smiled. 'He had an alibi though?'

'Well, his partner in crime vouched for him. It's not ironclad, but it seemed to tally with the report from the patrol car. After the trolley incident they were seen legging it down Main Street in the opposite direction to the bus stop and a while before Connor was spotted there.'

'What do you think? Was James Barber barking up the wrong tree?' Dan asked.

Shah frowned. 'If you'd asked me about all this a month ago I would have said the only reason the Gilchrists stood out any more than other possible witnesses was because we had no real suspects, and that of all the rat-faced, bigoted, hung-over and self-absorbed people we interviewed in the aftermath of Connor Leask's death, they were a fraction more dubious than most. The thing is, I wouldn't have said Jimmy thought any different, either. We all thought they were being shifty bastards, but like you say, it doesn't mean they had anything to do with Connor Leask's killing. I don't know whether he was barking up the wrong tree, but I was surprised that it only took one phone call to get him so fired up again. I regretted mentioning it to him almost immediately he started badgering folk about the investigation again, never mind when I heard what happened.'

'So Barber took this to other people too?'

'Oh, yes, he ruffled quite a few feathers. Not least Baroness Lise Eklund, and Sheena Baird.'

'Sheena Baird?'

'Daughter of Hugh. Former Detective Superintendent Hugh Baird. It was he who ultimately gave the order to close down the enquiry. Hugh Baird died, um, about six years ago, I think. Anyway, I gather Jimmy informed Sheena that her beloved father had had a long term affair with Baroness Eklund.'

Dan's eyebrows lifted. 'Why? Is it true? And if it is, what does that have to do with anything?'

'Don't ask me. I wasn't privy to what Jimmy was thinking at the end.'

Dan allowed this piece of information to sink in. It made him uncomfortable. Blurting out personal information to a family member: putting impropriety aside, that wasn't the James Barber Ellen had described to him. Even if it was true and Hugh Baird and Lise Eklund had been in a relationship with each other, what had it to do with Ronald Gilchrist and how did it tally with Barber's theory that the Gilchrists were involved with Connor Leask's death? Phoning Ellen Chisholm and trying to rope her into some kind of rogue investigation. Snooping round a dead man's garage while his family were singing hymns at his funeral. Was Barber mad at the end? Mad with grief, perhaps? Because none of this sounded like the behaviour of a rational detective. It sounded like a man with a personal vendetta.

Or a smokescreen.

14

The tide is out in the Firth of Forth, baring the low, barnacle-encrusted causeway alongside the monumental triangular concrete blocks that stretch from the shore out to Cramond Island. We used to call it the Toblerone. It was Robert's idea to come here. We walk in silence. Now and then one of us turns to survey the shoreline behind us, from the apartment developments at Granton past Cramond and across the mouth of the river Almond to the Dalmeny estate and west towards the bridges. Malcolm stops at one point to watch the planes banking over the Forth and descending towards the airport. Perhaps he's appraising the manoeuvres. Perhaps he's wishing he was in the cockpit. Though I suspect it's a departure he's after, not an arrival. Neither he nor Alistair has said anything about the police interviews. They took samples of all our DNA and our fingerprints. That same young detective constable interviewed me again: asked me over and over what happened when I discovered the body. Why I let Robert go into the garage. (She clearly doesn't have big brothers.) But Al and Malcolm, who never saw the body, who didn't know it was there until the police arrived, they were questioned for hours. And not just by anybody, either. By the detective sergeant who was in charge yesterday. The one who means business.

It's a bright day, the mudflats gleaming and the water further out in the firth the proper blue of a child's painting. We reach the island and head instinctively for the lookout that stands on the rocks overlooking the groyne. We stand inside the semi-circular building looking at the skyline of the city that was our childhood home, and our ghosts stand with us.

This was the most exciting place I knew in childhood. The fact that we couldn't always get out to it made it an adventure when we could. The fact that we might be cut off by the tide if we stayed too long made us daring. I could travel back in time, blimps in the air above me, U-boats threatening to penetrate the firth. Or I could be in Atlantis or Alcatraz.

'I can't remember when I was last here,' Malcolm murmurs.

'It hasn't changed much,' Robert says. 'Bit more graffiti to add to Al's.'

'Yeah, why did you feel the need to scrawl all over everything, Al?' It's a brave question, coming from Malcolm. Or a provocation.

'Dunno. I was angry.'

'At what? Walls?'

Al pauses. 'At everything,' he says quietly.

'Come on.' Robert turns and leads the way out of the lookout. We troop after him, Al casting a glance back to one corner where the walls are daubed with years' worth of frustration and self-expression.

We set off across the foot-worn path which rises towards the centre of the island, my seven-year old self hacking at the jungle alongside us. At a shout from a child on the beach behind us she drops to the ground and wriggles forward through the undergrowth until she finds a vantage point from which she can take aim.

'Wasn't there an old house here somewhere?' asks Malcolm. There is a dip in the centre of the island, wooded and thickly overgrown. I remember tumbledown stone walls, a hearth set with nettles.

'Maybe it's completely fallen down.'

Robert wrinkles his forehead. 'I don't remember a house.'

It was the enemy hideout. They came ashore in the night and managed to evade our searchlights and our dogs, but we tracked them down, surrounded them. It came down to a shoot out in the end, but there was nowhere for them to go.

I have little memory of being here with my brothers or with Mum and Dad. I was with James Mason and Steve

McQueen and Trevor Howard. My own company pulled to-gether from the films Dad loved to watch. I feel a sudden rush of emotion, thinking of the two of us on some mis-placed rainy Sunday afternoon, him in his chair with a rare glass of beer, me on the floor with instructions not to knock over my hot chocolate.

We reach the far side of the island where there is a whole settlement of small grey concrete or red brick build-ings, once embattlements that guarded the Forth, now made bright with graffiti. Many are still accessible through dark windows and doorways edged with rusting iron fix-tures. A network of cracked tarmac tracks and concrete steps half buried in the grass connects them. We climb the flight of steps to one of the larger buildings. Inside the walls are tagged in purple and green, broken glass and empty cans litter the ground. Deep channels cut into the concrete floor are stagnant with rainwater and clotted with the ash from bonfires, bird shit and God knows what else. Robert wrinkles his nose at the smell of urine. He won't go in.

'What was this, I wonder? Did they have some kind of tracks running round for equipment? Weaponry?' It strikes me that it's Malcolm's way to ask questions that don't need to be answered. It's safe. Should someone take him up on it, then it becomes conversation, but there's no slight to him if they don't.

Except that Alistair knows where the chinks in his ar-mour are. He takes aim.

'Dunno.' Bored. Dismissive. Who cares? Shut up!

'Maybe it was the shower block – drains?' I suggest.

'It's a toilet now anyway,' says Al, and he turns abruptly to go down the steps after Rob. I wait, but Malcolm does not budge. He stands with his back to me, staring through one of the slits in the wall. Eventually I leave him alone in the dank interior and follow the others.

What happened to us? Or was it always like this?

The detective who interviewed me asked me whether I remembered the dead policeman. Our family had been questioned about a murder in the area in 1993, she said. I was only seven, I told her, but she wouldn't leave it. She asked me to try and remember. Did I know of anything significant that happened around that time? Were there changes in the behaviour of my father or either of my two eldest brothers? She said there was no reason to worry, no reason to suspect they had been involved, then or now, but they had to ask these questions. She told me that, before he died, Dad had tried to contact the man who investigated that murder. That it was the man he tried to contact who was murdered in our garage.

Alistair and Malcolm were arguing about blame.

I didn't tell the detective that. I didn't tell her anything. I don't remember.

I climb up to an almost circular gun emplacement with its rusted iron track still in place on the concrete surface, weeds and grasses pushing through the cracks. Robert is staring out east towards the mouth of the Forth. I pause for a moment, while my seven-year old ghost looks down invisible sights and wheels round, sending a barrage of imaginary gunfire one hundred and eighty degrees over the firth. Then I sit down carefully beside him. I watch a tanker make its way slowly past the towns camped on the Fife coastline and on towards the open sea.

After a while we are joined by Al who has gathered a collection of pebbles and begins to hurl them off the gun emplacement. They chink and bounce on the rocks below. A couple reach the water, but the effort almost takes Al off the edge so he stops trying and sits down. Rob lies back looking up at the sky. Cool, spring blue with clean wisps of white clouds passing slowly across it.

When Malcolm joins us, stepping lightly onto the concrete platform, Robert squints up at him, shielding his eyes from the sun. 'I remember when I was last here. It was 1993.'

Malcolm and Alistair freeze momentarily. I hold my breath.

'The Cranberries were in the charts with Linger and I was in love with Dolores. She broke my heart that summer.'

Alistair snorts. 'Christ, what were you? Thirteen?'

'Eleven.'

'Hearts don't break,' Malcolm murmurs. 'They just kind of shrivel up. Like a sundried tomato.'

'Ooh, lah-di-dah,' Alistair sneers. He has run out of pebbles. Instead he picks at a loose bit of concrete and flings it hard onto the rocks below.

'Black pudding, then?' Robert offers. I wonder what he's playing at. He's still not himself. He's still angry and I can't tell how much of it is grieving for Dad and how much it's because Dad's funeral, his passing, has been tainted by this murder. It's as though he blames the others.

'That was the year we went to the campsite at Gairloch,' he says. And it's as though he has switched on a projector inside my mind. Flickering Hi-8 images of being crowded round the tiny table in the caravan playing beetle after fish fingers and beans; of being buried up to my neck in sand, feeling glad and proud to be at the centre of my brothers' world and just a tiny bit scared they might leave me there and forget about me. I can see the waves, high and bright with light just at the moment they overturn and fall. Malcolm and Alistair and Robert running along the sand in front of them. They are full of light too. Light and life. I remember being in the water, being lifted high by the three of them and flung into the air before landing back in the water with a splash. Again!

I want the others to remember too. I want us to share this, but they are silent. Al's knuckles are white. I can almost feel the tension in Malcolm's body: muscle and tendons poised.

'What happened?' I blurt out. 'What happened that summer?'

Only I don't. Only in my head. Because in the split second when I might have said it aloud I realise they will lie to me. Whatever happened that summer split them apart, but they will band together to keep it from me.

So instead, I say, 'We should be getting back'.

The others glance at the water. Alistair wipes his hands on his jeans and scrambles to his feet, then over the roof of the adjoining block and back onto the path. Robert, still supine on the gun emplacement, lifts an arm to me in a plea to haul him up. I hesitate. I try not to look over the edge at the rocks below and the moving water as I grab his arm with both my own and heave him into a standing position. Once he's on his feet I hold on for just a moment longer until I'm sure I will not topple over myself.

Robert peers at me. 'Ok?'

'Yeah.' I let go my grip on his arm. 'Getting a bit on the hefty side, aren't you?'

'Oi.'

'Middle aged spread, is that what they call it?'

'Watch it.' Rob swipes at me, but I'm too afraid to duck, and can only brace myself as the flat of his hand connects with the back of my head. Sensing my vertigo, he takes me by both shoulders and turns me physically, guiding me off the gun emplacement and back onto the path.

I will have to get them on their own.

15

'I don't think James Barber had ever given up on Connor Leask's murder,' Calder said as he got into Ellen's car outside the city mortuary, echoing her own thoughts. 'I think Ronald wanting to talk to him might have given him fresh hope and motivation. I think it made him go public with his interest in it, start asking around again, but I don't think he had ever let it go.'

'I thought the same. Before me, no-one had accessed the file for a number of years. And it would be the first thing you would do, wouldn't it? If it looked like there might be new evidence.' Ellen put the car into gear and pulled out into the traffic on the Cowgate. 'Unless you already had all the facts to hand.'

She turned up the Pleasance and drove in silence for a few minutes, before plucking up the courage to ask him what he had learnt. 'I take it the post-mortem confirms he was killed in the Gilchrists' garage?'

'Yes. He fell where he lay. Single blow to the back of the head.' Calder looked at her. 'I'm sorry.'

Ellen kept her eyes on the road. 'He must have carried notes with him. On his laptop, maybe. Whoever killed him took it.'

'That means they had to have time to dispose of it somewhere, even temporarily. Of course, we could be looking at more than one person working together.'

'Not the brothers, I don't think. Not much love lost there. Both Alistair and the guy who gave him an alibi on the night Connor Leask was killed were at the funeral, though,' Ellen said. 'Finlay Groat.'

'Let's check his statement when we get back. It would be interesting to know whether he remembered Barber's name, or admitted to doing so.'

Ellen glanced at Calder. 'Are we now assuming that

Jimmy's death is definitely related to his investigation into Leask's murder?'

'Not necessarily. Nothing else stands out so far and from what Vihaan Shah said Barber definitely riled a few folk in the last couple of weeks while pursuing the case. But that got me thinking. Say someone took advantage of that? If they wanted rid of Barber and they got wind of what he was up to? He wasn't exactly hush-hush about it. Maybe they saw a way to make us to think it was about the Gilchrists.'

Ellen mulled that over. She wasn't convinced. 'If that was the case, wouldn't you leave Barber's notes on the Leask murder for us to find? Make it more obvious.'

'Not if your name had come up in the process. Or you simply didn't have time to sort through his files and get rid of the ones that incriminated you.'

They left the city centre, cutting west and south past the Braid Hills. As ever, Calder's eyes sought the skyline. 'It would be nice to know exactly what Barber had on Leask's murder. And why he seemed so sure the Gilchrists were involved.'

'Alistair Gilchrist's prints were all over the garage.'

'But so far there's no evidence either of him on the murder weapon, or it on him.'

The spanner had been so thickly coated in rust that the forensic scientists claimed it must have left traces on the killer. Their examination had so far found nothing to indicate that any of the family members had come in contact with it recently.

'And as an electrician he has a good explanation for using his father's tools and workbench.'

'He's very defensive.'

'So's his brother, Malcolm.'

Ellen's phone went. She glanced at the caller ID as she passed it to Calder. It was Keisha Bell. Dan listened to what she had to say. 'Good work, Keisha. Get him in and put it to him. Take Liam with you.'

'Speak of the devil,' he said, ending the call. 'CCTV at the Western General shows Malcolm Gilchrist heading off

James Barber the day before Ronald died.'

'Bloody liar. He told us he only arrived in Edinburgh for the funeral the day before.'

'Hold your horses.' Calder could clearly tell she wanted to turn the car round and deal with Malcolm Gilchrist herself. 'Keisha and Liam can deal with it. We're here now. Let's see whether Starrett can tell us more about what Barber knew. Connor Leask was his case too, after all.'

Reluctantly, Ellen pushed on to the outskirts of south Edinburgh where she drew up outside a deceptively plain house on Frogston Terrace which backed onto mature woodland. They took a moment before getting out. Former Detective Chief Inspector Glen Starrett cast a long shadow.

'Have you met him before?' Dan asked.

'No. You?'

'Heard of him.'

Ellen nodded. Everyone had heard of Glen Starrett. He had a reputation. A good one. Most of it was based on the outcome of just one successful case, fairly early in his career. Starrett had put Billy Gaughan behind bars. Gaughan had run parts of Edinburgh in the 1980s. At the time, the city was known as Aids capital of the world, and some part of this was owed to the dirty needles being used to inject Billy Gaughan's heroin. The arrest earned Starrett enormous respect. The successful conviction sealed his reputation. Starrett became the poster boy for standing up to the hardest of career criminals, the face of the fight to keep the streets clean.

If you didn't know, Ellen thought, you would never think it from looking at him now. Starrett opened his front door to them wearing a pair of tartan slippers under some well-worn corduroy trousers and a faded rugby shirt. He took a moment to appraise them over the top of some tortoiseshell-rimmed spectacles, nodding slightly as he did so, then welcomed them in.

The house might not have been a looker, but it was large and set in its own sizeable grounds. Starrett led them through to a bright kitchen with apple-green walls and a large window above the sink and work surface that looked out over a pretty garden to the trees beyond. While Calder's eyes inevitably settled on the treeline, Ellen's attention was immediately drawn to a framed photograph of a woman on the old-fashioned dresser. She realised that the picture had been taken here, in the kitchen, but the way Starrett moved around the room, the glimpse inside the fridge as he pulled out a carton of milk, made her think that Mrs Starrett was no longer with them. There was a woman's summer hat on the peg by the door but it felt like a memento. A pair of ladies' gardening gloves and secateurs sat on the window-sill, more decorative than ever used. As he joined them at the table Ellen thought irreverently that if Mrs Starrett had still been around she might have made good use of the secateurs on her husband's eyebrows and nasal hair.

'So, you want to talk about Jimmy Barber.' Starrett leaned on the table for support as he lowered himself onto one of the kitchen chairs. Ellen noticed that the nodding had continued, albeit very slightly. It seemed to originate in his upper torso rather than his neck, a symptom of some condition, perhaps. He pushed a plate of ginger snaps towards Ellen with liver-spotted hands. 'Help yourself.'

She took one. She had a feeling a judgment would be made about her if she didn't. She didn't have much time for diets, but nor did she trust the offerings they were made a lot of the time. She had had her fill of soggy digestives when she was in uniform. And it undermined your gravitas if you had bits of jammy dodger in your teeth when you asked people to account for their whereabouts.

'Barber was in contact with you a few times over the past two-to-three weeks, I gather,' Calder said. 'What did he talk about?'

Starrett took a biscuit himself, fumbling it slightly between thick fingers that lacked dexterity. He sat back slowly. 'Connor Leask. He wanted moral support. He thought if we both made a case for it we could get the investigation re-opened.'

'What did you tell him?'

Starrett smiled, sadly, turning to Ellen. 'Same thing you did, probably. Told him if he had new evidence he should go through the proper channels.'

'He told you he came to me?'

Starrett nodded. 'Here's a piece of advice for you both: learn a language, go back to college, take up coding or get into archaeology or something. Golf is all very well, fishing, that kind of thing gets you out of the house, but it still leaves you too much time in here.' He tapped his head with his forefinger. 'Get yourselves an interest that uses your brain. Or you'll end up like Barber.'

'You called him the night before he died,' Ellen said. 'Did he give any indication of what he was planning to do?'

'No. I had just heard that Ronald Gilchrist had died. I called him to say I was sorry. I thought that might be an end to the matter. I should have realised when he told me he'd tried to see you again that he wasn't giving up. I gather he wanted you to go to the funeral for him?'

Ellen was puzzled. When had Barber tried to see her? She looked at Calder. His face was inscrutable.

'Do you think he planned to go himself, instead?' Calder asked.

Starrett shook his head. 'It looks a bit like it, doesn't it?'

'Why did you want to say sorry?' Ellen asked. 'Sorry for what?'

Without being condescending, the smile Starrett gave her left her feeling naïve. As though he could never explain what it would take her the rest of her career to understand. 'Sorry it turned out to be a dead end,' he said. 'Sorry I couldn't help. He thought we let it go too soon, back in the Nineties. I suppose I felt a bit responsible for his... frustration? Obsession? I don't know.'

'The investigation was officially closed down in 1997, but it was scaled back as early as 1994, is that right?' Dan said. 'Why was that?'

Starrett ran his tongue along the front of his teeth. 'We had nothing.'

They waited. He shrugged. 'You've seen the file.' He paused and Ellen felt a twinge of guilt. Did he know she'd seen the file before she should have done? 'Believe me, if we had the slightest shred of evidence to back up this theory of Barber's that the Gilchrists were involved, we'd have moved heaven and earth. It was frustrating. It was embarrassing, I don't mind telling you that. And I know Jimmy thought we just wrote Leask off, but it really wasn't like that. I wanted that murder solved every bit as much as he did. I just understood better where the Super was coming from.'

'Detective Superintendent Hugh Baird? It was his decision to pull back?'

'Yeah. And in fairness, Hugh was under a lot of pressure. I know he didn't make those decisions lightly.' A kind of reverence crept into Starrett's voice when he talked about Baird. 'Every time he had to choose between putting a man on that case or another he weighed up the pros and cons. You know as well as I do, we operate in a priorities-based environment. He'd had his budget cut. When he finally told us to put it in storage it was part of an audit of the whole department and our caseload at the time, the allocation of resources across every case we had. Jimmy didn't understand that.'

'But you think Baird made the right call?'

'There was a lack of evidence, meaning our chance of a conviction was slim. Yes, much as it pains me, I think he probably did. If Barber had been able to make a solid case against the Gilchrists it would have been a different matter. But all he had was a hunch.'

They fell silent. Ellen looked across at Dan. He was sitting slightly forward and she was surprised to see that he had drained the mug of instant coffee Starrett had given him. Was he afraid of being judged, too?

Before they interviewed people she had noticed that Calder would often pause and let his shoulders drop, as if he was relaxing into a conversation, settling in. It could give the impression he was letting down his defences, that he had no reason to suspect that person, or even that he was opening up to them. She had seen him do it when interviewing hostile witnesses. It put people at ease. She had seen him do it with suspects, to disarm them, make them underestimate him, because he was never less than alert.

But he was not doing it now. Instead, there was a tension about him. Ellen was surprised. She hadn't thought he was the type to be star-struck or awed by authority figures. She wondered whether it was a hangover from his early days in the job. Starrett was most definitely old-school. The type to have resented a fast-track graduate.

'The press put it down to a random hate crime,' Dan said. 'Though they didn't use those words at the time.'

'Yes.'

Starrett crunched on another ginger snap. When he finished Ellen noticed how quiet it was in the house. There was a melancholy about the place, she thought. About the man. Though she sensed that he still had enough steel in him to be furious if he knew she felt sorry for him. And perhaps she was projecting her own thoughts on him, anyway. By the time she was his age – and if she had a place like this – she might be glad of the peace and quiet.

'I consoled myself at the time with the belief that we would get the killer eventually,' Starrett said. 'Even if it was for another crime. Someone like that, unlikely they hadn't already been in some kind of trouble. Even less likely they would just stop, if they thought they'd got away with it.'

He made a good point, Ellen thought. That kind of violent act, if it had been random and impersonal, wouldn't be a one off. Someone fuelled with that kind of hatred wouldn't have kept it secret. Nor could they have switched it off. For the first time she had her doubts about the Gilchrist brothers. Even Alistair.

As if he knew what she was thinking, Starrett said, 'Perhaps we did. Get the thug responsible for killing Leask. Who knows? This thing Jimmy had with the Gilchrists – maybe it's the thing got Jimmy killed, not that he was right.'

'You mean he hounded them to the point one of them snapped?'

'Maybe. I don't know.' Starrett chose his words carefully. 'The thing you have to understand about Jimmy is that there was more riding on this than an unsolved case.'

Did he mean Jimmy took it personally because of his sexuality? Ellen wondered. She took offence at that. But

Starrett went on.

'I'm not saying he didn't want justice for Connor Leask, but there were other reasons why letting go of a case was difficult for Jimmy. He'd been compromised in the past, you see, and it haunted him. I don't know the details, just what Baird told me. Someone had held something over Jimmy, made him turn a blind eye. I gather he was young at the time, new to CID as was, and he was scared of losing everything he'd worked for. Anyway, it only happened the once, to my knowledge. When I knew him and worked with him he was nothing but diligent. Always very careful to do everything by the book. But it stayed with him and I suppose he felt doubly uncomfortable letting cases drop because of that experience. Subconsciously, he was always afraid he'd get the blame for looking the other way, as he had done once before.'

So there had been something in Barber's past. That half-remembered feeling she'd had was right. He'd had cause to be wary, to feel he had to work twice as hard to get things right.

'It made him overzealous, do you think?' she asked Starrett. 'That he might have got hung up on some of the details?'

Starrett shrugged. 'He was pretty intense when he spoke to me.'

'This idea that the attack was random, though,' Calder said. 'I have difficulty with that.'

'You haven't got to know Mr Leask very well, yet, have you?' Starrett smiled. 'He was quite a hothead, by all accounts. Liked to provoke people. When they said "random" I just thought it's entirely possible he pissed off the wrong person that night.'

Calder made to get up. 'Well, thanks for your time.'

Starrett seemed disappointed. Ellen wondered whether he had many visitors.

'Not at all,' he said. 'I have to confess: there's a bit of Jimmy in me, too. When he got in touch, I couldn't help being curious. It's in our natures, I suppose.' He winked at Ellen. 'I expect you were the same.'

'What do you do to keep your mind occupied?' Calder asked as they made their way to the front door.

'Local history's my thing.'

Calder opened the door and stepped out, car keys in hand. 'Thanks again.'

'Any time.' Starrett reached out a hand. Calder swapped his keys about and took it. 'The real trouble with Jimmy,' Starrett said, as they shook, 'Was that he was still trying so hard to put things right.'

He shook Ellen's hand next. 'We can't make everything right though, can we?' For a moment she caught a glimpse of the man he had been in the startling blue of his eyes. She felt her pulse quicken, told herself not to be stupid. He couldn't know anything about her. He was probably just thinking about his own history. The case his reputation was built on, even, and the criminals who filled the gap that Billy Gaughan left behind. She was not sure local history was the best thing for him to be spending his time on.

'Really, any time,' Starrett said again as they walked down the path. He raised a lazy salute to them as they turned onto the street but he hadn't disguised the keenness in his voice, and Ellen decided she really would not end up in a place like this, stuck out on the edge of the city with nothing stirring but the birds and the breeze in the trees.

'Poor guy,' she said. 'He seems kind of lonely. Did you see the picture of his wife?'

'He's a suspect,' Calder said, with more vehemence than she thought was necessary. She realised she wasn't the only one who was afraid of ending up like Barber and Starrett.

16

These are the people I cannot disentangle myself from, and yet they are strangers to me. These are the people who will come to my bedside and not know how or whether to make me laugh. They won't know what books to bring or what music I want at my funeral. What to say or what to do. I'll have to tell them everything. It's going to be such bloody hard work this dying.

I want them to care. If I must share my dying with them I want it to matter to them. I want it to bloody hurt.

I am angry with them today. They think I should stay. Because I haven't got anything urgent to go back to. I haven't got any children, and my job can't possibly be as important as Malcolm's. Because I'm the girl. Well, fuck that. I've got a hospital appointment and not one of you has even noticed I'm not well.

Saying goodbye to Mum is hard, though. Leaving her alone, even at Al's, suddenly brings it all home. It's as though, as long as we were all around, we could pretend Dad was just out of shot. There were enough of the rest of us to make believe he was still around somewhere. But he's not just out in the back garden, not just catching the last of the racing on the telly, not 'just' anywhere. When we leave, he will be gone too.

Guilt gnaws quietly at me. It makes me more pissed off.

Robert drives me to the station. We have time for a coffee before my train, then he will go back to the house and clear up – after the funeral, and after the police. He volunteered. His resentment is coming off him in waves. He is desperate to go home to Caithness, where he runs a small arts centre in the middle of nowhere, while his garage stacks up with half-started art projects of his own. It's way too bleak for me, all that flow country, but Robert craves it.

He needs to be able to see where the earth meets the sky.

I wait until we are both settled at one of the tables on the concourse outside Caffé Nero, then I reach across the table and take his car key.

'What happened in 1993?'

'Norna.' He runs an exasperated hand over his receding hairline. He looks around, at the suits inside with their pink papers and lattes. The people walking by: holidaymakers stressed and excited to be travelling and commuters in hassled autopilot. Then he makes a decision. He turns back to me and leans across the table. When he speaks, his voice is low and the words come out in a tumble, as though he's emptying them out, as though he can't rid himself of them quick enough.

'Most of it I found out from the papers, and later the internet,' he says. 'You know that bit on the corner of Corbiehill Avenue where it joins the cycle path? A man was stabbed there. His name was Connor Leask and he was a trainee procurator fiscal. I remember that night. I was supposed to be in bed but I heard the doorbell go and I crept out onto the landing. It was the police. Al and Finlay Groat had been reported for something. They got into a lot of trouble around then. Anyway, Dad was furious and after the police had gone he went out to look for Al. Malcolm was out with his pal Davey, too, so basically, all three of them – Al and Malcolm and Dad – were out and about in the area the night the man was killed. They were all interviewed as part of the investigation.'

It's little more than I had gleaned from that detective who interviewed me, but somehow hearing it from Rob makes it more real.

'None of them could have had anything to do with that guy's death, though.'

Rob's eyes flick to his left as a couple pause on the other side of the café railing to look at the departures screen. He leans even further across the table.

'Everything I read said it had been a random attack because he was gay. I think they were mainly questioned about whether they had seen anything, but it was pretty intense for a while. Dad was mad at both of them and Al got himself in more trouble for mouthing off at the police. Malcolm kind of shut down. It all went away after a bit, but it was horrible while it lasted.'

'So why was that detective killed in our garage?'

He glares at me. He's really pissed off, now. 'How should I know, Non? That's what the bloody police are investigating.'

He eyes my hand on his keys. I pull them off the table into my lap.

'But what happened to us in 1993?'

'What do you mean?'

It's my turn to be exasperated. 'I mean, what you were talking about on the island. What were you getting at? I remember Gairloch. We were a family. I remember you three burying me in the sand and playing in the sea, and running down the dunes and games in the caravan. You know that was the last time we were all together in the same place?' He knows full well but I go on. 'Al and Malcolm have hardly spoken to each other since then. They've done their best to avoid each other whenever Malcolm has come home, and that's not often. How did it all go wrong? Was it because of that murder?'

'Holidays aren't normal life, Norna. It's different when you're away and there's no school or work or friends to be cool in front of and you don't mind hanging around with your annoying little brother and sister and playing naff games. Things weren't perfect before that. Malcolm and Alistair always rubbed each other up the wrong way. They were always jealous of each other. Always fighting. You were just too young to remember. Maybe it got a bit worse that summer after we came back from holiday, but Malcolm was about to leave home for his bright, shiny future and Alistair was being made to go back to school to fail more exams. Al was all: "How come Malcolm gets to go to London and I'm stuck here? How come Malcolm gets money to train as a pilot and I have to get a bursary for college?" Even before then he and Finlay Groat had been constantly in trouble and Dad and Al were always at loggerheads. At one point someone chucked a brick through the shop window and Dad accused Al of doing it. Come to think of it, even Malcolm had started going out 'til all hours that summer. He'd finished school and he was just letting off steam but to listen to Dad you'd think he'd sold his soul to the devil. And Al being Al, he was peeved that Malcolm seemed to be pinching his bad boy image. Especially when Al went back to school and Malcolm had another month or so 'til uni started.'

I try to remember the things that Robert is telling me about but I can't. When I think about Gairloch I remember that Ace of Base were everywhere that summer, singing about wanting another baby on tinny little transistors hanging off people's tents, or in the cafés and petrol stations. I remember that when I went back to school in August my friends were full of Take That. I remember The Legends of Treasure Island and Adventures of Sonic the Hedgehog and Strange But True. Later, I remember sitting closer to Live and Kicking with my hands cupped around my ears to shut out the sound of Mum on the phone to Malcolm, berating him for not coming home for Christmas. But mostly I can't distinguish that summer, autumn and winter from much of my childhood and the dreams I moved in.

Robert looks up at the departures board and then in the direction of his keys, which are still tight in my hand on my lap.

'It'll get sorted, Non. The police will find who did it.'

'Tell me what else you remember.'

He sighs. After a moment his shoulders sag and suddenly he looks terribly sad. 'I remember that I thought it would be cool when I could get my hands on all Malcolm's things after he'd gone, but I missed him. I remember Dad insisting that Al stay at school til the end of the year because he still had to pass some exams if he was to go to college to learn a trade.' He frowns. 'He did get serious, actually. Al. He was already working for Lawrence Groat that summer. I think he'd started in the Easter holiday, helping out when Lawrence put up the storage unit at the back of the shop yard. He persuaded Lawrence to take him on because we weren't getting enough pocket money. Another reason he was pissed off when Dad gave Malcolm money for London.'

'Is that why Lawrence always treated us like we owed him something?' I shudder. 'Creep.'

Rob looks at me, curiously. Then his expression changes. 'He never did anything, did he?'

'Depends where on the scale "anything" starts. Running his finger down my spine, putting his arm round my waist and his hand on my bum, trying to hug and kiss me hello and goodbye. I got pretty good at avoiding it.'

'Bastard.' Rob's eyes darken with hatred.

'Dad seemed to think the sun shone out of Lawrence Groat's arse.'

'No. I don't think he did,' Rob says quietly. 'But they went back a long way and they'd always helped each other out.' A bitterness has crept into his voice.

'How d'you mean?'

'They grew up together, didn't they? They were like Al and Finlay. Dad's business took off first. You probably don't remember when he had more than one shop, do you? Lawrence was just working for a builder's merchant and Dad helped him set up on his own. Recommended him to the letting agents who used the shops if they were looking for someone to do renovations. Anyway, when it was his turn, Lawrence helped Dad out too.'

I suppose Rob must be right. Maybe I just hadn't recognised what Dad and Lawrence had as friendship. That network of favours and reciprocal recommendations, the backslapping and arse-licking. As far as I could see, Lawrence always lorded it over us. Us womenfolk at any rate. He used to call himself 'Uncle' Lawrence when he spoke to me. I shudder at the memory.

'Money was tight for a while,' Rob says. 'It would have been around then. That's why Dad let Lawrence help out with the storage unit. It would have been about then Dad started running the handyman service from the shop, too. It gave him an edge that the big chains like Homebase and B&Q didn't have, capitalised on the local aspect. It worked out well, too. Just at the right time for the property boom and all those people getting into buy-to-let.'

I don't remember any of this. I have a vague sense that things were quieter after Malcolm moved out. Al was not far behind. A year at the most. Then it was just me and Robert, then just me. And neither of us ever caused any aggro. Nothing beyond the usual teenage strops. I only remember one big row between Robert and Dad. I remind him of it now.

'What did you do?'

'Oh, yeah.' He had clearly forgotten about this. 'He caught me rummaging through stuff for the shop to do my Art project for Higher. He hit the roof.' He frowns, remembering.

'Is that why you don't finish anything now?'

He looks surprised. I'm afraid I've hurt him, but then he says simply, 'I don't have time for that kind of thing any more. Too many funding applications to fill in.'

I push his keys back over the table towards him. He grabs hold of my hand and grips it tight. 'It'll be alright, Non.'

I want to believe him, but I don't think he even does, himself. And besides, he's wrong.

17

Whenever he thought about it, Dan Calder kept coming back to the same question. Why was Barber at the Gilchrists' place? What good did he think it would do to go sniffing around their house? At the very least the man might have been arrested and charged with house-breaking. What could be so important that he had to go there on the day of Ronald's funeral? Was it just because he could be sure everyone would be out, but if so, what did he hope to achieve? He had never managed to speak to Ronald Gilchrist so how could he know what there might be to find at his house? He wasn't going to admit this to Chisholm but Dan was beginning to find Alistair Gilchrist's suggestion that Barber might be there to plant something on them entirely plausible. After what Starrett had told them Barber's behaviour had begun to seem less erratic, certainly, but more suspicious. Less like a man trying to compensate for the loss of a loved one or to solve the one that got away and more like a man trying to cover his tracks.

'Hello?'

'Yes, I'm still here.' Dan had been on hold for a good six minutes.

'I'm sorry, Baroness Eklund can't see you this week, she's in court. She's in London at the beginning of next week, but I could arrange an appointment for you to meet her next Wednesday?'

Dan made the arrangement. He had no intention of waiting to keep it but he could afford to let Eklund think he would for now. He moved down the list of Barber's recent contacts. Passing over Ellen Chisholm's name. She was an anomaly. Apart from her, everyone Barber had been in contact with in the last weeks of his life had been involved in some way with the original Connor Leask enquiry, or in Sheena Baird's case, related to someone involved in the investigation. Whilst they were still checking alternatives, it was looking pretty conclusive that it was something Barber had done or learnt as part of his renewed investigation into Connor Leask's death that had got him killed.

Dan looked at the list, weighing up his options. Farhana McLean was another slight anomaly. She had been Connor Leask's flatmate at the time he was killed, but she had played only a small role in the original enquiry. When Keisha had phoned to ask the nature of Barber's communication with her McLean had said that she and Barber had been arranging to meet, that she still had some papers of Connor's that Barber wanted. Dan looked at his watch. Keisha was cross-referencing witness statements and he could do with a walk. It wouldn't take long to collect whatever McLean had been going to give Barber.

*

McLean worked for a firm of solicitors and estate agents based in the centre of Edinburgh. Despite fresh décor the building smelt of its age: old stone and beeswax polish. It wasn't a bad smell. Dan followed McLean up a carpeted staircase and along the landing to an office at the back of the building which looked out onto a plain garden and the back of the New Town terrace on the parallel street. Her heavy desk was fastidiously neat, with every kind of stationery item from pens to treasury tags sorted into expensive-looking Scandinavian-style ceramic pots.

'I'm sorry to hear about James Barber. Was he a colleague of yours?'

'I never worked with him, no. Ms McLean...'

'Farhana, please.'

'Farhana.' He would have preferred to keep it formal. Calling a potential witness by their first name always seemed that little bit too intimate when he fancied them, and Farhana McLean was a beautiful woman. She smiled at him now and light danced in her deep brown eyes. He responded as he always did when he was attracted to someone. He ignored it.

'You said you had some papers of Connor Leask's to give to Barber?'

'Yes.' She got up and walked over to a filing cabinet in the corner of the room. As her back was turned and before he could stop himself Dan reached out and took a treasury tag from the container on her desk. By the time she turned round he was sitting back, the tag in his pocket. Farhana was carrying a cardboard file held together with string. She passed it over to him. 'It's stupid really. I should have chucked it out years ago.'

'Why didn't you?' Calder pulled off the string that held the file together and opened the flap, releasing a scent of stale paper and damp.

Farhana settled back in her seat. 'I didn't know I had it for a long time. The police had taken everything from his room and I moved out of the flat shortly after Connor died. I couldn't stand to be there any more without him. Didn't want to stay in Edinburgh even. His Mum had come and collected anything really personal or valuable, and we took his clothes to the charity shop but there was still a lot of stuff that had just become shared flat stuff, things that we'd had when we were at uni together. Some of our law books were mixed together. This was in with them. I just boxed it all up and moved it with the rest of my things. It all sat at my parents' house for a few years while I lived in London. When I got my own place back here again it spent another few years in my box room before I had a big clearout. When I saw Connor's writing it brought it all back. It felt callous to throw it out there and then. It's been on my list of things to do one day but...' She shrugged.

Dan had pulled out a sheaf of papers and was leafing through them. At first glance they comprised photocopied news stories, maps, transcripts of interviews.

'Mr Barber didn't say why he wanted it,' Farhana said. 'Are you re-opening the investigation?'

'Not at this stage. Not unless we find some new evidence.' He looked up. 'I'm sorry. It's James Barber's death I'm investigating and you were one of the last people he contacted.'

Farhana nodded. She was not naïve enough to have expected anything else, but still, Dan could tell she was disappointed.

'You were obviously very fond of Connor.'

She smiled. 'I loved him to bits.' Then the smile faltered. 'I don't mean this to sound morose, but life was never the same again after he died. It was a very brutal end to youth and innocence.' She laughed, a throaty, self-deprecating laugh, swinging her long hair back as if shaking herself free the emotion. 'We all have to grow up some time. It's just that, while Connor was still around, it was a lot more fun.'

'What was he like?'

'He was more full of life and energy than anyone I ever met. He could be a right nippy sweetie, though. And he wasn't afraid of confrontation. When I look back now I think we were sometimes lucky we hadn't got into serious trouble before. I remember one time being very scared when these guys started bothering us, calling me a Paki, you know the kind of thing. I just wanted to get out of there, but Connor insisted on challenging them.'

Dan frowned, thinking about what Glen Starrett had said about Connor. 'Is that why his death was said to be a suspected homophobic attack? They thought he might have stood up to the wrong person?'

'I don't know. It was more than possible, but I think they just exhausted the alternatives. I know they scoured his work and his personal life. They were all over Nichol and Mason for a while and they looked at the cases he'd been assigned to, but they couldn't find anything to suggest any of that was linked to his death.'

'Nichol and Mason?'

'Nichol Pelley and Mason Lennox. We were all at uni together. Connor had been seeing Nichol for a while not long before he was killed. When they broke up Nichol didn't take it too well. He kept coming round and phoning. Begging Connor to take him back one mintute, then hurling abuse at him for ruining his life the next. A couple of times we spotted him loitering in the street outside our flat and once Connor caught him following him round the local Spar shop.'

'He was stalking him? Did Connor do anything about it?'

'No. He just thought he would get tired of it eventually. Move on. Actually, I think Connor might have set him up with a friend of a friend to try and distract him. Anyway, he had an alibi for the night Connor was killed.'

'Was Mason another boyfriend?'

Farhana laughed. 'No. Mason's about as straight as they come. In more ways than one. But he went up for the traineeship, the same as Connor, and didn't get it. He was a bit miffed about that. Jealous, I suppose. He accused Connor of sabotaging his application.'

'Any truth in that?'

'I can't believe so. I think Mason's pride was dented. But Connor could be ruthless, I'll give him that. If he wanted something, he went for it. And he was ambitious. He loved the law. Criminal law anyway. He thought I sold out when I took property law. "Boring", he used to say whenever I started talking about it.' She mimed a yawn, patting her mouth.

'Do you know much about what he'd been working on?'

'Oh, yes, he was allowed to talk about his work,' she laughed. 'If I'm honest, though, I couldn't see that it was very much more interesting than what I was doing. I think even Connor was a bit disappointed, and frustrated, though he would never have admitted it.'

'Why frustrated?'

'The slow pace of it. And it's not straightforward is it? He could do all this work compiling information on a case and then it not even come to trial because of lack of evidence, or a technicality. Even if it looked very much like someone was guilty.'

Dan could identify with that frustration. He picked up Connor's notes again. 'This looks like it might be work-related. Did the police not ask for them at the time?'

'Like I say, they took everything from his room, but that folder was with my things. I used an alcove off the kitchen to work in because I had the smaller of the two bedrooms. Connor must have done some work there too. But most of the documents look like copies. They'd have got the originals from the Fiscal's office. And the typed versions of his own notes. These are just scribbles I think.'

Dan's eye was caught by a handwritten list of names, some with marks against them. Possibly witnesses Connor had to interview for a case. He wouldn't be allowed to bring this kind of data home now and leave it lying around.

'He was being mentored by Lise Eklund?'

'Yes, Lise got us our flat, too.'

'How do you mean?'

'The landlord was a friend of hers. Mitchell Kinley? She put in a word. Acted as a referee, I suppose. Nice flat it was, too. Cumberland Street basement with a private garden.'

Dan had heard of Mitchell Kinley. Kinley's was one of the biggest property firms in the city, catering to the elite end of the market both in conveyancing and letting. 'She sounds like a mentor worth having. Actually, I have an appointment to see her. Apparently Barber had been in contact with her recently, but she's a difficult woman to get hold of.'

Farhana stared at him. 'Then his death is connected to Connor's? It must be, mustn't it?'

'It just means he was interested in re-opening Connor's case before he died.'

'So maybe there is new evidence?'

'I don't know.'

But the list of names in Connor's file had made Dan think.

'Do you know how Barber got your contact details?'

'I'm easy enough to find. I haven't changed my name, and I'm on the list of partners here.'

If Barber knew what she did for a living, Dan thought. If he even remembered her name. From twenty-six years before. Dan could understand how Barber might easily recall Lise Eklund. She'd been a Procurator Fiscal, was now Senior Advocate Depute and a Baroness. She was a kent figure in their line of work. It would be obvious for him to contact his old colleagues, Vihaan Shah and Glen Starrett. Even

Sheena Baird was not a very big leap to make. But Farhana? It seemed more and more obvious to him now that Barber had never let the case drop. Why?

'How did Barber know you had these?'

'I told him when he phoned.'

'What was he calling you about, then, if it wasn't to get these?'

'He wanted to ask some questions about what I remembered from the time and to run some names past me. Actually, he asked whether we had socialised with Lise and whether I'd ever met Hugh Baird. He was a superintendent in the police.'

'Yes, I know. Had you?'

'No. I'd seen him once at a dinner. Connor pointed him out to me. He always knew who were the movers and shakers. Superintendent Baird was at the same table as Lise and Mitchell Kinley but they didn't really speak to us. I was only introduced to him properly at Connor's funeral. He was very sweet. He said they would do everything they could to find out who had killed him.' She trailed off, no doubt thinking that Baird's everything had not been enough.

Interesting that Barber should have wanted to know about Eklund and Baird, Dan thought. And just before telling Baird's daughter that her father had had a long term affair with Lise Eklund, too. Did this mean that Barber hadn't been contacting Eklund as a witness or for background information, but because she was a suspect? Dan didn't like that prospect at all. And he couldn't see what it had to do with the Gilchrists.

'Anyone else?'

'Well, he seemed interested in the fact that all three of them were friends – Mitchell, Lise and Hugh Baird. I'm afraid we didn't get any further. When I told him I had some papers of Connor's, we arranged to meet. He said we could talk more then.'

Dan shuffled the papers back together. As he closed the folder he noticed some faded biro in the top right corner where the words Land Registry had once been written then crossed out. The hand wasn't Connor's. The folder had once held Farhana's university notes.

'Were these all together in this folder when you found them?'

'Yes. Do you think they'll be useful?'

'I can't say. I was hoping they might help me to work out what Barber was thinking, but if he hadn't seen them they may not give me much insight.' He wrapped the string round the folder again. 'By the way, did you tell anyone that Barber had been in touch?'

'I told Mason.'

Dan had to remind himself. 'Mason Lennox?' The man Connor had bested to get the Procurator Fiscal traineeship. His supposed friend. 'When?'

'We met for drinks a week ago.' She was looking worried now.

'I'm just trying to build a picture of who might have known Barber was poking around Connor's case again. Did you also tell him you had this stuff?'

'Yes. He didn't think there would be anything useful in it. He thought I was grasping at straws.'

'He didn't ask to see it?'

'No.'

If Mason Lennox wasn't worried about new evidence coming to light in Connor's case he could go on the back burner just now. Dan wanted to talk to this Nichol Pelley at some stage, though. He might not have had anything to do with Connor Leask's death but if he'd been watching him, he just might know something that could help them.

It's Barber's death we're investigating, Dan cautioned himself, but resistance was futile now.

What he'd learned about Connor Leask told him that the man was driven, ambitious, purposeful. He might have been feisty but he was not chaotic. Dan didn't believe these notes had become mixed up with Farhana's belongings by accident. Connor hadn't mislaid them. He'd hidden them.

18

As a child I had a habit of narrating my own life. Norna strode into the canteen with her head held high. Norna took a moment to consider before answering clearly: sixty-two. The sunlight made Norna blink but she held her focus and took aim: the ball made light contact with the backboard and dropped pleasingly through the net. I was so busy living in a fiction of my own making that I didn't notice what was really going on.

Something happened when we came home from that holiday, no matter what Rob says. That summer our family got broken and I missed it. And now my brothers are in trouble. Real trouble.

The further I got from Edinburgh the greater the urge to turn round and go back. It's not the fear of missing out: Little Non being sent to bed before the others. It has nothing to do with my condition or my place in the order of things, and everything to do with the murdered policeman in the garage. And the man who died before him, twenty-six years ago, on a neighbouring street, when my brothers and my father were out there, somewhere.

The feeling that I left having forgotten to do something.

It's not that I didn't tell my family I am dying. There is something else.

Something I missed.

*

Astrocytoma. I feminise her. She has found the perfect home in my head. She stalks my dreams, leather-clad, firm-breasted, with a deadly high kick and fire in her eyes. But this is only a trick of the light, a metamorphosis. In her true form she is but a collection of cells, multiplying, a destructive force preying on living tissue. She is a parasite and I her unwilling host.

I watch the nurse scurrying back behind her protective shield and begin, automatically, to deflect the reality. I summon a large vat of a room, all matt metal and echoing space, which I fill with the throbbing of an enormous unseen engine. I stand in the middle and with the power of my mind command the domed roof of this cavernous vault to open, letting daylight pour into it. I will soar through the opening as the enormous metal roof retracts. Out into cool, clean air. Up into blue sky. I will be strong, I will be clean.

The humming around me gets louder. I can't lift myself off the ground. The sliding noise is not that of the large portals drawing aside. It is the sound of my coffin sliding behind the curtain into the fire.

Come on: blue sky, clean air.

I can't breathe. I can't move. I gasp for air, the mask on my face suddenly feeling like a restraint. Voices are coming at me. I can't hear what they are saying. I can't get out, I can't escape.

Come on. Blue sky...

Blue. Blue and silver. Gairloch bay under a summer sun. The feel of sand between my toes, and the rough grass of the campsite. The heat of the stepping stones over the burn that runs into the sea. My feet slap-slapping. Ice cream and sun cream, the two together, licked off my arm. Salt. Purple rings in the sand where the jellyfish beached.

And then a thought: how could Malcolm afford to rent a flat in London if money was tight?

Where did he get that money to train as a pilot?

*

Later, emerging into the daylight I stand in the car park with the smell of the hospital still raw in my nostrils. I lean on the wall of a raised flower bed. Panic has left me weak and I am afraid to stand straight. I can't bear to be sick again.

This is how it will be. This is how I will end my days, with this stench in my throat. Forcing me to live in the real world in the worst possible way.

This will be the memory my brothers and mother will have of me. The bitter, lingering shadow of death will push out any other thoughts of me. In time, perhaps, they will remember other things. But it will be the child they remember. It will be the girl making polythene-bag parachutes for toy soldiers, playing marbles on manhole covers, running through the woodland on Corstorphine Hill with Rambo marks on her face. Perhaps this is already the only way they know me. But that girl is gone. She is only a ghost. The adult they remember will forever be a dying woman. And who wants to remember that?

It's not how I want to be remembered.

Slowly the nausea subsides. I begin to walk, just one small, slow step at a time. I like the way it feels, the strain of using my muscles, the transfer of my weight from one leg to the other. I concentrate on each step and if I do that I can't think about how it might be that a man was killed and Malcolm suddenly had money. I can't think about how it might be that a man was killed and Alistair was suddenly a reformed character, working to learn a trade instead of spray-painting his frustration across suburbia. I don't think of these things. Instead, I focus on the air pushing against the walls of my lungs. With each step I feel stronger again. With each step I grow back into myself. By the time I reach the Downs I am alive again.

There is no sign of the man with the dog.

I climb onto the low wall at the viewpoint and lean out over the railing. Down below, the mudflats shine like metal, the river a narrow trickle of mercury between them. I have a sudden urge to take a run up and jump, to fall through the air like Butch Cassidy and the Sundance Kid. It's not real, this urge. Not suicidal. It's only the compulsion to do something that will equal the enormity of the terror and elation I feel.

I don't want to waste away. I have wasted so much. I don't want the comfort of strangers. And my brothers are strangers.

I need to do something.

There is no rickety film of my polar expeditions. No artist's impression of me staring out from a WANTED poster, nor yellowing newspaper report of the monster I vanquished. No shiny medal for the lives I saved or the disaster I averted.

There is one photograph, though. I can see it, clear as day. It shows me and my brothers sitting, in order, along the top of a sand dune, a clear blue sky behind us and smiles on our faces. The little girl on the end of the line beams with joy, and I remember. I can hear the drums in her head that beat in time with their footsteps on the tarmac track that winds through the campsite. I can feel the pride beating in her chest as she walks with her brothers.

Surely that wasn't all make-believe?

I need to find out.

19

Dan spread the contents of Connor Leask's file across the table and examined them, playing the treasury tag he had taken from Farhana McLean's office round his fingers as he did so. It was not immediately obvious what connected the items in front of him. There were a couple of photocopied newscuttings; copies of transcripts that looked like witness interviews, presumably from cases Connor had worked on; and assorted pages photocopied from the Edinburgh street atlas. Dan could see why Farhana McLean had called Connor's notes scribbles. For the most part they were nothing more than dates or question marks, underlinings or short memos made in the margins of the printed texts. In places Dan could see where the man had simply pressed his pen to the page while reading, marking a word or a name with a dot but presumably not considering it worthy of underlining. The initial impression was that of random research notes, thoughts in progress, and he could see nothing that looked like findings.

Dan placed the list of names he had first noticed when he was in Farhana's office in the centre of the table. It seemed a good place to start. He assumed it was a 'to do' list of witnesses Connor had been charged with re-interviewing for the Fiscal's office so it would offer an insight into what the man had been working on. There were three names listed together: Franjo Horvat; Dean Owens; Lee Quigley. Slight impressions under the last two but Horvat's name was both underlined and circled vigorously and Connor had drawn an arrow between this and another name, set apart from the others: Norris Ralston. Highlighted and underlined.

Ralston's name rang a bell. Dan walked over to Ellen's desk where the original case file on Connor's murder was sitting. He was sure they'd come across a reference to Norris Ralston there. He leafed past witness statements and suspect interviews until he spotted what he was looking for. Norris Ralston's name appeared in a document supplied by Connor's mentor, Procurator Fiscal Lise Eklund. She had been asked what Connor had been tasked with working on during his time with her and among other things she had listed an investigation into the possible shipment of drugs and money laundering through a building supplies company owned and run by a man named Norris Ralston.

Returning to Connor's notes, he rifled through the papers until he found something that made sense of the markings linking Norris Ralston to Franjo Horvat. It wasn't an interview Connor had conducted himself but a copy of a statement given by Horvat to the police. Franjo Horvat had been testifying against Norris Ralston.

He sat back. So what? All he had done was to confirm that the notes Farhana had given him related to Connor's work. It didn't shed any light on his death. Or Barber's.

Or did it? His eye fell on the list again and he realised that he knew one of the other names. Lee Quigley. It took him a moment to place it, but when he did, he felt a tremor of excitement run through him. Lee Quigley had been the name of the boy Barber had asked Vihaan Shah about two years ago. The accidental death in 1992.

Dan's brain was racing suddenly. Barber hadn't been doing a favour for a bereaved family member when he enquired about Quigley, he'd been following Connor Leask's trail.

There was no mention of the Fatal Accident Inquiry in the list Eklund's office had provided. Was this an omission? It seemed unlikely, but if Connor wasn't working on that inquiry why did he have Lee Quigley's name written down here?

Lee Quigley had been a teenager when he died. The same age as the Gilchrist brothers. Could that be a connection?

He searched Connor Leask's notes again for any mention of the Gilchrists but could find none. If Barber had been following Leask's trail when he came to the conclusion they were involved in his murder, there was no indication here.

Perhaps if he came at it from the other direction? Had the Gilchrist boys made mention of any of these names here when they were interviewed in 1993?

He pulled out Alistair Gilchrist's statement first and began to read.

Alistair admitted to having been in Davidsons Mains on the evening of Connor's death. He and his friend Finlay Groat had both owned up to painting graffiti on the wall at the back of the Safeway supermarket, and to 'moving' shopping trolleys and leaving them in peoples' gardens. They denied it was stealing. When one homeowner had threatened to call the police they had run off, they said. By the time Connor Leask was killed they would each have been back in their respective homes. Barber had put it to them that it was still early for a Friday night. Were they worried about getting enough beauty sleep? To which Alistair replied that he 'couldn't be bothered' staying out any longer. Dan could hear the feigned disinterest as he read the words on the page. His nerves jangled with recognition. This was exactly the kind of thing some of his schoolmates would have lived off for weeks. Quoting back the things they said to the officers, embellishing, imagining that they had actually made an impact when they told the officers they were part of the fascist state. Alistair Gilchrist, rebel king, striking a blow for the oppressed.

Though they were only near contemporaries, there was something about Alistair Gilchrist's testimony that made the thin white scar on Dan Calder's jawline tingle where it had split on the edge of a sink as his head was pushed down onto it suddenly. Made him remember the sharp pain as his hip bone connected with the side of a urinal. The blood soaking into his collar from the gash under his hair at the back of his head, where it struck the hand-dryer as he ricocheted off the sink. He reminded himself who he was now and straightened, letting his shoulders fall with his outward breath.

Dan hadn't been like the other boys in his class at

school, the boys Alistair Gilchrist reminded him of so keenly. He couldn't afford to be, it was too easy for everyone to put the blame on him. His dubious genes, that hint of other in his brown eyes, he was a born scapegoat. He had learnt the hard way that in any fight he would be the one to be punished.

Finlay Groat had been a little more forthcoming than his friend. He admitted that they had been in trouble before and that he didn't want any more.

GROAT: Some wifey saw us dump the trolley in her flower bed. She was screaming out her window that she'd call the police. I thought, if I get reported again my Dad'll skin me.

Finlay went to the fee-paying Edinburgh Academy.

GROAT: He keeps telling me he's not paying all that money for me to wind up in the gaol.

Finlay's father, Lawrence, had confirmed that his son had been home before ten o'clock on the night of Connor's murder. And that he had been furious with him.

Dan got a sense of Barber's approach as he read on. Unthreatening, unhurried, but persistent nonetheless. I've got all the time in the world, sonny, he seemed to be saying. I've got a good job, mortgage sorted. It's your future you're eating into here.

Finlay Groat told Barber that he and Alistair Gilchrist had parted company at about a quarter to ten, at the corner of Silverknowes Drive and Silverknowes Avenue. Dan knew that part of the city. He knew it the way a teenager knew it twenty-six years before. He knew it wouldn't take Alistair Gilchrist long to double back, cut along the cycle path and emerge at the edge of Corbiehill Drive.

Except that the positioning of Connor's body, and the knife wound to his chest suggested that his killer had come from the other direction. Dan sighed.

And why escalate so suddenly from petty crime to

murder? It didn't hold true.

Still, he could have seen something. Leave the animals to the animals, their father Ronald had said. Perhaps Alistair could identify the killer.

Had someone followed Connor Leask that night? Had they waited for the opportunity to get to him when he was furthest away from any likely witnesses? Or had he somehow invited trouble? Had he gone looking for it, even? Farhana had said he could be feisty. That he didn't like backing down, that he stood his ground against bullies and bigots. But Dan still couldn't account for why he had been in that area in the first place.

It's Barber's death we're investigating, he reminded himself, but he was certain now that the two were linked. Not least because the two dead men seemed to be following the same trail.

He looked again at the list of cases Leask had been assigned to work on. Barber had contacted Connor's former mentor, Baroness Lise Eklund shortly before he was murdered. It was time to let the Senior Advocate Depute know that, whilst she might be the law, she wasn't above it.

20

Ellen drove to Comely Bank and parked on the street opposite the high school, then walked the short distance along Raeburn Place into Stockbridge.

Ronald Gilchrist's hardware store had been in the middle of a row of shops. It was now a bistro which played on the hardware theme, with tables and seating made from reclaimed scaffolding planks. The decorative lighting made use of a variety of bits of piping and plumbing joints. Plants in large, labelled tins that once held wood stain and beeswax polish lined the cobbled alley down the side of the shop leading to a yard at the back which was now an outdoor seating area.

Jimmy Barber had come here the day before he was killed. A parking ticket in the glove compartment of his car showed that he parked outside the nearby Botanical gardens; a receipt crumpled alongside it showed that he had drunk a cappuccino in the bistro.

Ellen did not go in. She stood for a moment, watching the early evening diners through the window, then turned away.

When they had first concluded that Barber had never let the case go it had made her feel a little better. It suggested that his recent behaviour had not just been a series of desperate, irrational actions by a bereaved and lonely man. If he had been working on this for a long time, he must have had reason for his actions, surely? He must have been onto something. She wanted Calder to understand that if what Glen Starrett had said was true, then it was all true. If Barber had made a mistake once it had only been once and he had been manipulated, forced into it. It had never happened again.

Ellen had watched the interview Liam and Keisha had conducted with Malcolm Gilchrist, frustrated at not having had the chance to question him herself. She suspected Calder had deliberately kept her away from him. She scoured the interview for a reason to pull him back in, but she couldn't fault it. Malcolm claimed he had never lied to them. He had just returned for the funeral the day before. Yes, he had been in Edinburgh to visit his father in hospital before he died, but that was two weeks prior to the funeral and in between he'd been back at work. Flying between London and Frankfurt, Stockholm and Zagreb.

'I don't know why that guy wanted to see Dad. I didn't talk to him long enough to find out. I just wanted him to go away.'

'Why didn't you mention you'd seen him at the hospital when you found out he was the man who had been killed in your garage?'

'I don't know. There was so much going on. I was just trying to process it all. I couldn't work out how it all fitted together. Why he was there. Any of it.'

Why indeed. Vihaan Shah had told Calder that his memory of the case was shaped by Barber's last contact. She hadn't liked it when Dan made a point of telling her that, but alone, to herself, she could admit that they were all looking at everything through a funhouse mirror. And whether he was onto something or not, Barber's obsession with the Gilchrists made her uncomfortable. This was not the man she knew. True, it was not impulsive. It was the opposite of that. It was obsessive. It made her afraid. Perhaps she didn't want to be more Barber, after all.

Sometimes Ellen missed her old self. More than that, she missed her old, old self. The person she had been when spontaneity just meant doing things for fun. Before the impulse was one to strike back or strike first. The counselling had helped to smooth the join where the one had turned into the other, but there were still times when she felt it would be possible to fall into the crack between them. Days – and nights – when the shattered fragments of that time reared in her mind again, sharp and clear. Sitting with her friend Claire at the very farthest end of the beach, at the mouth of the Don, kicking at the charcoal remains of someone's fire, not telling Claire things she really wanted to tell her. A party at somebody's cousin's grotty flat in Torry. Blue paint on the rocks at the quarry, black water and rusted metal. And Donna. Donna walking the length of the languages corridor weeping when Gray from The Secret Sits got engaged, only to switch her undying love to Ryan the following day; Donna inserting herself between Ellen and Niall Rettie; Donna behind a car window, turning her face away. Donna swearing her to silence.

There was something else, too. Something she hadn't experienced for a long time. A need to check the space around her, to count heads, even when she was the only person there. It was always a moment too late – the sense that someone had just left the room. She never seemed to catch a presence, only a sudden absence.

Her mysterious other.

It was probably just a projection of her own emotional state, but still... Something made her sure she would never tell her mother she had these sensations. She knew what she would make of it.

Ellen got back into her car and pointed it in the direction of Silverknowes. Tracing Barber's final movements now.

As far as Ellen was aware, Robert was the only member of the family who had gone back into the house since the day of the funeral and Barber's murder. He had told them he was staying on in Edinburgh to tidy up and to secure the side exit to the garage. He had been as good as his word. Stepping into the living room she could see no remnants of either funeral reception or police presence. She nudged the door of the television unit closed with her toe and pushed back a vase that had been left teetering dangerously close to the edge of the bookshelf, but otherwise the place seemed spick and span, the floors vacuumed and surfaces free from crumbs, spills and forensic powder.

She went back out into the hall. Dust motes danced in the shaft of evening light from the window on the upstairs landing. She went into the kitchen. Everything had been put away and the place left neat for Linda coming home. A dishcloth had been folded neatly and left to hang over the tap. A fresh vase of flowers sat on the kitchen surface as a welcome. Robert had stocked the fridge. Ellen was touched. The place felt odd somehow, though. There was a slight fusty smell. Any stronger and it would have been cloying. She looked at the flowers. Perhaps they were turning already.

She felt the air move on her neck and turned. Robert had left the door to the garage ajar. Ellen stopped still. Why would he do that? Why would he so carefully clear away everything else but leave the door to the garage even a tiny crack open? It would be a glaring reminder of what had happened there.

She listened hard for a moment. Then in one swift movement she covered the distance to the garage door, reached in her hand and flicked on the light. There was no-one there. But there had been. The place had been turned over. She looked at the side exit and saw that, true to his word, Robert Gilchrist had fitted a new lock and a set of bolts, top and bottom. To do so, he might have hunted amongst his father's tools for a screwdriver but the disarray in the garage went way beyond that. The bags of outdoor games, the labelled boxes, all Ronald's drawers and shelves had been ransacked and various ironmongery and memorabilia left strewn across the floor. If Barber had been here looking for something, then he wasn't the only one.

But had they broken in, or did they have a key? She had come tonight because there was only a narrow window of opportunity before Linda came back. Had someone else known what she did, or had they just been lucky?

She thought about the vase she had righted in the living room, the cabinet door.

Shit.

The dust motes dancing in the hallway.

The intruder was still here.

Her pulse quickening, Ellen stepped quietly back into the kitchen, her hand on her phone. She held her breath. Suddenly the house seemed full of noise: the ticking of the clock on the kitchen wall, the sound of the refrigerator humming, the boiler in the cupboard in the corner. She couldn't hear past them. She moved to the kitchen door and very carefully stepped out into the hall, her eyes everywhere. She felt, rather than heard, someone's presence now, and assessed her options. They must have been upstairs when she came in. Had they stood on the landing listening to her move around the living room, ducking back into one of the rooms when she came back out into the hall? Should she be reassured that their fear of discovery seemed greater than the threat they might pose her?

'Police. Is there someone there?'

She moved quietly up the stairs, listening hard. There were four doors leading off the landing. Gingerly she began to work her way through them, pushing the doors back, taking a quick glance round each room. She had reached the third, the furthest from the stairs when she heard the front door slam shut. She flew down the stairs and was at the door in seconds. She ran down the drive and out onto the street. No-one in either direction. No cars speeding away, no-one legging it on foot. She peered at the shrubs and hedges of the neighbouring gardens. All was still. How could they have got away so fast?

They hadn't. The answer came to her immediately. She turned back to the house, scanning the windows for signs of life, as she reached for her mobile. She phoned it in, then slipped her phone back into her pocket, her eyes never leaving the house. Mentally, she pictured the rear of the property. Tall wooden fencing and enough pyracantha to do some serious damage to anyone stupid enough to try climbing into it.

She should wait there.

She should wait there, but what if whoever was in there had found what they wanted and was in the process of destroying it?

She paced the front of the building, looking up the path to the side door of the garage. It was still shut.

She returned to the front doorstep. Took a step up. Inside, the house was still. Had she imagined the whole thing? Just the wind, and her mysterious other playing tricks on her?

She took another step. The door to the living room was as she had left it. She stepped fully inside.

Nothing.

She moved quietly to the kitchen door, from where she could see through into the garage beyond. Nothing but darkness.

She had turned the light on.

Behind her, in the alcove under the stairs, half-hidden under a pile of coats she knew there was a golf set. She slid out a club and, armed, she tiptoed through the kitchen to the threshold of the garage. She hesitated just a moment too long, curiosity battling the urge to shut the door on whoever was in there and contain them until back-up arrived. When a figure launched itself at her from behind she didn't have time to turn before the blow to her back sent her flying down the steps into the garage. Instinctively she put out her arms but the force of the blow was strong and sudden. Missing the bottom step she tumbled to the ground, felt one wrist buckle on impact and her chin strike the concrete floor, knocking her teeth together. The door behind her slammed shut and everything went dark.

21

Ellen breathed damp concrete, cardboard and metal – though the last might have been blood; she had bitten her tongue. Her jaw throbbed. Struggling to her feet all she could think was that Calder was going to tear a strip off her for this. She felt her way towards the kitchen door. It wouldn't budge. She found the light switch and turned it on, then made for the side door, only to find that Robert Gilchrist had done a very good job securing it.

Her anger flared and this time she made no attempt to quell it. She let out a growl of frustration and drove her foot into the nearest cardboard box, hard. There was a muffled sound of china breaking.

That's what's going to get you into trouble, she heard Barber say, and suddenly, inexplicably, she felt tears prick at her eyes. What was going on with her?

She flexed her hands and feet, got her breathing under control.

And just like that, there it was again: the urge to count heads. One. There had only ever been the two of them there – Ellen and her assailant. So why did she feel as though someone else had just left the party?

Why had she not been aware of their presence?

And what bloody use were they?

If they seemed to manifest themselves in times of stress and tension they weren't much cop as a guardian angel if she only ever noticed when they'd gone?

She looked at the box at her feet and felt a flush creep up her neck. Given the state of the rest of the garage it would be easy to let the damage seem the result of the break-in but that wouldn't stop her feeling guilty about it.

The intruder had emptied boxes, tipped tools onto the floor and upended crates of assorted nuts and bolts, pipe fittings, shelf brackets. She knew that the reason the garage was so well-stocked was that Ronald had kept a lot of end-of-line goods after his hardware business was sold off. Things he hadn't managed to shift before closing down. Was this the main focus of the search, though? Or was it just that she had arrived before the intruder could really get to work on the rest of the house? Ronald Gilchrist had an office upstairs. Presumably that was where her assailant had been when she arrived.

She wondered suddenly whether they had got everything the wrong way round, whether, rather than being disturbed in the garage, it was Barber who had interrupted someone else, just as she had. Or even followed someone here? Someone who didn't need Ronald Gilchrist to tell them what they should be looking for. Whatever it was, the intruder had to have known that the police search was unlikely to have found it. The garage was the scene of crime and had been the focus of their search. They hadn't had cause to conduct a thorough search of the rest of the house. These things could take days and without any evidence showing Barber had gone beyond the garage Blackwood wouldn't authorise it. In here, though, it was fingertip. So why would someone think they could do any better?

She looked at the upended boxes at her feet. The ones labelled: Alistair – Keep; Malcolm – Uni. Alistair had been the one to propose the theory that Barber might have been here to plant something on them. If he was genuinely afraid of that, could he have come here to check for foreign objects that might later prove to be incriminating? She thought of the sudden pressure between her shoulder blades as her assailant had launched her down the steps. Ellen was five foot seven; she judged her assailant to be a little taller, and strong. It could have been Alistair Gilchrist. It could equally have been his brother Malcolm. Either would explain why there was no evidence of a break-in.

What if the person who did this wanted to make it to look as though the house had been ransacked in order to direct attention away from the family, to take the heat off Alistair and Malcolm? To throw the investigation off course?

In which case they clearly overestimated the success of the investigation to date. The Gilchrists might still be their prime suspects but so far there was no conclusive evidence tying them to the crime. Even motive was a bit of a stretch, unless they could prove Barber was right about their involvement in Connor Leask's death.

She heard knocking on the open front door. Calls of 'Police'. Back-up had arrived.

Ellen steeled herself. She was never going to hear the last of this.

22

They've let Malcolm go back to work, though he has to report in regularly. The pressure seems to be off Al too. He says they didn't tell him in so many words, but he reckons it's because the forensics came back on the clothes they were wearing the day of the funeral. He says there'll be no evidence that he had been in the garage or come into contact with the dead man. No blood on his clothes, hands, shoes. And there will be nothing of him on the murder weapon, he says.

'Whatever it was.'

Of course, he doesn't know what it was, but I do. I saw the spanner. They must have checked his hands and clothes for specks of rust too, because it was thick with it. For some reason, I didn't tell Al this.

Something else I know: it's not cheap to train as a pilot. I checked. I looked up the prices of property in the area where Malcolm lived as a student as well. Even renting would have cost him a pretty penny. According to Rob, money was tight around then, and yet Dad was happy to give golden boy everything we had? If you ask me, Al had good reason to be jealous of Malcolm.

Mum is glad to have me home. She's been putting a brave face on it but I can tell she didn't want to be here alone. The house feels strangely empty. I can't even feel any of our ghosts.

I pace round the house, touching things. If I was a dog I would be sniffing out the scents of who has been here, then re-marking my territory. It's uncomfortable knowing that all those people have been in the house, poking around, examining things. The intruder is bad enough, but the attention of the police feels more personal, somehow, because they have been actively analysing us, making assessments. Judgments. They won't confirm whether the break-in is connected to the dead man in the garage but I think it must be. The question is, are both things also connected to the man who died twenty-six years ago?

Or to the man who appears to be a link between the two dead men: Dad?

I feel there should be a song about this, a round or a shanty. Three dead men and a rusty spanner. Three men, two men, one man and a knife.

I have been reading about Connor Leask. I can't for the life of me think what he would have been doing around here. He sounds far too glamorous, far too trendy to have been spending Friday night in these parts. At a push I could imagine him at some posh house party over in Barnton, buttering up senior colleagues and city dignitaries, but it was way too early in the evening to be walking the long way home through the 'burbs after a few too many cocktails.

Upstairs in my old room I run my hands over Dad's and my old desk. There are indentations in the surface where the weight of a pen has pressed into the soft wood. Mine of course, Dad would always have put something under his papers to prevent marks. He was still using my old desk tidy, a faded red plastic thing. There's even a troll doll pencil topper on one of the pencils, and thinking of Dad sitting here using it makes me want to laugh and cry at the same time.

I know it's normal to be angry with someone who has died. For leaving you. But I can't help feeling a different kind of resentment. That he's stolen my thunder. He's used up everyone's tears. Numbed them. I thought about telling Mum last night when I got here, but I didn't. Partly because I had this awful feeling she might accuse me of being spoilt-brattish, as she used to say. As though I was a little girl stamping my feet and shouting, 'what about me?'. And partly because I'm saving it for when it will make more impact. Because, really, what about me?

Would they have searched in here, too? I can't tell. In my day, I would have known instantly whether anyone had been in this room. I knew every detail of how I left it each time I went out. Every crease in the duvet cover, the exact positioning of the trinkets on the bedside table. I can't imagine how we fitted a bed in here now. It must have been so cramped, but it was the one place that was mine. I realise now that my brothers never really had a space like that. Not Malcolm or Al anyway. Rob got plenty of room after they left.

It's laughable to think how fiercely I protected this space. The boys can't have had the slightest interest in my bits of coloured plastic. I was judging them by my own standards. I was the one who used to sneak into their room and fiddle with their things.

There was really only one thing I had that they would have loved to find. But I kept that very well hidden. Less a diary than a collection of my fictions: the adventures of Norna, the Intrepid. It wasn't called that but it might as well have been. My brothers would never have let me live that one down. I find that I'm blushing even to think of it. Or to think of Dad or a police officer finding it, anyway. It won't be there any more, though. I surely threw it out years ago, and anyway, it doesn't look like anyone bothered with my secret place.

My room was carved out of the roof space, with plasterboard walls and a dormer window, and a low cupboard cut into the sloping ceiling. In the corner, where Dad's filing cabinet now stands and where I used to keep a basket which held my old toys and keepsakes there's a small hatch through to the rafters. I call it a hatch, but it's nothing more than a bit of ply set into a frame and painted white. It was a precaution should someone need to crawl through to reach the pipes and cables behind there, or find a leak in the roof. That's where I stashed my diary. My brothers didn't even know it was there.

I find myself tugging at Dad's filing cabinet now. I can see why no-one else bothered. It has sunk deep into the carpet and has clearly not been moved since it was placed here however many years ago. It takes me some time and a lot of effort to haul it out far enough to be able to reach the hatch in the wall. It has no handle. I used to lever the ply out with a ruler. I try to do the same now but find that the whole

126

thing has been painted over. Some time ago by the looks of things. I feel an irrational surge of rage. It's Astro, shooting her flames. Or is it grief? I don't know which, but it feels suddenly as though this is an act of vandalism against my very childhood. Painting it over, rubbing it out.

I march down to the garage and grab a collection of implements from the scatter I left on the work surface when I half-heartedly cleared them from the floor, and return to my old room where I set about the hatch. I scratch the paint from the edges with a nail, then run a screwdriver along it, looking for purchase. When I have opened enough of a crack I force in a chisel and work it up and down, back and forth, all the time knowing that what I am doing is irrational, but I can't let it go. I can't stop.

Finally the last of the paint splits and the ply loosens. A waft of stale air hits me, and a long vacated cobweb drifts to the carpet. And to my surprise I find that there is a diary in here. More than one.

It's just that they're not mine.

23

If Dan Calder had ever stopped to picture what a Baroness should look like it would not have been Lise Eklund. A tall woman with a strong bone structure, she wore her hair very short in a shade he imagined might be called 'aubergine'. He had seen her photograph in the media but he had never met her in person and she made a striking impression. He watched from the public benches as she conducted a case against two men accused of the violent rape and murder of four elderly women. Eklund had received her peerage for her work campaigning for victims of violent crime and for the work of the charity she had founded to support them. Clearly it was something she was passionate about, but there was nothing impassioned about the way she conducted herself here. Her delivery was calm, measured. The court hung on her every word. There was something in the cadence of her voice and the shrewd gaze she passed around the room that commanded attention. When that gaze fell on Dan he experienced the uneasy sensation that she knew immediately who he was, as though she had been expecting him. He must be wrong, but that was part of her skill, he thought: she made people feel they could hide nothing. They deduced further that she must know everything about the accused too.

As the court adjourned for lunch, Dan slipped out of the courtroom and found Ellen waiting outside. He couldn't help glancing at the faint bruise on her jaw, and saw her bristle, defensively. He had gone easy on her, he thought. He figured she had given herself enough of a dressing down before he saw her. And sometimes less was more.

As soon as Lise Eklund emerged they approached her, showing identification.

'Baroness Eklund. Might we have a quick chat about

James Barber?'

Her irritation showed only in a tiny flicker of her eyelids. Her expression remained neutral. She looked at her watch. 'I can give you twenty minutes. It'll have to be over lunch.'

Dan and Ellen followed her across the car park and into the café in St. Giles Cathedral. She set quite a pace. Dan had never eaten in there but Eklund was obviously a familiar. Without waiting she ordered a panini and an espresso, and while Ellen ordered coffees for the two of them Eklund took a seat at a small table, forcing Dan to hunt for an extra chair.

'James Barber came to see you a fortnight ago,' he said, when they finally sat down. 'Do you mind telling us what that was about?'

'He was intent on digging up the Connor Leask enquiry again. Apparently he was onto a new lead.'

'Did he say what that was?'

'Only that he felt he was close to a breakthrough. It was all a bit cloak and dagger, which I tend to think means he had nothing.'

'How did he think you could help?'

'He said he wanted to double-check some of the background on Connor.'

'Such as?'

'The nature of the work he was doing for me, and the most recent cases he had been working on. Connor's...' She reached for the right words. '...Approach to his work.'

'What did you tell him?'

Eklund's panini arrived and she divided each half into two again with swift, forceful thrusts of her knife.

'Connor was in his second year of the Crown Office Procurator Fiscal Trainee scheme. I was his mentor. The scheme is highly competitive, so to get in Connor had had to demonstrate considerable potential, and to a certain extent he was living up to it. He was bright, capable, highly motivated. Sometimes a little overzealous. He found some of the decisions we have to make difficult. We have to be prepared to be unpopular.' She shot a flinty look at Dan and

Ellen in turn. 'Connor found that hard.'

'Connor was twenty-four. Was that young to be a trainee procurator fiscal?' Ellen asked.

'Not particularly. The trainee scheme is a fast track.' She took a large bite out of her panini and chewed it as though it were prey. 'I suppose Connor had a bit of an air of prodigy about him. He'd been young in his cohort at school and university, and being as bright as he was and as energetic, I suppose he gave the impression of being a bit of a wunderkind. I'm not sure it was wholly merited.'

Dan tried to work out whether Eklund was being bitchy, or whether it was just her style to be blunt. He thought the latter more likely, but there was a slight edge to the way she talked about Connor. Was it just resentment at having her lunch hijacked, at having all this brought up again, first by Barber, and now them? Or was there more to it?

'Were there any cases you had assigned Connor that Barber had a particular interest in?'

Eklund dabbed her mouth with a paper napkin, then downed exactly half of her espresso. As a way of concealing her thought process it was effective.

'He was particularly interested in what Connor had been working on in the last few weeks of his life.' She paused. 'Having said that, what Connor was working on was not always quite the same thing as what he had been assigned officially.'

Dan raised his eyebrows. When Eklund did not go on he said, 'You told the original enquiry that one of the cases he had been working on was an investigation into a building supplies merchant called Norris Ralston. Did Barber bring that up?'

She shot him a sharp, inquisitive look. 'Yes, he did.'

'What can you tell us about that case?'

'Well, it wasn't a case, for starters. It never came to trial.'

'Why not?'

'Insufficient evidence. It wasn't in the public interest to pursue it. I sent the DI in charge away with a flea in her ear and told her to come back when she had something more concrete.'

'Who was that?'

'Sharon Harkins.'

Ellen looked up from her notebook. 'You've a good memory.'

'Not really. I've only recently gone over it all with James Barber.'

'So he was definitely interested in that particular enquiry?' Dan asked.

'Yes.'

'Was that one of the decisions that Connor was unhappy about?' Ellen asked. 'Not pursuing a case against Ralston?'

'I can't think why. It was pretty clear to everyone that it wasn't worth pursuing. Harkins had placed far too much emphasis on the testimony of just one of Ralston's employees, and the man had done a runner. Without him the whole thing was little more than speculative.'

Dan thought about the page of names in Connor's file. The line drawn heavily between Norris Ralston and Franjo Horvat. He took a punt. 'Was the informant a man called Franjo Horvat, by any chance?'

Eklund glared at him. 'It was. If you already know everything, Inspector, I'm not sure why you're bothering me. Are you checking up on me?'

Dan was surprised. 'Not at all. It's just that I found that name in something Connor had written.'

'Well, if you've got Connor's notes, you know as much as I could about what he was working on before he died. And how he felt about it.' She said the last bit looking at Ellen, and with an emphasis that suggested it would be a failing on any of their parts to have any feelings at all. Dan had a sense of foreboding, too late to do anything about it.

'I gather Barber made certain allegations when he went to see Sheena Baird,' Ellen said. 'About you and Detective Superintendent Hugh Baird.'

'Did he? I wasn't aware of that,' Eklund said, her voice like ice. 'Would you care to repeat them?'

Ellen didn't flinch. Inside, Dan was doing enough flinching for both of them. 'Apparently Barber told Sheena Baird that you and her father had had a longstanding affair. I only bring it up because I can't understand what it would have to do with his enquiry into Connor Leask's death.'

'Well, I can't help you there, either.' Eklund looked at her watch and rose. 'I must be getting back.' She signalled a thanks to the waiter and put a note on the table. Dan had to hurry to keep up with her as she swept out of the café, leaving Ellen to pay their own bill.

'Before you go,' Dan said, as he followed Eklund out of the cathedral, 'Could I just run another few names by you?' He consulted his notebook for the names that had been in Connor Leask's papers. 'Dean Owens?'

Eklund shook her head. 'I don't know that name.'

'Lee Quigley?'

'Look, if you email them to me I'll get my assistant to check through our archives. I really must be going.'

'You can't think of anything that might have linked these names?' 'I found them in the same document that linked Franjo Horvat to Norris Ralston.'

'Knowing Connor,' Eklund said as Ellen caught up with them, 'The only thing it would take to link them was Connor's curiosity. Or his ego. The opportunity they offered him to prove himself. Listen.' Eklund stopped and turned to face them. 'I was very fond of Connor. He was a livewire. But yes, he was young. And impatient. He wanted to do everything. Solve everything. He was drawn to the idea of justice, but it was my job to teach him about law. About due process. About respect for the legal system.'

'You're saying he could be a bit of a maverick?'

'I'm saying he overestimated our role and our powers. Ralston was a case in point. Connor didn't want to let it go, he wanted to find new evidence so it could go ahead. He always wanted to do everyone's job, not just his own. Yours, mine, the jury's. He was difficult to mentor,' she said, and suddenly she seemed deflated. 'He was never going to be one of my success stories, even if he turned out to be his own.'

'Does the name Gilchrist mean anything to you? Did it come up in the Ralston enquiry?'

'As I say, send me the list.' She turned again and set off towards the court.

'What do you think happened to him?' Dan asked, matching her stride. 'Connor.'

'I assumed they drew the right conclusions. I assumed the investigation was done properly and they exhausted all other avenues of enquiry.'

'You weren't involved in the investigation?' Ellen asked. 'You weren't called on to assess the evidence at any stage?'

'No. As you would know from the original investigation files.'

And with that she was gone.

'Wow,' said Ellen. 'It's as though the wind just died down, suddenly.'

Dan smiled.

They stood in Eklund's wake for a few moments, then turned and began to make their way back to their cars.

'It's all very well all these clues leading us to Norris Ralston and his building-cum-drugs supply business,' said Ellen. 'But there's one big problem.'

Dan looked at her. He had a feeling he knew what was coming next but he asked all the same: 'You found him?'

'He's dead. He was finally convicted in 2001. Died in prison not long into his sentence. So even if Connor Leask's death was something to do with the investigation into Ralston, it's not him who felt threatened by Jimmy Barber digging it all up again.'

24

Saturday night at Al's place is a chaotic affair. Al is on the phone in the hall when I arrive. Mel welcomes me in and leads me through to the kitchen where she glugs some wine into a glass and thrusts it at me – 'Get that down you' – before picking up her own glass and chinking it against mine, a little too forcefully.

'Cheers. Oops!'

We go through to the living room where Kirsty is concentrating ferociously on a Wii dance programme. 'Hi Auntie Norna,' she shouts, without looking up or breaking her rhythm. All pink and sparkles and girl band dance routines, it's hard to believe she is Alistair and Melissa's daughter. As if to prove my point, Mel grins at me. 'This is how we danced in my day,' she says, and launches into her best Bez impression, glass still in hand, and we both laugh.

Kirsty loses her concentration. 'Mum! Look what you made me do.'

'Sorry love.' Mel slides onto the big leather sofa next to me. 'Time to stop now, anyway. Your Auntie Norna's here.'

'But I've got to practise.'

'Not all the time.'

'Yes, all the time. Katy Perry didn't get where she is by slacking off.'

Mel makes a face. 'Really?' It's the kind of 'really' that means, 'Seriously – that's who you want to be?'

'Yes, really.' Kirsty knows what her mum meant.

'Who did you want to be?' I ask Mel. I can't imagine, because when I was Kirsty's age Mel was the coolest person in the world and probably the only real, live role model I ever had so why would she ever have wanted to be anyone else? She and Al got together in school. He was the year above, but she seemed so much more mature, settled in herself. She had this retro Debbie Harry thing going on but it - and everything about her - was completely without guile or pretension. She was refreshingly direct about her opinions and she made Al laugh, which was no mean feat. She was also very nice to me.

She thinks for a moment. 'Carrie Ann Moss.'

'Who's that?' Kirsty asks, curling her lip in contempt.

'The woman in The Matrix.'

'Huh. As if.'

Mel raises her eyebrows at me as Kirsty stalks out of the room. 'Tell your brothers Norna's here. We'll be eating soon.'

Kirsty has left the door open and now we can hear Al in the hall.

'Come on, man. Is this because I retuned their radio?' He's trying to be jokey but there is an undercurrent. 'Is it because of what I said about Steve Wright in the afternoon?'

Mel gets up and pushes the door closed gently. 'Lawrence,' she says.

'Does Al still do work for him?'

'Yeah, he's been doing the wiring in those renovations at the old carpet factory.'

'Hey, Auntie Norna.' Josh comes in, leaving the door ajar again.

'Hi Josh, how are you doing?'

'Okay.'

Al's voice is raised now, no longer jokey. 'What the fuck, man?'

Josh seems to shrink into his shoulders a little. 'Mum, can I go out?'

'No, Josh...'

'I don't mind,' I say. 'We were just going to get a take-away, weren't we? And it's Saturday night. Josh and I can catch up later.'

There's the sound of Al's hand smacking against the wall in the hall. 'Fucksake!'

He appears in the doorway. 'Lawrence Groat has bloody cancelled my contract with him.'

'Oh, no, love.' Mel gets up and goes to him.

'Tried to blame it on the rest of the workforce. Said

they felt I wasn't quite fitting in.' He clenches his fists. 'Fucking police. Fucking...'

'Did you call Finlay?'

'No. I'm not going crawling to Fin. I've got other work. Lawrence can go fuck himself. Arsehole. After all these years I've worked for him. And he knows I had nothing to do with any of it.'

'I thought we were inviting Finlay over tonight?' She flicks a surreptitious glance in my direction. It irritates the hell out of me. The last thing I need is to be set up with someone. And isn't Finlay Groat married, anyway?

'He couldn't make it.'

I feel irrationally slighted.

I'm not the only one. I can practically hear the cogs and wheels turning in Al's head. Maybe Finlay knew what his Dad was about to do and decided to avoid an awkward evening. I can see the vein pulsing in Al's temple. He and Finlay have been friends forever. The thought that Finlay would drop him makes me angry on Al's behalf.

While his dad has been ranting, Josh has drifted into the hall and pulled on his jacket. Alistair notices him now.

'Where are you going?'

'Out.'

'No, you're bloody not. Your Auntie Norna's here and we're going to sit down like a proper family and spend some time together.'

Josh glares at his father and his father glares back. The Mexican stand-off is ruined slightly when Kirsty and little Sam crash through the middle of it. Sam runs to his mother while Kirsty reaches for her Dad's hand. Immediately, Al softens. Kirsty looks smugly at Josh and he glares at her resentfully.

Instinctively, I side with Josh. Kirsty is such a ghastly little sook. But maybe I'm jealous, too, because it used to be me who was the only one who could get through to Al when he was like that.

'How about you and me go and get the takeaway, Josh?' I ask. I squeeze Mel on the arm as I pass her, then quickly usher Josh out of the house, grabbing my coat on the way.

'You were going to tell me about that game you were developing.'

Both of us breathe a sigh of relief as the door shuts behind us. I nudge Josh's arm with mine, gently. We walk in silence for a bit. I can feel Josh's frustration and anger coming off him in waves, but he's different from Al. Softer. More easily hurt, I think.

'What are we going for?' I say. 'I forgot to ask.'

'I hate him,' Josh says, bitterly.

'Oh Josh...'

'He hates me.'

'No, he doesn't.'

'Yes, he does.'

'Why would he hate you?'

'He just does. He hates everything about me. He's always on my case. He never lets up.'

I think about what Rob said on the night of Dad's funeral, about Alistair and our Dad. And what he told me when he dropped me at the station. 'It sounds a lot like how things were between him and Grandad.' I look at Josh. He's fighting off the tears. 'You'd think he would remember what it was like. I'm sorry, Josh. I wish things were different for you.'

He rubs his eyes with the heels of his hands. Then, as we round the bend, he sees something up ahead and stiffens. A group of three boys lounge against the wall of the church at the corner of the main road. They've spotted us coming, one nudging another and nodding in our direction, and in that small gesture I understand the full nature of their relationship to Josh. I feel an immediate rush of blood to my head, a feeling of rage and protectiveness, but at the same time I know I have to make myself almost invisible. I stay on the side of him that keeps me between him and them, but drop slightly behind. I'm letting him be alpha.

As we approach them Josh puts his hands in his pockets and I am relieved to see him lift his head. At least he doesn't cower before them. Instead he looks calm, unflustered. He doesn't alter his pace, but he doesn't look at them either.

'Alright, Joshy-boy?' one of them says as we draw level. He's a big lad, heading fast towards fat, his hard eyes like studs in the upholstery of his face. I want to kick him in the balls. I see him sizing me up, taking in my scarlet hair and nose stud, my biker boots. Yeah, they'd hurt, I tell him telepathically.

Josh says nothing. He turns right at the junction with the main road and as we walk down to the crossing I can feel his renewed anger. His dad, these boys, the world is against him. I drop further behind him to let a woman pass. His hands are still in his pockets but I see now that there is nothing nonchalant about it. His right hand is balled into a fist.

No. I feel a sudden fear grip me. Not a fist. He's holding something.

Is he carrying?

I don't know what to do. Should I say something? Maybe it's nothing. Maybe he just wants to make it look like something.

We walk on down to the crossing and stop, waiting for the lights to change. It gives him the chance to look back up the road, as if he's only turning to me or to assess the approaching traffic as the light changes to amber, and the boys must still be where we left them if they are there at all, because Josh finally lets go whatever it is and takes his hands out of his pockets.

'Chinese?' he says.

'Yeah, does everyone like that?'

*

I wish things were different for Josh. I wish things had been different for Al, too. And though I don't yet understand why, I have a feeling I am going to wish things had been different in a whole lot of other ways.

If I was resentful before about Dad giving Malcolm money to go to London and to train as a pilot, that was nothing compared to my fears about where Dad might have got the money from.

There were three diaries hidden inside the loft space. Small, fake leather appointment diaries for 1991 through to 1993. They had been held together by elastic bands but the rubber had perished and it broke apart in my hands, leaving the frayed remains sticking to the covers. Sandwiched between the diaries was an envelope stuffed with fifty pound notes. I don't think I have ever handled a fifty pound note before. Let alone forty-two of them.

For the most part, the diaries are nothing to speak of. They record meetings and deliveries to the shop, they contain reminders for when to order new stock, and the reference numbers of purchases made. They detail the contact and address details for handyman jobs and the work needing done. They record who Dad sends to do the jobs if he doesn't do them himself.

And then every week, for two and a half years, he makes a note: Invoice paid – £250.

Every week. But that's all it says. It leaves me with a lot of questions. Was the money hidden with the diaries intended to pay these invoices, or had it been received in payment of an invoice Dad had raised? What were these invoices for? If Dad was just working off the books, why is the figure a neat round number and the same each time?

And what does it mean that the last of these notes is made on the night that Connor Leask was killed?

25

As Ellen Chisholm got out of her car a train rattled by in one direction and a tram hummed past in the other. The allotment plot occupied a roughly triangular tract of land between the tracks, a road and a golf course. Marion Carruthers, James Barber's sister, met her at the entrance.

'I'm sorry to call at the weekend, but I thought you would want to know,' she said for the second time. She had been flustered when she telephoned half an hour before. 'I didn't even know he had an allotment. I didn't think it was his kind of thing at all.'

A couple of people lifted their heads from their own plots as Ellen followed her along the narrow paths between them. Even if Marion Carruthers hadn't been there, she would easily have found Barber's plot. She could have followed her nose. The blackened remains of the shed and the melted plastic of the composter next to it still gave off a lingering scent in the damp air.

Neat squares of soil had been dug over and a rudimentary attempt at cultivation had been made but compared to many of the other plots it was basic. What was there – fruit bushes and the remains of the previous year's runner bean supports and other low maintenance vegetable plantings – looked exactly like what it was: a cover.

This was Barber's incident room.

With the reverence of someone afraid to tread on a grave Marion hung back at the edge of the plot. Ellen walked up the short path and stood beside the charred remains of the shed, letting her eyes adjust, as if to the dark. Where there were still walls she began to make out the round heads of pins, small fragments of paper still attached here and there, their contents beyond recognition. In the wreckage at her feet were the powdery remnants of more paper and cardboard, crinkled scraps she thought might once have been photographs. She looked around. There was no wifi at the allotment of course, but then Barber could easily have divided his operation between here and the nearest café that provided it. Anything he wanted printed could have been done at Prontaprint.

Whatever Barber had kept here threatened someone. Enough to destroy all this and Barber himself. Lise Eklund had dismissed Barber's cause by saying it was all a bit cloak and dagger and Ellen had to admit she had a point. Barber had a whole house in which to keep this material. Why go to such lengths to hide it?

'The allotment manager said they thought it was arson,' Marion whispered as Ellen rejoined her.

Ellen nodded. She would check with the fire service to be sure, but to her mind it couldn't be anything else.

'If you didn't know he had an allotment, can you think of anyone else who would have known?'

'No. I don't really know his friends. After Richie died I don't think there was anyone close.'

Ellen made a mental note to check with Vihaan Shah and Glen Starrett. They had both kept up with Barber. She didn't hold out much hope, though. They had each admitted that before the last few weeks of his life - when Barber had begun to pursue the Connor Leask enquiry again - they had fallen out of touch a bit. She had recognised in them the same guilt she felt at having lost contact with him. Ellen shook off the idea that Jimmy might have used the case, even subconsciously, as an excuse to make contact with people, to rekindle friendships without seeming too lonely or desperate.

'You said it happened on the Tuesday night?'

'That's when the allotment manager found out about it, but he had been away for a long weekend. He said it happened a few days before that. Possibly Friday. He put the note through Jimmy's door but I only got round to sorting out his mail yesterday. I haven't been back since you and I were there together.'

Friday. The day Barber was killed. In that case anyone who was already in their sights could have torched the shed. In theory. They would have to have known about the allotment, though, Ellen thought. That was the puzzle. If Barber had taken such care to keep the place a secret, the only explanation she could think of was that someone had followed him here. For that, they would need to have had a reason but they would also have needed time. They would need to have known Barber posed a threat to them and they would need to have been in Edinburgh some time before Friday.

She had been thinking a lot about the person who shoved her into the Gilchrists' garage, the sudden pressure on her shoulder blades and the sickening feeling of flying forward, unable to prevent her fall. Mostly she questioned why the intruder hadn't run when they had the chance? Whoever had been there had stood their ground until they could be sure she wouldn't even see them fleeing. It was a massive risk. They had gambled their escape against not being seen.

They were known to Ellen. Or recognisable from a description she could have given. Whoever they were, they had been in contact with the police already.

Ellen realised they were going to have to go back through everyone's movements right from the moment Ronald Gilchrist tried to contact Barber, hour by hour, day by day. It would be a pain in the arse, but it might just give them the break they needed. They were looking for someone who had the means and opportunity to trail Barber around town for at least one day in the weeks preceding Barber's death, to kill him on the day of the funeral, and to torch his shed. That had to narrow down the field.

Someone was still one step ahead of them. But now, that fact itself was going to make them vulnerable.

26

Dan drove to Musselburgh first thing on Monday morning to see former Detective Inspector Sharon Harkins, the senior investigating officer Lise Eklund had sent away 'with a flea in her ear' when the Norris Ralston case collapsed. Harkins lived in a grey stone terraced house on Eskside West, which looked directly onto the river. Dan parked across the road and stood watching the seagulls on the water for a few moments before heading across to Harkins' house. Of the three retired officers he had come across lately, he quickly gained the impression that Sharon Harkins spent the least time thinking about her former job. She led him through a house busy with colour and the evidence of a life well lived. In the time he was with her, her telephone rang three times and her mobile buzzed repeatedly with messages. Harkins herself had an energy that was infectious.

'A group of us are doing the Camino de Santiago next year,' she told him. 'For the Maggie's Centres. We're in training. I've just come back from five days on the St Cuthbert's Way. Have you done it?'

'No, though I do like getting out into the hills.'

'Munro bagger?'

'No. I mean, I'll climb them but I'm not into ticking them off a list.'

She nodded, approvingly. 'It's the experience isn't it? I'd recommend the St. Cuthbert's. And the other pilgrim ways. You don't have to be religious. Stretches of the John Muir are very good, too.'

'Where's next for you?'

'Southern Upland Way. Though last time I tried it I couldn't even get going. I met a local who said they'd changed the route to bypass a bull in a field and left half the signs pointing the wrong way. I ended up doing a loop round Gala and gave up and went for a cup of tea. Hopefully my companions will know where we're going this time.'

They sat down on opposite sides of a chunky wooden table in Harkins' kitchen. He wondered why it felt so different to Glen Starrett's and decided it was something to do with the fact that Harkins lived in the present.

'I almost feel bad bringing up all this stuff,' he said.

'Almost.' Harkins smiled. 'Go for it.'

'As I said on the phone, we're investigating the death of former Detective Inspector James Barber. In the process, it has become necessary to look into the case of Connor Leask. He was the trainee procurator fiscal...'

'Yes, yes, I know. You think Jimmy's interest in that was the reason he was killed?'

Dan was surprised. In the second before she explained, possibilities flitted through his mind. Had Starrett tipped her off? Was she more in touch with her old colleagues and the gossip being passed around than she gave the impression?

'He came to see me,' she said.

'Barber?'

'Yes. You didn't know? I thought that must be why you wanted to see me.'

'Your number didn't show up in his records.' He blanched, fearing for a moment that they had overlooked something.

'No, he didn't call. Just turned up on the doorstep one day. Jimmy knew where I lived. We kept up from time to time.'

Dan sat forward in his seat. 'Did he talk to you about Connor Leask? Did he tell you what he'd found out?'

Harkins shook her head. 'Only that he wanted to prove it wasn't a random attack. But then I didn't really ask. I was happy to answer his questions, but I wasn't willing to be drawn into his crusade. That sounds harsh. It's not meant to. Anyway, all he really said was that he thought he was definitely onto something this time, but he needed to make completely sure because he'd be the one hung out to dry if it all went tits up. But don't you know? I mean, he must have left notes. He certainly took some when he was with me.'

Dan's turn to shake his head. 'All gone,' he said, and though he instinctively liked Harkins, he watched carefully for her reaction all the same. What he saw made him smile. You could take the woman out of the service, he thought, but you couldn't take the detective out of the woman. Harkins' eyes flashed with interest before they turned to sadness.

'Well, good on Jimmy,' she said, quietly, after a moment. 'So he really was onto something. How can I help?'

'I was going to ask you about Norris Ralston. Is that what he came to see you about?'

'It was,' Harkins sighed. 'Bane of my career was Norris bloody Ralston.' She gave a little laugh. 'Sometimes I can't quite believe how much he got to me. The hours I spent trying to prove that man was crooked. It was an obsession. That's why I understood how Jimmy felt about Connor Leask. And why I didn't want to get involved. But then, when I think that they got Ralston in the end, that I was right, even if it wasn't me who nailed him, I don't feel so bad.'

'Tell me about it.'

'Short version? We'd had an inkling for some time that Ralston was using his building supplies business to move drugs and money. There were too many coincidences where his vans or his workers – or people getting work done to their properties using his supplies – kept cropping up, put it that way. The bit you'll be most interested in is when we caught our big break. Or thought we had. One of his workers agreed to act as an informant. He provided names, dates of shipments, partial details of what was being moved. He agreed to testify to all of it.'

'This was Franjo Horvat?'

Harkins raised her eyebrows. Dan indicated that she should continue.

'Franjo, known as Frank, Horvat. Well, that's it really. Horvat disappeared. We took the case to the fiscal...'

'Lise Eklund.'

Again the nod and the eyebrows. 'The same. She threw it out. Without Horvat we had little to corroborate our findings. We were back to square one. But how do you know Jimmy was interested in Horvat and Ralston? You said his notes were all gone.'

'Yes, but not all of Connor Leask's.' Again he watched for her reaction. Watched as she processed the information.

'So Jimmy was following the trail Connor Leask left behind? This is to do with something Leask had uncovered?'

Dan waited. Harkins went on, thinking aloud. 'The same killer? Jimmy wasn't killed just because he had found out who killed Leask. He had found out why Leask was killed. He had found out the reason someone wanted to silence Connor Leask in the first place?'

Dan said nothing. He had the feeling Sharon Harkins was not finished yet.

'Not Ralston, though. Ralston's dead. He died in prison sixteen, maybe seventeen years ago, not long after they put him in there.'

'What happened to his business?'

'Liquidated after he was convicted.'

'Did he have family?'

'His wife and daughter didn't wait around long after he was put inside. They emigrated. New Zealand, I think.'

'What happened to Frank Horvat? Did you ever find out?'

'Well, the general consensus was that he'd done a runner. Either in fear of reprisals from Ralston and his associates, or because he was a Croatian immigrant. He had fled the conflict in 1991 and there was a school of thought that said he was scared to testify because he was afraid he would be deported.'

Dan frowned. 'Was he illegal?'

'No, it's bollocks. I don't really hold with either of those theories. He never struck me as fearful. I don't think he would have talked to us in the first place if that was the case.'

'What then? You think someone got rid of him?'

'I wouldn't go that far. I think someone may have paid him off, though. He often asked what was in it for him if he helped us. I think he might have chanced his arm and gone to Ralston, told him what we were up to and struck a deal.'

'Did you look for him?'

'Oh yes. And I ran his name every now and then for years after the enquiry fell through. Nothing.'

'Leask was interested in him.'

'So I gather.'

'Did Barber ask about anyone else?'

'Mitchell Kinley. The property developer. Has he come up?'

Dan frowned. Kinley had come up, but not in the case file or in Connor's notes. Farhana McLean had told him that she and Connor rented a flat from Kinley. That Lise Eklund had helped to secure it for them. Eklund, Detective Superintendent Hugh Baird and Kinley were friends. Barber had been interested in that.

'He has, but I'm not exactly sure why,' he told Harkins now. 'What was Barber's interest in him?'

'He thought there might be a connection between Kinley and Ralston. He wanted to know if that had ever come up as part of our investigation.'

'And?'

'Yes and no,' Harkins answered, carefully. 'Kinley did use Ralston as the main supplier for his developments, and they belonged to the same rotary club. How much do you know about Kinley?'

'Not a lot. They're a fancy property company, that's about it.' He didn't tell her about the links to Eklund and Baird, or Connor Leask.

'Well, that's true now but it wasn't always. Nowadays they specialise in buying upmarket properties that have seen better days and restoring or redeveloping them for the elite market. Snapping up crumbling mansion houses and converting them into swanky flats, or splitting the properties into separate luxury town houses, that kind of thing. In the early days, though, Mitchell Kinley had a more mixed portfolio and he made a lot of his money from less prestigious developments. Those big regeneration projects of the 1990s, when whole swathes of unfit social housing were demolished and replaced across Scotland? Kinley made a fortune from local authority contracts doing just that. And as if that wasn't lucrative enough he was also using his contacts and – let's say his charm – to get his hands on land from which social housing had been cleared, which he then built less affordable private houses on. That was a big part of what he was doing at the time we were investigating Ralston, and as his main supplier, Ralston had been doing pretty well out of these deals too.

'Anyway, in answer to your original question, yes, Kinley came up, and we looked at him maybe a little harder than we did some of Ralston's other customers, but there was nothing to link him to the drugs or money laundering. I did have my suspicions that he may have offered support to Ralston when it came to legal matters, but I had no evidence of that either.'

'What kind of support?'

'Contacts, recommending a good lawyer, advice on his rights, on what our restrictions were, and so on. All I know for sure is that Ralston was getting help from somewhere because in the time we were investigating him he seemed to gain a lot of insight into law. And Kinley had friends in high places.'

Didn't he just, Dan thought. Procurator Fiscal Lise Eklund and Detective Superintendent Hugh Baird for two. He began to get that prickling sensation he had had outside the station that night when James Barber first mentioned Hugh Baird to him.

'And the later investigation which saw Ralston convicted – that didn't find any evidence against Kinley either?'

Harkins shrugged. 'Mitchell Kinley was never formally investigated to my knowledge. I don't think there was ever any suggestion that he was anything more than a legitimate building supplies customer.'

'Where is he now? I thought I read something about some philanthropic enterprise he ran.'

'Oh, yes, he's always had that side to him. He did back then, as well. He was quite the man of the people for a while. I think his charity is still going. It teaches skills for trades to teenagers who have come from deprived backgrounds and who are failing at school, or kids who've had a brush with the law or look like they might be heading into trouble. It's a sort of early intervention, it aims to give them a chance to turn things around or gives them opportunities they wouldn't otherwise have. They do day release from school in the summer term, then do paid work experience over the summer holiday. If they pass muster they get longer-term apprenticeships with Kinleys and other firms who've signed up to it. I don't know how much the man himself is involved now though. The property empire is run by his son. Last I heard, Mitchell had bought himself an estate somewhere and was playing at being landed gentry.' She smiled, sheepishly. 'I did look into the charity, actually. That's how I know all this. Call me a cynic, but when we didn't find anything in the business linking him to Ralston's money laundering I thought it was worth a peek. Clutching at straws, maybe. There was nothing untoward.'

Harkins' phone trilled again, and Dan thought it was probably time he let her get back to her busy retirement. One more thing, though.

'In your investigation into Ralston, did the name Gilchrist ever come up?' he asked.

'Jimmy asked me that. I didn't remember it but he had me do a bit of digging. I found two references to Gilchrists. The most significant was a Ronald Gilchrist on Ralston's list of customers. Hardware and handyman business in Stockbridge? But there was nothing to indicate he was anything more than a building supplies customer either. What is it?'

'Jimmy Barber was found dead in Ronald Gilchrist's garage.'

Harkins' eyes widened. 'Well then...'

Dan shook his head. 'It's not quite as simple as that. Ronald Gilchrist, the man who would have been Ralston's customer, is dead. The day Barber died was the day of his funeral. Seemingly he had tried to contact Barber before he fell ill, but Barber never had a chance to talk to him.' He reached for his coat and got up.

'Hang on.' Harkins was rising too, but instead of saying her goodbyes, she scurried away and he heard her pulling out drawers in a nearby room. While she was gone he thought about dropping Farhana McLean's treasury tag into the jar of pens on her hall table but he didn't have time before she returned with a sheaf of papers and a pair of spectacles propped on her nose.

'Somewhere... Yes, here we go.' She pushed the papers at him. 'You should have all this stuff anyway. I printed it off for Jimmy. List of young people who went through Kinley's charity scheme in the early nineties. Here.' She pointed to a name half way down one of the pages and Dan's pulse quickened.

'Alistair Gilchrist. Electrical. Any relation?'

'Yes,' Dan said. 'Yes he is.'

'That was the second of the two Gilchrists. I thought it less significant than the first, but if they're related, maybe there's something in it?'

Dan scanned the rest of the page. He was looking for it, but still, when he saw Lee Quigley's name a little further up the list from Al Gilchrist's he wanted to punch the air.

'What does this asterisk mean, next to someone's name?' he asked Harkins.

'I think it means he didn't complete the course.' Let's see. She put her spectacles back on. 'Oh, yes, that business threatened to shut the charity down. Lee Quigley didn't finish the training scheme but later he was found to have broken into a building site. You can imagine what certain sections of the press made of that. Kinley was taking young criminals and teaching them the skills and knowledge with which to profit even further from their actions and their ill-gotten gains.'

Dan's brain skittered, trying to make sense of it. Here was a link, of sorts. Al Gilchrist and Lee Quigley on the same training scheme run by Mitchell Kinley. Kinley and Ronald Gilchrist both customers of Norris Ralston. Lee Quigley and Ralston both in Connor's notes. But what did it all mean?

It meant one thing. It meant that if Connor Leask had known of Lee Quigley, then Al Gilchrist might have been known to him too. And if it came to finding a motive for Al Gilchrist to have killed Connor Leask, whatever that might be, it certainly couldn't be random.

27

Ellen listened as Dan Calder updated her on what he had learnt from Sharon Harkins, then pocketed her phone and rejoined Liam McGuire in the reception of Groat's offices and showroom in Bonnington. According to the glossy leaflets lying on the table in front of them, Groat's was an all trades company specialising in repairs, renovation, insurance claims, property adaptation and development. That was a lot of specialisms, Ellen thought, as she slipped the leaflet back onto the table. She didn't think she'd be needing Groat's services any time soon judging by the enormous pictures on the wall: models relaxing on the first-floor roof garden of a modern extension to an Edwardian house, and sharing champagne after dark, in an open-fronted garage conversion.

'I'd settle for having my own front door,' she said to Liam.

'Aye.' They pondered the images for a moment. 'Get through a lot of Windolene if you lived in one of those,' Liam said.

Ellen smiled. 'Yeah. And you'd think if you could afford a place like that you could afford some curtains.'

They both looked up as the door through to the back office opened and an immaculately dressed man in his early forties greeted them.

'Detective Sergeant Chisholm? Detective Constable McGuire? I'm Finlay Groat. Please, come through.'

He led them into a bright office decorated with yet more images of beautiful people in their beautiful homes. Ellen watched Finlay Groat with interest as he made a performance of putting away the paperwork on his desk. He could have done that before coming out to get them, she thought, or not bothered even, but he wanted them to see that he was making space for them, that he was removing any distractions, devoting all his attention to them. It was hard to believe he and Alistair 'Che' Gilchrist had once been partners in crime. Groat's schooling was evident in his cultured accent, the way he carried himself. Whilst it was not hard to spot the teenage tearaway in Alistair, who was all sharp angles and forthright fury, this man was smoothed edges, politeness, convention.

When Finlay Groat had finally settled she decided it was time to take control.

'We wanted to speak to you because we found your office phone number in the list of James Barber's recent contacts.' She had half-expected Finlay to fake confusion at this, pretend he didn't know who she meant, but he simply nodded.

'Your receptionist said that he made an appointment to see you last week. Could you tell us what you talked about.'

'Yes, of course. He wanted to go over my statement from 1993.' He looked at Ellen and Liam expectantly but neither said anything. 'About the night of that stabbing. I'm sure Alistair will have told you about how the two of us came to the police's attention at the time.'

'Perhaps you could tell us your version of events.'

Groat blew out air noisily. 'Like I said to Barber, I'll tell you as much as I can remember, but you'll have a better account in my statement from the time. We'd been mucking about round the back of the supermarket, that I do remember, to my shame. Someone threatened to phone the police so we legged it. I was on a last warning from my Dad... Anyway, we'd have gone past the pub where they said Leask was seen, though we didn't see him. We ran all the way down into Silverknowes. I think we split up somewhere around the row of shops on the main road there. I went home to get shouted at by my Dad.'

There was something about the way he put it that Ellen didn't like: a casualness in the way he used Leask's name, an offhandedness. Had Connor Leask's been a recent murder, Groat's mention of the pub and of Leask himself might have seemed like a slip, a giveaway. At any time it was callous. This was just a story to Groat. Tired and tiresome. It was frustrating, these layers upon layers of degraded information. It was impossible to tell what was memory, what had been gleaned from news reports after the fact and what had become contaminated with hindsight or speculation, or with sheer repetition.

'You didn't see Connor Leask at all that night?'

'Well, we saw people, especially on the main street outside the pubs and the chippie, but we were pretty wrapped up in our own drama. We just bombed it past them all.'

'Were there repercussions from that night?' Ellen asked.

Groat looked like he thought it was a trick question. 'Well, we were questioned, as you know, but we had nothing to do with it.'

'I meant as a result of your vandalism and the theft of supermarket trolleys.'

'Oh.' He gave a little laugh. 'I wouldn't call it theft. I mean, we...' He checked himself. 'Repercussions, yes. Not official. No charges were brought, but we both got hell from our folks. I know I did, anyway. And if I'm honest, being dragged into that investigation afterwards might have been the lesson I needed. I think that was probably the turning point for me.'

'You went straight?' Ellen said it with only a tiny hint of sarcasm, but Finlay Groat had the grace to look embarrassed.

'If you want to put it like that. Like I say, my Dad had made it clear, if I didn't change my tune I would be out on my ear. No more posh school, no more home comforts. I'd have to fend for myself. I don't think I really took him seriously until that night, but being questioned by the police was the scare I needed. I decided after that that I didn't want to be a rebel after all.'

'Why do you think James Barber wanted to go back over your statement after all this time?'

'I thought he was just re-investigating it.'

Ellen and Liam exchanged a brief glance. Had Barber

led Finlay Groat to believe he was still a serving officer or that he had an official role still? She didn't want to ask.

'What do you think now?'

Groat frowned at her. 'What do you mean?'

'I mean, the man reviewing that case has just been found murdered in the Gilchrists' garage. Has that changed your perception of things?'

'Al had nothing to do with it,' Groat said quietly. 'Not then. Not now.'

'You seem very sure of that.'

'I am. We did stupid stuff when we were boys but Al isn't a killer.'

'Then – again – why do you think James Barber was so interested in what you two were doing that night?'

Finlay Groat's mouth twitched in annoyance and for a moment Ellen thought she could see the common ground he and Alistair Gilchrist must once have shared.

'I think Al was an easy target and he didn't help himself the way he kicked off. But that was just the way he was. Gobby. And he had a temper, yes, but that doesn't make him a killer.'

'Was he ever violent?'

'No.'

Ellen left the answer hanging until Groat felt the need to justify it.

'He wrote some angry stuff on walls, and he might have taken it out on a bit of street furniture from time to time, but that's it.

'You're a loyal friend.'

Groat shrugged modestly.

'How did you come to be friends? You went to different schools, didn't you?'

'Only in secondary. We went to primary school together.'

'But you kept up after you went – where was it?'

'The Academy. Yes, we still hung out together after school and at weekends.' Again, they left him a pause to fill. 'Al was still my friend. In fact he was about the only one who didn't think I'd suddenly become a different person when I got sent there. A lot of my old friends shunned me, but Al didn't. I was grateful for that.'

'It was a difficult transition?'

'Most of them,' he placed a slight emphasis on the last word. 'The other pupils at the Academy, had started in primary, so when I joined in first year they already had their pals.' He hesitated. 'Plus, I wasn't really one of them. First generation private school, if you know what I mean.'

'Is that why you rebelled?'

'I suppose it was part of it. A lot of it was about my Dad, if you must know. Partly I was railing against his snobbery, against what he wanted me to be. But he also made it very difficult for me to fit into that world by being who he was. That was my snobbery, I suppose. The company wasn't like this then. Dad was still little more than a builder. He'd made money, sure, but he was... rough.' Groat looked apologetic. 'I saw things as very black and white then. It took me a few years to realise life is much more complex than that..'

'What was Alistair rebelling against?' Liam asked.

Groat thought for a moment. 'Both the same thing and the opposite, I think,' he said. 'I had all this expectation heaped on me. With Al, it was more like his dad had skipped that stage and gone straight to disappointment. All his life he was compared to his brother. He never stood a chance. Malcolm was this fantastic high achiever. Everyone thought he was a paragon of virtue, more fool them. They still do. You should have heard them at the funeral. So Malcolm flies a plane. Big deal.'

'What do you mean, more fool them?' Ellen asked.

'Just that if Malcolm's dad knew half of what he got up to he might have got a bit of a shock.'

They waited, but this time Groat was saying no more.

'Did you know Alistair's other friends? Ever come across a lad called Lee Quigley?'

Ellen thought there was flicker of something in Finlay Groat's eyes then. He sniffed. 'No. Are you sure he was a friend of Al's? I've never heard of him.'

Jealousy? Was that it? The idea that Alistair Gilchrist might have other friends.

'He did the same trainee scheme as Alistair, though he specialised in a different trade.'

'Sorry.' Groat shrugged.

'I gather Alistair works for you, now?' Ellen said.

'He's one of our contractors, yes.' Groat dropped his eyes and shifted uncomfortably.

'All above board, I hope?'

'Oh. Yes, of course. No, it's not that. It's just, well, my dad just cancelled a contract with Al, that's all. I feel bad about it.'

'Why did he do that?'

'It's just Dad being reactionary. I told Al that. We'll bring him back on board as soon as all this has blown over.'

'Does your father think Alistair had something to do with James Barber's murder?'

'I'm sure he doesn't. I think he's just afraid of what other people might think.' He sighed. 'It's cold feet. But it'll be ok. He'll get over it. And in the meantime, Al's got his Kinley's work to tide him over. Sooner you find out who did this the better, though. It wasn't Al. No way it was Al.'

*

'Loyal friend,' Ellen said again, to Liam this time, as the glass door closed quietly behind them. 'Is it unusual for them to be so close after all these years, do you think?'

'Don't they say something about bonds forged in childhood?' Liam said. 'Tell you one thing, though. He doesn't like Malcolm much.'

'No. So he flies a plane. Big deal. Bitter, much?'

'I wonder whether he's even more jealous of Malcolm than Alistair is. Groat's worked in his dad's firm all his life. Perhaps he adopted a kind of shared resentment of Malcolm as a child and Malcolm has come to signify all the chances he never had?'

'You're quite the psychologist, aren't you, Liam?'

Liam grinned.

'So, why do you think he was so evasive about why Barber was asking questions again? And why do you think he immediately assumed - when I asked about repercussions - that I meant repercussions from Connor Leask's murder?'

28

Ellen and Liam carried their takeaway sandwiches back to the car where it was parked on the bridge on Newhaven Road, and ate them leaning against it, looking at a short stretch of the Water of Leith below.

'Lot of connections to the building trade, aren't there?' said Liam. 'You reckon this is all connected to that Norris Ralston business?'

Ellen chewed for a few moments. 'The way I see it, if both deaths are connected to Norris Ralston and his involvement in drugs and money laundering there are two key possibilities. In Connor's case, he was disgruntled that the first investigation into Ralston collapsed. He appears to have been killed while he was trying to dig up more evidence. But Ralston was convicted, and died, long before James Barber was killed. So, possibility one: someone else benefitted from Ralston's criminal dealings, managed to erase any trace of their involvement before the later investigation and got away with it. They would have had a vested interest in getting rid of both Leask and Barber if there was a danger they might dig up some evidence against them.'

'Mitchell Kinley's name is starting to crop up a lot. We know Sharon Harkins looked into him but couldn't find evidence he was linked to Ralston. He was clearly a canny operator, though, and he had a lot of useful friends.'

'Which brings me to possibility two: it's not about Ralston per se, but it's about why that first investigation collapsed. Someone was protecting Ralston – and/or one of his associates. They failed with Ralston in the long run, but first time round they managed to silence Franjo Horvat, the key witness against Ralston, and then they took more violent action when Connor Leask started nosing around. Everything is rosy, until Jimmy Barber starts asking questions again.'

It wasn't a possibility she really wanted to consider, but she knew they had to. It seemed safer voicing it first to Liam over a cheese and pickle sandwich than in the incident room under the glare of Senior Advocate Lise Eklund's photograph. She had noted that Eklund hadn't denied her alleged relationship with Detective Superintendent Hugh Baird, the man who was ultimately responsible for the Connor Leask enquiry – and closing it down. And the two had been close friends of Mitchell Kinley.

Liam was clearly thinking along the same lines. 'Is friendship a strong enough reason to pervert the course of justice, do you think?'

'Friendship isn't always nice and fluffy, is it?'

She thought of Donna again. The schoolfriend who had betrayed her but whom she had not been able to abandon. She had felt the presence – or the departure – of her mysterious other often then. On the night of Donna's father's disappearance and throughout the police investigation which followed the discovery of his body.

Perhaps the mysterious other was no guardian angel at all, but quite the opposite. Perhaps it wished her ill.

Her mother would believe it was the spirit of her still-born twin.

'Whoever killed Barber must have been in a position to know he was asking questions,' said Liam.

'Trouble is, he doesn't seem to have been very subtle about it. He was stirring up all kinds of shit.'

'But top of the list is still the Gilchrists. No way they wouldn't have connected Barber with Connor Leask's death when he turned up at the hospital. And even if they were distracted by Ronald's illness I'd put money on Finlay Groat having told Alistair that Barber had been to see him. You don't think Ronald could have been involved in Ralston's dodgy dealings, do you?'

'I think it's worth looking into his business. Barber was at the old premises on the day he died. Ok, I'll play – who else knew he was poking around? Glen Starrett and Vihaan Shah, Barber's former colleagues and members of the team that investigated Connor Leask's death. Barber tried to get them to help him reopen the investigation. I don't know who Glen Starrett talks to these days but Shah is still on the job.

'Oh, but hang on. Two years ago James Barber also asked Shah to access information about Lee Quigley, the teenager who did Kinley's training scheme. If someone knew how the pieces of the puzzle fit together, they might have known he was sniffing around a long time before Ronald's call set him off again. That opens it up a bit. Though I do still believe it's someone known to us.'

'That lad, Quigley. He died while he was thieving scrap and building materials, is that right?' Liam said, waving the last of his BLT in the air, and causing some excitement to a large herring gull that was watching them from further along the bridge parapet.

'That was the assumption. He'd broken into a construction site late at night. He was crushed to death when a load of scaffolding poles collapsed. His death was ruled accidental.'

'Was it one of Ralston's sites?' Liam asked.

'Ralston was a materials supplier, he wasn't in construction. But we should check whose site it was.'

'Was he definitely on his own?'

Ellen looked at him. 'You thinking... Alistair Gilchrist?'

Liam shrugged. 'Maybe all this is a lot simpler than we think it is.'

She couldn't help hoping Liam was right. 'In the process of investigating Ralston's network, both Connor Leask and Jimmy Barber stumbled upon the murder of Lee Quigley? Why would Ronald have contacted Barber?'

Liam grunted. He didn't have an answer for that one.

'Ok, who else? Farhana McLean, Connor Leask's flatmate at the time of his murder. She knew Jimmy was asking questions and she told at least one other person. The DI is still trying to track down the ex-boyfriend. He had an alibi for the murder but Calder thinks he might have seen more than he let on at the time if he was stalking Connor.'

'You didn't tell anyone, did you, Sarge?'

'Only you.'

'Touché.'

They got back into the car and belted up.

'Ok,' Ellen said. 'Hypothetically, mind – let's just say Mitchel Kinley, property magnate and philanthropist, is involved in this, if Alistair Gilchrist did the Kinley scheme, d'you reckon he might have witnessed something? And told his Dad? Could that explain Ronald Gilchrist's call to Barber?'

'Why wouldn't Alistair just tell us if that was the case?'

'Because he still works for Kinley. He needs the job. Might be scared.'

'More than of having a murder charge hanging over his head?'

'It's not that crazy. Barber was killed and left at the Gilchrists,' Ellen said. 'What if he was killed there as a kind of posthumous punishment to Ronald for grassing? Or a warning? "Look what I can do."'

She put the key in the ignition. 'What do you say we go poke the bear?'

Next to her, Liam grinned. 'What's our angle?'

'Let's just see how he reacts if we put some names to him.'

*

They found Alistair Gilchrist at a small Kinley's development that had been built on the edge of Dalmeny to the west of the city. The billboards on the roadside promised 'A taste of rural life.' Ellen could practically taste it already: the adjacent fields had recently been manured. The girl on reception at the showroom led them through the pristine cul-de-sac and into one of the 'luxury five-bed townhouses' where the country air was thankfully absent and everything smelt newly of plaster, treated wood and plastic ducting.

Alistair Gilchrist was kneeling on the floor in a bare room fitting a plug socket into the wall. He sat back on his haunches when the receptionist brought them in.

'Some visitors for you, Al.'

'Thanks, Lisa.'

The girl reddened slightly as she took her leave and Ellen had to suppress an urge to roll her eyes. What was it with guys like Gilchrist? Something to do with that lopsided smile and the way it lifted his face unexpectedly from its habitual dark glower? Some kind of hypnosis in his black eyes that made a girl believe that she and she alone had been the one to light him up? Honestly.

Once she had gone, the glower was back, full force. 'What are you doing here?'

'We have a few more questions for you.'

'What if I don't feel like answering them?'

'Well, that's your prerogative. They're not very hard, though.'

Liam had been examining the room and the view of the development outside, the tips of the Forth bridges just visible beyond the houses opposite.

'You've been working for Kinley's on and off for some time now, isn't that right?' he asked Gilchrist. 'I understand you started out on one of their schemes. It led to your apprenticeship as an electrician.'

Alistair got to his feet and began gathering up off-cuts of electrical wire. He didn't answer but he gave a small shrug of acknowledgement.

'Did you ever come across Lee Quigley?' Ellen asked.

'Doesn't ring a bell.'

'He did the scheme too.'

'I don't know him.'

'Is this the kind of work you do for Groat's as well?'

'Sometimes.'

'Not at the moment, though, I gather.'

He didn't rise to the bait but she saw his jaw clench.

'Ever come across Norris Ralston?'

'Yep.'

'How?'

'He was one of the biggest building suppliers around for a long time. Everyone knew Ralston's.'

'But did you know him personally?'

'Not me. He was my Dad's generation. Him and Lawrence probably knew Norris Ralston to say hello to.'

'What about Franjo Horvat? He worked for Ralston. He was going to testify against him.'

Al gave an exasperated shrug, shaking his head. 'You're talking decades ago. I was a teenager.'

'Do you know Mitchell Kinley personally?'

'I've met him a few times. Graeme, too. I wouldn't call them mates. Look.' He glanced towards the door, before stepping closer to Ellen. 'I get that you have a job to do and you need to find out who killed that bloke and left him in my mother's garage, but don't think you can pin this on me or my family.' He leaned forward, his face barely a couple of inches away from Ellen's now. 'And don't think you can fuck up my life in the process.'

Ellen stood her ground. 'I've no intention of pinning anything on anyone. But I do intend to find out who killed James Barber. If we can also catch the coward who knifed Connor Leask...' She paused, letting her eyes drop to Alistair's open toolbox. '...That'll be a bonus. There's a suspicious number of connections between the two, and certain names just keep cropping up. Yours included. And your father's. And your brother Malcolm's.'

Alistair Gilchrist snarled. Ellen noted that he had a length of electrical wire coiled round his fist. Bring it on, she thought. Just give me an excuse.

With a sniff, Alistair backed away and threw the wire into a canvas bag that lay open on the floor. From where he was leaning casually against one of the plasterboard walls Liam winked at Ellen.

They were leaving when Alistair called out, 'Wait'.

'I do remember Quigley. He was a gobshite. He wasn't in the same team as me but everyone knew who he was. Thought he was the big man. They chucked him off the course because he didn't do any work, just gave them attitude. Thought he could get away with it because he knew someone or something. Obviously that was bullshit or he wouldn't have needed to go nicking stuff from sites. That's all I know.'

Ellen nodded. 'We'll talk again.'

Alistair scowled and turned away. She didn't catch exactly what he said, but it didn't sound like a polite good-bye.

She had glanced pointedly at Gilchrist's toolbox to wind him up, but it wasn't entirely a piece of theatre. They had concluded that, if the same person killed both Jimmy Barber and Connor Leask, in the twenty-six intervening years that person had lost the habit of carrying a knife. Moreover, they had not come prepared: they had used a spanner that they found in the garage.

They had never found the knife that killed Leask.

That was what Barber had been looking for. It seemed so obvious now. He had thought Ronald Gilchrist had the murder weapon that killed Connor Leask.

But why?

29

I walk with Mum, through the grounds of Lauriston Castle. It's not a castle really, just a wealthy Edwardian's aspiration, now in the gift of the city. I haven't been inside for years, not since primary school. I have vague memories of polished coconut shell goblets and pictures made of wool, sliced from a block of condensed yarn, to reveal the picture running through it like Blackpool rock. I like the grounds though, when it's peaceful in the middle of the week like this, and there are no family picnics or school parties examining insects in the undergrowth.

We reach a long straight stretch of level ground, and Mum holds out her hand. I take it and close my eyes, turning up my face to the dappled sunshine. I listen to the trill of the birds and our feet soft on the damp grass. The distant hum of the city. Light and shade flicker on my eyelids: yellow and black and orange. I concentrate on the motion of walking. I notice how thin Mum's hand has got now, the bones beneath her skin, the ring loose on her finger. I wonder whether she notices the same about me.

She guides me to the right. There is tarmac under my feet now and I know that we are near the car park. Something in the curve of the path, the scent in the air, chases memories through my mind before I can label them.

All I know is that I don't want this moment to end.

*

When we get home Mum puts on the television and heads into the kitchen to make us tea. Countdown is about to start and she has her paper and pen ready, but when I go through to the kitchen to hunt down some biscuits she is staring out of the window, seeing nothing. The window is cracked open and I can hear the chatter of garden birds over the muted hyperbole of the commercials in the other room. I find a packet of fig rolls. Seven-year-old me stamps her feet in disgust, but they'll have to do. I fetch a couple of plates as the kettle builds steadily towards boiling point, a mounting frenzy that sets my nerves on edge. Suddenly I can't stand to hear it, the urgency of its roar. I grip the plates in my hand as though I could snap them in half, try to shake the noise out of my head. I can't breathe. Finally the kettle reaches its crescendo and clicks off, but as the bubbling subsides it gives way to another sound that is even more terrible. I look up to see Mum bent almost double, gripping the counter. Huge sobs wrack her whole body rendering her helpless, and her cry in the quiet of the kitchen is like the wail of something much older, more primitive, something not quite human.

There is nothing I can do besides hold her.

After a while the wrenching sobs give way to a more pitiful weeping, bringing real tears. She ignores them. Straightens up, pats me on the cheek, and busies herself with our tea. Finally, rubbing her cheeks dry she goes through to the sitting room where she settles on the sofa and takes up her paper and pen. She has only missed the chat at the beginning of the show. She hasn't missed any of the word games. Here we go: D - F - L - A - U - E - P - X - R. She copies them down dutifully. It's a tricky one.

And standing in the doorway watching her, all I can think is, did she know?

Does she know?

Because I think Dad was blackmailing someone.

*

I leave Mum to her programme and head upstairs, into my old room, where I retrieve the diaries from the hole in the wall behind the filing cabinet.

I want to believe that Dad was only working off the books. That the payments noted in the diaries stop when they do only because Dad got a fright when he and the boys were interviewed by the police about the murder and he decided to clean up his act.

It's hard to believe that, though.

I turn the pages of the diaries again, hoping that something will leap out at me that will explain this series of 'invoices' paid. I have scoured the entries preceding the first Friday's payment in March 1991 but so far I can't see any reason for them. Throughout the diaries people are reduced to initials, and actions and events to individual verbs and nouns: pay MS; Meet LG. Most of it is day-to-day business: order plumbing supplies; stock take; 4 1/2 Chesser St. kitchen taps. The entry preceding the first of these payments is from the Wednesday and simply reads: Ferniehill Ter, patio slabs. The only thing that strikes me as odd about that is that I didn't think he did that kind of work. But then, Rob did say that times were hard around then; so maybe he was taking jobs on the side after all.

Jobs that brought in an extra thousand pounds a month. Really?

The back pages of the diaries contain random notes. Often Dad has recorded names of people he has met. I don't recognise many from 1991 and 1992, but there is a short list of people in 1993 who are less of a mystery: Det. Supt. Hugh Baird; DI Glen Starrett; DS James Barber; DC Roger Greaves; DC Vihaan Shah; DC Peter (?) Fox. Barber of course I know about now. I can only assume the others worked on the Leask enquiry, too. Why did Dad so carefully make a note of their names, though? Did he simply like to remember the names of the people he met? Was he tracing their hierarchy in the same way he traced our routes across the country – out of a need to know how one thing connected to another? Was it just because he liked to find out more about who he was dealing with?

Was he thinking of raising more invoices?

I hear movement downstairs and I jump guiltily. A part of me desperately wants to show these diaries to Mum, ask her to help me decode them like one of her Countdown puzzles, but how could I explain my fears to her? On the one hand, my family has always had me down as a day-dreamer with an overactive imagination; with this I'll be upgraded to full-on fantasist. What really stops me telling her, though, is the fear that she might lie to me – and she's not a good liar.

Then something occurs to me. Pay MS. I know who MS

is. That woman I met here on the day of the funeral, with the leopard-print scarf and fuschia lips. Margery Something. She used to do Dad's books. I could ask her about the money.

I tuck the diaries back behind the cabinet and survey the rest of the room. Someone has to sort through Dad's stuff so it might as well be me. Perhaps I'll find something that will help to explain it all. At the very least an address book that could explain some of the names and initials I don't recognise.

After an hour I have found nothing of much use in the filing cabinet or on the shelves or in the drawers of the desk. I look at Dad's computer. I half expect it to use floppy discs, it looks so ancient and boxy, and the way it's shoved away in the corner it doesn't look as though he used it much. It groans lazily as I coax it to life. It takes an age, but when it does, the wallpaper display hits me like a punch in the gut. It's the photograph – the one from Gairloch that last summer. The four of us on the top of a sand dune beside the campsite. Dad must have scanned it in. We are arranged in order. Malcolm hugging his knees in front of him, Al leaning back with his long, skinny legs stretching towards the camera. Rob has his arm around me and I'm leaning into him. We are all wearing massive grins, mine slightly enhanced by the pink smears of ice lolly around my mouth. Did Dad realise that this was the last time we would all be together in his lifetime when he scanned the image in? Was he aware of the years passing without us coming together every time he looked at it?

The computer is an open invitation to cyber crime, every piece of software on the brink of obsoletion if not already past it. Unsurprisingly Dad seems to have used it very little, and thankfully not for any internet banking or online shopping. There is a folder of correspondence – and by that I mean letters he typed, printed and posted by snail mail – but other than that he mainly seems to have used it for internet searches. His email account is barely touched. He has neither deleted nor replied to the Nigerian princes who wanted to share their fortunes with him or the people who promised to restore his hair and his libido.

His search history is fuller than I expected. At first glance it reflects Dad's fascination with science and engineering and with steam engines in particular. The rest is going to take more detailed exploration. I leave that for later and instead open the folder of correspondence. It's neatly arranged into sub-folders, including family. Dad took to typing his letters to us when arthritis made it increasingly uncomfortable for him to use a pen and rendered his handwriting almost illegible. The printed word enhanced the strangely formal register he adopted when writing letters and the overall effect made him seem a hundred years older than he actually was, like a Victorian patriarch. I hope this letter finds you well... An effect that was always slightly let down by the rest of the contents. Your mother and I have had a new washing machine installed. What a saga that has proved to be! Rob and I thought it was a hoot to text and email each other in the same manner from time to time. We liked to intersperse emojis and hashtags.

Dad never once wrote to tell us he was ill.

Let alone that he had a shady past as a blackmailer.

'Norna!' Mum calls up the stairs, and I jump again.

Well, he never told me, at any rate. I swither for a moment, then I click on the last letter he wrote to Malcolm and I see immediately that it's unfinished. It has never been sent.

Dear Malcolm,

I will get straight to the point. There are things that I should have said to you a long time ago.

I am very proud of you, and I always have been. Always. I know that you may have believed differently and I gave you good reason for thinking so. You may find this hard to accept, but everything I did was to protect you. Everything I did was only ever for you and your brothers and sister.

Fear pricks at the backs of my eyeballs. My chest contracts. I am suddenly very cold.

'Norna!'

'Just coming.' She won't have heard me. My voice is barely a croak. With my hands shaking, I shut the computer down, Dad's words still birling in my head. *Everything I did was only ever for you and your brothers and sister.*

It is surprising how quickly my fear turns to anger. Maybe they are simply shades of the same thing, because by the time I get downstairs I am raging at the thought I have been used as an excuse for something. I am hoping it's only blackmail Dad is referring to. That would be bad enough.

I join Mum at the table where she has put out bowls of soup and a loaf. All either of us seem interested in eating these days is soup, bread and biscuits. We take turns at the stove. Today she has made chicken broth.

'Had Dad and Malcolm fallen out before Malcolm left home?' I ask.

She looks startled. 'Where on earth did you get that idea?'

'Never mind.'

She doesn't pursue it, but I do, silently turning over the things I've read, worrying at them. Why should Malcolm think Dad was ever less than proud of him? Malcolm was always the bar by which the rest of us were measured. I thought.

'I forgot to say, Finlay Groat was asking after you, yesterday,' Mum says.

'Huh?'

'He popped over to see Alistair when I was there. He seems rather taken with you.'

'Isn't he married?' I say, with what I hope is a warning tone.

'Separated. It all seems quite amicable. He's a nice lad, Finlay.'

I give Mum a look.

'You haven't told me what happened with Angus,' she says, quietly.

I put my spoon down with a clatter. I try to say something but I don't know where to start. Anything I say is going to be a lie. I'm not going to tell her that he broke up with me because I never wanted to do anything any more because I had a headache. Or that when he heard I had a brain tumour he begged me to forgive him and to take him back, and that instead of telling him I couldn't let him watch me die I told him to fuck off and die and slammed the door in his face.

'Anyway,' Mum says, gently, 'Finlay's nothing like his Dad. Not that I mean to be nasty about Lawrence, but Finlay is a proper gentleman.'

'Not so free with his eyes and his hands, you mean. Not a condescending prick. Or a sex pest.'

'Norna!' Mum is shocked. 'Well. But we have a lot to be grateful to Lawrence for, though.'

'We do?'

'He helped us through some hard times. You know he only charged your Dad for materials when he built the store at the back of the shop. He recommended him to a lot of his clients and contacts, too, helped him get the handyman business off the ground.'

I think of some of the names noted at the back of Dad's diaries. Apart from the police officers it now seems nauseatingly sycophantic. An old boys' network.

'And he's put a lot of work Alistair's way, don't forget that. In fact, it was probably doing work experience with Lawrence that got Alistair interested in a trade in the first place.'

'He's not standing by Al now.'

That shuts her up. For at least ten seconds. 'I expect he's worried about it affecting his chances of getting elected.'

'His what?'

'To the council. He's thinking of running next time round.'

I have nothing to say to this that won't offend Mum even more than I already have. Instead, I ask, 'What's the surname of that woman who used to work for Dad? Margery something?'

Mum purses her lips slightly. 'Shanks. Margery Shanks. Yes, quite. Point taken.'

I'm not sure what she means by that, but clearly Margery is not top of Mum's Christmas card list. 'I met her on the day of the funeral,' I say. 'She said something about your lovely taste in home décor.'

Mum humphs indignantly and I can't help smiling.

After our old ladies' supper I go back up to Dad's office and boot up the computer again. I begin to trawl through his internet search history. A joyless journey that at first consists largely of pistons and crankshafts, valve gears and coupling rods. But further back, a more disturbing pattern emerges. If Dad was interested in science, he showed more than a passing interest in forensic science.

It appears in his search history in little bursts every now and then over the years. Nothing for ages and then a flurry of searches into Locard's Exchange Principle, blood typing and DNA analysis.

Into forensic anthropology.

Knife wound analysis.

Comparison samples.

30

Dan Calder didn't want to believe that James Barber was guilty of perverting the course of justice – or worse – but it wouldn't have been the first time the man had been compromised. Dan had checked. What Glen Starrett had told them was true. At least, there was record of a 'mistake' made early in Barber's career as a detective. It had been put down as an oversight, blamed on naivety in a young officer. Barber had been disciplined and sent for some retraining, but Dan could read between the lines. It looked very much to him like entrapment, that someone had put Barber in a compromising position, manipulated his actions. He understood why the shadow of doubt had lingered over Barber, why there might have been rumours about blackmail or a bribe, someone holding something over him. Glen Starrett had told them it made Barber careful after that. It also made him vulnerable.

Something had been nagging at Calder. It had its origins in what Farhana McLean had said to him about Connor's notes, that they were just scribbles and his finished, typed work would have been obtained from the Fiscal's office. Dan had looked. There was nothing like these notes in the original investigation file. Nothing that even touched on the same enquiries. Perhaps that shouldn't be surprising if, as he had suspected, Connor had hidden those notes for some reason. If, as Lise Eklund said, what Connor was working on wasn't necessarily what he'd been officially assigned. But in that case, how had James Barber ever known to ask anyone about Lee Quigley? What did he have in his own files that led him down the same trail as Leask? And where had he got it from?

According to the fire officer who looked at Barber's shed – and the statements made by the other allotment tenants – it looked as though the fire had been started in the early hours of the morning on the day of the funeral. The day James Barber was killed. He could have done it himself.

Dan couldn't shake off the idea that Barber already knew what Ronald Gilchrist had to say to him.

Or the possibility that he knew, and he didn't want to hear it. That what he was really anxious to know was whether anyone else knew what Ronald knew.

Not that any of this helped them catch his killer.

In the meantime, Calder wanted to talk to Connor Leask's former boyfriend, Nichol Pelley, but the man was proving difficult to find. Farhana McLean hadn't had up-to-date contact details for him but she had suggested that Mason Lennox might, and Dan's heart had sunk when she told him he now worked as a criminal defence solicitor. He always got a prickly sensation when he encountered criminal defence solicitors. A feeling that battle was about to commence, however cultured, however polite. It didn't seem to matter whether they were in an interview room, a courtroom or a bar. It was in their nature. Or was it in his? The sense that he was up against hostile forces? That he had to fight his corner? Either way, he had no reason to think that a meeting with Mason Lennox would be anything but adversarial. He wanted an address; he was fully expecting a lecture on data protection. Thinking the personal approach might yield more success, he took a deep breath and entered the nondescript office building that housed Lennox's firm.

*

Mason Lennox peered at him over spectacles that magnified the grey bags under his eyes. 'Have we met before?'

Dan raked through his mental database of court appearances. 'I don't think so.'

Lennox smiled a tired smile. 'What can I do for you, Inspector?'

'Well, it's really Nichol Pelley's contact details I'm after, if you have them. We haven't managed to track him down. I gather you acted on his behalf at one point?'

'Yes. Drugs charge. Not really my thing, but since he

was an old friend...' Lennox chewed the inside of his cheek for a moment. 'Do you mind me asking why you want to talk to him? Is he under suspicion? In which case, I'd like to be present when you interview him.'

'No, he's not under any suspicion.' Dan hesitated. 'Why? Is he unfit?'

Lennox let out half a laugh. Rubbed the side of his face wearily. 'It's more of a preventative measure.'

'I don't want to interview him formally. If he can give me some information that might help our investigation I'll take it from there, but otherwise...'

'As I understood it you were investigating the death of James Barber, not Connor Leask. How can Nichol help with that?'

'It's possible Barber spoke to him in the weeks before he died. He'd been tracking down former witnesses.' Dan left it at that. It was not the whole truth, but he didn't want to let Lennox know that they had made a definite link between the two deaths. Lennox already knew that Barber had approached Farhana McLean so he had no reason to question Dan's suggestion that he might also have found and approached Pelley.

Lennox took a long time to think. It gave Dan time to take in the office. It had none of the gravitas that age had given Farhana McLean's office. Instead, it might have been any tired local authority department Dan had ever been in. Social work or housing. In contrast to McLean's neatly organised files and stationery, Lennox's room was cramped and full, his desk a cityscape of files and boxes. Dan felt his hand stray to his pocket. The treasury tag he'd taken from Farhana's desk was burning a hole in it. He needed to find somewhere to deposit it. But not here. This wasn't unconnected enough. The whole point, he'd worked out, the thing that drove this compulsion seemed to be about putting things where they had no business being. He forced himself to ignore it.

'I suppose I could arrange a meeting,' Lennox said eventually.

Dan fished out his card and handed it over, but he remained seated.

'Barber didn't come to see you?'

Lennox shook his head. Either Barber didn't think him worth a second look or he'd not got round to him yet.

'Farhana said he was interested in some files she had found of Connor's? They were useful, were they?'

'I don't know, yet.' Dan wondered whether Lennox's decision to become a defence solicitor had anything to do with losing out to Connor for the Fiscal traineeship. A sub-conscious 'See if I care. I never wanted to work prosecution anyway.' He had minded at the time.

'Why did you think Connor had sabotaged your application to the procurator fiscal traineeship?'

Lennox blinked. 'I didn't think it, I knew it. We were both relying on our academic references. Connor instigated an investigation against me for plagiarism in my final thesis, during which time our tutors couldn't act as my referee. It was thrown out, of course, but by then the applications had closed.'

'You must have been furious.'

'I was. But not enough to kill him.'

Dan smiled. 'You have an alibi, I know that.'

'I got over it. And to be honest, I wasn't suited to it. The fast track.'

'But Connor was?'

'On the face of it, perhaps. But Connor was never going to survive in the fiscal service long term.'

'Why do you say that? Everything I've learnt about him suggests he was a brilliant legal mind.'

'Mind, maybe, but not temperament. Even if they hadn't got rid of him, I'd have given him five years, tops, be-fore he burned out. He couldn't pace himself. He was too fired up all the time, too much in a hurry to make a name for himself. He didn't just want to be a PF. He wanted to be the PF. A star.'

'"Even if they hadn't got rid of him"?'

Lennox looked surprised, as though he hadn't realised what he'd said or what it sounded like. 'Didn't you know? They were on the point of terminating his traineeship.'

This was news. 'I didn't know. Why?'

Lennox frowned. He was as surprised as Dan that he hadn't heard.

'He constantly challenged decisions the fiscal service made, but the way I heard it, it came to a head when he accused them of deliberately finding reasons to drop certain cases. He was facing gross misconduct.'

Dan's mind was whirring now. Eklund had said nothing about this. 'Was this accusation aimed at anyone in particular?'

'Lise Eklund, his mentor. And a police officer, a Superintendent. Hugh Baird. I remember because Farhana said something at Connor's funeral about how all was forgiven. They were both there, eulogising. Connor thought they were in cahoots, if I remember rightly.'

'Did he say why he thought they were manipulating the outcomes of cases?'

'I'm not sure. I know he had a beef with the system as a whole. He felt that it was too easy for investigations to be swayed by financial or political concerns. That these dictated priorities and affected decision-making.'

'Do you remember any cases in particular he might have been referring to?'

'Only the one that brought it all to a head. It was a fatal accident enquiry which Connor took it upon himself to re-examine. Apparently he found some detail that Eklund had overlooked. It wasn't enough to get the enquiry reopened, but it had the potential to show her up as less than thorough.'

It showed Connor up as a thorn in Eklund's side, Dan thought. An accidental death. He made a note to check the Lee Quigley case for Eklund's involvement.

'You don't think this had something to do with his death?' Lennox said.

'I don't know. Do you think it might?'

'I think the only knives Baroness Eklund sticks in anyone are metaphorical. She's certainly looked daggers at me across the courtroom plenty of times.' He hesitated. 'Connor could make enemies as easily as he made friends, and often people went from one to the other pretty quickly.'

Something about the way Lennox spoke of Connor Leask struck Dan. 'You don't think his death was a random attack.'

'No, of course not. Neither do you, clearly.'

'A lot of people still do.'

Lennox took a slow breath. Suddenly he wasn't a defence advocate anymore. He was Connor Leask's former university friend. His face sagged a little.

'Farhana always stuck up for Connor, but he could be a right bastard sometimes. If he wanted something, or if he believed he was right about something he just went for it. Anyone in the way, any difference of opinion...' He made a sweeping gesture with his hand. 'Same if he didn't want something anymore. He was a shit to Nichol. He had a kind of tunnel vision. If he had something in his sights he was fearless about going for it, and that meant he stuck his nose – and his dick – where they weren't wanted. I think he could easily have made someone nervous or angry enough to kill him. I was never comfortable with the idea that it was random in the sense of an impersonal attack on him just because he was a gay man. Even if it was only the result of something that happened that night, I'm convinced it was more than a spontaneous stranger attack. It was about Connor being Connor. He got to someone.'

31

Ellen listened as Calder told her by phone what he had learned from Mason Lennox.

'We need to talk to Eklund again,' she said.

'We need a bit more before we do that. Blackwood would have our guts if we went charging off accusing an Advocate Depute of withholding information, let alone raking up suggestions of malpractice from nearly thirty years ago. How did you get on?'

Ellen and Keisha had just left Linda Gilchrist. It hadn't been her first choice to bring Keisha; she had a sneaking suspicion Dan was trying to get them to bond, setting her up as some kind of mentor to the younger detective. She didn't much feel like being anyone's mentor – she wasn't a hundred – and she didn't think Keisha was all that keen on the idea either. Ellen was pretty sure she'd much rather Dan took her under his wing. Probably rather Dan took her all sorts of places. She felt guilty for that, told herself to stop being so bitchy, even if no-one could see inside her head.

'Linda wasn't able to tell us much about Ronald's business,' she told Dan. 'She didn't recognise the name Ralston, but she's referred us to the woman who used to do Ronald's books for him. We're just about to go and see her now.'

They ended the call and Ellen and Keisha got out of the car. It took Ellen a moment to place the figure she saw emerging from Margery Shanks' house as they approached. Her hood was up, hiding the scarlet hair, and without that identifying feature Ellen's memory had to work harder. In the process she found that she took in things she had not noticed before: features that were thin enough to be called gaunt; a weariness in her gait; the way she winced when the bright beams of an oncoming car swept over her face. It was more than grief, more than tiredness. Norna Gilchrist looked ill.

'Hello Norna. Have you been to visit Margery Shanks?' she asked as they drew level. Norna looked startled. Presumably, she was racking her brains in the same way Ellen had just done. 'Detective Sergeant Ellen Chisholm,' Ellen reminded her. 'We met at your mother's house.'

The other woman nodded. She had barely paused. Ellen could see she wanted to keep walking. She stepped in front of her, blocking her way. 'Nothing wrong, is there?'

'No, of course not. I just... She was very kind to me at my dad's funeral. I didn't have a chance to thank her properly at the time.'

Ellen smiled. She couldn't think of any other reason to detain her. She watched Norna Gilchrist walk away up the street and wondered why she didn't believe her.

Margery Shanks took a while to come to the door. When she did, her face worked quickly through a small range of expressions and settled on plastered smile. She was wearing a lot of make up, but even under the matt tan Ellen could see that she was flushed. Her antenna quivered.

'Ms Shanks? Detective Sergeant Ellen Chisholm. Detective Constable Keisha Bell. I wonder whether we could have a word please? We just have a few follow-up questions from the statement you gave the day after Ronald Gilchrist's funeral. It won't take long.'

She had picked up on Norna's description of the day, the referral to Ronald's funeral, rather than the murder of James Barber. It seemed to work. Margery Shanks relaxed a little.

'Yes, of course. Do come in.'

Despite their protestations, Shanks insisted on making them both tea. She seemed to take an age, faffing in the kitchen. Ellen noticed that when she brought the tea things through on a tray she patted each object as though to check it was in place. A nervous habit, perhaps. A little OCD. Shanks glanced at the clock on the mantelpiece as she sat down. When she was finally settled on a deeply impractical cream suede sofa, Ellen smiled at her and began.

'Ms Shanks, when you were interviewed in the aftermath of the funeral you told officers that you had worked for Ronald Gilchrist, is that right?'

'Well, yes, I worked for Ronny, a couple of days a week. I did his books.'

'Do you still keep any documentation from Mr Gilchrist's business?'

'No, I'm sorry. Everything was kept in the shop. Ronny would have taken it after it closed.'

'Perhaps you could tell us something about his business, then. It was a hardware shop primarily, but he also ran a handyman business, is that right?'

'Yes. He'd had three shops, but he had to close two of them. It was getting harder and harder to compete against the big DIY chains. Homebase had just opened up the road. Ronny had to think about ways to adapt the business, things that would give him a competitive edge.' It didn't sound like something she would normally say. It sounded like something learnt. 'So he started running the handyman service. That really took off.'

A sudden bang from the hallway made Keisha jump and Ellen turned to the door. They heard a man's voice.

'Margery, love?' His tread was heavy on the floorboards.

Margery Shanks looked panic-stricken and relieved in equal measures. She called out quickly: 'We're in here, sweetheart.'

The man who pushed the door open was big, an impression emphasised by the oversized raincoat that flapped in his slipstream. His hair was a little too long and swept back over the crown of his head in a silver lick. His eyes darted between the three of them comically for a couple of seconds. Neither Ellen nor Keisha made any attempt to break the silence. Ellen was too busy trying to work out what it was that had stopped him in his tracks. Was he surprised to find them there at all, or afraid he had arrived too late? Had Margery spotted them outside talking to Norna, or even before that when she was on the phone to Calder, and called him for support?

'The detectives just had a few more questions for me,' Margery squeaked.

'Mr Groat, isn't it?' Ellen said. 'Actually, I'm glad you're here. It saves us another journey.'

It hadn't been their intention to speak to Lawrence Groat that day, but Ellen found that she suddenly wanted to, very much. A lot of it had to do with how little he seemed to like the idea. But also, she thought, Lawrence Groat was in the building trade, too. And he had been at Ronald Gilchrist's funeral.

'Perhaps you could give us a minute to finish up with Ms Shanks and...'

'I don't mind if Lawrence stays. I'd like him to,' Margery said.

'Alright then.' They waited until Groat had sat down. Ellen made a tiny nod in Keisha's direction. She wanted to be able to observe.

'We were talking about Ronald Gilchrist's business,' Keisha said with a placid smile.' Lawrence Groat cleared his throat, but without looking at him Keisha said, 'Ms Shanks. The business finally closed in 2016, is that right? Did you continue to do the books right up until that time?'

'Yes, yes I did. Then when Ronny decided to retire I did the same.'

'In your time with Mr Gilchrist were there ever any irregularities? Any payments or purchases unaccounted for, anything that seemed out of the ordinary – stock ordered or sold, or handyman jobs that seemed unusual?'

'No. Nothing like that.'

'Was there ever a time you thought he might have been doing a bit of trade on the side? Not putting it through the books?'

'No. Never.'

'Has anyone else ever made enquiries of this kind? This man, for example.' Keisha held out the photograph of James Barber.

'That's the man who was killed.'

'Yes. James Barber.'

'No. I never came across him before.'

Ellen was watching Lawrence Groat. Keisha was freezing him out of the conversation and Ellen could see that he didn't like it. He was used to being acknowledged, at the very least. Deferred to, more likely.

'Do any of these names mean anything to you?' Keisha asked Margery. 'Dean Owens?'

'No, no I can't say that rings a bell.'

'Lee Quigley.'

'No.'

'Look, what's this all about? Who are these people and what do they have to do with that Barber chap?' Groat was belligerent, but it was Margery's reaction that interested Ellen. The way in which her forehead creased and she blinked, fast. The furtive glance she threw in Lawrence's direction while he blustered.

'Norris Ralston?'

'No.'

'No? What about you Mr Groat?'

"Course I knew Ralston. Everyone in our line knew Ralston. He was the biggest building supplies merchant in the region in those days.'

Ellen's mind snagged on the phrase. 'In those days.' Was that odd? Why not just 'back in the day'? Or 'in his day.'? Did it matter that it seemed more specific to the time of Connor Leask's death? Margery, too, had seemed to assume she had asked about the past, when she had simply asked her to tell them about Ronald's business.

'I remember now, of course. Yes, Ronny did some business with Norris Ralston,' Margery said. 'It was such a long time ago, I'd forgotten.'

'You mentioned before that Ronny had to find ways to adapt the business,' Ellen said. 'To compete with the big chains.'

'Yes. Things were challenging for a while, but he managed to keep the business afloat. Lawrence was a great help, of course.'

Lawrence Groat's gaze flickered, and not with bashful pleasure at the flattery.

'How do you mean?' Keisha asked. 'Did Mr Groat help him out financially?'

Groat was not going to let that pass. 'I didn't give him

money, if that's what you mean. I did him a few favours. Got my lads to put up the store and workshop in the back yard in between jobs and charged him at cost for the materials. Put in a word for him with some of my customers and clients. It was nothing more than he'd done for me in the past.'

'And of course your sons were great friends,' Ellen said. 'They alibied each other on the night Connor Leask was killed.'

'What the bloody hell do you mean by that?'

'Lawrence, dear.' Margery cooed. His jaw clenched.

'But I gather from Finlay that you've just sacked Alistair from his current contract with you.' Lawrence's ample nostrils quivered. 'Do you believe he killed James Barber?'

'Not at all. But I have to look after the welfare of the team. There were complaints. Some of the other lads on the site felt uncomfortable with him being there whilst all this is going on. I may be semi-retired but I'm not about to see the company I've slaved to build up go down the tubes because you lot can't get your act together. If you solved this tragic death we could all get back to business.'

'In the meantime, Alistair Gilchrist has his work with Kinley's, is that right?'

'I believe so.'

'Do you have any connection with Mitchell Kinley yourself?'

'We've done some business in the past. What's that got to do with the price of bricks?'

'You actually backed up their alibi, if I remember rightly. Alistair's and Finlay's, on the night of Connor Leask's murder. Could you remind me: you were at home...?'

Groat grunted. 'I saw the little toerags as the taxi was dropping me home. I knew they'd been up to something. They came sprinting off the path from Davidsons' Mains. When I got in my wife told me the police had been looking for them; it wasn't the first time they'd been in trouble. Finlay got into the house a few minutes after me and I gave him hell. End of.'

'You can't account for Alistair Gilchrist's movements after that?'

'As far as I know he went home too. Look, I've always done my best by Alistair Gilchrist because Ronny was my pal and Finlay didn't have any brothers of his own and they were close. I don't know whether that was always the right thing or the best thing, but it's the way it was.'

'Well, thanks very much,' Ellen said, standing up. She wanted to think.

Margery rose too and saw them out. Ellen and Keisha nodded briefly in Groat's direction as they left. He had not got up.

As they stepped out into the dusk, Ellen asked Margery, 'What did Norna Gilchrist want, by the way?'

Margery looked flummoxed and something in her reaction made Ellen wonder again whether she had phoned Lawrence and told him to come. But this time she thought it might not have been the sight of the police outside her door which had put the wind up her. What if it was Norna Gilchrist? She thought of how flustered Margery had been when they arrived, the pink of her cheeks under the foundation. Had Norna Gilchrist said something to rattle her?

Then Margery seemed to rally. She made a decision. 'She wanted to ask about money,' she said.

'Money?'

'Yes. She wanted to know where Malcolm got the money to go off down south to university and where he got the money to train as a pilot.'

32

Over the next day the idea that Norna Gilchrist knew more than she was letting on grew and solidified in Ellen's mind. Why was she asking about money? And money for Malcolm to go away at that. Ellen had checked. Malcolm Gilchrist left to go to university in London in the autumn of 1993. He had been due to study in Edinburgh, but at the last minute he'd changed his mind and applied for a place in London during Clearing. After graduating he enrolled on training for his pilot's licence. Neither of these options was cheap. Even now it cost upwards of forty thousand to train as a commercial pilot, sometimes up to three times that amount. Ellen had found one article in the Telegraph that claimed that by the time they qualified some pilots were in debt to the tune of a hundred thousand pounds. The numbers might have been different, but the relative cost would have been much the same even a quarter of a century ago. So where did Malcolm Gilchrist's money come from? And was the timing significant?

She cautioned herself against going off on tangents. If Ronald Gilchrist had been working off the books, offering his handyman services for cash in hand, then it made him no different to thousands of other tradesmen across the country and it was the business of Her Majesty's Revenue and Customs, not hers. It had precious little to do with James Barber's death. Or did it?

If the money came from Ralston... If Jimmy Barber, and Connor Leask before him, had made that connection...

She picked up the phone.

Linda Gilchrist answered. 'Norna's not here, I'm afraid. She's gone to the cinema with Josh.' She couldn't remember which film. 'Some superhero movie, I think. At Cineworld.'

*

Ellen waited outside the entrance to the multiplex watching the throngs. She was almost surprised to see how busy it was; she couldn't remember the last time she'd been to see a film at the cinema. Liam went regularly, she knew. He was into films. Liked to see them as soon as they came out, and liked to talk about them afterwards. People had to avoid him if they didn't want spoilers. If it was known he was pacing the station bursting to share his views on the latest Star Wars installment or this year's Oscar bait they had been known to duck into fire escapes, stationery cupboards, the wrong toilets. It wasn't always to avoid spoilers, either.

After a while Ellen spotted Norna Gilchrist weaving her way through the crowds with her nephew at her side. They were talking animatedly and Ellen questioned the view she'd had of Norna the night before. She looked better today. More alive.

An appearance that waned when she caught sight of Ellen.

'Could I have a quick word?' Ellen glanced apologetically at Josh Gilchrist. He too had shrunk back into a sullen scowl. He stuck his hands in his pockets and mooched over to the corner of Frankie and Benny's while Ellen took Norna aside.

'Margery Shanks seemed a bit upset after you left,' she said. 'Is there something we should know?'

'Upset? No. Why should I have upset her?'

'Margery said you were asking about money. The rather large amount of money Malcolm would have needed for university and pilot training.'

'Did she tell you that?'

'Yes. Is there a significance to the money?'

'I don't know,' Norna said. 'Probably not. Mum thinks it's why Alistair is jealous of Malcolm.'

Now they were closer Ellen could see the hollows in Norna's cheeks, the weary lines around her eyes. She looked and sounded exhausted, but Ellen couldn't tell whether it was only tiredness making her seem absent-minded, or whether she was deliberately obfuscating.

'Why should Alistair be jealous? Where did the money come from?'

Norna seemed distracted momentarily by a group of girls who burst loudly out of the multiplex singing a song Ellen didn't recognise.

'Norna? Why were you asking about the money? Where did it come from?'

'Dad gave him it. It was from savings, I suppose.' She glanced over to where Josh was loitering.

'How did it come to your attention?'

'I've been sorting out Dad's things, that's all. It's not important. Just family stuff.'

Was that all it was? A sibling's radar for fairness? Ellen might not have her own siblings but as a child she had seen how her cousins measured out juice to the precise millimetre so as to be sure the drink was distributed fairly. They still did it. The only difference was that they did it with wine and whisky these days.

Norna looked at Ellen suddenly. 'Why were you at Margery's?'

Ellen held her gaze. 'I wanted to know about your Dad's money, too.'

'Why?' And when Ellen didn't answer: 'What did she say?'

'That she was never aware of anything untoward.'

'Why would there be?'

Again, Ellen didn't answer. Instead she said, 'I understand there may be personal issues that arise, questions about family matters that you want answered in the aftermath of your father's death, but I'm advising you not to do anything that might be seen to interfere with our investigation. Do you understand?'

'Of course.'

'And if you come across anything that might be relevant to our enquiry, anything at all, please contact me.' She handed over a card, which Norna pocketed hastily, blocking the transaction from her nephew's view.

Ellen nodded once, signalling that their meeting was over. She watched Norna walk over to Josh, then turned her collar up and left.

Outside it was beginning to spit with rain, the low

cloud having banished the last of the day's light early. It felt more like November than April. As she walked away, Ellen wondered whether it was significant that Norna hadn't pressed her on why she should be enquiring about her father's finances - when he was already dead by the time Jimmy Barber was murdered.

33

I don't see how I could have upset Margery Shanks. She didn't seem upset when I saw her. If DS Chisholm looked at her the way she looked at me I'd say it's far more likely it was her got Margery's frilly knickers in a twist. If DS Chisholm was telling the truth, that is, and not just trying to get me to spill the beans on what Margery told me.

Which wasn't much.

Josh nudges me and holds out a packet of Haribo. I smile and shake my head. I glance at our reflections in the front window of the bus. I like it. This. Me and Josh. 'Mood-kill,' he called DS Chisholm after she'd gone; we'd been having such a good time up until then. She didn't completely ruin the evening, though. He asked me what she wanted and I found that I wasn't really sure. I told him she was asking about Margery Shanks.

'Who?'

'She used to work for Granddad. She was at the funeral. Bright pink lipstick and a leopard print scarf? Big hair. Barbara Cartland eyelashes.'

'Barbara who?'

'Never mind. Before your time. Before mine.'

'That's going back a bit then.'

'Cheeky bollocks.'

I'm older than you think.

In the reflection I could pass for not much older than Josh. Certainly no less alive. I look well. For a moment I imagine being able to step through the window, swap places with that version of me. I always liked the idea of parallel universes. I would take Josh with me of course. In that other version of us he would be confident, popular. He and Al would get on.

I think I had the naïve idea that I could create a new version of life here now. Suddenly make myself a bigger part of my brothers' lives and leave them with memories of my own choosing. Solve whatever happened to us. How arrogant of me. And besides, Rob was probably right: nothing happened. We just weren't anything special to begin with.

Margery Shanks said the same thing, more or less.

'Sometimes brothers just don't get on. Malcolm was always going to go places. Ronny was very proud of him but he didn't favour one over the other. It's just that the support they needed was different. Malcolm couldn't get the kind of experience or training he needed by working for your dad or Lawrence, could he?'

I had an uneasy feeling when she talked about them, the way she talked about them. It was too familiar. When I think of how Mum pursed her lips at the mention of Margery's name and the way Margery spoke about 'Ronny' I feel dizzy.

Rob was right. I should have left well alone.

Margery said that Dad started the handyman side of the business in spring 1993, and that does tally with when Lawrence built the store and workroom in the yard at the back of the shop. Thinking back, I'm sure Rob said the same. But in Dad's diaries he was clearly doing odd jobs well before that. Three years before that. Patio slabs and kitchen taps. I asked Margery about that, and about the invoices, but she said that without seeing the diaries herself and being able to cross-reference them with the books, she wasn't sure what the entries might refer to. 'I was good with the figures,' she said, 'But I'm not that good in the memory department.'

These awful thoughts I've been having about Dad – is it just Astro messing with my head? It makes far more sense if that money was for odd jobs off the books. Maybe he and Lawrence were working together, Lawrence taking the money and paying dad a regular wage. Everyone keeps saying they helped each other out.

'You don't need to get off here,' Josh says as I press the button for the next bus stop. 'I'll be ok.'

'Yeah, I know, but I want to see your Mum. It's not all

about you,' I say.

Though it is, really. I'm afraid that if I don't walk him home he won't go home, and if I do at least I can provide cover while he gets past Al and goes to his room.

It turns out I don't need to run interference, though. It's already taken care of. We let ourselves in to the sound of laughter from the living room. Finlay Groat is here and his presence has made Al happy.

'Alright Uncle Fin,' Josh says before making good his escape.

Uncle Fin?

'Norna, you know Finlay,' Mel says, and she's so pleased with herself for being able to introduce us like this. Suddenly I feel about twelve.

'Hi, nice to see you again,' I say. 'I'm not stopping,' I tell Mel. Not now anyway. 'I just wanted to see Josh home. We had a great time; he's good company.'

'How are you getting home?'

'I'll just walk. It's not far and it's not late.'

'I'll give you a lift,' Finlay says, getting up, and I suppress a sigh. 'I was about to head off anyway and you're on my way.'

The last thing I want is to have to make polite conversation with Finlay Groat but it's a battle I won't win gracefully so I say, 'Sure, that'd be great, thanks.'

I wait on the path while Al and Finlay do some laddish hail-fellow-well-met leave-taking. I guess the business with Lawrence and the severed contract has made them self-conscious because it's all a bit over-the-top.

Finally we can go. After that little display, and because I've developed some mean preconceptions about Finlay, I expect a performance about the car. Holding the door open, fussing over the controls, that kind of thing. Making sure I notice how nice it is, in other words. Peacocking. There is none of that. Instead, Finlay slides into the drivers' seat and starts the engine. 'You and Josh get on well,' he says as he reverses out of the drive and the smile he gives me as he puts the car in first is open, genuine. 'It's great you can be here for a bit.'

'Yeah, I'm enjoying spending time with him. We're into some of the same things. It's nice to have someone to talk to.'

'I know Al worries about him a bit.'

Not that he lets Josh know. 'How so?'

'Well, that he spends so much time alone at his computer, playing games.'

'Sometimes he's playing with people on the other side of the world. He's got people he regularly plays with in Canada and Japan and Iceland. You know he speaks a bit of Korean?'

'Really?'

'They talk as well as play. He's got a better world view than I ever did at that age.'

Finlay is thoughtful. 'I don't think Al knows any of that. I think he was worried Josh was a bit of a loner.'

There is so much I could say to that; the word loner immediately makes my blood boil. Finlay disarms me.

'I told him, that's not a bad thing in itself, as long as you're happy in your own company. I should know. I was a real outsider when I was Josh's age. Al was pretty much my only friend.'

I look at him in surprise. 'How come?' He's so suave, so confident, it's hard to believe.

'Didn't fit in at school. Didn't fit in at home.' He puts on the indicator to turn into our street. 'This thing with my dad...'

So he feels it too, hanging over us.

'...He'll come round.'

He pulls over to the side of the road. 'And if he doesn't, I'll be the boss soon enough.'

He gets out of the car before I can stall him and walks me up the path. Awkward.

'Well, thanks,' I say. 'Maybe see you at Al's sometime.'

Finlay glances up at something over my shoulder and smiles, gives a small wave. I turn to see Mum peeking through the living room curtains. 'Great. She'll get ideas.'

'I don't mind,' he says.

I ignore that, but the ignoring creates a pause in which

he clearly wants me to invite him in. If I don't get rid of him quickly Mum will appear at the door and she'll have him inside eating fig rolls in no time.

'Well, maybe we could meet for a coffee sometime,' I say, putting my key in the lock. 'Thanks again.' I step inside, give him a swift grin and shut the door behind me, breathing a sigh of relief.

34

Nichol Pelley had a ravaged look about him. A former drug user (former according to Mason Lennox anyway) Dan had learned that he was also HIV positive. A long-term survivor. Damaged, but more by bitterness than the disease. Dan had to remind himself that the man had graduated with Lennox, Connor Leask and Farhana McLean. His life had taken a very different path to their glittering legal careers. Then again, he was still alive at least. More than could be said for Connor.

Lennox had set up the meeting but Nichol had told him he didn't need representation. 'I told him I've got nothing to hide. I had an alibi the night Connor was killed.'

'Yes, I know. I'm not here because you're a suspect. You might be able to help me, though.'

'Here' was a city park. The choice had irritated Dan at first. He felt as though they were acting out some kind of childish spy fantasy. After a few minutes in Pelley's company he changed his mind, though it was true that Pelley had chosen the location with a lot of care. It offered multiple escape routes and it gave him a kind of anonymity. The man was paranoid. Determined that Dan should learn next to nothing about him and even the relatively small amount of information that might be gleaned from a choice of café or even a street corner seemed to him to be too much. When Pelley wrapped his arms across his front as though he was trying to hold himself together Dan asked him, 'Are you cold? We can go inside somewhere. I'll buy you something to eat.' Pelley shook his head defiantly, as though the offer was some kind of trick. Dan suspected this was also the real reason he had not wanted Mason Lennox to join them: he feared Lennox might give something away about his life. International man of mystery, Nichol Pelley.

'How much do you remember from 1993? The year

Connor was killed.'

Pelley shrugged. 'Try me. Do my best.'

Dan nodded. 'I'm not accusing you of anything, remember, but I heard that after you and Connor split up...'

'After he dumped me.'

'After that, you tried to see him a few times. You turned up at the flat, and watched it sometimes. You followed him.'

'Might have done.'

'I was wondering whether you ever saw or heard anything that might help me work out what happened to him?'

'I didn't follow him that night. I was miles away. I told you.'

'Yes, I know. But it's possible his murder was related to something he'd been working on. It's possible he angered someone or put himself at risk. Did you ever see him arguing with anyone? Or was anyone else hanging around him who might be significant?'

Pelley's mouth hung open. 'What, you think he was targeted?'

'Would that be so surprising?'

As he processed this Pelley's face hardened. 'They said it was a homophobic attack. Like that explained it all.'

'Yes, I know. I don't believe that, though.'

Pelley looked at him and Dan saw a glimmer of the sharp intelligence Nichol Pelley had once had, before addiction got the better of him. 'That the only reason you're looking into it again, then? Because it's something else? Something more interesting. Would you be bothered if it was just some passing bastard who didn't like gays?'

The question hit home. Dan heard Barber's anger again, at the way Connor's death had been written off as a 'random gay-bashing'. They thought that was good enough reason. We let him down. Was it any better, he wondered, that they were only interested in Connor's murder now because of Barber's death? Was it any better that it had only piqued his interest when it occurred to him it might not be random?

'Honestly? I don't know. I was twelve when it happened. I might never even have remembered it if I hadn't been reminded of it by one of the detectives who investigated at the time. It's his death I'm really investigating.'

'Huh.' Pelley nodded as if to say, I knew it. After a moment: 'Least you're honest about it, I suppose. Not like those bastards at the time.'

'Actually, for what it's worth, James Barber really did care. He never stopped looking. Even after he retired, right up until his death. That's why I'm asking. It's possible he got close to finding out who did it and that's what got him killed in turn.' He was overcompensating, he knew. But Pelley was fidgeting, his legs bouncing and his eyes on the few other people using park, the paths that led off onto the nearby streets. Dan didn't want him to go. Not yet.

'Don't know who that is.'

'James Barber? He was the...' Dan stopped. He had been about to say DI, but Barber had been a DS at the time. He wasn't in charge. Dan kept forgetting the case was not Barber's alone. He cast his mind back to the transcript he had read. 'Of course, you were interviewed by DI Starrett and DC Shah, weren't you?'

Pelley shrugged. 'Dunno. Some big shot and a Paki.'

'Sheesh. No honour among the discriminated against, then?'

'Fuck off. We done?'

'We haven't even started, yet. You haven't told me anything.'

'Nuh. Didn't see anything like that. And if I did, why should I tell you?'

'Because I thought you wanted Connor's killer to be found.'

Pelley shrugged. 'Doesn't make any difference to me.'

'What was all that about, then? Giving me a hard time, saying I was only looking into it because it was more interesting than a hate crime?'

'I was just joshing with you, man.'

Dan stared at him. Then put his hands on his knees and pushed himself up off the bench.

'Wait. Don't be like that.'

Dan ignored him, set off towards one of the park exits.

'Come on, man.' Pelley hastened after him. 'Look, I'll tell you what I can.'

'I thought you didn't see anything.'

'I didn't see any arguments. But I did follow him, okay. I saw where he went.'

Dan stopped and turned to face Pelley. 'And?' When Pelley said nothing, he began to walk again, lengthening his stride. Dan Calder had long legs, and he was fit. Nichol Pelley had to scamper to keep up.

'Look, you've got to understand,' he panted, 'Connor Leask ruined my life.'

Dan wheeled round. Pelley had his full attention now. For a fleeting moment he thought, did Connor infect him? Did Pelley kill him because of that? The suspicion must have shown in his eyes, if not the reasoning.

'Nah, man, I didn't do it. That alibi was sound, man. It's just, when I saw him with his new boyfriend, it flicked my switch, you know? I chucked a brick through the window, but that's all. I never did anything else. And I backed off when Connor threatened to hand me in to the cops. I left him alone after that.'

'I don't know what you're talking about. What window? What boyfriend?'

'That boy with the floppy hair. The one who worked in the hardware shop. The pretty one. They interviewed him.'

Dan searched Nichol Pelley's face for signs he was being had.

'Connor was going out with a boy who worked in a hardware shop? You're sure about that?'

Pelley looked away. 'Well, Connor was after him. I never actually saw them together outside the shop.'

'So what did you see? Connor going into a hardware shop? Maybe he just needed a light bulb or a tin of paint?'

'No, it was more than that. See, it wasn't the first time he'd gone there. The first time he didn't go in, he just pretended to look in the window, and he waited a bit in the alleyway at the side. He only went in the second time because that boy was there. I saw him talking to him at the counter.'

'It's a bit of a stretch to call him a boyfriend, if that's all you saw.'

'He was Connor's type. He liked boys like us. He saw himself as some kind of liberator. He outed me, man. He said he was setting me free, said I should be allowed to be who I was. Easy for him to say. He ruined my life and then he dumped me and went off chasing after someone new so he could do it all again.'

'So you threw a brick through... the shop window? In broad daylight?'

'No, I went back later that night. But Connor had seen me watching through the window when he was talking to the boy and he knew it was me. He told me he wouldn't go to the police if I promised to leave him alone. And I was to stay away from the shop as well. Keep away from his precious new boyfriend.'

'Do you know this boy's name?'

'No, but they interviewed him, I told you. I saw him in the police station when they took my statement.'

Dan's mind was racing. How much of what Pelley was telling him could he trust?

'Do you think he might have done it, then?' Pelley asked him.

'Why would he?'

'If Connor did the same to him as he did to me.'

'Go out with him, then dump him? Happens to us all.'

'No.' Pelley's eyes flashed with anger. 'You don't get it, do you? I wasn't like Connor. He liked boys who still weren't sure about their sexuality. He seduced me, and then he told everyone. He made out he was helping me, but I wasn't confident like him. I didn't know for sure what I was or who I was and I wasn't ready. I didn't have the support he had. My folks, they disowned me.'

'But that's you,' Dan said. 'These are your motives, not anyone else's. You threw a brick through a window in a fit of jealousy, you're accusing Connor of ruining your life...'

'I had an alibi.'

'Yes, you keep telling me that, too. I think I'd better get it checked again.'

Pelley rocked back and forth on his feet for a moment, then, with a defiant 'Fuck you,' he took off. Dan almost laughed as he jinked across the open playing field, indecisive about which route to take, then finally plunged into the trees at the far end of the park.

At least Dan hadn't had to give him any money.

As he walked back to his car he thought about what Pelley had said about Connor Leask. If it was true, Connor had risked imprisonment and a certain end to his sparkling career in law, because although Nichol Pelley was over the age of legal consent by the time of Connor's death, Malcolm Gilchrist had been a long way off twenty-one in 1993. And that's who Pelley was talking about, Dan was sure.

It meant that Malcolm knew Connor before that night in the pub – the night Connor was killed. That didn't tally with what he had told the police at the time and it didn't tally with what he was telling them now.

Dan needed to get that CCTV footage digitised as a matter of priority.

35

I feel as though my opacity is waning. As though I didn't collect enough energy on the way through the previous levels. Astro is mining my reserves, fuelling her campaign for domination. I lug the bags from the boot of the car. They are heavy. I have to put them down on the pavement so I can use both hands to shut the boot. It's not very far from here to the charity shop but even so I know it would be more sensible to take two trips. I just want to get it over and done with in one. I hang the bags with the longer straps over my shoulders and then lift the remaining ones. I get approximately thirty yards before one of the straps slips off my shoulder and pulls me awkwardly to one side. I have to stop and readjust. Several times. I can hear Dad tutting, muttering about the inefficiency of my strategy. But he's just a figment of my guilty conscience so I ignore him.

I'm exhausted by the time I reach the charity shop. The bags are bulky and I have to make two attempts to get through the door, then I knock over a set of low shelves just inside the doorway, sending bric-a-brac flying. The woman behind the counter comes running.

'I'm so sorry. I didn't see it for all the bags.'

'Not to worry, no harm done.' She rights the shelves and pushes the objects back on. 'I can rearrange them later. Give me something nice to do. Here, let me give you a hand.'

I wish she wasn't being so kind. She takes two of the bags off me and leads me through to a cramped back room. The shop smells fusty and stale. I feel nausea rising. I desperately want to lie down all of a sudden. Or scream.

'What do we have here?'

'Clothes mainly, some other bits and bobs.' I have a sudden fear that she will reject Dad's things and send me back out onto the street with them. 'Are they any good to you? They've all been cleaned.' I can't carry them back.

'Yes, I'm sure they'll be grand. They look in good condition. Thank you.'

Relief floods through me. I feel tears pricking at my eyes. For God's sake, not now! Not here. I leave the bags with the woman and back out of the storeroom into the main shop, trying to conceal the fact that I am close to tears from the few customers in the shop. I bash into a clothes rail but luckily I don't knock anything over this time. I need to be careful. I concentrate hard on looking at things arranged on cheap white shelves against the walls: ugly crockery and mismatched glasses; old DVDs of celebrity exercise videos and box sets of Top Gear. The smell is coating my sinuses now. What is the point of all this crap? It didn't help Dad and it's not going to help me. I try to force back the self-pity but like the stench it has permeated my being, making me both weak and furious at the same time. Fifty pence for a cheap pink plastic bangle; a pound for a copy of A Royal Duty by Paul Durrell; three pounds fifty for a hideous pair of women's tartan trews, displayed on a circular railing arranged by colour. I mean, what the fuck? I can see where Dad's things are going to go. His jumpers over there in the corner, his shirts on the rack against the back wall.

It's too much.

I need to get out of here but there are people in the way. They are old and slow and I can't get past them. I can't bear it any longer, though. I try to push past a rack of blouses, but I lose my balance and stumble into it. The rail careens into a spindle stand. Polyester and cat calendars spew onto the floor. The spindle falls into the window display, taking a tailor's dummy down with it, and dislodging the pictures mounted on the back panel. A wailing sound rises through the shop. I wonder whether it's an alarm. I must have set something off. Everyone is staring at me and I realise the sound is coming from me. I'm holding my head in both hands and I have no control over the noise that is coming from my mouth. I see the woman who helped me before, shocked and uncertain now. She doesn't know what to do and neither do I.

Then I feel some hands firm on my shoulders, a voice

tender in my ears.

'Come on, love. It's alright.' An elderly man pulls me into an embrace. 'There, there.' No-one says 'there, there', do they? But he does, and it's oddly soothing. The smell of his soap helps to blot out the fug of the shop, and it's good to be held. Again. What is it with the comfort of strange men? I can't talk to my family, I can't tell them what's happening to me. I can't look to them for the comfort I need and yet I find myself overwhelmed by gratitude for the kindness of strangers, and I succumb completely to it.

I don't know what he says to the people in the shop, or what they say to him. I don't know how he gets me out of the shop, but he does. The next thing I know I am sitting in the corner of a café, blubbing quietly to myself while he orders us tea at the counter. He buys cake too, slices of sweet lemon sponge and gingerbread. I blub some more.

He doesn't fuss and he doesn't chide. He shows not the slightest embarrassment at sitting here with a hysterical stranger. He stirs the tea, then lets it steep for a while before pouring it out. He cuts the cakes so we can each have a bit of both. Gradually, the sobs subside and I gain control of my breathing. It helps to watch his measured movements. His hands are spotted with age, calloused. A gardener? He is wearing a polo shirt under a puffy jacket and a pair of cords. Stiff walking boots complete the outdoor look. His face is kind. Wise, I think. He looks like he's seen a bit of the world. After only five minutes I feel as though I have known him for ages. I am imprinting on him like a duckling. I want to follow him around and let him give me tea and cake and hugs for the rest of my life.

I am quite pathetic.

'Did I do a lot of damage?' I ask eventually.

'No, I don't think so.' He looks as though he's about to say something else. A hint of a smile plays at the corner of his mouth, but he doesn't know whether it would be appropriate to make jokes.

Then he's serious. 'The things you were dropping off: your Dad's?'

I nod, purse my lips to still the tremble in my chin.

'I'm sorry to hear that,' he says. 'I did the same thing when I lost my wife. Well, I mean that I took her belongings to a charity shop. I stopped short of wrecking the joint.'

A laugh escapes me. And then I'm mortified again. 'Oh God.'

He puts his hand over mine, smiling, and gives it a squeeze. 'It all just got a bit much, did it?'

'I just couldn't see the point of it suddenly. It felt so hopeless.'

'Too little, too late.'

'It's selfish,' I say.

'No. You're grieving.'

'It is. If I'm honest, I don't even know how much it's about Dad at all. It's me, too, you see.' I struggle to find the words.

There is shock on his face? 'You have cancer?'

I nod. 'Brain tumour,' I whisper.

'Oh, love, I'm so sorry.'

'Don't.' I can feel the tears coming again and I hate myself for them. This wallowing is exactly what I never wanted to do.

'How long have you known?'

'Not long. I thought I was just working too hard. Spending too long in front of a computer screen, not getting enough fresh air and exercise. I started running again and I thought it was helping. In many ways I haven't been so fit in years. Turns out there's not much point.'

'Is there nothing they can do?'

I shake my head. Shrug. 'They said there was only the ghost of a chance that surgery would be successful. And it carries its own risks. Big ones.'

I'm half-expecting a lecture on denial, on not giving up or some spraff about post-diagnosis depression, but instead he just stares at me for a moment before saying, quietly, 'That must be messing with your head.'

At first I wonder if this is a pun; I almost laugh, but then I realise he's completely serious. 'Bad enough losing your Dad,' he goes on. 'I went a bit loopy when my wife died, but you're dealing with this as well. Do you have other family?'

'I haven't told them.' His eyebrows lift slightly. 'I can't. Not just yet. Not just after Dad.'

'Haven't they noticed something's wrong?'

I shrug. 'Everyone's dealing with their own stuff, aren't they? And anyway, I'm not sure how much they ever really see me or hear me. I don't mean that in a bad way. Just, you know, we see what we already think we know about a person. The image that's already fixed in our minds. To them I'm little sister. I don't think they'd even believe me at first. They'd think I was being melodramatic or that I got ideas in my head because of Dad. They've always said I have an over-active imagination. It would be hard work, telling them.'

I smile, ruefully, and suddenly I realise that I am not crying anymore. It feels good to talk about it. It's an enormous relief, in fact. I take a piece of gingerbread. It doesn't taste as I expect it to, as I remember it, but I'm used to that now. I enjoy the stickiness, and the sugar will give me a lift. The tea is Earl Grey. It tastes amazing.

'So you've been holding all this in, trying to cope with it by yourself?'

'The doctor recommended I get in touch with Macmillan.'

'You should.'

'I will. I will.'

If my outburst in the charity shop was not really about Dad, this is, of course. How tragically, patently obvious I am. It's not that I see this kind man as a substitute. He's nothing like Dad. And Dad and I could never have done this. We could never have sat here sharing confidences over tea and cake. No, this man represents a kind of idealised father figure. Perhaps the father I wish Dad had been. Maybe the reason I feel so drawn to him is precisely because he is nothing like Dad. Because I'm not sure I like who Dad was anymore.

He is talking about his wife, saying something about memory and the tricks it plays and the things that get lost in its folds. 'You go through a phase of trying to make sense of things. Your mind runs riot a bit. In a way, I suppose you're doing that for yourself and your Dad. Double the crazy thoughts and the desperate feelings.'

'I feel guilty. I wasn't there, you see. I had a hospital appointment but I couldn't tell my family why. I feel as though they all blame me for not coming up when he was still alive. Not saying goodbye.'

'It wouldn't be anything to be ashamed of, even if you hadn't been able to face that. You need to stop finding reasons to beat yourself up.'

'Some days I can't properly picture him in my head. I feel terrible about that.'

He nods. 'I know. I had that too. Carry a picture of him, if you're worried about it. It's not cheating. This isn't a test.'

This matter-of-fact piece of advice is like a revelation to me. I smile at him, gratefully.

'Because they feel guilty people don't talk about these things,' he says. 'So then we think we're monsters because we're the only one. Another thing I found was that I went through this phase of almost trying to find reasons to – not be glad my wife was dead – but, to take her down off her pedestal, if you like. Find imperfections in her. They say anger is a part of the process, so I suppose it was to do with that, but of course I felt tremendous shame about that as well.'

Is that what I'm doing, I wonder? Painting Dad black. Finding fault with him because I'm angry with him for dying? Or for stealing my thunder? Dying at a time when it prevents me from getting the sympathy I want from the family.

In other words, are all these thoughts I've had the product of my overactive imagination, my tumorous and grief-stricken brain?

No, I think. Nice theory. It might work better if it wasn't for the dead policeman in the garage on the day of Dad's funeral, and the fact that he and my two eldest brothers were suspects in the murder of a man twenty-six years ago. And as soon as I remember that, all the doubts and suspicions come flooding back.

I decide that this nice man doesn't need to know

about that, though.

We hug as we leave the shop, and this time I deliberately don't ask his name, because if he's called Roger or Nigel it will completely ruin his fairy godfather image. Clarence, I could deal with.

I set off back to the car feeling so much lighter than I did on the way to the charity shop. As I walk, I wonder whether part of the reason I am so vulnerable to the kindness of strangers is because, at some level, I'm afraid that my family will not be supportive. I'm scared that they are so wrapped up in themselves and their own dramas that they won't even care.

By the time I get to the car, that thought has hardened into a dark intention. I want to shock them. I tell myself it is not just a vengeful whim, but it would be for their own good. If I ebb away so will they. If I go quick, if I go hard, if I go by my own choosing, I can make them stop, wake them up. It will hurt because they won't have time to numb themselves. But I don't want them numbed to my death. They are already numb to their own lives.

36

There was an excited huddle round Liam's desk when Ellen got into the office. He waved her over. The CCTV footage from the Mains Arms had been digitised.

'This is the bit that's mentioned in the case file.'

It was poor quality and Vihaan Shah had been right about the landlord's mistrust of his staff because the camera was trained down the length of the bar, taking in the optics and the fridges containing wine and bottled beer, the taps and most importantly the tills. In the strip of the frame that was left they could just make out Malcolm Gilchrist as he joined the throng at the bar and waited to be served. Ellen could see why Connor might have liked him. What struck her most was not Malcolm's looks, though. It was nervous energy of youth. He seemed never to be still: a flick of his fringe; a self-conscious glance; a sudden smile for the barmaid. Even in grainy monochrome this Malcolm Gilchrist had something the older man had lost, something that had been locked up or polished away. And not for the better.

'There, that's Connor Leask,' Liam said, pointing to a man with his back to the camera and only partly in shot at the bottom corner of the frame.

They watched as the scene played out in stop-motion. Spots of light appeared and disappeared. Positions changed, faces turned, including Malcolm's and Connor Leask's, allowing them very briefly a glimpse of Connor's face in profile. Malcolm appeared to be laughing, then he wasn't. Connor had gone.

They watched until Malcolm had gathered his drinks and left the screen. It was exactly as Vihaan Shah had described. It didn't look like much.

'Play it again,' Calder said.

Liam scrolled back. They watched the episode again.

'Keep it running… Ok, go back again.'

Calder leaned forward, poised.

'Connor appears seconds after Malcolm and he waits behind him, but look, there's a space at the bottom here, right by the bar, only he doesn't take it. He doesn't make any attempt to get to the bar himself. I think he's waiting with Malcolm. I think they've come to the bar together. And look now, there are five drinks. You can just see the edge of a pint here. Malcolm takes three of the drinks, he leaves two behind and comes back for them later. When they were interviewed Malcolm and his friend said they met two lassies. They said nothing about Connor. But who was the fifth drink for if it wasn't for him?'

'And why did neither of them mention they'd been with him that night?' Ellen thought again of Norna Gilchrist and her enquiries about her brother's money. She felt a sudden flash of annoyance. Did the woman know more than she had told Ellen when she asked? What was she doing, poking around asking questions?

'Get hold of Malcolm Gilchrist,' Calder said to Liam. 'I want him back in here.'

He stood for a moment, looking at the picture frozen on the screen. 'Do we have an address for Malcolm's friend? What's his name?'

'Dave Ayers. He's a self-employed delivery driver.'

'Let's go have a word, shall we?' he said to Ellen.

*

They arranged to meet Dave Ayers at a roadside burger van just off the A92. Calder's phone went as they neared the layby.

'Malcolm is flying, apparently,' he said when he ended the call. 'Liam is arranging for someone to meet him when he lands.'

'Where?'

'Newcastle. Lucky for us. Could have been the other side of the world.'

'I want to interview him,' Ellen told him.

Calder nodded slowly. She wasn't sure it was assent.

There was only one other vehicle in the lay-by besides

the burger van. Dave Ayers was half way through his day's deliveries of online purchases.

'I was due a break,' he said. 'I don't know what use I'll be, though. I barely remember what I had for dinner last night, let alone what happened twenty-six years ago.' He leaned on the bonnet of his van and peeled back the wrapper on his burger, then took a big bite. A trickle of grease leaked down his chin. He wiped it off with the back of his hand.

'Are you and Malcolm Gilchrist still in touch?' Ellen asked.

'Nah. Malcolm went off to London. I heard he got his degree then trained as a pilot. My mum kept me well-informed.' He grinned. If his mother's intention had been to inspire him to be more like Malcolm he clearly wasn't bothered. 'But I never saw him after he left. He didn't even come out for drinks at Christmas like most folk did when they came home. Left us all behind.'

'How much do you remember about Connor Leask? The man you were with in the bar that night. The man who was murdered.'

'Not much. We bumped into him, like, but he didn't stick around. Probably only remember him because he was killed, to be honest. I don't mean to be nasty but it was a bit of excitement, really, sort of knowing someone who got stabbed and getting interviewed and all that. These days I suppose the kids would be bragging about it on social media.'

Ellen and Dan exchanged glances.

'You must have known him well enough for Malcolm to buy him a drink?'

'Eh, if I remember rightly he bought us a drink first. I think Malc was just being polite.'

'He bought you a drink? When was that?'

'When we first arrived. I think he was already at the bar. When he saw us he offered to buy us a drink.'

'Was he with someone?'

Ayers frowned. Shook his head slowly. He didn't remember.

Ellen waited as he took another chunk out of his burger. When he had chewed through it enough that there was no danger of him spluttering it over her, she said, 'You didn't tell the police any of this at the time. You said you didn't know him.'

Dave Ayers blinked at her. 'Didn't I?'

He stared across the fields that bordered the dual carriageway for a moment. 'No, right enough. I don't suppose I did.'

'Mind telling us why?'

'Malcolm didn't want anyone knowing that he and that guy knew each other.'

'Why not?'

''Cause he was gay, wasn't he?'

'Malcolm?'

'Nah. Well. I meant the guy who was murdered, but I dunno about Malcolm. I wouldn't be completely surprised. But he was desperate for his dad not to think he was. Said his dad would skin him alive if he thought he was queer. That's why he asked me not to say. Doesn't seem that big of a deal, now, does it?'

'You said you were with Malcolm all night at the pub. Was that a lie, too?'

Dave Ayers flushed slightly.

'It might have been bending the truth a bit. As I remember, I met a lassie. Malcolm went off with her pal. But I had a girlfriend, see, so when Malcolm said we should just say we were together all night, I agreed. Look, we were silly young boys. Some of it was just a kind of excitement about the whole thing. Being questioned by the police and that. We were caught up in the drama of it all. We got the feeling we needed cast iron alibis, you know what I mean? Probably been watching too much TV. In our heads we were more involved than we were.'

'Do you know for certain that Malcolm went off with this girl?'

Dave thought for a moment, then shook his head.

'How did you know Connor Leask?'

'Well, we didn't know him. I'd seen him once before

that night, at Malcolm's dad's shop. I didn't like him. I suppose he wasn't much older than us but at the time it felt like he was. I thought he was trying too hard to be "down with the kids" as they say. He was kind of overfamiliar with Malcolm. Maybe I was jealous, a bit.'

'Jealous?'

'Malcolm was kind of cool. A lot of people wanted to hang out with Malcolm, but he was my pal. I guess I thought that guy was trying to muscle in. It was the summer after school finished. I suppose I was a bit sensitive about things changing. Having to grow up and go out into the big, bad world and all that. Wanted things to stay as they were.' He shrugged. 'Funny, isn't it? I wouldn't be a teenager again if you paid me, now.'

*

Dan and Ellen sat in the car in the lay-by after Dave Ayers had driven away, double-tooting his horn as if they were old pals themselves.

'So, Malcolm Gilchrist has just lost his alibi for the night Connor Leask was killed,' Ellen said. 'And he had plenty of opportunity to kill Jimmy Barber, and more than most to change his clothes and clean up after himself.'

'Mmm.' Dan was thumbing through his contacts. He found Vihaan Shah's number. 'Makes you wonder who else's alibis are not all they were cracked up to be.'

Shah picked up after a few rings. Dan put him on speaker and cut to the chase, explaining that they had watched the CCTV footage, and that they had just questioned Dave Ayers. 'You told me about the encounter between Malcolm Gilchrist and Connor Leask at the bar. I take it you saw the CCTV footage yourself?'

There was a fraction of a pause before Shah answered. 'Yes. Why?'

'Did you see all of it? From the beginning of the night?'

Shah had to think. 'Just the bit with Connor Leask and Malcolm Gilchrist. Barber showed it me. I remember because, as I said, it was quite exciting at the time. I think it was the first time I'd been on a case where CCTV was used.'

'Was there another clip of the two of them? From earlier in the evening?'

This time the pause was different. Ellen knew that kind of pause. The kind when your heart dropped like a stone, when your blood drained and you were suddenly very afraid you had made a terrible mistake.

'Did we miss something? What have you found?'

'I don't know how significant it is,' Dan said. He was trying to make Shah feel better. 'They met earlier in the evening. Connor Leask bought Malcolm and his friend a drink. It looks like Malcolm was returning the favour when they had that moment at the bar. We think they already knew each other.'

'Shit.'

'It's not mentioned anywhere in the file. Who would have seen all the footage, can you remember?'

'I'm sorry. Like I said, Barber showed it to me. I don't know if anyone else saw it.'

When Dan had ended the call they sat in silence for a few minutes, Dan staring across the fields towards the Lomond Hills. Finally he twisted round in his seat to face her.

'Two things. What was Connor Leask doing at Ronald Gilchrist's hardware shop in the first place? Leask wasn't a DIY kind of guy. Okay, maybe he spotted Malcolm out and about in Stockbridge and took a fancy to him and followed him to the shop when he was working there one day, but the way Pelley described it, it sounded more like he was staking the place out.'

'Are you thinking this is a link to the Ralston business?'

Dan nodded. 'It would make sense.'

'If Barber knew about it, it would explain why he was so convinced the Gilchrists were involved. What's the second thing? You said, "Two things".'

'How did the original investigation team miss the fact that Connor and Malcolm already knew each other? Or, if someone on that team didn't miss it, why would they dismiss it without record? There's no other CCTV footage even mentioned in the file.'

Ellen frowned. 'What are you getting at? You think they didn't miss it, but for some reason they covered it up?'

Calder didn't say anything, but she could tell from the look on his face that that was exactly what he thought. And who he thought might have done the covering up.

37

Malcolm Gilchrist had lost some of his suave elegance. Ellen could see it in the bags under his eyes, and there was a slight tremble in his hands that had not been there before. She wondered whether he had been drinking a lot lately or taking some form of medication. He had asked for legal representation, but without hostility. Sitting opposite him now she could see no evidence of defensiveness. Instead he seemed resigned to what was coming. Defeated.

'How well did you know Connor Leask?'

'Hardly at all.'

'But you had met him before the night he was killed. Before you met in the Mains Arms.'

He swallowed. When he spoke his voice was hoarse. 'He came into the shop a couple of times.'

'This was your father's hardware shop, in Stockbridge?'

'Yes. I worked there a bit that summer.'

'What did he come in for?'

That seemed to throw him a little. 'I can't remember.'

'But you got chatting.'

'Yes.'

'What sort of things did you talk about?'

Malcolm frowned. He shifted, impatiently, as though he knew this was just a preamble. 'I don't know. What I was going to do at uni, stuff like that. Why? How is this important?'

'Did he ask you about the business?'

Malcolm looked genuinely surprised. 'I don't know. Maybe. I can't remember.'

'Ok, so you chatted... And you arranged to meet in the Mains Arms for a drink?'

'No.'

Dave Ayers had told them they met Connor by chance. It was interesting, though, the vehemence with which Malcolm denied arranging to meet.

'I was there with a friend.'

'Dave Ayers.'

'Yes. We bumped into him. Connor. By accident.'

'Do you think it was an accident?'

Malcolm didn't know what to say to that. Ellen took a sheet from the file in front of her and slid it across the table to him. It was a still image from the CCTV footage. It showed Malcolm at the bar in the Mains Arms. His expression was unclear, but his body language was defensive. The back of Connor Leask's head could be seen at the bottom of the frame, a hand extended towards Malcolm. Malcolm stared at it. He seemed to leave the present. His whole body sagged towards the image on the table in front of him, and Ellen saw his eyes moisten.

'What did he do to upset you?'

'Nothing.' Malcolm's voice was quiet, broken. 'I didn't like the way he looked at me.'

He covered his face with his hands, and when he pulled them away again he had made a decision. 'That's not true. I did like the way he looked at me. But it frightened me. I wasn't ready for it. To answer your earlier question, no, I don't think it was an accident he was there. I think he came deliberately so he could meet me. But it wasn't arranged.'

'Dave said you asked him to lie for you. To say that he'd been with you all night, when in fact he lost contact with you not long after this incident occurred.'

'I didn't ask him to lie. Just not to say. I didn't want my Dad to find out. If he thought I was ... He wasn't very open-minded. Though he found out anyway. I suppose Al told him.' The bitterness was clear in his voice.

Ellen thought about what Norna Gilchrist had said about their father giving Malcolm money and Alistair being jealous. She reached out a finger and laid it on the photograph. 'So, did something happen between you after this?'

Malcolm nodded, but it was difficult for him to speak. Eventually, wringing his hands as he spoke and his shoulders rigid with tension, he said, 'I followed him outside. He was having a cigarette. He ... kissed me. It would have led to more, only then Al and Finlay Groat appeared.'

Ellen straightened. She glanced at Liam, sitting next to her, then in the direction of the camera.

'They were laughing. I ran off. I don't know what happened to Connor after that. I swear.'

This shattered version of Malcolm Gilchrist, shiny barriers broken down, it would be so easy to believe him, she thought. And Alistair was there. Alistair and Finlay Groat. That alibi had just gone up in smoke too.

She said, 'I still don't quite understand why you didn't tell the police this at the time.'

'I told you. My Dad.'

'But you said he found out anyway. And from what I hear, he can't have taken it very badly. He gave you money to go to university, to train for your pilot's licence.'

Malcolm looked at her in shock. 'He gave me money to get rid of me. He said it was for my own good. But he couldn't even look at me.'

'Why was it for your own good?'

'Well it wasn't, was it? It was for his good. He was ashamed of me.'

'Did you kill Connor Leask?'

Malcolm's solicitor opened his mouth to protest – he had been told they only wanted to clarify a witness statement – but Malcolm got in first. 'No.'

'Did you kill James Barber?'

'No.'

'Really, DS Chisholm ...'

Malcolm waved the lawyer down.

'Where did you go after you left your brother's house on the day of James Barber's murder?' Ellen asked. 'Did you go to James Barber's house? Or to his allotment?'

'What? No. I don't know where that is. Either of them.'

They kept up the pressure. 'Why did you lie to us about seeing Barber at the hospital?'

'I've told you already. I forgot. My dad was dying. I had other things on my mind. I was only in Edinburgh for a day, then I had to fly out again.'

'What did your father want to talk to Barber about?'

'I don't know.'

'Do you think he thought you had killed Connor Leask?'

He stared at her.

'Well it's possible, isn't it? It makes sense of him giving you all that money to go away. For your own good.'

He clammed up then. She could see it, practically hear it, the clanging shut of the gates.

'Were you afraid he was going to give you up? Were you afraid he had given you up?'

38

Finlay Groat has asked me out for a drink.

'I told you,' Mum says. 'Didn't I tell you?'

'I'm probably what passes for exotic in Finlay's world. It's about as crazy as his mid-life crisis is going to get to go out with a girl with bright red hair.'

'Don't forget the nose piercing,' Mum says, drily. A moment later: 'So you are going then? Out. With Finlay?'

'It's only a drink. I expect Al will be there too.'

He isn't, of course. When he invited me, Finlay made an ambiguous reference to the fact that he and Al often meet for a drink at The Laird's, but he was only testing the water. If I had said I'd love to join them, I daresay he would have rung Al, but since I didn't, he didn't.

I am not the slightest bit interested in Finlay Groat. I am going because there are things I want to know and I think Finlay may be able to help me find the answers. I've been thinking a lot about what Margery Shanks said.

I watch him ordering our drinks and then carrying them carefully back to the table. I can see why Mum thinks he's a catch. He is rather good-looking I suppose, in a sturdy, dependable sort of way, and what's really nice about him is that he's completely without airs and graces. There's a down-to-earth humility about him.

'You're very different from your father,' I say as he puts the drinks down and settles opposite me.

He looks at me for a moment with a kind of measured gaze, as though he's trying to work out whether I mean that as a good thing (which it certainly is), or whether I mean it as some kind of class comment.

'I am different from him,' he concedes, eventually. 'But I've also benefitted from him being the way he is and the things he achieved because of it. He did all the hard graft, so that now I'm starting to take over the business it's in good shape and I can afford to take a more relaxed approach with my staff and meet my clients on more equal terms.'

He's being very careful about what he's saying. I want to ask him why he can't overrule his Dad on Al's dismissal if he's already started taking over the business, but I have only had one sip of my very nice wine and I decide it would be a shame to begin the evening on a sour note. I shouldn't be drinking at all, of course.

'Mum says we have a lot to be grateful to Lawrence for. That he helped Dad out when things were a bit rough in the early nineties. Did he tell you that?'

Again there is that searching look.

'Perhaps he was too modest to tell you?' I say. 'Anyway, Mum seemed to think it made a big difference at the time, the fact he recommended Dad to clients, helped get the handyman stuff set up.'

He makes no sound, it's very gradual, but I swear I see Finlay letting out a breath of relief. Was he worried I was talking about money? Would he have asked for it all to be paid back, with interest, if he found out his Dad had been giving hand-outs? Or does he know more than he's letting on?

Invoice paid.

'Well, that's good to know,' he manages, eventually, with a little bashful look. 'I think your dad did the same for him, though. If it wasn't for Ronny's business nous and the advice he gave Dad, Dad'd still have been at Ralston's when that went down the tube.'

Ralston is a name I recognise from Dad's diaries, but I don't know who he is.

'Builders' Yard,' Finlay supplies, as if he can read my mind.

'Did you always want to work in the family firm?' I ask. I don't think that was ever something I or my brothers would have considered. And though we each did a stint behind the counter at one time or another I don't remember there ever being any pressure to actually take on the business. Even for Al. Whether we weren't to be trusted, or whether we were simply allowed to choose our own futures, I don't know.

'It was never really discussed,' Finlay says. 'I started working for Dad in the holidays, then after uni, and just kind of stuck. I'm not complaining. I don't know what else I'd be any good at.'

'It can't be as simple as that though. You must have had to study business or construction or something, didn't you?'

'I studied architecture. But I also worked on the shop floor, so to speak. In every department, from mixing concrete to handing out sales brochures. I made a point of getting involved in every aspect of the business, finding out what it was like, hands-on, day-to-day.'

'You earned your position.' I'm thinking: you know the business inside out, everything that goes on there. Went on.

'It's good for the business if I have first-hand experience of every operational system, every workflow. I can see where the glitches and the gaps are. I can make it more efficient.'

'You're not so different from your dad, then. You both worked your way up.' I smile, but Finlay doesn't seem to like the comparison. 'I worked my way up. Dad – I don't know what verb I'd use for Dad.'

There's an edge to his voice. Not for the first time, I have an inkling that Finlay doesn't much like his father.

'Sorry,' he says. 'The police asked me about the things I used to get up to with Al. They asked what I was rebelling against.' He smiles. 'They clearly didn't think I had much to complain about and on the face of it I'd have to agree with them, but at the time I wasn't all that happy. I had all this teenage rage, mostly directed towards my father. I guess their questioning brought it all back.'

My stomach vaults at the thought the police were asking him about Al. 'The other day you told me you didn't fit in at school or at home. That's sad.'

'Like you said, I'm not really like my dad. It was his choice to send me to that school; he wanted me to be like those other boys, have the kinds of opportunities they did, but then he resented me for it. Because no matter what he did he was never going to fit in with the other parents. They were happy enough to make deals with him, sure, but he was never going to be one of them. He used to blame my Mum. Said she didn't make enough effort to get in with the other mums. The things he called her, he was a bastard to her.'

Wow. Not so careful now. There's proper hatred there and I wonder whether he knows what he's saying. He makes me think about Josh and the hatred he professed for Al, and what Rob said about Al being just like Dad now. The image of Josh holding his hand in his jacket pocket as if he were holding a knife comes to mind and I can't stop the thought that follows. The idea that Al might have carried a knife, too. I don't want to be thinking about that.

Or about the searches into forensic science that Dad made on his computer.

'I'm really only just hearing about what you and Al got up to. I don't remember much first-hand.'

'No, you were just a wee thing. Al doted on you, though.'

I feel ridiculously pleased to hear this from Finlay, even though I know full well it's true. 'Yeah. I adored him, too. Still do,' I add.

I may not remember much about the petty crimes Al and Finlay committed or the trouble they got into, but I do remember Al's moods, as Dad called them, and his frustration. There were times when I was the only person who could approach him. Little Non. I didn't mind it when he called me that then. I would find him sitting on his bed or in the back garden, listening to his music, and I would climb onto the bench or the bed and get as close to his unresponsive body as possible and burrow my hand into his and wait. Eventually, he would pull off his headphones or pull me onto his knee and just hug me. Sometimes we just sat together. Sometimes he played me his music. I didn't always like it, but I was entranced by the act of him sharing it with me. If I took pencils and a notepad with me we might draw together. Once I found a replica of a drawing we did together on the wall of the underpass under Silverknowes

Road and it was the best secret. I missed him terribly when he left, but on occasion I would come home from school to find him loitering outside the house. 'Alright, Little Non?' He would ask me about school and how things were with my friends and he would tell me about what he'd been doing on his college course or his apprenticeship and try to explain electricity to me, and then he'd saunter off without going into the house. I felt special.

Finlay is watching me. I smile. 'You've got me remembering the past now.'

'We were pathetic really,' he says. 'Me and Al. It's laughable.'

'Well, from what I've heard, a couple of shopkeepers might disagree.'

He blushes. An actual blush. It's endearing.

'In fact I don't know how you weren't arrested if half of what Rob says is true.' Something occurs to me. 'That's not down to your Dad, is it?'

'I wouldn't be surprised. I'm sure he was quite capable of greasing a few palms. Do you think less of me?'

What makes you think I have a high opinion of you to start with? But I confess, I am warming to him. 'Why should I?'

'Spoilt brat, Daddy bailing him out of trouble.'

'Well, if it got Al out of trouble, too, I'll let you off. As long as we're only talking shoplifting the odd packet of crisps and tagging underpasses, and not the murder of a trainee procurator fiscal.'

It's out before I can stop it. What a bloody stupid thing to say.

Finlay stares at me. There's nothing searching in it this time. I see a glint of anger and a warning in it.

'That's not something to bandy about lightly,' he says.

I feel chided. Foolish and ignorant.

'No, you're right.' I don't know why, but I won't say sorry.

Finlay looks down into his beer. He says nothing for a few minutes, just turns his glass round and round, watching the patterns of amber light it casts on the dark wood of the table.

'That was a nightmare. I can't believe it's all come back again.' He looks up and I almost get a fright, his eyes are so hard. 'Don't go asking questions like that, Norna. You don't remember. To you it might seem almost a fiction, but for all of us it was very real.'

It stings, that. The fiction bit. It stings in the way things do when they are close to the bone. When you know someone is right but you don't want to admit it.

My first instinct is to try to find excuses for what I said, to rationalise my interest in what happened. But even as they flit through my head my reasons sound pathetic at best: *It felt like something everyone else knew about and I didn't; I thought if I understood what happened, if I got to the bottom of this, I would understand what happened to us and I could somehow heal the rift in my family.*

Terrifying at worst.

I think my father might have killed a man he had been blackmailing and that at least two of my brothers know about it.

I hoped to discover it was not my father but yours. I wanted to find someone else to take the blame.

I can't even articulate in thought my fears for Al.

I say nothing.

39

Farhana McLean had left a voicemail message for Dan while they were talking to Dave Ayers. He'd listened to it as Ellen drove them back to Edinburgh. Ellen was angry with him again, he knew. Barber had clearly meant a lot to her and she was still finding it difficult to hear any suggestion that he had been less than perfect. If Barber had done something to suppress information during the original investigation, though, it might go some way to explaining his zeal in trying to find the killer later on. Guilt and a desire to make amends might also have made him reckless and irrational. Dan thought about what Barber had said to him. We let him down. He thought about the way Barber had hissed in anger when Dan brought up his sexuality and asked whether that was why Barber was so keen to find an answer. If Barber was touchy on that subject, in 1993 he must have been doubly sensitive. What if he had understood the position Malcolm would be in if his father suspected he was gay, and glossed over what he had seen in that CCTV footage in order to protect him? And what if he had later discovered that the very boy he had protected with his actions had turned out to be the killer?

He could tell Ellen was tempted to believe Malcolm when she came out of the interview, but all it had done for Dan was to confirm what Nichol Pelley had said about Connor.

Farhana MacLean's message said that she had found some more papers of Connor's. She would be working late, she said, and not to worry about calling by the office any time before ten to collect them.

He thought about not going at all. She could have dropped them off herself, or left them at her office reception. He didn't like being at someone's beck and call, however beautiful they were.

He went though.

Farhana came and let him in herself. The receptionist had long gone and she was the only one left in the building, she said. She flashed her stunning smile and Dan resented the effect it had on him.

'You made me think,' she said, as she led the way back up to her office. 'The other day, when you were asking about how I ended up with all that stuff. I went back through all my old law textbooks, and I found them stuffed inside my Gretton and Reid.'

Dan thought she could have brought the papers down to reception with her. He waited, standing, as she retrieved a few sheets of folded paper from the handbag behind her desk. His eyes strayed to the small pot that held her treasury tags and he felt a flush creep up his neck. He could have returned the one he'd taken, he thought, but that wasn't how it worked. And he couldn't now, anyway. He had dropped the tag down the side of Dave Ayers' passenger seat when he leaned into the van to say goodbye. It would accompany him on his deliveries around Fife, a displaced fragment from a stranger's life, an oddity maybe, but unremarkable nonetheless. One degree of separation if only anyone knew it.

'Again, I don't know how much use they'll be,' Farhana said, 'But it's definitely Connor's writing and he seems to have been quite excited by it, judging by the underlinings and circlings.'

'Thanks,' Dan said, taking the papers from her.

At first glance they seemed to be maps or plans of some kind, and again Connor had scribbled notes in the margins in his mixture of shorthand and initialisation peppered with question marks, arrows and other marks.

Dan sighed internally. He had never had much love for cold cases and this reminded him why. The lack of fresh evidence, the dearth of CCTV footage and recorded data. The things he resented when it came to his own personal life, in fact, were the very things he missed when it came to trying to do his job. As Dave Ayers had proved, there were times when new details came to light. When the lies people had told then, the things it seemed important to hide, no longer seemed to matter. But on the whole memories were warped and clouded, evidence degraded, the facts silted up.

There was a melancholy about it, too. Looking at these documents he couldn't understand someone like Glen Starrett's interest in local history. It only made Dan feel despondent to dwell on the past. Some of it was to do with Connor himself. For some reason, his death echoed in a way that present day killings did not. Perhaps it was because Dan had a very tangible sense of all the life Connor had missed out on, not least because their paths were bound to have crossed. When a murder happened in the present it was about the immediate impact, the loss felt by the relatives, but that stolen future was still only notional.

He couldn't help liking Connor. There was something about the way his energy and his zeal still rang out despite the intervening years. Something to do with Leask's refusal to be curbed by societal mores or other people's scruples, misguided though it clearly was at times. The attraction of opposites, Dan supposed. He suspected his liking for Connor would not have been reciprocated. Where Connor was passionate and driven, Dan was measured. Connor was outgoing, he wanted to challenge everything. Dan kept his cards close to his chest, he slipped under the radar. Years of melting into the background, trying to quietly fit in, had made him like this. He thought that Connor would have despised that.

He realised that Connor reminded him of Ellen Chisholm.

He thanked Farhana again.

'I was about to knock off actually,' she said. 'Do you fancy a drink?'

It was only a tiny bit of strategy, Dan knew, getting him to come here so she could ask, but it put him off. He had no time for tactical relationships.

'No. Thanks,' he said pleasantly, smiling to soften the words, but without giving any reason or excuse.

As he drove home, he tried to tell himself it was

because it was the right thing to do, that he was only following the rules. Because he did like her. He would have liked to go for a drink, and maybe more. Definitely more. But it would be inappropriate, wouldn't it, while she was a witness in a case he was working on? He wanted to believe it was just that. But he knew it also had something to do with the hardened knot of distrust inside him. As much as his declining her invitation was to do with good working practice it was also the result of a deep-seated and obsessive need to know where he stood at all times. He cursed himself. What the hell was wrong with him?

*

He let himself into his flat and without bothering to turn on any of the lights he went through to the kitchen and opened the fridge. After a moment of bleak consideration he decided an omelette might be possible. He took out a couple of eggs and some tomatoes that needed eaten and put them on the counter. He had already lost interest. Instead he pulled out the folded papers Farhana McLean had given him and in the light from the fridge he looked again.

A couple were photocopies of pages from the city A to Z, others looked like extracts of town planning documents of some kind. They showed areas of the city marked out in line drawing and overlaid with large sections marked out for development. In the margin of one of the plans Connor had scrawled the initials 'L.Q.' Suddenly Dan was interested. Lee Quigley? He pushed the food aside and laid the papers out on the counter, only now switching on the main light.

From the initials Connor had drawn an arrow pointing to an area of the plan which he had circled. Dan scanned the page for a clue to what he was looking at. He recognised some of the street names as being part of Wester Hailes in West Edinburgh. That was where Lee Quigley had died. Did this plan cover the construction site he was attempting to rob when he died? If there had been a legend for it it had been cropped out in the enlargement process but Dan spotted a footnote at the bottom right-hand side of the page. He squinted at the tiny writing. He could make out a copyright symbol and the words, 'Kinley Developments'. His pulse quickened.

On the city map he looked for the area covered by the plan, and found it circled, with the same initials underlined in the margin. There were other areas circled on the map, with question marks and number references: 6-11/90; 4/89-7/92. Dates perhaps? Periods of time during which building developments were scheduled? If they reflected the Kinley plans these could be the regeneration projects Sharon Harkins had mentioned. Ugh. Definitely something to delegate.

He thought again of Glen Starrett with his interest in local history. He hadn't much liked the man, he realised. The way he had answered them when asked what he had told Barber: Probably the same thing you did. Like Farhana, there was nothing deeply manipulative about what Starrett had said. Dan just didn't like the way he had said it in order to show them he knew things. Starrett knew Barber had approached Ellen and he wanted them to know that. Maybe it was a retired copper thing – wanting not to be seen as decrepit or obsolete. Trying to prove he was still in on the action.

Dan sighed. His ego was taking a bashing tonight, because he knew his dislike of Starrett was also just another of his hang-ups. He was giving an old man a hard time for wanting to show them he wasn't past it, all because he, Dan, didn't like the idea of other people knowing things about him.

Well, Ellen seemed to think Starrett needed company. If they got nowhere with the dates on these maps themselves, she could go and ask him.

His stomach growled. A takeaway was becoming an attractive option. Eating out, even. He looked at his sparse front room: it might be nice to go somewhere with a bit of life. He thought about the impressions he'd formed of Harkins' and Starrett's lives from their homes; if he didn't know himself he'd draw some pretty dismal conclusions from his own. His friend Doug had laughed when he first visited. 'I love my brick,' he'd said in cod Oirish accent, looking at

Dan's collection of stones on the shelf above the radiator. Dan had laughed too. He got the reference, to Father Jack in the TV sitcom Father Ted, but coming from Doug, a kindred spirit whom he'd first met one night in a bothy in Torridon, he got the point too. Since then, he'd made a bit of an effort. A couple of candlesticks, some framed landscapes – and more rocks, in pen and ink this time – but if he was honest, he did love his stones: quartz from Morar; granite from the Cairngorms; gneiss from Wester Ross. They were more evocative than any photograph of the places he'd been.

He returned to the map in his hands. Towards the bottom edge there was a circle over part of the Moredun area of the city. Here the initials in the bottom margin had a question mark attached: 'D.O.?'.

Dean Owens? The one name on Connor's list they hadn't yet made a connection to.

Connor was less sure of it, too. Dan grabbed the second of the enlarged planning documents. There was no mark to show a precise location here but again, 'D.O.?' in the top left hand corner.

Dan picked up the phone. 'Keisha? Did you manage to find anything on Dean Owens?'

'Umm.' There was a pause while Keisha swallowed something and got her head back into work mode. 'If it's the same Dean Owens, there was a missing persons report filed in 1991. It's on my desk ...'

'Thanks Keisha.' In his excitement, he'd cut the call before thinking to explain. Or to apologise for interrupting her evening. Some people had lives, he reminded himself. He'd buy her a coffee tomorrow morning by way of thanks.

*

Half an hour later he was back in the office, take-out noodles hastily scoffed, leafing quickly through the missing persons report that Keisha had unearthed. There was nothing in it to indicate why he had come to Connor Leask's attention, or to link him to the part of the city Connor had marked. Owens had last been seen soliciting in Leith, where he lived. Nowhere near Moredun.

Soliciting? That came as a surprise. He was nothing to

do with the building trade, then.

Dan sat down at his own desk and began to go through the earlier documents they had got from Farhana, looking for anything that featured the initials D.O. or the name Dean Owens, or that referred to the Moredun area. He found one photocopied article about the proposed replacement of post-war prefab housing in south Edinburgh written in 1989. Another concerned a former limestone mine in the area. There was nothing else about Dean Owens.

There had to be a reason why Connor Leask had linked Dean Owens with Quigley, Horvat and Norris Ralston. Dan began the same search online. Owens' name yielded nothing significant. He found some nice pictures of prefab housing in South Edinburgh but that told him nothing. When he typed in Limestone mines, Moredun, though, he hit the jackpot.

In 2000 there had been a landslip in the Moredun/ Gilmerton part of the city when abandoned limestone mines underground had become waterlogged and the supports had collapsed. Dan found pictures of whole streets with great cracks running down the centre of them, houses literally broken in half.

When the houses were demolished the following year a set of remains had been found in the wreckage underneath Ferniehill Terrace. The remains of an unidentified male, estimated to be in his late-teens or early twenties.

Was this Dean Owens?

If it was, though, Connor Leask had worked out where Dean Owens' body was seven years before it was found. He had worked out that he was dead, even. Long before anyone else had. Or before anyone else would admit it.

Dan looked at the list of names on Connor's page again: Franjo Horvat; Lee Quigley; Dean Owens. They were looking at three suspicious deaths.

He looked at the article about the proposed replacement of the prefab housing and then at the photocopied blueprint on which Connor had marked Dean Owens' initials. It was another plan for a housing development. He held it up to the light and peered at the tiny writing running along the bottom right hand corner. It was the same footnote as on the Wester Hailes plan. The scheme was to be managed by Kinley Developments.

40

It's late when Rob calls.

'What's this Mum says about you and Finlay Groat?' He sounds furious.

I take a moment to process. 'It was only a drink. And he's separated.'

'Stay away from Finlay Groat.'

'Jesus, Rob. When did you become such a presbyterian? You're not the boss of me.'

'You said it yourself about Lawrence. The Groats are horrible people.'

'You can't blame Finlay for his father. He's nothing like him. And anyway ...'

I let out a frustrated growl and cut the call before I say something I'll regret. Something about him leaving the mother of his child for a woman twelve years younger.

Bloody Rob. I'll say one thing though. There's nothing like a bit of fraternal disapproval to make Finlay seem suddenly very attractive. And what does any of it matter, anyway? It's not like I'm in it for the fairytale ending.

I'm not dead yet, for Christ's sake.

My phone buzzes: it's Rob again. I ignore it. I go back to poring over Dad's diaries.

The money stopped coming in the week after Connor Leask was killed, but I can't understand the connection. How could the money have been coming from Leask? Why should my Dad have had anything to do with him? Had he carried out work at his flat? Had he discovered something about him whilst replacing a washer on a tap or putting up a shelf? Something that would have crippled the man's legal career, perhaps? It doesn't make sense though. Leask would still have been a student when the invoices are first recorded. He came from fairly well-off parents but it's a stretch to imagine him being able to afford two hundred and fifty pounds a week. Certainly without anyone noticing when they combed his bank records after his death. As surely they must have done.

If it wasn't Connor Leask my father was blackmailing, who was it, and why did it stop when Connor Leask was killed?

Why did that policeman think my Dad had something to do with his death?

And why can't I leave this alone?

I think about what the charity shop man said about the crazy things that went through his mind after his wife died, and what Finlay said when he told me not to ask the questions I'm asking. The trouble is, I have nothing else to do with my time, and I need a distraction. Is that the worst reason ever for possibly uncovering information that might destroy your family? Because I realise now, there is a much greater chance of me doing that than fixing things.

I think about taking the diaries and the money to the police. To that Detective, Ellen Chisholm. I know she was suspicious when she saw me outside Margery Shanks' place. I imagine taking them to her and her telling me gratefully that it's the piece of the puzzle they've been looking for, explaining to me that it's not what it seems but that in fact it exonerates Dad, and Malcolm and Al. But of course, that's not what would happen at all. She would take them from me, tell me nothing, and I might even find myself charged with obstructing their inquiries.

I flick through 1993 again and come to the list of names at the back and something else occurs to me. Why would Dad have wanted to bring it all up again? If he was blackmailing someone, if he had done things he felt he had to justify to Malcolm in that letter, why suddenly ask to see that detective? Was he going to confess?

If he was going to do that, wouldn't he have finished the letter to Malcolm first?

These are the things that are rolling round my head when the display on my phone lights up again. I hadn't realised it was quite so late: nearly two in the morning. This time it's Mel.

'What is it?'

'Norna? Is Josh with you?'

'Josh? No. It's the middle of the night.'

'I know,' she wails. 'I just thought, I hoped he'd maybe come round to see you, then stayed over. He hasn't come home.'

I'm on my feet. I have to rack my brain to work out what day of the week it is. I think it might be Thursday or Friday but I'm not completely sure. 'Could he be out with friends?'

'I've tried the ones I know. Norna, I'm really scared. He and Al had a massive row. He stormed off. I've never seen him like that before.'

I think of Josh's hand in his pocket. The solid shape that was still there when he removed his hand.

'I'm coming over.'

I pull on some clothes. I hesitate at the front door, wondering whether I should leave a note for Mum. Surely all this will be sorted by morning. There's no point worrying her, but if she hears the car, she might worry about me. I scribble a quick message – Couldn't sleep, gone for a drive – and leave it on the hall table.

I drive slowly, looking around, just in case. Looking for the lanky figure of my nephew, willing him to appear, lolloping down the street towards home, his anger spent.

Why didn't I say anything about the knife? It was a knife. I know it was a knife.

When I get to Al's, Mel is in the open doorway before I've even turned the engine off. She's frantic.

'Al and Finlay have gone out looking for him.'

'Finlay?'

'Yeah. Al called him to see if Josh was there.'

For a selfish moment I feel jealous to think that they tried Finlay before me. That Josh might have gone to him instead of coming to his Auntie Norna's. Then I remember he did neither.

'What happened?' I ask.

'They had a flaming row. I mean they clash a lot, but this was ... Josh said he wished he was dead. He said no-one would care if he was. Al ... He told him to stop being such a self-centred snowflake.'

'Oh, shit.'

'I know. I think he just didn't realise it was so serious. I mean, he's been having a crap time himself. What with your Dad and Lawrence and the police asking all these questions.'

'And you've no idea where Josh would have gone?'

Mel shakes her head and her chin trembles. I pull her into a hug. She's freezing cold. 'Come on, let's get you warm. You can't think straight just now.' I guide her through to the living room and put on the heater. Then I can't think of what to do next. All I can think is how badly wrong I got it the other day. There I was, thinking I was cool Auntie Norna, there to listen, there for Josh, and I ignored what was right under my nose.

Mel is still clutching her phone. 'I don't know who else to try,' she says. I don't really know his friends. He doesn't bring anyone home.'

I think about the three knuckleheads we passed the other day. I have a horrible feeling Josh doesn't have many friends this side of his computer screen, but there's no way I'm going to tell Mel that.

There is a sudden commotion outside and we both rush into the hall as the front door bangs open and Al staggers in. He is carrying Josh in his arms, weighed down by him, and there is blood all over them. Josh's head is lolling over the side of Al's arm and Al is breathing heavily, irregularly, like he's on the point of crying. He is barely holding it together.

'I'll call an ambulance,' I say.

'It's on its way already.' It's Finlay, coming in behind Al. 'We wanted to get him into the warm.'

'What happened to him?'

'He's been stabbed.'

My blood runs cold. 'How?'

Al is on the floor now, Josh still in his arms, and he's given in to tears. Mel is with them, but she seems to have swung into action. She is putting blankets over them, pulling up Josh's eyelids, then listening to his breathing, talking to him. 'Josh, darling. It's Mum, can you hear me? We're going to get you to hospital. You're going to be alright. Just hold on.'

I can't see a way to check Josh's coat pocket without anyone noticing and wanting to know why. 'Where did you find him?'

'He was on the path up to Corstorphine Hill.'

'How on earth did you find him there?'

'Al did Find My Phone with Josh's number.'

'Who did this, do you know?'

Finlay shakes his head. 'Happened before we got there.'

We see the blue light glinting off the bevelled glass in the front door and hear the ambulance draw up. Finlay goes out to meet the paramedics and tells them what he knows as they walk up the path. They take over then, and because the hallway is small and crowded Finlay and I are pushed back into the living room. I can only see glimpses of Josh on the ground, behind the green of the paramedics' uniforms and the hunched forms of Al and Mel, who cling to each other in front of us. The voices of the paramedics are calm, their questions and their instructions clear and unhurried, but it seems unreal. I am so intent on what's happening that I don't notice how much I'm shaking, or that Finlay's arms are round me.

Mel goes with Josh in the ambulance. Al follows in the car. I tell them I'll stay here for Kirsty and Sam.

After they've left I stand, numb, in the hallway. There are smears of blood on the floor and the skirting boards where Josh and Al had slumped. Little round bits of plastic that must have come off something the paramedics stuck onto Josh. His coat has been discarded together with one of the blankets. I kneel on the floor and feel for the fabric of his pockets. There is nothing there.

'What happened?' I ask Finlay again.

He shakes his head, hopelessly.

'Whose knife was it?'

'What do you mean?'

'I think it might have been Josh's.'

I tell him about the other day and the thugs by the church, Josh with his head up and his hand in his pocket.

Finlay is staring at me. He can't make me feel worse than I do already.

'But you don't know it was a knife?' he says.

'No. I didn't see it. At first I thought he might just have been trying to make it look like that for their benefit. But...'

But I do know. I'm shaking again.

Finlay pulls me into an embrace. 'Oh Norna, why didn't you tell me? I wish you'd told me.'

So Uncle Finlay could save the day?

I push him away, taking a deep breath. 'I better clear all this up in case Kirsty or Sam wake up and come down.'

Finlay offers to stay with me but I can tell he doesn't really want to. I tell him to go. It seems very quiet once he has left. The house feels eerily vacant.

When the doorbell rings I just about jump out of my skin. Two police officers are standing on the doorstep.

41

'If we are looking at three suspicious deaths, Malcolm is the least likely of the Gilchrist men to have been involved, isn't he?' Ellen said as she and Calder approached the Advocate Depute's office.

'I might be barking up the wrong tree entirely,' Dan said. They didn't have conclusive evidence that the body under Ferniehill Terrace had been Dean Owens, and unless they could find Franjo Horvat – dead or alive – he had to admit this theory was shaky to say the least. 'And it's still hard to see how Dean Owens connects to the others. They each have direct links to Ralston or Kinley. He doesn't.'

'Not through the building trade, perhaps. But rent boys see and hear things. He could still be a threat to someone.'

'Meantime, apart from Ralston himself the only one of the names on Connor's list that we know for sure is dead is Lee Quigley. If we can find out why Connor was so convinced his death was more than an accident, it might help us either validate or rule out this line of enquiry. Have to say, I'm not much looking forward to this, though.'

He rapped on the door to Lise Eklund's office and didn't wait to be asked in. She did not look pleased to see them.

'Make it quick,' she said, when Dan explained that they needed to corroborate some information given in a statement by another witness. She sat back in her chair and fixed Dan with a cold, blue stare. He turned to Ellen, who didn't see the point in beating about the bush.

'Had you decided to terminate Connor Leask's traineeship just before he died?'

'I'm sorry? How is this relevant to James Barber's death? That's the case you're investigating, isn't it?'

'It is. But everything we've found so far suggests that

it was Barber's interest in Connor Leask's murder that led to his own death.'

Eklund's jaw tensed, but she did not protest.

'Last time we spoke you told us that Connor had difficulty accepting some of the decisions your department had to make,' Ellen said. 'We have spoken to someone since then who suggested that it went further than that. That Connor actively questioned decisions that were made, highlighted evidence that had been overlooked, that he believed inappropriate decisions were being made about which cases went to trial.'

'Is that a question? Yes, I told you before, Connor challenged everything, all the time.'

'Did he ever go so far as to accuse you or anyone else in the department of withholding evidence or suppressing it? That would have amounted to gross misconduct, wouldn't it? On Connor's part, I mean.'

Up until that last bit Ellen had almost managed to sound as though they weren't casting aspersions, but she just couldn't resist, could she? Dan didn't expect Lise Eklund to take it well and was surprised by her response.

After a brief pause she said, simply: 'Yes, he did, and it did amount to gross misconduct. We were about to terminate his traineeship.'

'Why didn't you mention that to us before?'

'Which bit? Connor's accusations, or that he was about to lose his position with us?' She did not wait for Ellen to answer. 'The first, because I do have some pride and my own career to worry about; the second because I didn't see the point. Connor is dead. He died a long time ago. If he had lived, who knows what he might have become? Losing the traineeship might or might not have had much effect on his future, but it didn't have anything to do with his death. I'm sure of that.'

'How did he take it?'

Meaning: did he threaten you? Did he threaten to expose something if you terminated his contract? Dan winced internally.

'He didn't know yet. We hadn't told him. That's why I

say it can't be a factor in his death'

Eklund knew what Ellen's question had meant. She had been a prosecutor for long enough. 'Look, let's just stop pussyfooting around, shall we? I had no reason to want Connor dead and I think you'll find that the original investigation file records wherever I was that night. You have no doubt checked my whereabouts on the day James Barber was killed, too, and found that I cannot have killed him. So, is there anything else I can do for you, and if not, can I please get on with my job?'

Dan took a breath. He had the feeling of being about to dive into deep water. 'There was a case of accidental death that Connor thought was suspicious, in Wester Hailes, am I right?'

The Baroness turned her raptor eyes on him. 'There was.'

'A young man called Lee Quigley, who had been a participant on one of Mitchell Kinley's construction training schemes, was assumed to have broken into the site looking to steal materials, but lost his footing and triggered the collapse of some scaffolding pipes which crushed him.'

Lise Eklund made no comment.

'Do you know why Connor was so convinced it wasn't an accident?'

'The boy had done some work experience with Norris Ralston. I assume Connor thought he might have been another possible informant.'

'Did Connor ever show an interest in another of Kinley's Developments? In Moredun?'

'Not to my knowledge.'

Dan weighed up his options. Was there anything to be gained from keeping Connor's discoveries to themselves? He thought not.

'We have come by some notes of Connor's from the time. Some pertain to Quigley's death at the site of one of Kinley's developments in Wester Hailes.'

Eklund pursed her lips.

Dan went on. 'Connor appears to have made a similar connection between another of Kinley's developments in the Moredun area, and the disappearance of a young man called Dean Owens. At the time of Connor's death in 1993 Dean Owens was still listed as a missing person. In 2001 the remains of a young man fitting Dean Owens' description were found after a landslip. In Moredun.'

A tiny jolt of surprise ran through Eklund but she recovered quickly. 'That is remarkable, I agree. Perhaps I underestimated Connor's investigative skills, but it doesn't mean Kinley was involved in anything criminal.'

'It looks suspicious.'

'It's circumstantial.'

The three of them sat in silence for a minute. It was stalemate.

Ellen tried one more time. 'Did Connor Leask ever accuse you or Superintendent Baird of trying to cover up evidence that Mitchell Kinley was involved in criminal activity?'

'If he had, he would not only have faced dismissal from the traineeship, he would have been sued for defamation.'

Ellen faced down her glare. 'Even so, what I don't understand is why none of this came up in the original investigation into Connor's death. It's a legitimate line of questioning, isn't it? To look at a murder victim's relationships at work, at any recent behaviour that might have got him into trouble, made someone angry. It's standard procedure. So why is there nothing of this in the original investigation file?'

Eklund had paled slightly. 'I can't help you there.'

'Would Hugh Baird have tried to protect your reputation, do you think? I don't say that he deliberately suppressed information that might have led to the discovery of Connor's killer, or even that he was trying to protect Kinley from Connor's accusations, but if he thought that it was irrelevant, might he have dismissed certain evidence that could have harmed your reputation.'

Eklund was very still for a moment. She had to clear her throat before she spoke again.

'Connor accused me of not wanting to pursue the Ralston case because of his links to Kinley. He made the same accusation about the enquiry into Lee Quigley's death. I had been called in on the fatal accident enquiry. It seemed cut and dried. I didn't actually know he was anything to do with Kinley at the time, but Connor later accused me of choosing to interpret the evidence in a way that suited Kinley's best interests. There was a bit of bruising on Quigley that couldn't be fully explained by the accident. But he'd been clambering over a construction site in the dark. He could easily have tripped and fallen before the accident that killed him. Connor was convinced someone had knocked him out. When he raised the issue, we did re-examine it, but it was tenuous.

'True, we were about to terminate his traineeship, but it was because Connor had become impossible to mentor, with his conspiracy theories and the fact he was putting more effort into his extra-curricular sleuthing than he was into his job. It was not because of any malpractice on our part. And I don't believe for a minute that Hugh Baird would tamper with evidence, to protect me or anyone else.'

But she didn't look too sure about that.

Hugh Baird died six years ago, Dan thought. He wasn't the man in the Gilchrists' garage wielding a large spanner. He didn't kill James Barber. The trouble was, if he had concealed information relating to Connor Leask's death, he might have unwittingly destroyed evidence that could have helped them to find out who did.

42

I have this sense of the path ahead being erased as I walk towards it. What will happen when I reach the point where it disappears?

The police officers who came to Al's took my statement and left for the hospital to get everyone else's, but they didn't leave immediately. I watched from the front door as they sat in the car for a while. Every now and then one of them said something, but mostly they seemed to be listening. They must have been on the radio to someone else. Then they both turned and looked at the house and me for what felt like a long time. I don't know why, but it sent a shiver of fear through me.

I stand on the pavement outside the hospital and listen to the dialling tone and imagine Rob, all those miles away at the top of the Scottish mainland. Mainly I picture drizzle and a bleak landscape with seagulls wheeling over red sandstone stacks. He took me to John O'Groats, of course. A more dismal place I don't think I've ever seen. Though this comes a close second.

Come on. Answer.

Churning seas and brown earth and flat skies, and Rob's garage full of projects he never finishes.

'You cut me off last night.' He is both aggrieved and astonished.

'I know, I'm sorry ...'

'I'm serious, Norna. About the Groats. Dad told me Lawrence ...'

'That doesn't matter now,' I snap. 'Josh has been stabbed.'

I've shocked him into silence. 'Oh my God,' he rasps eventually. 'Is he ok?'

'I don't know. I'm at the hospital now but they don't know how bad it is yet. Will you come? Please come. Al's in bits, Mum's looking after Kirsty and Sam. Please will you just come.'

'I don't know, Non.' I picture him running his hand back across his head, exposing that receding hairline. 'I'll have to see if I can get away. Is Al there?'

'He's inside with Josh.'

'I'll give him a ring.'

'Right. Well …'

'I said I'd try, Non. I'll call you in a bit.'

'Okay then.' I don't seem to be able to keep the petulant note out of my voice. I hate myself for it.

I stand for a while after Rob has gone, staring at the ugly multi-coloured building in front of me. Then I try Malcolm. He takes even longer to pick up.

'Hi Norna.' He sounds weary and distant. I picture him having just got off a long-haul flight somewhere.

'Where are you?'

There's a pause before he answers. 'In Edinburgh.'

'You're here? How long have you been here?'

'Don't, Norna.'

I process this information, the fact he hasn't even been to see Mum. The tone of his voice. I picture DS Ellen Chisholm. The dead man in the garage.

'What did you call for?' Malcolm's voice brings me back to life. I realise I've stalled.

'Josh has been stabbed. He's in the Infirmary. I'm here now.'

Malcolm doesn't say anything.

'Al could use some support.'

Still nothing. 'Malcolm? Are you still there?'

He clears his throat. 'That's terrible …'

'Will you come? To the hospital?'

'Let me know how … Things go. Will you? I've got to go.'

I stand there with the phone to my ear long after he's gone, as if he might just reappear on the other end. I'm too numb to feel angry.

When the old boy with a roll-up wedged between his missing teeth starts wheeling his saline drip towards me I realise it's time to go back inside.

I follow the yellow line on the floor back to Josh's ward. He's asleep, with Mel dozing in the chair by his side. Al isn't back from the canteen, which is probably a good thing. I was afraid he was going to send the machines haywire, he was giving off such a charge. It's the first time I've really seen Al like this. Rob told me his anger was scary sometimes, but I haven't truly felt it until now. I hope for their own sake that whoever did this gets locked up before he can get to them.

'How's he doing?' Finlay Groat steps quietly into the room. His voice is low so as not to disturb Josh or Mel. I see that he's brought a Nintendo 2DS, at the same time both thoughtful and flashy. And completely stupid to have in a hospital where valuables vanish into thin antiseptic air. I want to hug him.

'They still don't know the full extent of the damage, but he's out of danger. He was awake earlier. Not making much sense, though. '

'How could you tell?' He smiles. 'What about you?'

'I'm okay.'

'I went back to where we found him, but by the time I got there the police were there and they had tape blocking off the path.'

'Why did you go back?'

'To look for the knife. You said you thought it was his.'

'Yes, but ... What were you going to do if you found it?'

'I don't know. I was worried he'd get into trouble.'

I look at Josh, who makes so little impression beneath the covers he seems to have melted. 'I don't think it could be worse.'

We sit for a while, occasionally making polite conversation. The ward is quiet because the hospital sends as many people home for the weekend as possible. When Al comes back he and Finlay talk for a bit. Mel wakes up and goes to the loo. Finlay tries to explain what a DS is to them both. They thought it was a police officer. Josh sleeps.

When Finlay offers me a lift home I accept gladly. He puts on some music in the car: Richard Hawley, 'Nothing Like a Friend'. It makes me feel sad and nostalgic. I feel like I'm in a film, watching the streets pass from the windows of the car.

'Do you mind if we just pop by my Dad's?' he asks as we get near home. 'I need to pick up some prospectuses for tomorrow.'

'Are you working tomorrow?'

'Sunday viewings. It's the only time a lot of clients can make it.'

'Of course. Do you do them yourself, then? You don't have staff to do that?'

'I still do my bit. Mainly the high-end stuff, I have to admit. So is that okay?'

'Sure.'

It's not really. Lawrence is possibly the last person I want to see right now. Second only to another police officer.

'I'll just wait in the car,' I say as we draw up outside the house.

'No, come in. He'd kill me if I left you out here. He'll want to hear how Josh is. We'll just pop in.'

We don't, though. Just pop in. For some reason, after Lawrence has enquired after Josh and Mum, and when he presses a sherry on me and then brings out some nibbles, I stay. And after he's regaled me with tales of his and Dad's 1970s fashion faux pas and I've begun to feel as though I've rooted in his voluptuous armchair by the fire, when he offers a bit of supper I accept. And I find that he's not as awful as I'd imagined him to be.

Not until he helps me on with my coat and gives me a goodbye hug when we take our leave, anyway.

It's late by the time Finlay pulls up outside our house. I can tell from the low light downstairs and the curtained windows upstairs that Mum and the children have already gone to bed. I click off my seatbelt and turn to Finlay, who is waiting without expectation. 'Do you want to come in?'

His face lights up, but he checks himself, quickly. 'You're shattered, though,' he says. Then, 'I'll come in for a bit, but no silly business.'

He's a funny man, is Finlay.

'Rob disapproves of me hanging out with you,' I tell him as I unlock the door.

'So I gather,' he whispers as we tiptoe inside, and I'm glad it's dark in the hall because I flush with embarrassment to think that Rob must have said something to Al and Al to Finlay.

Finlay is right. I'm shattered. Astro is karate-chopping the backs of my eyeballs and high-kicking the walls of my skull as if she's trying to break out. I don't last long.

When I wake a few hours later I have a vague recollection of the conversation petering out and a sense of quiet companionship as we listened to some music. I find that he has left one corner lamp on but switched off the others. He's washed our wine glasses, and brought the travel rug from under the stairs and laid it across me.

And I think to myself: Rob can go stuff himself.

43

It was Sunday. Ellen was not good at weekends. A little better at holidays, if she had a project, or if she went away. With an itinerary. And even then only after the first couple of days. Often she was only just getting the hang of it when it was time to return to work. This was the trouble with not having a boyfriend, she thought. Having Chris around had meant always having something to do on a Sunday. During the week she didn't miss him at all and on a Saturday she could usually find someone to hang out with, but when an empty Sunday came along she had to remind herself that it hadn't been perfect; that while they had had fun together she had dreaded his sister's wedding and resented the assumption she would attend his niece's christening. The suggestion of a joint holiday with his parents had sent their relationship into a tailspin. She thought of calling Claire, but wasn't Sunday the day people with children had lunch with Granny and Grandad or did other sacrosanct family type stuff? It felt somehow out of bounds. And what kind of company would she be, anyway? She felt closed in on herself. Both vulnerable and spiky at the same time. She didn't feel much like socialising.

She was at serious risk of doing some work.

One of the hardest things Ellen had had to learn in the early days was that it wasn't always urgent. She found it hard to accept that time was wasted by lies and missed opportunities, near misses, concealed truths. And by people knocking off for the night. She had to be told to go home sometimes, to take a break. She had to learn to accept that it could take weeks or months to uncover the truth, and that sometimes they didn't. She thought she had got the hang of that now, but working on a case that had its origins twenty-six years in the past was testing her patience.

Working on the murder of the man who had taught

her patience was testing it further. Having his integrity questioned, was testing her temper.

Ellen went and stood at the bay window of her top floor flat. If she looked north, to her right, she could see a small triangle of the Firth of Forth and the Fife coastline beyond between the apartments on the spit of land jutting into Newhaven harbour. It was a murky day but even the weather lacked conviction. Rain was spitting at her window half-heartedly. There were few people out and about, despite it being almost lunchtime.

If Barber was not to be trusted, who was?

She could handle him being wrong. Mixed up and grieving as he still must have been at the end. But she could not face the idea that he was corrupt. He had been the first person she had trusted since ... Well, since she stopped trusting anyone.

She went through to the kitchen to fetch a pad of paper and a pen, automatically stepping round the bag of Chris's stuff that still sat in the narrow hallway, only afterwards noticing that she had done so. She went to nudge it further against the wall with her toe, but as she did so the realisation hit her: he wasn't coming back for it. Not today, not next weekend, not ever. That bag had been sitting there for – she made the calculation – almost ten weeks now. A couple of t-shirts and a pair of boxer shorts, a toothbrush, a stick of deodorant and a paperback. He was never coming back for any of it. He'd moved on.

Well, so had she, hadn't she? After all, if she hadn't even registered that so much time had passed, she must have, mustn't she?

Or did that just say more about why he had left in the end?

She picked up the bag and stuffed the whole lot into the kitchen bin, then returned to the window where she sat down on a large floor cushion with the pad on her lap. From memory she began to trace Barber's movements in the days preceding his death. Inevitably there would be details she would not remember, but she had found that sometimes this helped. Away from the incident room and its clutter of facts she found that she could sometimes cut through the layers of information that built quickly around a murder case.

She started with Barber at one end of the page, dead in the Gilchrist's garage, and at the other, Ronald Gilchrist attempting to contact him. Barber had made three attempts to see Gilchrist in the hospital, each of which had failed. In desperation, he had turned to her in the hope she might be able to access the family. She had wondered why her? Why not Vihaan? Why not any of the other officers who had served under him. She had quickly realised: it was the old Ellen he was hoping to persuade. He wanted to tap into some of that old reckless impulsiveness.

For a moment she was distracted, thinking about Calder and the look he had given her when he'd owned up to meeting Barber outside the station the night before Ronald Gilchrist's funeral. Something Barber had said about her? Or was she being over-sensitive?

She made a note of Barber's visit to the station and the phone conversation he had had with Starrett the same night. He had not let go of the case, despite Gilchrist's death. Earlier that day she noted his visit to the site of Ronald Gilchrist's hardware shop. He had been walking in Connor Leask's footsteps.

Where had he been before that? That was the day he went to meet Sharon Harkins. Asking about Ralston. And about Kinley. She thought of the maps and plans that Calder had received from Farhana McLean and his theory that Connor had worked out where Dean Owens' body was buried. Keisha had traced the forensic anthropologist who had examined the bones found in the landslip to a retirement village in the Borders. It hadn't been straightforward estimating the length of time the body had been there, she said, given the effects of the limestone and waterlogging.

It was proving even harder to find any trace of Dean Owens for comparison.

Had Barber drawn the same conclusion as Connor about Dean Owens? Did he know how the boy fitted into all this? What was it Glen Starrett had said? Maybe it's the thing got him killed, not that he was right? Starrett had been talking about the Gilchrists and Barber's obsession with them, but what if it was simply the case that, while focusing on Connor Leask's death, Barber had stumbled upon something else?

She wondered whether Barber had discovered who killed Connor before he died. She hoped he had. She wanted that for him at least.

Thinking about Glen Starrett gave her an idea for what she could do with her afternoon. Calder had suggested that Starrett's local history knowledge might provide them with a picture of the Moredun area in the early 1990s, and even the layout of the old mine, help them to determine where the remains that might be Dean Owens had been dumped originally, before the landslip had disturbed much of the ground. Starrett was also someone who had known Barber, and for whatever reason, that felt important right now.

After a quick phone call she was on her way to his house, stopping off to buy a packet of chocolate mini-rolls on the way.

*

Starrett looked tired, greyer than she remembered, but pleased to see her all the same, and again she had the sense he didn't receive many visitors. This time he led her through a glass-panelled door off the kitchen into a dining room where he had already set up a laptop and laid out some maps. A notebook and pen sat at the ready. She stood in the doorway, making small talk while he made them coffee.

'You're not from Edinburgh, yourself?' he asked.

She shook her head. 'Aberdeen. Though it's been a long time since I lived there.'

'Your boss, though. He's a local boy, is he not?'

'Yeah. Only been back in the city for a couple of years, though. He was in Glasgow for ten years. Dundee before that.'

'What's he like to work for? He didn't give much away the other day.'

'No. He doesn't.' She didn't want to talk about Calder.

Starrett fumbled with the packet of mini-rolls, his thick fingers not as dexterous as they must once have been, but she didn't think he would appreciate an offer of assistance.

'This you taking my advice about taking up a hobby?' he asked with a wink when they settled at the dining room table.

She grinned. 'If you make a good enough case for it today, I'll think about it.'

'After you phoned I made a quick search. I couldn't find very much about the landslip you mentioned.' He pressed the touchpad of the laptop and the screen sprang to life. 'This is the best I could do, really. There are a couple of other articles but mainly they're about whether the Council was culpable for the collapse – it was decided they weren't, by the way – and how much the homeowners had to fork out on top of the insurance to get their houses rebuilt.'

Ellen skimmed through the article on the screen. She thought it was probably the one Calder had already found, primarily concerned with the geology of the area, describing the waterlogging and the resulting landslip, illustrated with diagrams and photographs showing the damage to the streets and houses. She peered at the caption to one of them: Ferniehill Terrace.

Starrett spread one of the maps out on the table. It was an orange OS map of the city. Large scale.

'Do I get to know what this is about? I take it it's not the Barber case.'

Ellen took a moment to answer. She made it look as though she was peering at the map, but she was really thinking about how much she could say. She remembered Calder's terse words: He's a suspect.

'A body was found. When they demolished the houses after the landslip. They couldn't tell how it had ended up there, or when exactly.'

'Another cold case? Have you switched jobs?'

She smiled. 'We think Jimmy might have been looking into it.'

'So it wasn't about Connor Leask after all? You think it's to do with something else he was investigating?'

'He never mentioned this to you?'

Starrett shook his head. He knew the limits to what she could say and he didn't push it. He bent over the map, pointing. 'Well, this whole area would have been riddled with old shafts and caverns. The kinds of places teenagers love to hang out. Easy to get lost or trapped in. Got a cause of death?'

'No.' The remains were to be re-examined but she didn't hold out much hope. And besides, they weren't going to identify the killer or killers by MO alone. Lee Quigley's death, if not an accident, was made to look like one. Connor was stabbed on the street. Jimmy was struck on the back of the head.

Starrett straightened up. She noticed the tremble again. 'Why didn't he just apply for a job working cold cases and get paid for doing all this?'

Ellen smiled. 'Why don't you, if you're into history?'

'Ach. Different thing. Here.' He pulled the laptop closer and moved his fingers across the touch pad. 'You said something about the prefabs as well. This is more what I'm into. Take a look at that.'

He turned the screen to face Ellen. On it there was a black and white aerial photograph. It showed a large building in the centre, and fanning out from it in an oval formation were rows and rows of small, neat houses.

'That's the old school at Moredun and all those are prefabs. The scheme was built after the Second World War.'

'But it's all gone now?'

'Mmm. But there are still a few prefabs dotted about, in Gilmerton and Craigour.'

'When was the area redeveloped?'

'Mid-Nineties.' He looked disappointed. He'd wanted her to be interested in the pre-fabs, not their destruction, but it had made Ellen think.

'Not the early Nineties?'

'No.' He frowned quizzically, but didn't ask. 'It had been proposed in the late Eighties I think, maybe early

Nineties, but there were protests. A lot of people wanted to keep the prefabs, make them viable. It's not just the buildings themselves, though a lot of people are really fond of them, but whenever they regenerate an area the existing community is displaced, scattered. It's never the same again.'

Connor Leask died in 1993. If the area hadn't been redeveloped until the mid-Nineties, the plans he'd made notes on, the ones drawn up by Kinley Developments, must only have been speculative. Ellen sighed. If they were not actually doing any building at the time, the theory that someone might have disposed of Dean Owens' body on one of Kinley's building sites had just gone up in smoke.

'You're thinking hard,' Starrett said. There was a hint of a smile in his voice.

Ellen rolled her eyes and sighed, frustrated. 'I need to stop. I'm just going round in circles.'

The phrase made her think of the old Noel Harrison song again. It had taken her days to get it out of her head after Barber's murder. It had not helped her sense of frustration and confusion. The memory of him lying on the cold concrete floor, his congealing blood thick in the cracks, made her push her toes into the floor.

'What was he doing there? I mean...'

'You do need to stop. You just said it. You'll get as bad as him.'

'I know, but how could he be such an idiot?'

Starrett didn't have time to answer. Ellen made an apologetic face at him as her phone rang.

'Take it.' He put their empty mugs on the tray and pushed himself up using the table for support.

It was Liam on the phone. 'Something's come up I think you're going to want to know about.'

'Hang on.'

Starrett knew what she was going to say already.

'I'm going to have to go, sorry.'

'How it goes,' he said, patting her on the arm. 'Thanks for the chocolate rolls.'

He saw her out, and waved her off with the same lazy

salute he'd given them before.

'What is it, Liam?'

'Got a call from a mate of mine from North West. Apparently there was an incident on Corstorphine Hill on Thursday night in which a fifteen-year-old was stabbed with his own knife.'

Ellen stopped abruptly at the bottom of Starrett's drive.

'Boy by the name of Josh Gilchrist? Alistair Gilchrist's son.'

'I'm on my way.'

Liam hadn't finished. 'And get this, the knife used to belong to his father. And to his grandfather before that.'

'It's a Stanley knife.'

'It is indeed.'

44

After Strontian the road became even more narrow and winding. Dan's suspension creaked in protest as he lurched over deep ruts in the road caused by the late frost and recent spring rains, but Dan didn't care. This was the kind of country he loved. Ardnamurchan in the west of Scotland: remote, rugged, sparsely peopled.

It was the rhododendrons that told him he was nearing his destination. He turned into a discreetly signposted driveway and followed it up the hillside until it opened out onto a circular gravelled area around a small green with a disused fountain in the middle. Mudle House was a former Victorian hunting lodge, a stone building complete with turrets and even a faux rampart.

Dan got out of the car and pulled on his jacket. The air was cold and moist, but it was fresh. He could almost taste the pines. He crunched across the gravel and pressed the doorbell. A deep clanging echoed within. After a few minutes, he tried knocking instead and this time it was the sound of his fist on the heavy door which resounded. There was no answer. He glanced over at the garage block but the doors were closed. He couldn't tell whether anyone was home.

After a few minutes more he decided to try the back of the house. In a place this size, it might be easy not to hear the door. Turning the corner of the house he stopped. A terrace and landscaped gardens gave way to open land that ran right down to the lochside where there was a small jetty and a boathouse. The view was spectacular. Moorland and mountain, the sea in the distance and the islands of the Inner Hebrides. This was Dan's idea of paradise. Actually, he could have done without the landscaped gardens and the big house. A small bothy, though, and all that stretching out in front of him – heaven.

He hadn't intended to come here. He'd set off with his walking gear but something tugged him north and westwards, past the Rannoch moor and on through Glencoe.

There was no sign of anyone as he continued round the house, peering into a large drawing room through French windows that led off the terrace. Everywhere was in darkness. He passed a kitchen and came to an external door leading into a porch that was clearly used as a kind of boot room. He tried the handle and to his surprise it opened. He hesitated, then curiosity got the better of him.

'Hello!'

No answer. The building smelt old. Familiar in a way that made him think of youth hostels. Something to do with the combination of cooking and damp stone, fresh air and socks drying on radiators. He was in a small passageway between the kitchen itself and what must once have been the pantry and scullery, but now seemed to be used as storage space for a variety of hunting and fishing equipment.

Stepping into the kitchen he felt the difference in the air and looked instinctively towards the obligatory Aga. Someone was here, or had been recently. It was warm.

Even as he thought it, he heard a sound in the passageway behind him and turned. Too late. The blow struck him on the back of the head, hard. He was out before he hit the floor.

45

Ellen listened to the automated recording for Dan Calder's voicemail for the third time and decided to give up. She had left a message the first time. He would pick it up eventually. Still, some of the old impatience stirred inside her. Of all the weekends he could have decided to go stomping up a hill, he picked this one. She turned to where Liam was waiting for her at the entrance to the hospital.

'How is the boy doing?'

'He's out of danger. They say he'll make a full recovery.'

'Do we know what happened, yet?'

'They took a preliminary statement after he first regained consciousness. Sounds like he stumbled upon a group of kids who thought it would be a bit of fun to put the frighteners on him. He got scared, pulled the knife on them, but in the struggle he was the one who got stabbed.'

'Tell me about this knife, then?'

'It was recovered from the scene of the attack.' Liam held out his mobile phone and Ellen took it. On the screen was a photograph of a Stanley knife, a heavy-duty one, old-fashioned. Ellen flicked through the next few images. The blade was red with blood and there were smears of it on the handle and pooled in the dimples of the textured metal and between the letters of the impressed brand name. In some shots she made out what looked like tiny fragments of fabric. Then she came to a close-up of initials scratched into the handle: A G. The 'A' was clumsy, overworked. It had once been an 'R'.

'What's Alistair saying?'

'He has no idea how his son got the knife. He hasn't seen it for years.'

'But you've sent it for testing?'

'Well, technically it's not ours to send – yet – but yes, they've agreed to put a rush on it.'

'Well, let's see what his son has to say for himself.'

They paused outside Josh Gilchrist's room and looking at the boy in the bed for a moment Ellen had a flashback to another time. To another person – a teenage girl – lying in a hospital bed. She wondered whether Josh would be famous now amongst his school friends. Whether they would treat him with the same kind of reverent awe that Donna had received. She shook herself free of the memory.

Alistair Gilchrist was hovering at his son's bedside. His wife sat, holding her son's hand in hers but although there was another chair there Alistair seemed too pent-up to sit. He was pacing. He stopped when Ellen and Liam appeared, and growled at them. 'What are you doing here?'

'We'd like a few words with Josh.' She looked at the boy. 'If you're up to it? We have some questions about what happened.'

'Why? What's this got to do with you?'

'Al.' His wife's voice silenced him.

On the bed Josh had turned his face away from his father.

Melanie Gilchrist stood up and took Alistair by the arm. 'Go easy on him,' she said to Ellen and Liam. Ellen was about to ask her to stay – her son was only fifteen after all – when she realised that Norna Gilchrist was also in the room. She was sitting quietly in the corner to the right of the door. She looked wan and Ellen thought she was on the edge of tears.

Ellen turned back to Melanie Gilchrist briefly and nodded at her gratefully. She waited until she and Alistair had left the room then sat down at Josh's bedside.

'How are you?'

'I'll mend.'

'Are you up to telling me what happened?'

He took a moment but when he spoke his voice was steady enough. 'I went out, up the hill. To the tower?'

'I know where you mean.'

'I wasn't going to do anything. I just wanted some space. From my dad. He was doing my head in.'

Ellen could understand that. 'Go on.'

'I heard voices when I got nearer. They had some cans and they were smoking and stuff. I turned back but they must have seen me.'

'How many?'

'Four. I think.'

'Did you know them?'

'I think one of them goes to my school. I didn't really recognise the others. It was pretty dark and they mostly had their hoods up.'

'So you went back down the hill. They followed you?'

'Yeah. I didn't realise at first, then I started hearing noises and I heard them sniggering. I think they thought it was some kind of game. But I ...' He broke off and his face contorted. Suddenly he looked like a little boy and Ellen thought about how frightened he must have been up there in the woods on the hillside, in the dark, being pursued, taunted.

'That must have been pretty scary.'

He turned his face away. 'They followed me right the way round. They were calling me names and throwing stuff, sometimes at me and sometimes in the bushes so I didn't know which direction they were coming from. They started gaining on me when I got nearer the edge of the woods. I thought, they're not going to let me get out.'

'What happened next?'

'I had the knife in my pocket and I got the blade out. I just meant to threaten them with it. I never meant to stab anyone. But then two of them jumped me and I panicked.'

'How did you end up getting stabbed?'

'When they saw the knife one of them grabbed my arm and tried to take it off me. I held on, and he kind of twisted my arm round. They were laughing at me and the other one was beating on me and I was trying to fight them both off at the same time. I couldn't keep hold of the knife. He got it and I don't know what happened next. I thought he just punched me and then it was as though he was dragging me down to the ground. I don't remember much after that.'

Ellen waited. Josh Gilchrist had begun crying silently. She thought he probably didn't even realise he was doing it.

When she thought he would be able to answer again, she asked him, gently, 'Where did you get the knife from?'

'I nicked it from my Dad.'

46

The first thing Dan saw when he opened his eyes was a pair of hairy legs sprouting from some suede moccasins that had seen better days. His head hurt.

'Who the bloody hell are you and what are you doing in my kitchen?'

The legs disappeared into a charcoal grey towelling dressing gown. Dan didn't want to look much further than that. 'Police,' he said, feeling for his ID.

There was a pause. 'Well, why the bloody hell didn't you say so?"

It was a fair point. 'I hadn't got round to it.'

'Well, come on then, let's get you up.'

Mitchell Kinley bent to grab hold of Dan's arm and he caught a strong whiff of stale whisky. Kinley had a large, affable face, very little hair – on his head at least – and the kind of tilt to his eyebrows that made him look permanently amused. Perhaps he was amused.

'What did you hit me with?' Dan asked as Kinley hauled him to his feet.

'Hunting stick.' Kinley indicated the stick. It had a stake at one end for driving into the ground, and at the other the handle opened into a leather seat. Dan felt his head, gingerly. There didn't seem to be too much damage done. He'd had worse.

'You're not going to arrest me are you?' Kinley said.

'I haven't made up my mind yet.'

'I've got some very good brandy. That'll sort you out.'

'A drink of water would be fine.'

Kinley poured them each a glass of water and downed his in one, then poured another.

'Bit of a night, was it?' Dan asked. It was three in the afternoon and Kinley had clearly just got up.

'Was out on the boat all night. Nothing beats a bit of

night fishing. Do you fish?'

'No.'

'Well, you haven't tried night fishing.'

Sitting on a boat getting pissed, in other words, Dan thought. 'Did you catch much?'

By way of answer, Kinley swung open the door of his fridge-freezer. Three large fish gawped out at Dan. He wasn't sure what to say to that. 'Very good.' He fought back a wave of nausea. 'Mr Kinley – '

'Mitch, please.'

'Mitch. I came because I'd like to ask you some questions. You may be able to help with a current enquiry.'

'Right. Fire away.'

'You don't want to get dressed first? I can wait.'

'Oh. Sure. Yeah. Well, listen, you go through and have a seat and I'll join you in a minute.' He jabbed a finger down the passageway.

Dan followed the finger and found himself in a large wood-panelled hallway. It had its own fireplace, set high on a rough, slabbed platform, with small recesses set into the stone surround. An open door led into the drawing room he had seen from the terrace. From the outside he had not been able to make out much of the interior. He found, to his surprise, that it was elegantly but sparsely furnished. He had expected paintings of pheasants, and stags' heads mounted on the wall. Sharon Harkins had told him that Kinley was playing at being Laird. Instead he found the room almost bare apart from seating, lighting, a well-stocked bookshelf and a large open fireplace. Instinctively he was drawn to the windows, and as he waited for Kinley to join him he stared out at the expanse of land, sea and sky.

When Kinley arrived he brought with him a flask of coffee, a plate of sandwiches and a packet of biscuits. 'Help yourself,' he said.

'Do you stay here by yourself?' Dan asked.

'Lot of the time,' Kinley said, tucking into a ham sandwich. 'Wife doesn't much like it here, to be honest. She's fine when the whole family is here and it's a bit of an event. Christmas, and the grandchildren's school holidays. But she'd rather be in the city. That suits me fine.' He winked at Dan. 'So what can I help you with?'

Dan had had plenty of time to think about how to put this to Kinley, without it sounding as though he was accusing him of anything, but it wasn't going to be easy. 'Does the name James Barber mean anything to you?'

'Nope. Who's he, then?'

'He was a retired detective. I thought he might have tried to contact you sometime within the last month, about an old murder case he had been involved with.'

Kinley shook his head. 'But then, I don't get mobile reception here, and half the time I turn off the ringer on the landline.'

That explained why they hadn't managed to get hold of him either.

'Barber was reinvestigating the murder of Connor Leask in 1993.' He looked for a reaction. 'Leask was one of your tenants? A trainee procurator fiscal, mentored by Lise Eklund.'

'Lise. Oh, yes, she's a great pal of mine. Lovely girl.'

Dan had to pause to take that in. 'This is a bit awkward. It seems Connor Leask had been doing a bit of detective work himself, before he died. I suspect it started with a case he had been given at work, and then he couldn't let it go. You're familiar with a man called Norris Ralston?'

'Oh, yeah. Dodgy Norris.'

'Dodgy Norris?'

'Mmm. They got him in the end, didn't they. He's dead now, though, I think?'

'Yes. Died in prison. I have to ask: did you know he was dodgy before he was arrested?'

'I heard some rumours. When it all came out I was shocked at the scale of it. And the drugs: that was a surprise.'

'Were you ever questioned as part of any investigation into Ralston?'

Kinley stopped chewing and looked at Dan, suspiciously. 'Do I need a lawyer here?'

'I hope not. I haven't come all this way to have to sit

and wait for a lawyer to turn up.'

Kinley shrugged. 'Yeah, someone came along and asked me questions. I told them what I could. They went away. End of story.'

'Did you do a lot of business with Ralston?'

'Yeah, we had a good thing going for a while. When I started to scale up I struggled to meet all the up-front costs of the developments. I negotiated a deal with Norris – he gave me discounted building materials and labour in return for a cut of the profits. It was good arrangement.'

'And you never had any suspicions he might be involved in anything illegal?'

'Well, I wouldn't have been surprised to hear he did a bit of trade on the side, as it were. Or got some of his stuff from suspect sources, you know, looting beaches for pretty pebbles or using wood from endangered trees.'

'He was involved in your charity, too? The training scheme.'

'Yeah. It's not too hard to sign folk up to that. Good for the public image and it's tax deductible.' He grinned at Dan. 'I'd rather be able to choose what my hard-earned money gets spent on, wouldn't you? Can't trust the politicians to spend it wisely. Present company excepted, of course. This kind of diligence, that's what I like to see in a public servant.'

Dan smiled. From someone else that might have sounded offensive, but there was something disarmingly forthright about Mitchell Kinley.

'Do you mind if I ask you about Lee Quigley?'

'Who's that then?'

'He did one of your training schemes.'

Kinley looked blank. 'I didn't get involved much personally. I did a bit of press and a few motivational speeches but that was it really.'

'I gather Lee Quigley caused a bit of embarrassment to the charity, though. He was asked to leave, and subsequently caught stealing from construction sites. The press got hold of it.'

'Ah, that I do remember. That was him, was it? So,

what's he up to now?'

Dan was surprised. 'He's not up to anything. He's been dead since 1992. He was killed on a construction site he was thought to be trying to rob while on probation, not long after all the news stories came out.'

'You're losing me, Inspector. What's your interest in him, then?'

'Honestly? I'm beginning to wonder. But both Connor Leask and James Barber seemed to think his death was linked to Ralston in some way.'

Kinley shrugged. 'Can't help you there, I'm afraid. But if you ask my son Graeme he'll give you access to all our records. If that lad was placed with Ralston it'll say.'

'Thanks. Do you remember the landslip in Moredun?

Kinley frowned. 'Yeah?'

'Were they your houses that got damaged?'

'No, I did do a development that replaced the old prefabs near there. Mid-Nineties. But mine survived the slip.'

'When did you build, exactly?'

'First sod cut in ... Ninety-five I think? I'd have to check.'

Dan frowned. 'Are you sure it wasn't earlier than that?'

'Absolutely. I was itching to go ahead much earlier only there was some local resistance. Dragged on. Sentimental crap, if you ask me.

'Look, son. If I'm completely honest, I greased a few palms in the council from time to time, but that's about the extent of it. I'm not bent and I never was. I heard a few rumours about Norris Ralston but I never got close to finding out how true they were and I never knew anyone else who had cause to use his services. I will admit a little birdie tipped me off when he was being investigated and as soon as I heard that I distanced myself from him and that was that.'

A little birdie? Hugh Baird or Lise Eklund, Dan suspected.

'What did you do for labour and materials after he was arrested?'

'Plenty other suppliers out there. And the labour was

always Lawrence's side of things, anyway. To all intents and purposes it was a separate business by then. Drylaw Build and Repair.'

'Is this Lawrence Groat?'

'That's right.'

'I thought his business was self-titled?'

'It is now he's gone up in the world. Drylaw doesn't exactly chime with a classier breed of customer in Edinburgh. But back then he was cheap as chips and we did good business.'

'I'm confused. His company supplied the labour for your projects?'

'Yes, well it became his company in the end. There were rumours about that too. Started out as a side-shoot of Ralston's. Lawrence worked for Norris. Maybe Norris saw the way the wind was blowing, maybe it was some kind of tax dodge, but he had the company transferred into Lawrence's name not long before he was arrested. It meant that when they seized the business they couldn't touch that.'

He could see Dan wasn't following. 'Which meant there was some money left in the pot for Ralston's wife and daughter. Considering Norris's assets had been frozen Charlene and Trinny left for New Zealand surprisingly wealthy women. The general consensus in the Rotary was that Lawrence paid out in exchange for full ownership of the business.'

'So Lawrence Groat did very nicely out of Ralston, then? And his conviction. Just so I'm clear, both when it was under Ralston and when it was under his own name, Lawrence Groat managed the labour for your projects?'

'More than that. He site-managed the developments.'

'So he would have had copies of your plans?'

'Of course.' Kinley slapped his thighs. 'Right, well. Anything else? My fishing permit's up to date.'

It was probably his loch, Dan thought.

'Ready for that brandy?'

'I should get going, really,' Dan said, getting up. 'Thanks, though.'

As Kinley walked him to the door, he asked, 'I don't

suppose the name Franjo Horvat means anything to you?'

'Frank Horvat? Yeah, I remember him. Big surly bloke, could put vodka away like it was pop. Handy to have on site, though.'

'He was a labourer?'

'Oh, yes. Good one, too. It was a shame when he left.'

'Where did he go?'

'Home I assume. One of those Eastern Bloc countries it was, I think.'

'So he worked for Groat, not Ralston?'

Kinley shrugged. 'Same difference.'

Dan stepped out onto the gravel and pointed his key fob at his car. Kinley looked amused but he refrained from saying anything about car thieves or the lack of, half way up a hill in the middle of nowhere.

Something was nagging at Dan. A turn of phrase Kinley had used. 'Earlier, you said something about not knowing anyone who needed Ralston's services. What did you mean by that?'

'You know. He had a reputation. Someone you could go to if you were in a bit of a fix. I assumed you knew that.'

'What kind of a fix?'

'Well, since he was done for money laundering, I would think money trouble. Wouldn't you?'

Dan thought about it, but he was not so sure he would. He thought Ralston might have been fixing problems more prosaically. He thought he might have been simply making problems go away.

Or someone working for him was.

*

He mulled it over as he drove. By the time he reached the Corran Ferry the idea had solidified. Ralston was a building supplies merchant. He wasn't a builder. He provided materials for construction sites, but he didn't work on them. Lawrence Groat did. Groat did all sorts of building jobs, big and small. Garages and extensions, refurbishments and renovations, new builds and rebuilds.

He got out of the car and stood on deck for the duration of the short crossing, stretching his back as he looked down Loch Linnhe, watching the movement of the hills and the glowering sky reflected in its glassy surface.

Did Ronald Gilchrist know what Lawrence was up to? Was that what he had wanted to tell Barber? He and Groat had been close friends and colleagues for years. Perhaps he had witnessed something? Or Alistair had. If Dan was right and all this came to light Lawrence Groat would lose everything. Even the suspicion that he might have been involved in something like this, the damage to his company's reputation might be enough to destroy him.

He had been at the Gilchrists' house the day Barber was murdered.

Dan followed the short line of traffic that rolled off the ferry as far as Onich, then pulled off the road beside the tea room and stores. He took out his phone. The signal wasn't great but it was one bar better than nothing and he saw that he had several missed calls. He listened to the message Ellen had left him and suddenly all his theories fell away. He called her.

'What's this about Alistair Gilchrist's knife?'

She told him about Josh and the knife he had been carrying. 'We're having it checked for Connor Leask's DNA.'

'Have you taken him in for questioning?'

'I was about to.'

Dan stared at the black clouds amassing over the mountain across the water. He should know which one it was, he thought. He'd walked it's eastern flank once, from Ballachulish. He tried to piece together the news from Ellen with what he had learned from Kinley.

'If his kid's in hospital, he's not going anywhere. It can keep 'til tomorrow. We don't know for sure it's the knife that killed Connor Leask and I've got some questions of my own for him.'

'Where are you?' Ellen asked.

'Onich. I've been to see Mitchell Kinley.'

'What?'

'I know. I was there before I knew it.' He told her what Kinley had said about Ralston's reputation for problem solving. He told her something of what he had been thinking on the drive. 'I don't know how much any of this is relevant now. Let alone, how close to the truth it is.'

'It would explain how Dean Owens fits in. I mean, say he'd been killed as a result of a sexual encounter with a client that went wrong? Would that be the kind of trouble you went to Ralston for? Or Groat? Do you think it was what Jimmy and Connor Leask were onto?'

'Maybe. But if your knife theory is correct, we need to make sense of why Alistair Gilchrist might kill Connor Leask to stop it getting out.'

'Alistair worked for Groat. Ronald did work for him too. The business was struggling in the early Nineties. Linda and Margery Shanks both said it was Lawrence Groat they had to thank for seeing them through those hard times. They needed him. More than that, they owed him.'

'Mmm. Or they were implicated.'

47

Al is not in Josh's room when I arrive at the hospital for visiting hours. Apparently he's gone down to the shop to get Josh a magazine and some chocolate. Mel is here, with Kirsty and Sam. Kirsty can't decide whether to sulk because of the attention Josh is getting or whether she can use the whole episode to her own advantage.

God, I'm mean.

The same detectives wouldn't investigate murder and this kind of incident, would they? So why have those detectives been asking questions? DS Chisholm and that rumpled DC who was kind to Mum, but whose benign charm might be a cunning disguise. It's not about Josh being attacked, is it? It's about the knife he was carrying. And the fact it used to be Al's.

I try to think my way through it. I feel I must have the solution, but my brain is mashed. It feels like constant white noise. Unidentified invoices and lists of the names of police officers, and Malcolm and Rob not even caring about what's happened to Josh, and Josh carrying a knife that used to belong to Al that used to belong to Dad. I mean, what kind of a fucking heirloom is that? It's making me question everything I think I know about all of us.

I decide to go and find Al. I hear the footsteps in the corridor before I have even left the room. Purposeful. DS Chisholm is back, with two uniformed officers.

'Hello, Norna.' They stop at the door. 'How is he?'

'He seems much better.'

'That's good. Is your brother around?'

'No, just Mel.' I don't know why I lie. Instinct, maybe. 'I was about to head off myself.'

DS Chisholm is peering at me. 'How are you?' she asks.

'Fine. Could do with a kip.' I never say kip.

I force a smile and walk past them down the ward,

trying to go at a normal pace. I will Al not to appear before I am safely out of sight, past the nurses' station and out in the main corridor. There I break into a jog. Round the bend into another corridor and I'm running now.

Downstairs I meet Al coming the other way. He's just passing the canteen. 'What's the matter?' I see panic flash across his face.

'It's not Josh,' I pant, pushing him into the canteen. 'Police. Looking for you.'

He squeezes his eyes shut. Nods. It's not the reaction I was expecting. I don't like it.

'What's going on, Al?'

He guides me over to a quiet corner behind the recycling bins and the trolley they collect used trays on.

'They're going to question me again about the murder in 1993.'

'Why?'

'And I'm going to have to tell them I lied about not seeing the man who was murdered that night.'

'What?'

'I didn't do it, Non. You have to believe me. Will you look after Mel and Josh for me if I'm away a while?'

'Why would you be away a while?' My voice has risen an octave.

'Josh told me they were asking about the knife. It was mine. I know what they're going to think.'

My head is spinning now. I think I'm going to be sick. 'Why does that make a difference? What do you mean you saw that guy? How come you never said?'

'I saw him with Malcolm.'

I stare at him. I don't know what he's telling me. 'You're not saying Malcolm did it.' I feel my anger rising. Not just at Al, the idea that he would put the blame on Malcolm as if this was just about a broken window or because someone else started it. It's not just because I'm sick of the squabbling and bitching and the tit-for-tat: it's that sense of being left out of everything again. The feeling that all along, everyone else has known what's going on and stupid Little Non has been none the wiser.

Al gets hold of me by my shoulders. His grip is strong. It hurts. 'I saw them together,' he hisses, and the truth dawns.

'So?'

He lets go of me with a sigh and clutches his head with both his hands. I feel the imminent approach of the detectives.

'Afterwards,' Al says. 'Quite a bit afterwards, I realised that I couldn't really be sure ... I never really knew that what I saw was ... consensual.'

I gape at him.

'And if it wasn't ... Malcolm came home really late that night. He wouldn't talk to me, not to anyone, but he was really upset. He didn't really talk to me properly ever again after that. And I can't honestly say I blame him.'

This is when I realise we are truly broken. That summer – did I somehow believe that it would come again? As though it was unfinished, or suspended. Something we would return to, given time. We never will.

'I was a complete shit. I was angry with him, you see. I know it sounds stupid, but I was embarrassed by it and I knew I was never going to hear the last of it from Finlay, and that made me furious with Malcolm. I never actually said anything but I made all these comments. And I treated him like he was, I don't know ...'

I do. I remember something. Al making a show of not wanting to touch something Malcolm had touched. As though he was infectious.

Al looks over my shoulder and his expression hardens. The detectives have found us.

DS Chisholm gives me a meaningful look as Al walks towards them.

And then the three of them are gone.

48

They left Alistair Gilchrist to stew in one of the interview rooms while they worked out their approach. They could be waiting for ages for the forensics to come back and without Connor Leask's DNA on that knife they were relying on the fact Gilchrist had lied to them about seeing Leask on the night of his death, and on Gilchrist being nervous enough to trip up.

That morning Dan had asked Liam to follow up on the Kinley development dates.

'He was telling the truth,' Liam said. 'The development in Moredun didn't go ahead until the mid-Nineties. But he'd first proposed it in the late-Eighties. And get this, he'd started buying up land and properties then too, ready for when he got the go-ahead. Or maybe as leverage so he'd get the contract, or could stand in the way of anyone else who might. Yeah, call me cynical. Anyway, in the early Nineties he owned a fair amount of property in that part of town. And guess who was managing the upkeep for him?'

'Lawrence Groat.'

'And guess who Lawrence Groat sub-contracted to do maintenance?'

'Ronald Gilchrist.'

*

Alistair Gilchrist sat opposite them looking wary.

'When we first interviewed you,' Chisholm began, 'You suggested James Barber might have been in your garage to plant evidence. Did you mean the knife? You were trying to get your defence in early, were you? You didn't realise your son had already found it.'

'I didn't mean anything in particular. I just couldn't understand why he was there and he seemed to have it in for us. But what has the knife got to do with anything? Other than the fact my son just got stabbed with it? What about that, eh? What are you doing about that? Or are you just intent on getting me for something I didn't do quarter of a century ago?'

'James Barber was only killed a couple of weeks ago.'

'For the last time, I had nothing to do with that.'

Dan was always amused when people said that. For the last time. As if they had any choice in the matter. As if they weren't going to be made to go over it again and again.

He pushed a photograph of the knife across the table towards Gilchrist. The man flinched: it had his son's blood on it.

'Can you confirm this is your knife?'

'Yes. At least it was. I haven't seen it for years.'

'And before that it was your father's by the look of things. The initials scratched into the handle were R. G. but you altered the R to look like an A.'

'Yes.'

'Did he give it to you?'

'No. I took it. I didn't think he would miss it. It was with a lot of old tools he never used any more.'

'When did you take it?'

He shook his head. 'I can't remember. It was years ago. When I was at school.'

'Roughly? Before Connor Leask was killed or after?'

Gilchrist chewed his lip. 'Before.'

Dan nodded. 'When before? When you did the Kinley scheme in, what ... fifth Year at high school? When you started doing Saturdays working for Lawrence Groat? You'd have needed tools for that. What about when you were working for Groat in the summer holiday of 1993? Or just before you went out on the night of August 20th 1993.'

'No. I didn't have it that night. I didn't carry any more.'

'You didn't carry – any more?'

Gilchrist sagged a little in his chair. 'Look, I admit it, it wasn't about needing tools when I first took it. I took it because it made me feel good to carry a knife.'

He cringed as he said it, his face contorting with pain to think of his son lying in a hospital bed after being stabbed. Perhaps he thought about what it had been like

276

for Josh, hurrying down the hillside, fingering the knife in desperation, but not feeling at all good about carrying it.

'I'd have been about thirteen. It made me feel, I dunno, more confident. More like a man. I was a stupid wee laddie, that's all. But I stopped, I swear.'

'Are we going to find Connor Leask's DNA on it?'

'No. I never used it on anyone. I used it to carve some graffiti a couple of times. And to cut kindling to start fires. I never used it as a weapon. I swear. And I had stopped carrying by then. After I did the scheme and began working with Lawrence I started my own tool kit. I would have kept it with my other tools.'

'But you did see Connor Leask that night, didn't you?'

He hesitated, his Adam's apple rising and falling.

'We know you did. Malcolm told us. '

Alistair looked momentarily, and genuinely, astonished. Then he nodded. When they asked him again, for the benefit of the recording, he said, 'Yes'.

'What were you doing at the pub?'

'We were going to try and get in. I knew Malcolm had gone with his mate. We thought we might be able to persuade him to buy us some drinks.'

'If you threatened to embarrass him? Make a scene?' Alistair nodded. 'Why did you lie about seeing Connor Leask that night?'

'I knew the police wouldn't believe I had nothing to do with his death. That Barber was just looking for a reason to put me away.'

Ellen leant forward. 'Do you really believe that? Still? You're not a teenage rebel any more. You can't seriously believe that you seeing Connor Leask that night would be enough to get you charged with his murder?'

'We didn't know what else they knew.'

'What do you mean?

'He'd been to the shop. Dad's hardware shop.'

'You saw Connor Leask there, too? We know he met Malcolm there.'

Alistair's eyes flickered with interest for a moment before he returned to his own memories. 'He came in one time when I was doing a shift. He made out like he knew us. Or knew about us. He started asking all these questions about Dad's work and how business was going. Made all these comments about the business expanding and how it paid to have good contacts. The implication was that Dad was involved in something dodgy. Him and Lawrence Groat.'

'Can you be more specific about what he said?'

Gilchrist shook his head. 'I can't remember. Like I said, it started with lots of questions. He wanted to know if we knew some guy – ' He shot bolt upright suddenly. 'That guy you were asking about. The one with the foreign name.'

'That's convenient,' Dan said, and the sceptical expression on his face belied the tremor of excitement he felt inside. Because he believed Alistair Gilchrist. On this point at least.

'Was your Dad there?' Ellen asked.

'No. I never told him, either,' he added quickly. 'He didn't know anything about it. The thing is, I threatened him.'

'Connor Leask?'

'Yeah. I told him he should watch his mouth or, I don't know, he'd better watch his back, or something. I was acting the big man. But I know I threatened him with violence. That's why I was so scared when he actually got stabbed that night. I thought if he'd told someone I threatened him and then if you lot found out I'd seen him that night, that would be it. I would be put away for it.'

'So you got Finlay Groat to provide you with an alibi.'

'Yes. No. Well, most of it was true. We just missed a bit out.'

Dan let a silence open up. It gave him time to think. Alistair's story had the ring of truth to it. But he felt he was still holding something back. And just because he hadn't told his father about Connor's visit to the shop, that didn't mean Ronald hadn't known what Connor was up to. Or Lawrence Groat, for that matter. Then again, if they were right about the knife being the murder weapon – and Ellen said she could feel it in her water – why would he put it back amongst his tools? And what would Ronald know about it? It couldn't be why he contacted Jimmy Barber twenty-six years later.

Alistair Gilchrist wasn't appreciating the thinking time as much as he was. He had started to fidget.

'If we find Connor Leask's DNA on that knife, how are you going to explain that?'

'It can't. It won't. I had nothing to do with it, I swear. I told you, I don't even think I still used that knife by then. I wanted my own stuff, not second-hand stuff from Dad. I was starting to take things seriously. I'd done the Kinley's training and I knew I wanted to get a trade. I had my place at Drylaw's. For the first time in my life I had some sense of direction.'

That's what it is, Dan thought. That's what he's holding back on. He realised that when it came to his own actions Alistair was adamant, but when it came to the knife he lacked conviction.

He thinks it is the knife that was used on Connor.

'You make it sound as though you were quite the re-formed character, but you were still out nicking shopping trolleys and vandalising underpasses of a Friday night.'

'Okay, I didn't just stop over night. Well, I did after that guy got stabbed. That was it. It really freaked me out. I kept waiting for someone to tell the cops about me threatening him. I didn't know whether he'd told anyone. I was looking over my shoulder the whole time.' He looked up, a thought striking him. 'So, I definitely wasn't carrying then. And I don't remember deliberately getting rid of the knife so I must have already stopped carrying it around, or I would remember that.'

'Who else could have got hold of it, then?'

'Who says anyone did?'

'Your father? Perhaps he reclaimed it?'

'No. Why would he? He had loads of stuff. That's why I took it in the first place. I knew he wouldn't miss it.'

'Did you ever find out what it was all about? The things Connor Leask was saying about your father?'

That stumped him.

'You didn't ever ask him? It didn't strike you as odd that a man comes sniffing round your father's business, and then a few days later he's killed?'

'My Dad didn't kill anyone. He was only out that night looking for me. It was my fault he ever got dragged into all that in the first place.'

'Is that what he told you? Give you a hard time about it, did he?'

Alistair did not reply. He looked away. Dan took that for a yes.

'Twenty-six years later your Dad contacts a detective, wanting to tell him something, and a few days later the detective is dead?'

'Well, Dad can't have done that, can he?'

'You weren't curious about what he wanted to see Barber about?'

'I didn't know he had asked to see him. I just thought Barber was sniffing around again. Taking advantage of the fact Dad was ill.'

'Your father didn't say anything to you after you'd asked Barber to leave the hospital? He didn't give you any indication why he wanted to speak to him?'

'I don't think Dad even knew he'd been there. Not the time I told him to go away, anyway. But Malcolm and Rob were there another time he tried. Ask them.'

'Could Malcolm have got hold of your knife?'

His eyes flickered. 'Malcolm wasn't interested in anything of mine. We moved in completely different circles.'

Malcolm, Dan thought. The empty vessel. Malcolm, who had kept his shame bottled up for all these years. It had solidified now, settled in him, like a stratus of rock, but back then it would have been raw, molten.

Dan waited, tapping his finger lightly on the photograph of the knife.

'Malcolm wouldn't ... Why would he?'

Alistair's denial lacked conviction. He thought his own brother had killed Connor Leask.

'You tell me, Alistair.'

Alistair stared at the photograph on the table for a

long few seconds.

'I think I'd like to speak to a lawyer now.'

49

The bypass is hell. Rain blatters against the windscreen. I can't get enough distance between me and the car in front to give me respite from the surface water either. If you let so much as a few metres open up, some aggressive nutter swerves in front and the car behind starts hounding you to get a move on. It's terrifying.

I am sure there is an earlier exit that will lead me to Malcolm's apartment but I can't make the links in my head so I end up going right the way round and then driving back in towards Haymarket. By the time I get out of the car my head is pounding. Please let me not have missed him. If he goes now, I don't think he'll ever come back.

As I make my way to the apartment I have that dis-orientating sensation of things rushing towards and away from me in the aftermath of being in the car. I have to steady myself against some railings. People go by without lifting their heads. It's only because of the rain, because they are cold and wet and want to get inside, but it adds to an eerie feeling that I exist outside of their realm, that I am translucent or unreal, a glitch. I breathe, deep and slow, and hope it doesn't get the better of me. Yet.

I hold down the buzzer for the apartment and wait.

'Who is it?'

'It's me, Norna.' I'm so relieved Malcolm is still there I practically fall into the building. Malcolm is waiting at the door to the apartment. He's wearing normal clothes, not uniform, but his flight case is sitting just inside the door.

'Norna, what are you doing here? You're soaked through.'

'Don't go. You can't go.'

'I'm not going anywhere. I'm not allowed to.'

'They've taken Al in again. I think they might charge him. Josh was stabbed. It was Al's knife. From years ago.'

As I babble Malcolm's eyes harden. It's like a shield coming down in front of them. 'You have to talk to the police,' I say.

'I have. Why do you think I'm stuck here? They hauled me in, off a flight into Newcastle the other day. Christ, it was embarrassing.'

'You have to help.'

'Norna.' He turns away from me.

'He didn't do it. He didn't kill anyone.'

'Can you be sure of that? Really?'

'For God's sake, Malcolm!'

'Norna!' He glares at me. 'I get that you want everything to be lovely. And you've always been Al's little sister. But there are things you don't know.'

'I know about the money Dad gave you. I know about you and Connor Leask.'

He looks at me as though I've slapped him. For a moment we stand there saying nothing. Then the bitterness creeps back into his face again. 'I suppose Al told you. Well, you can have a good laugh about it together when you visit him in prison.'

'Why would we laugh about it?'

'He did, then.'

'He was a sixteen year-old fuckwit. He was more worried about his own macho image than anything else. He admits he behaved like a prick. He regrets it, I can tell.'

He snorts.

'Is that why you never brought anyone home to meet us? Because you were afraid of how we would react?'

He won't look at me.

'He thinks you did it.'

'What?'

'He thinks you might have killed Connor Leask. He didn't say it in so many words, but he said that later on he wasn't sure if what he saw was consensual. It was, though, wasn't it?'

Malcolm can't speak. I watch as he struggles with what I've said. Then he nods. His face crumples and he sits down hard on the nearest chair. He puts his head in his hands and sobs.

After a moment I pull another chair closer and sit next to him. I reach for one of his hands and pull it into mine and then I sit and wait, like I used to all those years ago with Al.

Eventually, Malcolm's sobs subside.

'The reason I never brought anyone home to meet you,' he says, quietly, 'is that there never has been anyone. Not since then.'

As his words sink in I feel a profound sense of desolation. I thought I had wasted my life.

Slowly, Malcolm begins to talk. He tells me what happened with Connor that night. He tells me how terrified he was that Dad would find out.

He tells me about the shock of discovering that Connor had been killed. The fear. And the guilt.

'Somehow, I did feel responsible. I felt as though I had caused it in some way. He'd only been there because of me.

'Al must have told Dad. He gave me the money to leave and told me to stay away for a bit. He said that it was to help me make a fresh start, get past what had happened, but that was bullshit. He just couldn't bear to have me around. He couldn't even look at me.'

I think of the letter I found on Dad's computer. The one he never sent. I am very proud of you, and I always have been.

'Before that summer I'd always seen myself on this straight line.' Malcolm laughs bitterly. 'No pun intended. Do your homework, do your exams. Go from school to university and into work. No-one ever really taught me to think for myself. I just did what you were supposed to do. So, after ... I just went back to that. A to B to C to D. Onward. It was just how it was. I just kept going. And maybe that was a good thing. If I'd stopped to think about it too much ...'

He tells me that before he left home he had a row with Mum. A 'scene' he calls it – one of her words. He was feeling wretched, as though no-one would miss him. She was tetchy, annoyed with him. Griping over last-minute washing, nagging him about his packing, snapping at him for the silliest things. He was the first and he wasn't to know, as I do, that this was the sign that she minded his leaving. That she did this with all of us when we went away. Malcolm thought she was angry with him. Disappointed, and ashamed, like Dad. He told her they would all be glad when he was gone. It wasn't fair. Al could do anything, he said, and she just hugged him and fussed over him. Even when he was in trouble with the police.

'Well, someone has to,' she said. 'Dad is so cross with him all the time, he needs to know he's loved. And you've always been fine. We never had to worry about you. We always knew you'd be alright, make a success of yourself, do well. You didn't need us for anything. You were so independent.'

I can hear her say it as he tells me. I recognise that defensiveness, the way she turned it round on him. It's so familiar to me, but he was the first. He didn't know she couldn't hear the plea, only the accusation.

Malcolm says, 'You go past a stage when you can just clamber on a knee and demand attention. Especially if there is always someone else there.' He trails off.

'Dad was proud of you,' I tell him, but he shakes his head.

'He was proud of my pilot's licence. Captain was a word Dad could understand. Tell all his cronies about.' He sits up straight, rubs his eyes with the heels of his hands. 'It doesn't matter.'

It does matter. All of this matters. I feel my anger rising again, and this time it is reserved wholly for whoever did this to Malcolm. And to Al. The person who killed Connor Leask. And I don't care any more if finding out who that was makes Dad collateral damage. I don't even care if it turns out it was Dad that did it.

*

I persuade Malcolm to come home with me. In return I promise not to tell Mum that he's been here for the best part of a week. When we arrive she falls on him like he's some kind of lost prophet. Dinner tonight is going to be a step up from soup and biscuits.

'Have either of you heard from Rob?' she asks. 'He's

supposed to be on his way too.'

My heart leaps. I feel guilty for doubting him.

Mum doesn't seem excited, though. Something is troubling her.

'I had that Tina on the phone,' she says, and I can tell now that she's trying to keep her voice light. 'Apparently he'd gone to Fiona's to say goodbye to Calum and he must have left straight from there, but she'd been expecting him to stop off home again before he left. "He wouldn't go without saying goodbye to me," she said.'

Mum is a bit sniffy about Tina, the implication being that she doesn't realise her place. Hasn't accepted that Calum is more important than her. I feel a sudden wave of sympathy for the woman, and remorse for the way none of us has accepted her role in Rob's life. We had bonded with Fiona and we took sides when they split up, when there might not even be sides to take.

I've spent so much time lamenting what happened to our family in the past that I've neglected to notice how I'm contributing to the rift now. I resolve to change this.

'I told her he probably just set off, thinking he'd already said his goodbyes,' Mum says. 'The thing is, he hasn't arrived.'

'Mum, it's a five hour drive, more if he stops for any length of time.'

'I know that. But this was Saturday night,' she said.'

We both stare at her and I get a tingle of fear down the back of my neck.

'Maybe he stopped off in Dundee,' Malcolm says.

Yes, that must be it. Rob went to art college in Dundee and still has friends there.

'If he hadn't told you he was coming, maybe he hadn't intended to arrive here yet anyway.'

'I'll give him a ring,' I tell Mum, patting her on the arm.

Malcolm and I go upstairs. I get sheets and towels out for him, then pull out my phone and try Rob. There's no answer. But then, we haven't exactly been communicating well by phone lately. He might easily want to avoid another argument. And he could be driving.

I grab a corner of the sheet to help Malcolm put it on.

'I think you're wrong about something,' I say after a bit. 'I promise I'm not just sticking up for him, but I don't think Al did tell Dad about you and Connor Leask. When he told me at the hospital this afternoon it was, I don't know, like he was giving something away. He said he was going to have to tell the police he lied about not seeing you both that night, and the way he said it, I think he's been covering that up for years.'

Malcolm looks at me. 'Well someone told Dad,' he says.

50

While they waited for Alistair Gilchrist's lawyer to free up some space in his busy schedule, Calder and Chisholm took a quick trip to Stockbridge.

'Something I want to run by you,' Calder had said, mysteriously.

As they walked towards the bistro where Ronald Gilchrist's hardware shop had once been Ellen posed the question that had been troubling her since the interview.

'What if the knife is just an attempt to frame Alistair? Or Ronald?'

Calder turned to look at her. 'You believe him?'

Ellen made a face. 'I don't know. But something feels wrong. If Ronald knew what Ralston and Groat were up to, could the knife be insurance, in case Ronald ever did feel like telling?'

Calder thought as they walked. He didn't speak until they stopped in the alleyway at the side of the bistro.

'You mean someone deliberately used his knife on Leask? That suggests premeditation, doesn't it? Plus, they'd have to be sure they could place Alistair or Ronald in the same locus as Connor and get away themselves. It's unlikely.'

Ellen waited patiently for him to pause. 'I agree. That's why I think they didn't use Al's knife for the murder. But they did take his knife afterwards.'

She watched the realisation dawn in Dan's face.

'They switched the blade.'

'Yes. It's possible, isn't it? I've asked the lab to check whether it was tampered with.'

'Did they say how long it would take?'

'They said it would get done when it got done. Maybe if you asked?'

She could tell Calder liked this idea. Almost as much as she did.

'So?' She looked up and down the alleyway.

'Ah. So.' Dan led her into the back yard behind the shop. The outdoor tables and chairs were empty. The metal shutters of the kiosk where they sold ice creams and hosted barbecues in the summer were rolled down. Dan stopped in the middle of the yard and looked at the ground for a moment.

'My turn to theorise. Slightly harder to prove than yours.'

He pulled some folded sheets of paper out of his inside coat pocket and spread them on one of the café tables. Ellen looked at them and nodded. She recognised them as copies of some of the documents from Connor Leask's files.

'We know that Connor made a note of the locations where two bodies were found. One was no mystery. Lee Quigley was found contemporaneously where he died, on a building site that it was assumed he had been trying to rob. The other, Dean Owens, was different. Connor managed to predict where his body would be found, eight years into the future. We don't have his missing workings. Maybe Barber had some, maybe they've been destroyed. So, exactly how Connor got there we can't be sure, except that it seems likely he was following a lead that began when he was charged with interviewing Franjo Horvat, the key witness in the case against Norris Ralston.'

He paused to check that she was following.

'When Horvat failed to show up it was decided that there wasn't enough evidence and the case was thrown out. Connor being Connor, doesn't leave it at that. He has a zeal for justice and his job is boring and here is a whiff of intrigue that just might spice it up a bit. He sets out to find out where Franjo Horvat has gone. Don't you think?'

'Reasonable to assume. I would.'

Dan gave a small smile. 'Somehow, Connor arrives at this.' He spread his hands across the pages on the table. 'A link between Dean Owens and Lee Quigley. A link between them and Ralston and Franjo Horvat. He marks the location of Quigley's death and what he believes is the likely location of Owens' body. Both are Kinley developments.

But both were contracted to Drylaw Build and Repair, Lawrence Groat's part of the company. While Liam's been looking at Kinley, I've had Keisha going through Groat's work scheme, charting all the places he was working in the early Nineties. They changed the name to Groat's in 2000 by the way.'

'The year before Ralston was convicted. Interesting timing.'

Dan agreed. 'This is where Lawrence Groat was working at the time Franjo Horvat disappeared.'

Instinctively Ellen looked at the maps on the table, before she realised that Dan was not showing her another location on the map. They were standing in it.

'He built the storage unit as a favour to Gilchrist,' she said. 'It was one of the things Linda Gilchrist and Margery Shanks both mentioned when they said he helped Ronald out. You think Franjo Horvat is here?'

'Apart from this, they were doing snagging on a previous job and there were other, bigger developments in the pipeline. It's possible that – if this is anything more than my fevered imagination – Horvat's body could have been kept in storage and then dumped later. But in terms of actual, physical building work going on at the time Horvat was last seen alive, work involving digging, this is it. And it gives us another link to the Gilchrists. It would explain why Connor was sniffing around here.'

'And Barber.'

'And Barber. Groat redeveloped this whole yard. There used to be a garage over there, directly in line with the lane, but it meant there was no access to this bit here except through the back of the shop. They knocked down the old garage and built the unit over there, adjoining the back of the shop. It meant delivery lorries could come right the way down the lane and unload straight into the unit, which led straight into the shop, and it gave them a workshop space.'

'Did Ronald know? Was he involved, do you think? Is that what he wanted to tell Barber?'

Dan shrugged. 'It's Gilchrist's yard. Groat can claim he has nothing to do with it.' He folded up the maps and tucked them back into his coat pocket. Anyway, it's all just speculation at this stage. Blackwood is going to need a bit more, before he lets us start tearing up the cobbles.'

'It won't do much for their trade, if it comes to that,' Ellen said, nodding towards the bistro. A couple of members of staff had moved to the window and were watching them curiously. 'They must be wondering what we're up to.'

'We can say we're part of Glen Starrett's local history society. Reminiscing about the olden days.'

They made their way back up the lane to the street. 'Alistair could have known about it,' Ellen murmured. 'He helped Lawrence build the store. And he was angry when Connor started sniffing around the business. He threatened him.'

'Something bothers me about your knife theory,' Calder said as they walked back to the car. 'That kind of insurance only works if the person knows about it, doesn't it? I mean, if Ronald doesn't know that he or his son can be framed for the murder of Connor Leask, what's to stop him going to the police about what Lawrence and Ralston are up to? And if he does know, why not just get rid of the knife?'

Ellen chewed this over for a few minutes, then shook her head.

'Something bothers me about your theory, too,' she said as they got back into the car.

Dan smiled. 'You and Blackwood, both, I dare say.'

'No, it's not that. I completely buy the whole thing and I would get the diggers in tomorrow. No, it's that, if this is what they did with people who were a problem: make it look like an accident or make them simply disappear, why wasn't Connor Leask disposed of in the same way?'

'Well,' Dan said. 'They made it look like a "random gay-bashing" didn't they? At that time, barely a step up from an accident, it would seem.'

His phone rang. 'Liam,' he told Ellen as he put it to his ear. 'We're on our way back,' he told the DC. 'Has his lawyer turned up, then?'

Liam wasn't calling about Alistair Gilchrist. Ellen felt Dan go very still as he listened to what Liam was telling him. When he finished the call he said nothing for a couple of seconds, then turned to her.

'Robert Gilchrist's body has been found in his car up a forestry track off the A9 in Sutherland. It looks like suicide.'

51

The traffic is much lighter than it was earlier, as is the rain. More of a drizzle now. Still, the motion of the windscreen wipers unsettles me and I find myself sneaking along the back roads, down Marine Drive and along West Shore Road, reluctant to have to negotiate too many other vehicles or junctions. It's dusk and people have their lights on. I wince as they draw near. I feel as though the light is flaring at the sides of my eyes.

Malcolm said something earlier that made me think. After we finished putting on his duvet cover he looked around his old bedroom and said, 'It's funny, the way it all came back just as suddenly as it went away.'

At first I wasn't sure what he was talking about. Memories or feelings perhaps. Then I realised he was talking about Connor Leask's murder and the police interest in him and Al and Dad. 'What do you mean it went away suddenly?'

'Just that. They were all over us. That Detective Barber in particular. I was sure he thought we were hiding something.'

I decided not to point out that they were.

'Then suddenly it was all over. Dad said we didn't have to worry about it any more. They were satisfied we had nothing to do with it.'

I thought about the names in Dad's diary from the time. Barber, Shah, Starrett, Baird, Harkins. Police officers. I had assumed he wrote them all down during the investigation, but what if he knew something about one of them already? What if he'd been blackmailing one of them? Could that be why the money stopped coming in at the same time as the murder? When Connor Leask was killed, did someone see their chance? Did the spotlight fall on Al and Malcolm and Dad in order to make Dad stop the blackmail? Was it someone turning the tables on him? Did it make them even?

The blackmail stopped, the suspicions went away. Dad got in touch with Detective Barber, it all came back.

My moment of inspiration didn't last long. After all, how could the person Dad was blackmailing have known about Malcolm and Connor Leask? Or about Al's knife? Or that either of them even knew the murdered man or were out that night? No. My theory was rubbish.

Much more likely it all went away for exactly the same reason every other charge against Al and Finlay Groat went away – Lawrence pulled some strings.

Finlay's house is a large detached stone house in Cargil Terrace. Victorian, I think, though I'm not very good at these things. It's posh, anyway. Lawrence must be proud. I walk up the path and ring the bell. I'm not completely sure how I'm going to play this. Tell him the truth about the diaries and enlist his help? Play up the fact that I'm concerned that my Dad might have been involved in something, and make out that I'm working through bereavement issues, trying to make sense of it all? The charity shop man seemed to think that was quite plausible. For a flickering moment I even think I might tell him about Astro. I remember the relief when I told the charity shop man. But I'm scared of Finlay's reaction. I don't think I could bear it if he felt sorry for me. What if he backed away in horror?

The alternative is to focus on what's happening to Al and just straight-out ask him for help with that. Tell him that the police now know they both lied about not seeing Connor Leask that night. Act like I'm both warning him and at the same time trying to find a way through this for both him and Al. Even ask him outright if his Dad knows a police officer who might be able to help.

The door is opened by a woman.

'Oh,' I say, inelegantly. 'Have I got the right house? I was looking for Finlay Groat.'

She looks at me curiously. Not entirely amicably.

'Finlay isn't here at the moment.'

'Oh.' I suddenly feel sick. The light from the porch

behind her is bright white. I can feel it piercing my eye sockets.

'Are you alright?'

'Sorry. It's just ... I'm Al's sister.'

She softens considerably. 'Oh, I'm sorry. Look, come in. You don't look all that well, actually.'

'It's been a pig of a day.'

She leads me through a spacious hallway into a room that is thankfully low-lit. There is some kind of classical music playing softly in a corner and it looks as though she was doing some kind of studying or writing when I arrived. There is a mug of something steaming on a desk in the corner and files and books stacked up on it.

'I'm Vivienne,' she says, extending a slim, bangled hand, not to shake mine but to wave me onto a chair. 'Finlay's wife.'

'Norna.'

'Do you suffer from migraines?' she asks me. 'I saw you wincing under the hall light. Can I get you some painkillers, or a glass of water?'

I nod, gratefully. While she fetches me water I fight down my anger towards Finlay and try to focus on how I might turn this to my advantage, but I am too tired and too nauseous to think straight. In the end, when she comes back I blurt out the truth.

'Al's been arrested. Or at least, he's being questioned. About a murder that happened when they were younger. Finlay and Al both alibied each other, but it seems they lied about something and now it's cast doubt on their whereabouts.'

She regards me calmly for a few moments. 'I'm sorry about your Dad, by the way. Lawrence and Margery told me. I heard about what happened at the funeral, too. The retired police detective. Is this connected to that?'

I nod. 'He investigated the murder.'

'And you say Finlay lied to the police? To protect Alistair?'

'Well, they both withheld information.'

This is not going well. The emphasis she put on that

last bit, about Finlay lying to protect Al, I don't like that. I remember that somewhere in the house there is a child. Finlay's child. She's going to want to protect that child from all of this. At any cost. I should never have come. But even as I think this, I find I want to disabuse her of any illusions she might have about Finlay and his father.

'I don't know how much you know about what Finlay was like then? He was pretty wild. He and Al used to get into a lot of trouble. That's probably why they lied. Because they were already known to the police. Finlay told me his dad was threatening to chuck him out if he didn't mend his ways. He said Lawrence used his connections to get them off a shoplifting charge once before, but he made it clear he wasn't going to keep bailing him out.'

She sniffs. 'Ah, Lawrence's pet polis.'

She surprises me. 'You know about that?'

She rolls her eyes. 'Oh, yes. Lawrence has a friend for every occasion. Parking fines, troublesome neighbours, planning permission. You name it. He's always happy to put in a word.'

'Do you know the name of his pet polis?'

She shakes her head. 'You don't want that kind of help from Lawrence, believe me.'

I have a sudden snapshot of what it must be like for her to be Lawrence Groat's daughter-in-law. The thought makes my flesh crawl on her behalf.

As if reading my mind she says, 'I can move very quickly when I need to.'

'I think Lawrence might be involved,' I blurt out.

'In what, exactly?'

'In the man's murder. Both of them. I think he made it go away at the time, but then that detective started asking questions again. It's possible my Dad had found out what was going on ...' I run out of steam. Is this really what I think? If Lawrence had been involved in Leask's death and Dad had been onto him, wouldn't there be invoices paid from Lawrence in the aftermath of Connor Leask's murder?

'Lawrence is a sleazebag,' Vivienne says. 'I don't doubt that he's greased a few palms in his time, and he definitely enjoys trading in favours, but I don't think I'd go so far as to accuse him of murder.' She looks faintly amused, and she pities me.

All I've done now is to risk alerting Lawrence to the fact I'm making accusations.

'Wait a minute. You said Lawrence and Margery told you. About my Dad. About the man in the garage.'

'Yes.'

'Margery Shanks?'

'Yes.'

'Are she and Lawrence …?

She smiles. She thinks I'm being coy, or that I can't find the right word for people their age. 'Bidey-ins?' she suggests. 'Yes. For a long time now. Finlay was none too happy about it at first. He suspected it started up well before Lawrence and Joan split up. That's Finlay's mother.'

I nod, absent-mindedly. Mum's pursed lips when I mentioned Margery Shanks. She was snooping around our house on the day of Dad's funeral. Did she know about the knife? Did she know about the diaries? But why would she be looking for either?

Unless they incriminated Lawrence.

DS Chisholm said Margery was rattled after I had been to see her. I shiver, slightly.

I told Margery about the diaries.

Lawrence already knows I've been asking questions.

I get up, suddenly resolute. It's time to put an end to this fantasy. Stop playing detective and let the real ones do their worst. I'm going to give the diaries to DS Chisholm.

'Here,' Vivienne scribbles an address on a piece of paper. 'It's one of their properties. Fin's been staying there. We've been having a few problems.'

'Thanks.'

'Are you sure you're ok driving? I could call you a cab?'

I shake my head, though she's probably right. The drive home is pretty awful. I'm terrified I'm going to get pulled over at any moment.

I go straight upstairs to Dad's study. Malcolm has clearly made himself at home. His laptop is set up on the desk and he's piled up all the stuff of Dad's I was going through and dumped it on top of the filing cabinet. I can't see what he's done with the diaries. I tense with irritation.

I go downstairs to accost him but as I reach the bottom step the doorbell rings.

It's stupid, but the first thing I assume when I open the door to find two uniformed officers standing there is that I was spotted on a traffic camera. I expect them to produce a breathalyser. When they ask to come in I know that's not why they're here, and when they tell me to sit down once we're all gathered in the living room together, my blood turns to ice.

52

Liam had been assigned the job of liaison with the police in Wick. The post mortem on Robert Gilchrist's body would be carried out the following day they said, but it looked pretty clear cut. Gilchrist's car had been found on a rutted track deep inside a large area of forestry land east of the main road north. A tube had been attached to the exhaust pipe and fed through the front window. By the time a forest ranger found him, the car had burned through the fuel supply.

They had a rough time frame between when Robert had said goodbye to his ex-wife and son and when rain began to fall in the early hours of Sunday morning, leaving a rectangle of dry ground under Robert's car.

Dan wasn't taking anything at face value. He asked for the call history on Robert's phone to be sent through. When it arrived one name stood out.

Over the past few days Robert had exchanged several calls with Lawrence Groat, the last one on the day he died.

'How did we miss him?' Dan asked as they drove through the city.

'He was eleven in 1993. He had nothing to do with the investigation into Connor Leask's death,' Ellen said.

'He was in the hospital visiting his father when Malcolm saw off James Barber. What if Ronald told him what he wanted to tell Barber?'

'Then he lied to us. Withheld vital information, anyway.'

'He insisted on going into the garage after his sister found Barber's body.'

'So, what are we saying? That he killed Jimmy to stop him ruining his dad's reputation? That he killed himself because he couldn't cope with the guilt? Because he put his brother in the frame, not only for that murder, but for Connor Leask's?'

Dan didn't know what he was saying. He believed Ronald had told Robert what it was he wanted to tell Barber. And that it concerned Lawrence Groat. The rest he wasn't sure about at all. He parked across Groat's driveway because there wasn't anywhere else and because there was a sign on the gate saying STRICTLY NO PARKING.

'They haven't found a note,' Ellen said. 'There wasn't one in the car or the house. Not that that necessarily means anything. But you'd think if he was feeling guilty about dropping his brother in it he'd at least try to clear that up.'

Dan strode up Groat's front path and ignored the doorbell in favour of his fist on the door.

It was the first time he had met Lawrence Groat. The description Ellen had given of the man hadn't endeared him to him and the reality did nothing to improve matters. Groat drew himself up when they showed him their warrant cards. He took the time to appraise Dan before he stood aside to let them in, as if he was considering him for work. The look he gave Ellen was completely different.

Dan refused the hand Groat extended. They weren't there on business matters.

'Over the past few days you have exchanged a few telephone calls with Robert Gilchrist. Do you mind telling us what they were about?'

Groat settled into a large armchair and made himself comfortable before answering. 'What does Robert say?'

'We're asking you.'

'His father and I were friends, as you know.' He nodded at Ellen. 'Robert had some questions about his father's business activities. I don't know what he was driving at. He seemed to think Ronny might have been involved in something illegal. It was news to me.'

The man was odious. Dan wanted to wipe that smug look off his face.

'You don't think there was anything in it, then?' Ellen asked.

Groat ran a hand over his thick silver mane. 'Robert implied that his father had confessed something to him, so it could be true. It wasn't something I was aware of, though.

Do you mind my asking why you're interested?' He feigned a sudden realisation. 'You surely can't think this has anything to do with that man's death?'

'Can you tell us where you were between the hours of eight p.m. on Saturday evening and two a.m. on Sunday morning?'

Groat raised a quizzical eyebrow. 'Certainly. I was here.'

'Can anyone corroborate that?'

'Yes. That is, until midnight when I went to bed alone. My son was here for most of the evening. And Norna Gilchrist.'

53

They had found traces of Connor Leaks's DNA on Josh's knife.

Ellen left Keisha talking to the nurses on duty at the nurses' station, knocked on the open door and went into Josh's room. Evening visiting time was about to begin and she wanted to see him before family arrived. He pulled off his headphones and she heard the rasp of something angry before he turned off his music and pushed his mobile aside. His bed was surrounded by cards now. She picked up a couple and read the messages inside. Rounded letters with bubbly hearts for full stops and dots. Kisses and empty wishes. She looked at Josh. He was watching her under lidded eyes. He did not need to say anything. She knew how it went.

When it was Donna lying there, all those years ago, Ellen had ranted internally at the cards and flowers. The people who professed to be thinking of Donna, praying for her even, when for the past five years they had ignored her at best, or rolled their eyes when she talked, mimicked her walk, her speech and her gestures. Hypocrites.

It was not a righteous anger. She hated Donna. But now she would never be able to ditch her. Now, she could never walk away, because everyone would think she was being a bitch after what had happened. Poor Donna, what she must have been through, and Ellen was supposed to be her friend.

Donna, of course, lapped up the attention.

She looked at Josh. 'Only another year or so and then you never have to see any of them again,' she said. 'It'll pass quickly enough.'

His look of astonishment turned quickly into a grin and he seemed to relax.

'How are you?'

'Okay. Doctor says they'll let me out tomorrow. I have to be careful for a while though. How's my Dad?'

Ellen nodded, slowly. 'We questioned him again, yesterday. I can't pretend he's not still a person of interest to us.'

'But you don't think he did it?' He hauled himself to a more upright position. 'Do you?' She realised no-one had told him about his uncle.

'Tell me about the knife, again. Where exactly did you get it from?'

'It was in a box of stuff in the shed. He never used any of it any more. I don't think he ever even opened the box since he brought it from Gran and Grandad's. The Sellotape was all yellow and crinkly.'

'Was the box labelled? Did you know what you would find inside?'

'No, but I thought it might be tools, or stuff from Granddad's shop, because it was heavy and I could hear the sound of metal clanking if I shook it. I wasn't looking for a knife. I was just being nosey, but when I found it ...' He shrugged.

'Was there anything else with it?'

'How do you mean?'

'Was it just in amongst other things in the box or was it packaged separately? What else was in the box?' They had searched the shed with Melanie Gilchrist's permission, but she wanted to hear it from Josh. Alistair had had three days to get in there before they did.

'It was just random stuff. Like, screwdrivers and pliers and stuff. Most of it looked really old. The knife was at the bottom. It was in a plastic bag so it wasn't as rusty as some of the other stuff. It still worked when I pushed out the blade.'

'Did you clean it?'

Fear was creeping back into Josh's eyes. 'I gave it a wipe.'

'Inside, or just outside?'

'Mainly outside, but I pushed the blade out and wiped that. It was just rust.' Though he didn't look too sure about that now.

He looked over her shoulder suddenly, and his face lit up. Ellen turned to see Norna Gilchrist standing in the open doorway. The look on her face suggested she had been there long enough to hear some of what had been said.

'Can I talk to you?' Norna said.

'Sure.' Next on my list, anyway, Ellen thought.

Norna did not move from the doorway. 'I'll come back and see you afterwards,' she said to Josh.

Ellen got up. 'Take it easy tomorrow.' The boy nodded, but he was already reaching for his earphones again.

She followed Norna along the ward and out into the main corridor. Norna hovered there for a bit, looking nervously at the hospital staff and visitors passing by. She looked terrible. The dark circles round her eyes seemed to have deepened, and her skin was very pale, almost translucent under the harsh lights. She seemed to be having trouble keeping her eyes open. Ellen took her by the arm and guided her gently towards the lifts.

She took her down to the main hub of the hospital and found a row of chairs against a wall in the dimmest of corridors where there was sufficient space for them not to be overheard. She had used this spot before.

'Are you on something?'

Norna looked surprised. 'Not like you mean. Medication.'

Ellen took a moment to consider this, then decided they could deal with it later if she needed to take an official statement.

'I'm sorry about your brother. Robert.'

Norna looked for a moment as though she didn't understand. She searched Ellen's face. Perhaps she was just trying to gauge whether she meant it, the sympathy. Eventually she nodded.

'What did you want to talk to me about?'

Norna took a minute to answer, her eyes on Ellen the whole time. There was something haunting about them, Ellen thought. Something far away and old. But she didn't look stoned.

'Some of this might be a bit muddled,' Norna said, eventually. 'I found something of my Dad's. Diaries. From the early Nineties. Hidden in a wall cavity in the house.'

'That sounds pretty clear so far,' Ellen said. 'What's the significance of these, do you think?'

'The diaries have names in. I recognised some as people Dad knew through work, but there are other names too. And he listed the names of the police officers who investigated the murder of Connor Leask, including the man who died in our garage.'

She sounded as though she was feeling her way, Ellen thought. Watching Ellen for a reaction, trying to work out whether or not she was doing the right thing. Ellen found herself sitting very still, as though the slightest movement might startle Norna Gilchrist and she might fly away.

'It's not very clear why he collected the names. I suppose it might just be a kind of contact book. Except that – I think he might have been blackmailing someone. Or maybe more than one person. There are regular entries in the diaries where he's written "Invoice paid - £250".'

Ellen lifted her eyebrows slightly. 'That was a lot of money in the early Nineties. How often?'

'Every week. For two and a half years. Always the same amount.'

'And you're sure the money was being paid to your dad?'

Norna tilted her head to one side. 'I think so. There was money with the diaries. Quite a lot of money.'

'When do these entries start?'

'Beginning of 1991.'

Ellen did the arithmetic. 'They come to an end around the time Connor Leask was killed?'

Norna nodded. She looked pained. 'They finish exactly when he was killed.'

'Is Connor Leask's name in the diary?'

Norna looked surprised. She had not thought of that. 'No.'

Ellen drummed her fingers lightly on her thighs, thinking. Unlikely Gilchrist was blackmailing Leask then?

Surely his name would appear somewhere if that were the case. Could these payments be connected to whatever Connor thought Gilchrist was up to? Not blackmail at all, even, but a service provided? She thought about what Calder had learned from Kinley. His theory about the service Ralston was providing to people in a spot of bother. She had an urge to get up and pace the corridor, but Norna Gilchrist didn't look as though she would manage it.

'You realise you're putting your dad in the frame for murder?' she said, gently.

Norna nodded. 'I just want it all to be over. You know, I didn't know about any of this stuff until the day of Dad's funeral, but I realise it's been hanging over our family for years. It totally destroyed Malcolm, what happened that night, and afterwards. It's wrecking Al's life, now. Rob ...' Her voice broke. She seemed to grow older and more distant even. 'And then what's it going to do to Josh and Kirsty and Sam if there's still this doubt hanging over their Dad? I just want the truth to come out and then maybe at least they can move on.'

If only it was that simple, Ellen thought, but she kept it to herself.

'Is this what you went to see Margery Shanks about?'

'I didn't tell her everything. I asked her about Dad's income and whether he did any work off the books. She said she didn't think so. Only, now I've found out that she's with Lawrence Groat. And I think she was snooping around the house on the day of Dad's funeral. I found her upstairs coming out of his office. Maybe she knew about the diaries.'

Or the knife, Ellen thought.

'Or the knife,' Norna said. 'You think Josh's knife was the one that killed Connor Leask, don't you? I heard you asking Josh about it. And Al said you knew he lied about not seeing Connor and Malcolm that night.'

Ellen waited.

'If Dad did have something to do with it, I think it was at Lawrence's bidding.'

'Why do you say that?'

'Lawrence was always doing all this stuff for Dad.

Building him the store at cost, giving Al his first job, and the apprenticeship, recommending him and Dad to clients and all that, but I think he had his own agenda. Vivienne, Finlay's wife said it, too. She said he loved to trade in favours, and he had people everywhere, people he could "put in a word with" if you needed help with something. And there's more. Vivienne says that Lawrence had a "pet polis" – her words. And Finlay told me that his dad definitely used his connections to get him and Al off at least one shoplifting charge. And Malcolm said it all went away really suddenly in 1993. Them being questioned, I mean. What if Lawrence used his connections for that too?'

And what bit of me telling you not to interfere in our investigation did you not understand? Ellen thought.

'Why would Al keep the knife if he'd used it to murder someone?' Norna's voice was urgent now. 'And why would Margery be snooping unless there was something that would incriminate her or Lawrence?'

Ellen had to agree. After talking to Josh, she was inclined to believe that Alistair hadn't even known the knife was there until now. And she remembered how unsettled Margery Shanks had been after Norna had been to see her.

'People do snoop,' she said to Norna.

Norna shook her head. 'They're involved, I'm telling you. Rob said something on the phone. I wasn't properly listening; I thought he was just being overprotective.' Her face twisted in anguish. 'He didn't like me spending time with Finlay. He started to say something about Lawrence, something Dad told him before he died, but I cut him off.' The last bit came out as a wail. Ellen bent to fish some tissues out of her bag, but Norna grabbed her arm, fixing her eyes on Ellen, red-rimmed and terrible. 'Rob knew something. You should ask Lawrence where he was when Rob died. It wasn't suicide. There's no way.'

'We have asked Lawrence Groat his whereabouts on Saturday night,' Ellen said, gently. She looked meaningfully at Norna, half hoping she would contradict Lawrence Groat, but as she watched her she saw confusion give way to understanding.

'He was with me.' Norna looked appalled.

Ellen looked at the thin coat Norna Gilchrist was wearing. 'I take it you haven't got these diaries on you?'

'No.' She had sunk down in her seat, the urgency gone. 'I'll bring them to you. I have to ask Malcolm where he put them. He's been using Dad's office.'

'How did you get here?'

'Bus.'

'I'll give you a lift. Come on. I'll need to let my colleague know. You can pop in and see Josh quickly, then we'll head off.'

Ellen saw Norna into Josh's room and had a quick, whispered conversation with Keisha in the corridor while they gave aunt and nephew a few minutes together.

Ellen wished they had the results from the post mortem on Robert's body. She thought about what Norna had said about Lawrence Groat's network of favours. It made a lot of sense if they were looking for two people working together, and it certainly hadn't been Margery Shanks who pushed her into the Gilchrists' garage.

Her phone rang. She didn't recognise the number, but she knew the voice.

'DS Chisholm?'

'Yes.'

'Can we meet? Now? There's something I'd like to give you.'

Ellen hesitated, then she made the arrangement.

She stuck her head into Josh's room. 'Change of plan,' she told Norna. 'I've been called away. DC Bell will take you home after she's taken a quick statement from Josh.'

'Can you get him to confirm what he told me about the knife,' she said to Keisha.

Then she set off, wondering what it was that Baroness Eklund could possibly want to give her.

54

Eklund had been in court. She came out to meet Ellen. 'Let's walk.'

She said nothing more as she led the way through the tourists on the Royal Mile, down onto the Canongate and then through the archway onto St John's Street and into the spacious courtyard between the university buildings.

She didn't beat about the bush.

'You've been particularly interested in my relationship with Hugh Baird.'

Ellen felt like a schoolgirl being reprimanded. She didn't like it. She opened her mouth to justify her interest, her professional interest, but Eklund cut her off.

'As was James Barber before you. I didn't much care for it. The way he kept prodding, asking what kind of a handle Hugh had on what was going on. Insinuating, I thought, that Hugh might have manipulated the course of investigations. But of course, Barber knew how hands-on Hugh was. He worked for him. He was there, on the ground.'

Was this coming back on Jimmy again? Then Ellen had another thought. 'Do you think he was trying to provoke you?'

The Baroness put her head on one side. All the better to see Ellen with.

'Pushing you on your relationship with Hugh Baird, pushing you on Connor's criticism of you? I think he wanted to provoke you into backing his attempts to get the investigation reopened. Asking nicely hadn't worked. Going through the proper channels hadn't worked. He was trying to make you feel it was in your own interests to clear it up. I don't think he thought you or Baird were involved at all.'

The light shifted in Eklund's eyes. Ellen might almost have said she was pleased. Impressed even. Eklund laid her briefcase on a bench and clicked open the catches. She took out a slim file and handed it to Ellen.

'We can only go by the information you provide to us.'

Ellen glanced at the file. It was the fatal accident inquiry into the death of Lee Quigley.

Her phone buzzed in her pocket. She looked up at Eklund as she reached for it.

'Keep it. It's a copy,' the Baroness said, closing her briefcase and nodding curtly. Ellen watched her go as she put the phone to her ear, wondering what it would be like to be as indomitable as that.

It was Keisha. Upset. 'She gave me the slip. Norna Gilchrist. When I was taking Josh's statement. She didn't wait for me.'

Ellen cursed silently. 'She can't be too far ahead of you. She came on the bus. You might still catch her. And if not, get to the Gilchrists' house and collect the diaries from Norna there. I'm not having her playing Scooby Doo any more.'

She was sorely tempted to charge Norna Gilchrist with obstruction.

'On second thoughts, I'll meet you there.'

55

I don't' like DC Bell. She's the one who interviewed me after I found the body in the garage. The one who kept on about what happened in 1993, as if I might suddenly remember that, oh yes, I forgot, my brother killed someone. Silly me, it slipped my seven-year-old mind. There's a kind of do-goody urgency about her, like she wants to win a prize. I wish I'd brought the car, but I don't think I'm safe driving any more.

Immediately after telling DS Chisholm about Dad's diaries and Lawrence and everything else it felt like a relief. Like I'd discharged some of the responsibility for what to do with it all. But already I'm beginning to feel a nagging remorse and the jittery beginnings of panic rising. I think about what she said to me: You do realise you're putting your father in the frame for murder.

I provided Lawrence with an alibi. I feel – tricked.

'I'm just going to the loo,' I say, leaving Josh and DC Bell to it.

I fell for Finlay's bullshit. I feel – furious.

Oh, and here he is, the man himself. As I emerge from the toilets I almost bump into him, striding down the corridor. He's brought games magazines this time. Good old Uncle Finlay.

'Norna, I'm so glad. I've been trying to call you. I'm so sorry to hear about Rob.'

I can't speak.

'I'm sorry about Viv, too. I should have given you my current address. We are separated, honestly, I would never have asked you out if I wasn't free to.'

I make an effort to pull myself together. I don't want him to think I was upset about him and Vivienne. 'I felt like a right eejit when she opened the door,' I say, though I can hardly bear to look at him, still.

'Yeah, I know that feeling. How's Josh?'

'There's a police officer with him. DC Bell. Taking a statement.'

'Oh.' He makes a face. 'That rather earnest one who treated us all like suspects on the day of the funeral.'

'We were all suspects.'

He swithers, looking at the magazines he's brought, then down the length of the ward. 'Have you had a chance to see him?' Then, when I nod, 'Fancy getting out of here, then? I'll leave these at the nurses' station.'

'I can't. I've got to wait for DC Bell. She's giving me a lift home.'

'So? I'll give you a lift.'

'I've got to give her something.'

'Oh. Well. Can't she come and collect it another time? Is it urgent?'

I haven't forgiven him, but the thought of bailing on DC Bell is rather appealing. She won't get any prizes for that.

We leave the magazines and I have a sudden urge to giggle as we make our way to the exit. It's like playing truant.

'How is he? Josh?' Finlay asks as we walk across the car park.

'Good. He's getting out tomorrow.'

'That's great news. What about you?' He glances at me and I can see concern in his face. 'How's the head?'

'The head?' It's too defensive.

'Viv told me you had a migraine or something. She said you didn't look well at all. I have to say, you are looking a bit peaky.'

'Just how separated are you? You seem very chatty.' I am beginning to feel uncomfortable. Surely Vivienne won't have told him about our conversation about Lawrence? He wouldn't be being so nice to me if that was the case, would he? Then again, I'm not sure he's ever been his father's biggest fan.

'We're trying to keep it civil for Harry. Harriet. My daughter.' He smiles. 'You'd love her. She'd love your hair, too.'

Christ, we've only met up a couple of times. What's wrong with the man?

The irritation must show on my face because he apologises quickly. 'Sorry. Too much? I'm an idiot. It's just, with you being Al's sister, I feel like I've known you forever. Almost like we're family.'

Right, that's not creepy at all, I think. 'It's okay,' I tell him. 'I'm just knackered.'

'Mmm. It's been a difficult few weeks.'

Difficult doesn't begin to cover it. A well of grief rises in me then gets stuck. It's been like this since I heard about Rob. Like I need to cry but can't. Need to feel but it's suppressed. As though there's something blocking it all. Maybe it's Astro, or the drugs I'm taking to hold her back. Astro. How childish is that? Suddenly I hate myself. For everything. For my whole, stupid, life. What have I been doing? I make up all this crap, I invest all this time and energy in inventing things, telling myself stupid fucking stories to make life more interesting. Then, when something real happens I can't feel it. I can't seem to take it in. It's like my brain just automatically shuts off from it.

We get into the car and Finlay drives in silence for a while. Up Dalkeith Road and then cutting along Melville Drive. Oh, you went that way, did you? I hear Dad say, and his voice in my head is so achingly familiar I want to cry. I'm besieged suddenly, by myriad fragments of memories of the man I loved for no other reason than he was my dad. And overwhelmed with shame for telling on him to DS Chisholm, and for all the terrible things I have thought about him over the last few weeks. The way I have hated him for leaving us in this mess. For not being the man I thought he was or the man I wanted him to be. The pain of it is almost unbearable. I feel the pressure building in my chest and my head, the same as it did in the charity shop. I cling to the memory of what that kind man said, about the things he felt guilty for afterwards, but his guilt must have been nothing like this. He took his wife down off her pedestal. I hung my dad out to dry, believing him to be part of some criminal underworld, extorting money, working illegally. I readily assumed he was a blackmailer. I even thought him capable of murder. Dad, in his brushed cotton shirts, smelling of Imperial Leather. Making crap jokes and not getting any of ours. Yes, he struggled to accept Malcolm for who he was; yes, he was slow to praise; yes, he got angry sometimes. When we let him down, when we were rude or lazy or when we took things for granted. When Al got into trouble with the police. He wanted us to be better. How could I have believed the worst of him when he worked so hard to make us good?

What if Dad's diaries don't prove anything about Lawrence? What if they only incriminate him? What if they think Rob would have done anything to hide the truth? I told DS Chilshom that Dad had told Rob things before he died. I can't breathe properly.

I notice suddenly that we are near the turn-off for home but instead of taking it, Finlay drives on.

'Where are we going? You missed the turning.'

'I can't take you home to your mother like that. Let's get a bit of fresh air.'

Like like what? I pull down the visor and look in the mirror. Oh. Finlay's right, I look like crap. My eyes are red-rimmed – they almost match my hair – and I look like I've seen a ghost. Mum would collapse if she saw me like this. She would think someone else had died.

Finlay drives down to the very bottom of Silverknowes Road and turns into the car park overlooking the Firth of Forth. He parks at the far end, beside a wooded area. I get out of the car and walk down the wide grassy slope that separates the car park from the promenade. When I get to the bottom I stop by the low concrete wall bordering the scrappy stretch of beach and breathe deeply, looking out onto the water. There is a brisk wind coming off the Forth and I pull my coat around me. Still, the air is good. Finlay is right. I feel it clearing my head, washing some of the panic from my face.

'Better?' he asks, coming to stand beside me.

I nod. 'Thanks. Sorry I'm such a mess.'

'Don't be daft.'

We look across the water for a while.

'What's happening with Al?'

'I don't know.'

Finlay says nothing for a moment, then lets out a frustrated sigh. 'I wish you'd told me about the knife earlier. Why didn't you tell me?' He seems genuinely upset about this, and it irritates me for some reason.

'I told you, I didn't know for certain it was a knife he was carrying. And even if I had, what difference would it make? How could we possibly have known they would think it was the same knife used to kill that man?'

'I'd have recognised it as Al's knife. We could have got rid of it and Josh wouldn't have got stabbed.'

'Are you saying all this is my fault?'

'No! No.'

What does he mean, he would have recognised it as Al's knife and got rid of it? He can't think Al killed that man. He was Al's alibi on the night of that murder.

Only they lied, didn't they? They lied about that night. About not seeing Malcolm with Connor Leask. What else did they lie about?

I remember Finlay telling me that he went back up the hill to look for the knife after Josh was stabbed. He said it was because he was afraid Josh would get into trouble but it wasn't that, was it? He was already afraid it was Al's knife. And of what that would mean.

I make an effort to breathe slowly. I stare across the water at Cramond Island. It's only been a couple of weeks since we were there, the four of us. I picture Rob stretched out on the gun emplacement. He was angry. Whatever it was Dad had told him before he died, I think it made him feel the same way I've been feeling. It made him question everything he thought he knew. It made him scared. I wish I'd listened to him. With all my heart and every part of me I wish I'd listened to him. Every nerve and muscle I have is straining at the impossible. If only I could walk across there now and find him stretched out on that gun emplacement, take it from there again ... what wouldn't I give?

I feel Finlay shift by my side. Rob said Dad told him

something about Lawrence. He said the Groats are horrible people.

And I was with them when Rob died.

My phone is vibrating in my pocket. I glance at the screen. It's DS Chisholm. I put the phone to my ear, turning my back on Finlay and taking a few steps away.

DS Chisholm is angry with me. 'I told you to wait for DC Bell.'

'I got another lift. I didn't think it would matter.' I want to tell her that I am now very much afraid that it does.

'Where are you?'

'Just down at the front. You know, the car park by the promenade at the bottom of Silverknowes.' I glance up at Finlay. If he's at all disturbed by the amount of detail I'm giving Chisholm he doesn't show it.

Wind buffets the phone at both ends. I cup the handset and move into the relative shelter of the trees. I begin to walk up the path that runs alongside the wooded area back towards the car park, as slowly and calmly as I can, but my chest has tightened. I glance behind me to where Finlay is still standing by the wall. How did he know that Rob disapproved of us? I don't think Rob told Al. I don't think Al told Finlay.

'Go home and wait there, please.' DS Chisholm is saying. I can hear traffic and people in the background. She sounds as though she's walking too. 'DC Bell and I will come and collect the diaries.'

I stop to look back towards the promenade. I feel suddenly very cold. I don't think it's the sea breeze, though it's whipping the surface of the firth, sketching graphite patterns in the shallow waters where the tide is advancing up the beach. Finlay is standing very still, watching me.

I don't think the diaries are there any more. I left them on the desk when Mel called about Josh and with everything that's happened since then I never went back to them. I assumed it was Malcolm who moved them when he set up his laptop, but Finlay was in the house on Saturday night.

I start walking again, up the path towards the car,

more quickly this time. 'Why did you already check Lawrence's alibi for the night Rob was killed?'

'You know I can't tell you that, Norna. I've warned you about this. You have to leave it to us.'

'I know.' Finlay is now only a few metres away, pounding up the path behind me. 'Sorry.'

'Norna? Are you alright?' DS Chisholm sounds concerned now.

'Yes.' The effort it has taken to climb the path to the car park has left me breathing hard though, and shaking. My head is throbbing.

'Everything okay?' Finlay has reached the top of the path, his face a mask of concern. I stare at him blankly.

'Who's that?' DS Chisholm asks.

'Finlay.' I manage a weak smile. 'Finlay Groat?'

The detective makes a noise that I know is in place of a swear word. A whole series of them, probably. 'Alright. Look, don't say anything to him, okay? Just go home, and ...'

'Yeah, we're just heading home, now.'

I stare at Finlay. A rabbit in headlights. His face is still a mask of concern, but now I think, that's exactly what it is: a mask. Behind it there is no emotion. I see his eyes move over the area around us. There is only one other car in the car park, the owner nowhere to be seen. The promenade is empty. I can't see the road beyond the trees on the brow of the hill.

'Norna?' DS Chisholm is still on the line.

'Yep. See you in a minute.' I cut the call.

Finlay and I stare at each other for what seems like an age.

'So, what does DS Chisholm want you for?' he says, eventually. He'd looked at my screen.

Astro is pounding at the back of my eyes, firing smoke-canons across my already muddled brain.

'I found some diaries of Dad's,' I tell him. 'She's coming to collect them.'

'Why? What's in them?'

He's not worried. He knows the diaries aren't there any more. He just wants to know what I've made of them.

I think about the list of police officers at the back of Dad's diary. And about what Vivienne said about Lawrence's pet polis. I think about that dead man in our garage. The man Dad thought could help. If Lawrence could make that happen...

Finlay knew exactly what he was doing when he took me to his Dad's on Saturday night.

'Oh, Norna,' he says. 'I told you, this isn't a game. You can't muck about with the police.'

The wind rushes in the trees behind me. I have backed myself into a corner. I should have kept pretending.

'You said you weren't like your father,' I say, and my voice sounds far away. I force myself to stay present, but I can feel my mind shutting down, shutting out the reality.

'I'm not like him.' Finlay is very close now. I realise that as he has advanced I have retreated, so that we are standing now at the entrance to the path through the woods.

I think of the contempt, bordering on hatred, with which he spoke of his father when we met in the pub. Then I think of the hatred Josh expressed for Al, and Al before him for our dad, and I realise how much it is simply a facet of feeling unwanted, unloved, unacknowledged. How close it is to a desperate need for approval.

'You were there, that night. You saw Malcolm with Connor Leask. Why has everyone been lying about that? I don't understand. Did you tell your Dad? Is that it? Did Connor Leask have something on your Dad? On mine?'

He looks away for a moment. Impatience – annoyance – something passes across his face.

'Yeah, I told my dad what we'd seen,' Finlay says, a bitter note creeping into his voice. 'Your Malcolm and that poof going at it behind the pub. I thought it was hilarious. I thought Dad would find it funny too. I thought he would be pleased. It gave us something on him. Malcolm was underage. I thought we could use that. We could have ruined him.'

You ruined Malcolm, I think. I can feel the rage building in me. You destroyed him. But I'm too scared to interrupt him. As long as he is talking I have some time.

318

'Why? Why did you need something on him?'

'My Dad was a crook, Norna. You know that, I know that. He thought I didn't back then, but I did. I had one of my school chums to thank for that little nugget of information. Then I started paying more attention. I started looking through the business accounts, and listening in. I heard him and Ralston talking. Then Connor Leask came along, asking questions, poking around. I was ashamed of my dad but I still didn't want to give it all up: the money, the school, the holidays. I couldn't stand the idea that Dad might go to prison and everyone would know about it. I thought if we had something on him, he'd back off.

'But you know what Dad focused on? He focused on the fact I even knew who Connor Leask was. He focused on the fact that I'd come into contact with him at all and I hadn't said. I told him I'd been at Ronny's shop with Al when Leask came in asking questions. What had I told him? he asked me. As if I was the liability.'

Mentally, I try to put together a picture of where I am in relation to the road, the nearest houses. There's the promenade, of course, but I could never outrun Finlay on that. I know that beyond the wooded area behind me there is a stretch of rough scrubland mainly used by dog walkers, that stretches all the way to Cramond. If I can get across there...

'He was furious with me. Called me every bad name he could think of. He kept asking me how often I had seen Leask and where. Did Leask know who I was? Did Alistair know what all his questions were about? What had Leask said exactly? He told me I was stupid. That he should have thrown me out the last time he threatened to, or let me suffer the consequences. A short stay in the cells might have knocked some sense into me, he said. Did I realise what Leask could do to us? He could ruin us. Did I think that was funny? Watching my life go down the tubes?

'Then he hit me.'

Even now, I can see the impact that had on Finlay. It's as though the shutters on his eyes are pulled back and the bitter pain and resentment, the rage that has sat behind them all these years, is revealed.

'As for Al: he was supposed to be my friend, but he told me to shut up. About Malcolm and that poof. He's still my brother, Fin.'

The mockery in his voice, the self-pity and jealousy – before I am aware of what I'm doing, I swing my arm, suddenly. I'm still holding my mobile and I smash it into the side of his head as hard as I can. The impact sends pain shuddering through my arm and into my shoulder and I cry out in agony. I don't have time to waste, though. Finlay has reeled over to one side, his hand flying to his cheekbone, but he is coming back up fast.

'What the fuck, Norna?'

I lash out again, this time bringing the bottom edge of the device down hard on the bridge of his nose.

Then I run.

Finlay Groat? Ellen covered the remaining distance to her car, then tried to get Norna Gilchrist back for a third time. No answer.

What was it Norna had said? she thought, as she got into her car and started up. Lawrence used his contact in the police to keep Finlay out of trouble. That made sense. Young Finlay was a loose canon. A teenage misfit, a trouble-maker.

Was he more than that, though? Could that be why Connor Leask's death was not like the others? Where they had been planned, his was impulsive; where they had been concealed, his was not. Not really. Hidden in plain sight, Dan had suggested. Made to look like a hate crime, a random act of violence. But was that a plan, or damage limitation? There had always been an opportunistic element to Connor Leask's death. A rashness. Hatred, yes, but personal.

Alistair had said that when Connor Leask was in the hardware shop he acted 'as if he knew us'. She had taken 'us' to mean the Gilchrist family. But Connor hadn't just been talking about Ronald Gilchrist's business, he had made insinuations about Groat's too. What if Finlay had been there with Alistair?

Alistair had said 'we' again when he talked about not knowing whether Connor had told anyone about Alistair threatening him.

Could this explain the spontaneity? Could it explain why Connor was left where he was stabbed? It would explain how the blade that was used could have found its way into Alistair Gilchrist's knife.

Finlay could easily have planted it on him.

She called Calder.

'Someone's in,' Dan said as he and Liam drew up outside Finlay Groat's place. There was light in the first floor window of the modern townhouse he had given as his temporary address.

They rang the buzzer and Dan stepped back to look up. He saw Finlay Groat appear in silhouette at the full length window on the first floor and stand for just a beat too long before he raised a hand in acknowledgement and disappeared. A moment later the buzzer went to let them in.

They found him hovering in the open-plan living room. The room was lit only by a small table lamp and the streetlight outside and it was gloomy in the dusk, but Dan could still make out the marks on his face.

And the bag sitting open on the leather recliner.

'Are you going somewhere?'

'I'm moving back in with my wife. Good news.' Finlay attempted a smile. It clearly hurt.

Dan didn't believe him. 'We're looking for Norna Gilchrist.'

Finlay hesitated, and Dan could see him processing his words. Gauging how much of the truth to attempt?

'I gave her a lift home from the hospital earlier, but that was a while ago. She said she was meeting your sergeant. DS Chisholm?'

'Did she do that to you?' Dan got in his face, looking at the gash across the bridge of Finlay's nose and the fresh bruises blooming around his left eye and cheekbone.

Finlay laughed, shook his head. Winced. ''Course not. Have you seen the size of her? I left the bathroom cabinet door open. Turned round too fast. Overexcited about going home, I guess.'

Dan and Liam stared at him.

Finlay's face was suddenly a picture of concern. 'Anyway, Norna's not in a fit state to hurt anyone is she? Is that why you're here? Has something happened? Is it the tumour?'

'I'm sorry?'

'Her brain tumour. Didn't she tell you?'

'Norna Gilchrist has a brain tumour?' Dan was thrown by the change of topic. Sensed that they were being manipulated, pushed off course, but curious all the same.

'Yes. I mean, I know she was worried about telling her family so close to her dad dying. It's horrendous timing. And with Rob now, too. But I'd have thought she would have to tell you. It must have a bearing on any evidence she has to give, doesn't it? And I know it's been affecting her. Both her behaviour and her memory. And when she saw Viv the other night she said it was affecting her vision.'

Dan watched Finlay closely, trying to work out where the truth ended and the lie began. He was quite sure of the dissembling that ran all the way through it. 'How bad is it, do you know?'

'Inoperable, apparently. It's been taking its toll on her, you know, trying to keep it under wraps. It's making her a bit doolally.'

Liam had turned away from Finlay and was slowly doing a circuit of the room. He paused beside a low table and bent over, peering. 'You've got blood on your phone.'

'Oh.' Finlay put his hand to the cut on his face. 'It's not started bleeding again, has it?'

'Who did you call?'

'Just … Someone from work. To tell them I might not be in tomorrow.' He indicated his face. 'Can't really see clients looking like this.'

Dan looked at the gash on the bridge of Groat's nose, at the bag sitting by the door. He felt a sense of unease. It was one of those moments when you had to call it, one way or the other.

'I'd like you to come with us to answer some more questions about the murders of Connor Leask and James Barber.'

'Oh. Alright. When would you like to …'

'Now, I said.'

'Well, but my wife is expecting me.'

'Is she?'

'I'll give her a ring,' Liam said, the picture of solicitation. 'Let her know.'

'Really, there's no need.' Finlay was thrown by the sudden shift in tone and pace. 'Look, I don't see what the urgency is.'

They were both feeling their way, Dan thought. He kept his voice neutral. 'We're investigating two murders, twenty-six years apart and you are one of a handful of people who link the two. If we can eliminate you from our enquiries, that would be an enormous help, but right now, you're being heavily implicated.'

'What?' Groat managed an amused smirk. 'Who's saying that? It's nonsense.'

'Look at it from our point of view. We know you lied about seeing Connor Leask on the night he was killed, and you could easily have had access to the murder weapon.' He watched Groat for a reaction to this, but the man gave nothing away. He had settled on a baffled frown, his mouth held slightly open in disbelief. 'You knew James Barber was reinvestigating Leask's murder. You were at the Gilchrists' house on the day he was killed and you had ample opportunity to enter the garage: as a frequent visitor and friend of the family, no-one would have batted an eyelid.'

'That's ridiculous. Besides, we were all at the funeral when he was killed. I couldn't have …' His words petered out.

'You know his exact time of death, then?' Dan asked him. 'Because we don't.'

'Oh, this is crazy. Is this all Norna?'

'But the urgency, as you say, is that Norna Gilchrist has gone missing, and you are the last person known to have been with her.'

Groat said nothing for a moment but Dan could almost hear the cogs and wheels turning. 'Missing,' Groat said, eventually. 'So you think this is serious. Shit. You think something might have happened to her? Then, of course, what can I do to help?'

'Well, you could tell us the truth about when you last saw her for a start. You say you dropped her home but she hasn't been home. Where exactly did you last see her?'

'I didn't actually say I dropped her home. I said I gave her a lift ...' He blinked under Dan's stare. 'I took her down to the shore to get some air because she was in a state. I didn't want her mother seeing her like that.'

'And, what? You just left her there?'

Groat wriggled uncomfortably. He looked away. Dan took a step closer and peered at the marks on his face again.

'Yes, look, alright, she did this.' Groat waved a hand over his bloodied face. 'She was rambling. Like I said, she was in a right state. I thought the air might do her good, but she just got worse. She got all jumpy; it's like she was having some kind of psychotic break. She was going on about how she had some diaries to give to DS Chisholm, as though it would solve some mystery, and then she started saying that she knew Al and I had seen Malcolm with Connor Leask. I told her that was true; I didn't see any reason to hide it any more if it's all out in the open and everyone knows about Malcolm now, but then she whacked me with her phone and ran off. I called after her but she just kept going. I told you, her head's messed up with the tumour.'

Dan was looking at Groat's hands. They were balled into fists by his sides, the knuckles white but the skin unbroken. Dan couldn't see his nails. 'Why didn't you tell us this earlier?'

'It's embarrassing, isn't it? And like you say, with all this murder stuff going on and Rob committing suicide and Norna making crazy stuff up and lashing out like a lunatic, it's, well it's scary. Plus, I know she didn't mean it. I don't want to get her in trouble. If it was anyone else I'd have pressed charges, believe me, but I know she probably can't help it. Look, I'm worried now. If you say she's gone missing, we need to get out there and look for her. She could be lying unconscious somewhere and it's getting pretty dark.'

This is a man who sells people the dream of a perfect life, Dan thought. The kind of man who could spin a poky old flat into a bijou city-centre studio with period features. He sounded plausible, genuine even, but that meant nothing.

This was a man with a bag packed and no intention of going to work tomorrow.

This was a man Dan wanted to keep where he could see him.

58

This feels like where it all began. Like a dream. If I could wake up from this now, none of it will have happened. I'll be on Clifton Downs, and I've slipped or tripped and fallen. And there's someone coming. Their footsteps beat an alarm …

Only I'm not on the Downs. And this time, it really is my phone I'm worried about. This time my phone is more important than anything, because it contains a recording of Finlay Groat confessing to killing Connor Leask.

Nearly.

Sort of.

Doesn't it?

I struggle to a sitting position. There is still light left in the sky, but not enough for me to make out the features of the figure coming towards me. I almost cry with relief when I hear his voice.

'Oh, no. Oh, love, come on, let me help you up. Is it the head? Have you had another wee spell?'

I almost laugh at that. This is not what you could call a wee spell.

'Something like that,' I say.

The charity shop man helps me to my feet. 'Steady on.' He takes hold of my elbow guiding me across the rough ground. I've lost my bearings. It's not until we reach the road that I realise we are at the Cramond car park. I must have run nearly the whole way across the scrubland before I tripped and blacked out. Perhaps that is the very thing that saved me. Perhaps when I fell, I fell out of sight and Finlay couldn't find me. I look into the darkness behind us and wonder whether he is still there. For a moment I think I glimpse torchlight way off in the distance and I shiver. The charity shop man pulls off his padded jacket and wraps it round my shoulders.

'It's a bit late for tea and cake this time. If you'll allow me, I can rustle up a bowl of soup, though. And maybe a wee nip of something medicinal, eh?'

'No, please, I'm fine. I don't live far from here, actually.' I realise I don't know how long it has been since I ran from Finlay. 'Actually, would it be a terrible imposition to ask you to take me home? I'm supposed to be meeting a police officer there.'

'Were you attacked?' He is shocked.

'No, it's nothing like that.' With a growing sense of disquiet I realise the truth in that. Finlay didn't do anything. He didn't even say anything. It was all in my head.

'It's to do with something else,' I say, but I'm confused now; full of doubt.

He guides me towards a battered old Golf parked rather jauntily at the edge of the car park. This late, I don't suppose it matters how he parks. As he holds the passenger side door open for me I have the sense that something is missing. I feel as though we've left someone behind, but I can't work out who that would be.

He pulls on his seat belt and starts up the car, then leans over and reaches into a compartment under the dash.

'Here.' He proffers a tin of butterscotch. 'A cliché, I know, but it'll keep your blood sugar topped up.' I smile. I am tempted to say something about getting into cars with strange men. Accepting sweeties from strangers. But that would be rude and ungrateful.

'Righto. Where to?'

I give him directions, then sit back. The butterscotch is creamy and sweet. The car is warm and the seat comfortable. As we pull away, though, I realise what it is that is troubling me. A dog, I think. That's what is missing. He should have a dog.

Why else would he have been walking that patch of ground at this time of day?

59

Ellen made her way back to her car and turned off the torch on her mobile. She had covered the woodland between the car park and the waterfront, walked up and down the promenade in both directions shining her light to each side and over the low wall onto the beach. There was no sign of Norna. The one dog-walker Ellen had encountered had seen no-one.

While she had been searching, she had gone over and over the things Norna had told her, matching them against what they already knew or suspected. Had Ronald Gilchrist found out what Lawrence was involved in? Had he been blackmailing him? She would have to check but she thought that the date Norna told her these invoices started appearing would tally with Dean Owens' disappearance. Norna had told her that they stopped exactly when Connor Leask was killed. Had Lawrence made Ronald think one or other of his sons could be framed for the murder? Well, he wasn't bluffing, was he?

If Calder was right about the body of Franjo Horvat being under Gilchrist's back yard, that gave Lawrence even more leverage. With Margery Shanks in charge of his books and reporting everything back to Lawrence Groat, Ronald must have found himself well and truly outmanoeuvred.

It was Lawrence Groat's 'pet polis' that was nagging at her. Lawrence's alibi was never questioned in the Leask enquiry. Lawrence had never been implicated in Ralston's criminal activities, either. Someone must have been protecting him. Advising him at the very least.

She slid into the driver's seat and dialled Calder's number. 'I can't find any sign of Norna Gilchrist, but it's too dark to search the whole area myself. We need a team out here. Has Groat said anything?'

'He's said rather a lot, but where it leaves us I don't

know. He claims he left Norna down by the front, but not by choice. Says she whacked him with her mobile and ran off. He's got bruises on his face but there's nothing to suggest he attacked her. It's possible he's telling the truth. Did she say anything to you about having a brain tumour?'

'No. Is that what he says?'

'Yeah. I'm pretty sure he's making a case for her being an unreliable witness, but it's a funny thing to say if there's no truth in it at all. It would be easy enough to check.'

Ellen thought of the dark circles under Norna's eyes, the weariness and slight confusion, the way she struggled with her words sometimes. She remembered Norna wincing under the hospital lights. Admitting to being on medication.

'I'll ask the family. I'm going there now.'

When she got to the Gilchrists' house Malcolm was pacing the hall. 'You didn't find her?'

She waited until they were in the living room. She could see that Keisha had been busy making tea, trying to keep them calm. 'She wasn't with Finlay and there's no sign of her down at the front. Is there anyone else she might have gone to see and just not thought to let you know? Old school-friends or neighbours?'

Malcolm turned to Linda. She shook her head. 'I don't think she's been in touch with anyone since she came home. Just family. And Finlay.'

'Can I ask, does Norna have any health issues that we should know about?'

'No-o. Why?'

'She hasn't been seeing a doctor lately for anything?'

Linda frowned. 'She said she had an appointment shortly before Ronald passed away. It was why she couldn't make it up to Edinburgh. She didn't tell me what it was for.'

Linda had drawn herself up defensively. Perhaps she had given Norna a hard time for not coming home to see her father on his deathbed. Ellen made her voice gentle.

'Finlay Groat told my colleague that Norna had a brain tumour. Could there be any truth in that?'

'No!' Linda cried, but it was more in horror than denial.

'I'm sorry,' Ellen said. 'I thought you might be able to tell us whether it was true. It seems an odd thing for him to say.'

She could see they were processing the information in the same way she had. Picturing the dark rings under Norna's eyes, suddenly realising how thin she was, how haunted. They had put it down to grief and worry. Now they were reassessing everything they had seen of Norna in the past few weeks.

She could understand why Norna might not have told them. She couldn't understand why she had told Finlay.

'Did Norna mention some diaries to you? She told me she thought they might be useful.' She didn't want to give too much information away.

'Diaries? No.'

'Never mind. The main thing just now is to find her.'

She drew Keisha into the hall.

'Have you had a look upstairs?'

'Yes, but I couldn't see any diaries. I didn't want to poke around too much, though.'

Ellen nodded. Standing there, outside the kitchen, she remembered doing the same when she thought the intruder was still in the house. That could easily have been Finlay, she reasoned. He would certainly have the strength to have pushed her so hard. And the stealth. And he would have known about the knife. Perhaps he had realised that they might find a trace of his DNA. Something he might not have known back in 1993.

How would Barber have known about the knife, though? It was the same question Dan Calder had kept coming back to: why was Barber in the Gilchrists' garage if he never spoke to Ronald Gilchrist? How could he know that there might be a murder weapon concealed there? Unless he already knew what it was that Ronald had to say.

As she left Keisha with the Gilchrists and walked back to her car Ellen felt a profound sense of dismay. Had Calder been right all along to distrust Jimmy Barber? Was he Lawrence Groat's 'pet polis'?

She put the key in the ignition and started up. Even

if she assumed he was guilty, that he did know about the knife and was concerned that Ronald was about to confess all, she still found it hard to believe that the man she had known would have been flailing about as he had. Recklessly breaking into a family's home on the day of a funeral, attempting a search on a day when he couldn't hope for more than a couple of hours' peace? Far better to wait until the funeral was past, when the place was still contaminated with a great many people's trace evidence but when Linda Gilchrist was out or away and he wouldn't be disturbed.

Sneaking around on the day of the funeral was stupid, and whatever he was, Barber had never been stupid.

No. She refused to believe it. He had wanted the investigation reopened. He wanted Connor Leask's killer caught.

Keeping her eye on the road ahead, she reached into the glove compartment for the file Lise Eklund had given her and laid it on the passenger seat, flipping it open. There was only one thing she needed to check. She slowed as she approached the big roundabout at Crewe Toll and glanced down at the page.

It told her everything she needed to know.

As the lights changed she stamped on her accelerator and swerved quickly in front of the car that had been waiting in the next lane to turn right. The driver punched the horn, but Ellen ignored it. She was too busy on her mobile.

'Ellen?'

'Dan, can you check whether Finlay Groat called anyone after he claims he last saw Norna.'

'He did. Liam noticed blood on his phone.'

'Have you got the number?'

'Ye-es.' She could tell he was looking for it. She didn't have time.

'Check it against Glen Starrett's.'

Calder began to speak again, but she didn't stick around to hear it. She knew what he would be saying, anyway. He would be telling her to wait. Not to do anything stupid.

60

I wake in a strange room. In the gloom lit only by the street-light outside I make out striped wallpaper and heavy, dark furniture. I am lying on top of a quilt that smells musty with age and lack of use. My head is throbbing.

I haul myself into a sitting position and everything swims. My stomach lurches but I manage to stem the urge to retch. When everything stills I notice that my coat has been hung over the back of a chair which is tucked into a desk against the far wall. Behind the desk a number of black and white photographs are mounted in serried rows, but it's too dark and too far away for me to make out any detail from here. Very slowly, I turn and slide my legs over the side of the bed. As I haul myself upright my vision dissolves into white noise. I put my hands out and lean on the wall for support, fighting to control the panic, breathing in through my nose and blowing out through circled lips. Gradually my vision returns. I turn slowly, still breathing carefully, and take a few tentative steps.

I lift my jacket rather than bend and risk losing my sight again, or the contents of my stomach. I feel inside my pockets. My phone isn't there.

Shit. Did I lose it when I was running across the scrubland? I try to remember whether I still had it when the charity shop man found me. Maybe it fell out in his car.

I can just about make out the contents of the photographs clustered on the wall now. At first all I see is how similar they are, and how dull. Picture after picture of men standing in groups looking pleased with themselves. My left eye is sticky. Each time I blink it takes longer to open again than the right. Then I register the uniforms. I begin to look more closely. I pick out charity shop man in each one: here shaking someone's hand; here receiving some kind of award. My eye goes to the caption at the bottom of one of the images. Detective Chief Inspector Glen Starrett.

I hear a noise outside, then the sound of a key in a lock. The door opens and he is standing there. He looks different. It isn't that he has changed, it's that something in him has changed.

'You're the pet polis,' I say.

He comes in and shuts the door behind him. 'Have a seat, love.'

I don't want to sit. 'You're Lawrence's inside man. You made it all go away, every time Finlay got into trouble. What else did you cover up for Lawrence? What did you do for him? Did you kill Connor Leask to stop him ruining Lawrence?'

He's shaking his head. 'I didn't kill Leask.'

My dad was onto you. He knew what Lawrence was up to.'

He sighs. 'I don't think your Dad knew about me, no. He wasn't as clever as he thought he was. He did not bad out of Lawrence for a couple of years, but he didn't really know what he was dealing with. They were friends; he might even have convinced himself he was just giving his old pal the benefit of the doubt. He wasn't a match for Lawrence. Not really. I'm a rank amateur when it comes to Lawrence. He's always known how to find out what matters to people. What they're willing to protect. He's always known how to get people to do exactly what he wanted.'

He is distracted momentarily by the sound of a car on the street outside. Relaxes when it has passed.

'My dad did know about you,' I say. 'He wrote your name in one of his diaries.'

He looks at me steadily and though he is not the same as before I can see something of the way he looked at me in the café after I trashed the charity shop. I think there is a tiny glimmer of empathy there. And I am still alive after all.

'Is that why you were at the charity shop? Were you following me?'

'You'd been asking questions. Got Margery quite flustered apparently.'

'If I hadn't told you about my tumour, would you have

killed me then? Were you just hoping to keep me quiet until I died of natural causes?'

'I never wanted to hurt anyone.'

'But you did, didn't you? You killed my brother. You killed Rob.'

'He knew too much. Your dad should have kept his mouth shut.'

I let out a cry.

'He told Robert all about Lawrence. Your dad saw him do something bad once, you see. He saw him putting a boy's body in the ground. Lawrence persuaded him it had been an accident. A one-off. It wasn't of course, either of those things, but your dad was encouraged to believe that.'

'Lawrence paid him to keep quiet.' I am crying now. Bitterly. Wretchedly. He fishes out a hanky and tucks it into my hand.

'That implicated him, too, of course. Once you start these things, it's nigh on impossible to get out of it. But he had you four to think of and money was tight.'

He is distracted by the sound of a car again. Is he just nervous, or is he waiting for someone? For Lawrence?

'Lawrence told Dad about Malcolm, didn't he?'

He looks surprised. 'Yes. He told Ronald that he'd been seen with Leask and that Leask had been killed with a Stanley knife. Didn't need to say more. Your dad knew what he was implying. Lawrence told him, "Don't worry, it's gone. They won't find it." We thought that was true, too. That's what that idiot Finlay told us. It was only when Jimmy Barber started sniffing around again that he owned up to what he'd really done with it.'

Finlay.

I feel the blood draining from my face; sparklers crackle at the outer limits of my field of vision. Perhaps I should feel vindicated but my stomach turns to ice. It's not just because I fell for his charms, let him dupe me into providing him and his dad with an alibi while Starrett got rid of Rob; but all those years ago he planted that knife on Al. And all these years in between he's eaten at his table and played with his children and hugged our mother. Why did he do it? Because Al stuck up for Malcolm? Because Al said to him, 'He's still my brother, Fin'?

'Robert phoned Lawrence, did you know? Told him to get Finlay to back off from you or he'd go to the police and tell them everything Ronald had told him.'

I think I'm going to be sick.

Starrett seems distracted again. I didn't hear anything this time, but he walks over to the window and looks out.

'I don't get it,' I say. 'If this is what Lawrence does with people who know too much, how come he didn't just get rid of my dad?'

'Your dad was part of it. His business was, anyway. Even if he didn't know it. And besides, they were old friends.'

He glances out of the window again. He doesn't make a sound but I feel a change in him. He turns suddenly and walks past me, leaving the room and pulling the door shut behind him before I have time to react. I hear the key being turned in the lock.

I go to the window and look out. The street is quiet. At first I can't understand why he should have reacted like that, what made him look in the first place. In the gap between the trees and shrubs that border his property I can see only the houses opposite, hunkered down for the night. There is a car parked on the street, but apart from that all is quiet. Then I hear the sound of the front door opening beneath me and a moment later Starrett appears. He marches down the drive and straight over to the car. He stops beside it and stands expectantly, and sure enough the window is rolled down. It's DS Chisholm. I feel a surge of hope, then a plunging sense of betrayal. Has she been working for him all along? For Lawrence?

Is it all happening all over again?

61

Ellen pulled up outside Starrett's house on Frogstone Drive and thought. She tried to piece together the mixture of instinct, knowledge and reasoning that had brought her here, tried to knit it into something she could explain to Calder and Blackwood. To herself. Even to Starrett. Enough to justify a late night call on an old man. An old man with connections in the force. Who might be able to influence her career, or destroy it. An old man who might be all he claimed to be. But just might not.

Barber would not have had the clout to manipulate the Connor Leask investigation. Starrett, though, he would have been in a position to bend things, skew things, portray it as a lost cause to Baird. He was the only one in a position to handle evidence, to hand out orders and to manipulate Baird into thinking it would do his reputation no good to pursue something that was dead in the water.

The only person who Barber would have allowed to lure him to the Gilchrists' house.

We can only work with what you give us, Eklund had said. Starrett's name was on the fatal accident inquiry.

That reverence Starrett had seemed to have for Baird and the difficult decisions the 'Super' had to make. Bullshit.

But then Starrett was coming down the drive. He crossed the road and walked to her car. He didn't bother to rap on the window. That might have drawn attention. She opened it anyhow.

'Are you coming in?' He spoke pleasantly enough, but there was something about him, she thought. A change in his demeanour. A little less of the old man, a little more of the hard man.

'My apologies, it's very late.'

'Not a problem. It's not as if I have to be up early for

work, is it?'

And you're a bit of a night owl, aren't you, Ellen thought. No wonder he'd looked tired when she went to see him last Sunday. He'd been driving through the night. Caithness and back.

'Well, if you don't mind, I'll be along in a minute. I just have to make a quick call.'

He eyed the mobile in her lap. 'Call from the house. It's warmer. I'll put the kettle on. Be nice to have a chat.'

Ellen felt her nerves tighten. She wasn't very good at these kinds of games. She despised coded messages and having to read between the lines.

'I'll follow you in.'

'You wouldn't be hiding behind your DI, would you? Smart girl like you. I thought you were the type to take the initiative. You went straight to the Connor Leask file, after all, didn't you? While he was still havering about.'

So he did know about that. She knew Starrett was trying to wind her up. The best thing to do was not to rise to the bait. Be more Barber. She held his gaze, smiled.

He sighed, theatrically. 'Pity. It's so hard to have a proper chat, alone, these days. I suppose you'd say it was the need for corroboration.' He looked her directly in the eyes. 'But it makes it very difficult to have a frank discussion, and there is so much we have to talk about. I didn't have a chance to ask you the other day, about why you chose to join up in the first place. What it was that inspired you to join the force.'

Ellen had to fight the urge to react, to keep the fear from showing in her eyes.

'It's a service, isn't it? I don't think we call it a force any more.'

'Think for yourself.'

That hit the mark. Still she sat tight. She was thinking. Hard. She knew she needed to wait. If she went in there now, alone, she could blow everything. She saw a twitch of annoyance in the corner of Starrett's mouth. He hummed, impatiently, looking up and down the street, checking to see whether any of the neighbours was watching them.

Then Ellen caught another movement out of the corner of her eye.

In the upstairs window of Starrett's house she saw Norna Gilchrist.

Starrett bent to lean into the car, but whatever he was about to say she cut short. 'Alright. I fancy a ginger snap.' She opened the door, catching Starrett off guard. He had to step back quickly to get out of the way and stumbled slightly. Perhaps the aged and infirm act was not complete fabrication after all.

Norna Gilchrist had backed away from the window as soon as they had moved.

'Get that kettle on,' Ellen said. 'If you don't mind, I'll just make that call.'

She lifted her mobile but Starrett's hand shot out before she could dial. The grip on her wrist was so sudden, so tight that she gasped. She felt the joint click. His thumb and middle finger dug into the soft flesh between the bones, while his forefinger slid up the side of her hand. If he pushed just a little bit harder he would break her wrist. He reached up with his other hand and took her mobile from her.

Starrett wasn't pretending any more. 'Who knows you're here?'

'No-one.'

He slipped the phone into his pocket. 'I'll put that kettle on, then.'

Ellen walked ahead of him into the house, her mind racing. She heard the snib click on the front door behind them, but noted that he didn't lock it. She paused in the hall, glancing up the stairs quickly, estimating the layout and the location of the room in which she had seen Norna Gilchrist.

'In here.' Starrett motioned her through to the room in which they had sat looking at pictures of prefabs and maps of old Edinburgh. It seemed like a long time ago. She realised now how much of that had been a diversion. The way he had turned her attention to the prefabs and directed it away from the properties Groat already maintained on the site, his suggestion that the body might have been some kid who'd been mucking about in the old mine shafts and tunnels. He'd known Dean Owens was a teenager. Everything he had told them from the start was a carefully constructed version of the truth. He was too clever to lie outright, but the subtle emphasis he had placed on certain things was enough to skew their thinking. It was he who had made them think Barber was obsessed with the Gilchrists. It was he who had made Calder doubt Barber.

'You told us Jimmy Barber was compromised once, forced into turning a blind eye to something, dropping charges. It was you who put him in that position, wasn't it?'

He cocked an eyebrow at her, mock impressed. 'We gave him money. He didn't ask for it or accept it of course, but it was enough that it might look like he did. A bribe and a promise and something went away. He seemed to be pursuing something and then he wasn't. There was a disciplinary, it was put to bed, but a doubt lingered.'

'Yeah, I'll bet you made sure it did.'

'It's all about information management.'

'It was you who controlled access to the CCTV footage, too, wasn't it?'

'Bit of a juggling act, that. It was handy having an extra bit of leverage, but I couldn't risk it being too obvious that Connor knew Malcolm already, that he'd been sniffing round the businesses.'

'Jimmy thought it could still all come back on him. You'd have used his sexuality against him as a way of suggesting the case had been mishandled, wouldn't you?'

'I never should have had to do that, if he'd just left well alone. Back then it was just a matter of time before Baird would drop it. He was always so numbers focused. It was better for all of us that Barber never found out I had anything to do with it.'

'He did though, didn't he?'

Starrett shook his head. 'Only at the very last moment.'

Ellen swallowed. Her feet were pressing into the ground, her hands spread like starfish. There was only one reason Starrett was telling her all this. He thought it didn't matter.

62

The window is one of those ones where you have to press down a button before you can turn the handle. It's locked. I feel along the sill and the top of the frame for the little metal key but, of course, Starrett hasn't been stupid enough to leave it here. I look around the room for something I can use in its place. Inside one of the drawers in the desk I find a stapler and a pair of scissors. My hope is short-lived. The scissors are too thick to fit the metal slot in the button and the staples are too small and fiddly. I waste a moment wishing I was the kind of girl who carried a nail file, then another contemplating whether or not I could pick the lock using the rod in my nose piercing – gross, and unlikely – before my eyes fall on the photographs again. I take one off the wall and turn it over. The backing is held in place by metal clips about half a centimetre wide. They might do. There is the hook the picture was hanging on too, one of those brass ones fixed to the wall by two thin nails. I use the scissors to lever both the hook off the wall and a couple of the metal clips out of the picture frame. Then I set to work on the window lock.

It takes a little time to get a feel for the different indentations in the mechanism, and longer to find the combination of clip and nail that works but eventually I feel a tiny click and I'm able to twist the button to the right. I've done it. I feel exceptionally pleased with myself. Then I remember where I am. I hear Finlay's voice in my head – To you it might be a fiction; to us it's very real – and my resolve hardens. I'm going to see that bastard gets what's coming to him.

I turn the handle one hundred and eighty degrees so I can open the window fully, and lean out. To the right the roof of the porch offers me a kind of staging post. From there I think I will be able to dangle and then drop down. It might hurt, but nothing should break.

I reverse out of the window, clinging onto the frame until I feel the porch roof under my feet, then I slowly transfer my weight to it. I tiptoe across it and look over the other side in the hope of finding a trellis, something I can climb down, but no luck. I'll have to do this the hard way. I lie down on my belly and shuffle slowly backwards until I'm bent in the middle and my legs are dangling over the side. It is at least grass beneath me. I shuffle further backwards, bracing my knees against the wall to lever myself further over the edge. I steal myself not to yelp when I land and, here goes ...

Pain shoots through my ankles and up through my shins into my knees and hips. I lie on the ground panting heavily until my vision clears again and I can begin to move my joints. No real damage done, thank God.

I haul myself up, all my instincts telling me to run. Run. But I don't. I think about the woman who listened to me at the hospital. I know people can appear one thing and be another. I think about Dad and his secrets. Finlay, who has been my brother's best friend for ever, a pretend uncle to my nephews and niece, who stabbed a man to death and would happily let Al take the blame. The charity shop man, who comforted me and locked me in a room and killed a man and left his body in my Mum's garage. Who killed Rob.

I know Starrett has been protecting Lawrence all these years. I know there are bent coppers.

But I trust DS Chisholm.

I trust DS Chisholm, and if she is in there with Glen Starrett, then she's in trouble too.

I work my way round the house to the back. Beyond the rectangle of light from the kitchen window it is almost completely dark here. At one point I trip over something and land softly on what feels like a rug or a mat. Where the light hits it I see that it's a large quantity of that black fabric you put down as a barrier to weeds. I think nothing of it at first. Then a terrible thought strikes me. Is that for me? Still I can't quite believe it. Not because I don't think this man is dangerous, but because I think he's cleverer than that. I think his intention was to make my death look like the result of my tumour and the effect it has had on me. I wonder why he didn't take advantage of the fact I had fallen, and just bash me on the head with a bit of fallen branch and leave me for dead on that patch of ground. Maybe Finlay told him about the appointment I had with DS Chisholm. Did he need to know what I'd told her?

I move into the shadows well beyond the light cast from the window and look back towards the house. I see them now. Beyond the kitchen, through a glass-panelled door. It's a dining room, I think. Starrett has his back to me and they are talking, but it's like a stand-off. There's a tension between them. Chisholm is playing for time, just as I did with Finlay.

Although Starrett is facing away from me, I check the framed picture on the wall, and the glass cabinet. Will he see my reflection if I get closer to the window? There is wind in the trees; it ruffles the clematis near the back door. He will certainly hear it, feel it, if I open the door. I peer around me for a weapon of some kind, but the bit of the garden I can make out is obsessively neat and tidy, all tools locked away carefully. Inside the kitchen, though, I can see a knife block sitting on the counter. It is nearer me than him but I will have to act fast.

Then I see something else. Something DS Chisholm must not have seen. Tucked into the back of Starrett's jeans there is a gun.

63

If she could lull Starrett into a false sense of security, Ellen thought, make him sloppy, she might be able to overpower him. But he was showing off, and that annoyed her.

'I think Jimmy knew about you long before the end. He didn't keep any evidence at the house. No notes, nothing. Because you were a regular visitor.'

Starrett wasn't looking impressed any more, mock or otherwise.

'Jimmy worked out the link, didn't he? He'd worked out your connection to Groat. And Ralston.'

His eyes flickered. It was a lucky strike.

'Because it all stems from there, doesn't it? How far back does it go? Did you make a deal back in 1988? He helped you put Billy Gaughan away and you looked after him when he took Billy's place?'

He looked at her steadily. 'I'll give Barber his due,' he said. 'He took it on the chin, his earlier blunder. Learnt from his mistake. I don't think he even tried to find out who set him up.

'One bad thing, that's all it takes. To make you careful. To make you vulnerable. You'll understand that.'

Ellen felt the electric sting of fear. The impulse that ran through her limbs. She wanted to believe that Starrett was still talking about Barber. At worst, that he was implying that they – she – had made mistakes during this investigation. He knew that she'd gone into the Gilchrists' house alone. And she was here alone, wasn't she? But that wasn't what he meant. Rash or regrettable as these things were, they weren't bad. They might make a successful prosecution more difficult, make them jump through a few more hoops, but he wasn't talking about any of that. He was talking about why she'd joined up.

'One. Bad. Thing. That's all it takes.'

At least if he thought he could intimidate and coerce her, killing her was not his top priority. He wanted to come to some kind of arrangement.

'I don't know what got into Jimmy at the end,' he went on. 'He could have been sensible about it. That's the difference between us, I suppose. After the job, after he lost Richie, he didn't care about his reputation any more. Me, I still do. But I told him I was tired. Made out I felt the same as him. "Let's not go down without a fight, though," I said. "Let's take the bastards down with us." And he fell for it. I told him I knew where we would find the knife.'

He shrugged. 'So, what do you care enough about, Ellen?'

She would call his bluff. He wasn't going to get her, the way he got Barber.

'I take it Connor Leask had worked it all out?'

He tutted with annoyance. 'We could have dealt with Connor Leask. It would have been easy to make him think Baird and Kinley were behind it all, make a fool of himself, and in the process his career would go up in smoke. It wouldn't take much to discredit him completely. We didn't need to get rid of him. Murder is a last resort. An act of desperation. You know that. Lawrence knows that. There's usually a better solution than murder. The people who paid Ralston and Groat to make their problems disappear didn't realise that. That was the beauty of it. Once you know someone's that desperate, you've got them.'

'So what happened? If you weren't scared of Connor Leask, if you weren't desperate to get rid of him?' Then she knew. 'Finlay. Finlay happened, didn't he?'

Starrett scowled. 'Finlay's a useless piece of shit. He thinks he's so much smarter than his Dad. Thinks he's progression, evolution. He doesn't know the half of it. He was a liability then, and he's a liability now.

'We made the best of a bad lot, though. It gave Lawrence the opportunity he'd been waiting for to turn the tables on Gilchrist. It was easy to threaten his sons. They implicated themselves. And Gilchrist played right into Lawrence's hands. Of course, he never believed either of them was guilty, but he packed one of them off down south with a load of money he couldn't account for, that wasn't too clever.'

'And let's not forget the body in the back yard of his shop.'

'Well, well. You are clever, aren't you.'

When he looked at her then, there was no sign of the old man she'd spent time with just a few days before. Instinctively, she looked away. And as she did so she caught a movement outside the window, a pale face and a lick of red hair.

'That was Calder, actually,' she said, turning back to him quickly. 'And Connor Leask. Between them they worked that out. Barber, too.'

A look of doubt crossed Starrett's face.

'And of course, Finlay's DNA will be all over that knife.'

Starrett's expression had hardened again. 'Let's stop fannying about, shall we,' he said, taking a step towards her. 'Are you going to be sensible about this?'

Ellen took a breath. 'Probably not.'

Before he could answer, Starrett was distracted by a noise upstairs. The slight rattle of a door in its frame. His eyes darted upwards, then back to Ellen.

'Yes, I know Norna's here,' she said. 'I saw her at the window.'

She watched as Starrett processed that. It gave her a moment's satisfaction to think he might realise it was that which had made her change her mind about coming inside with him, not the power of his persuasion.

'I don't think that was her, though,' she said. 'It sounded more like the wind to me.'

Starrett frowned. Then he understood what she meant. He started towards the door and in an instant Ellen's arm shot out and grabbed a large silver candlestick from the mantelpiece. Before she could raise it to strike at him, Starrett was pointing a gun at her.

She froze for a second. Then they both snapped round as a gust of wind blew the back door back on its hinges and Norna Gilchrist rushed on Starrett, a knife held high in her hands. The gun went off, Ellen swung the candlestick and both Norna and Starrett dropped to the floor.

64

They stood at the edge of the site, watching as the claw of the digger made first contact with the ground, teasing up the cobbles and the grit beneath, leaving long striations in the sandy earth, like monstrous teeth marks.

The DNA results from the knife had confirmed their suspicions, but it hadn't taken much to make Finlay spill his guts. He wanted to cut a deal. Which was lucky, because his father was so far saying nothing and Glen Starrett had clammed up tight.

'I was mad,' Finlay had told them when he recounted his father's reaction to hearing that Connor Leask had been asking questions, prying into the business. 'On some level I knew it wasn't really me he was angry with, but he was blaming me. It wasn't fair. It wasn't my fault. I took his car. It was partly to piss him off. I was ready to wreck it, too, though. I think I even considered just putting my foot down on that stretch of road past Lauriston Castle, straight into the wall at the bottom. Bang!

'But why should I pay? I realised I was looking out for Leask as I drove. I started looking deliberately, driving round the streets. I couldn't believe my luck when I saw him. He was walking up the road all by himself. I parked up round the corner. I had this knife on me. I got that idea from Al, of course. I always wanted to be like Al.'

'All because he wanted to impress Daddy,' Ellen had said when they emerged from the interview room after three hours.

'It was more personal than that. It sounds like he wanted to punish Leask too, for getting him into trouble. Making him look stupid. And of course he was angry that Alistair didn't want to make anything of what they'd seen. I think he took that out on Connor too.'

'How much do you think Ronald Gilchrist really

knew?' Ellen asked now, looking at the hole gouged in the courtyard at the back of the bistro. 'He saw Lawrence Groat disposing of Dean Owens' body, but did he know Franjo Horvat was here? Did he know it was Finlay who killed Connor Leask?'

Dan shrugged. 'He knew he was implicated in Owens' murder. He was the man sub-contracted to do the patio where Owens' body was dumped.'

They had found Ronald's diaries in the side pocket of Finlay's bag. Putting together the information from there, with the record of the landslip and the location where Owens' body had been found, it was reasonable to assume that the last job he had recorded before the invoice payments began – Ferniehill Terrace, patio slabs – related to the disposal of Owens' body.

'If he got wind of the questions Connor Leask was asking about Franjo Horvat I'm guessing he might have worked out that Lawrence had done the same again, here. The man was caught in a trap. From what Norna said Starrett told her, I think it's likely we'll find that his business was part of the money laundering, if not the drugs supply chain, too. It was all so tightly intertwined it meant that if Ronald ever said anything, he and one or other of his boys would go down, with or without Groat.'

'Starrett said that Lawrence Groat always knew how to manipulate people,' Ellen said.

The post mortem on Robert Gilchrist's body had revealed bruising around his mouth where he had been subdued prior to his death being staged to look like suicide. They were still working on connecting Starrett to the murder – Keisha and Liam were ploughing their way through car hire firms and traffic cameras as they spoke – but it was only a matter of time.

'All those searches Ronald made into different forensic science techniques, though. He must have kept hoping to clear their names somehow.'

'Not that he was completely blameless,' Dan said. Ronald had had a choice, he thought. He could have gone to the police as soon as he saw Lawrence Groat dumping Dean

Owens' body but he didn't. He accepted money to keep quiet. Starrett, too, had had a choice. Dan thought about the photograph of Glen Starrett's wife on the dresser in the kitchen. It wasn't just about protecting her, he thought. It was about apple green walls and a nice garden and a reputation that was passed down through generations of new recruits.

But then, what did he know? What did he have that someone like Lawrence Groat could use against him? What did he care about so much that he would do anything to protect? Was it better to have something you would put everything on the line for than nothing at all? Nothing more than a collection of pebbles.

He looked at Ellen. What did she have? She had given a full account of what happened at Starrett's house, but he still didn't understand.

'What was Starrett hoping to do?'

'Norna thought his original plan was to try and keep her quiet until she was too ill to be lucid. If it became necessary he could dump her somewhere and make out she'd wandered off, confused, and got into difficulty. Finlay would have backed him up.'

'But he can't possibly have thought he would get away with that, not after you turned up.'

Ellen stared fixedly at the digger. 'No, but I don't think he really wanted to kill either of us. Until Barber, he hadn't killed anyone. He just covered up for Norris Ralston and Lawrence Groat.'

Dan watched her as she spoke. He hadn't liked Glen Starrett the first time they met. He hadn't liked the impression Starrett gave that he knew things about people. What did he know about Ellen Chisholm?

She's worked hard to sort herself out. Barber's words came back to him, not for the first time since he had spoken them to Dan the night before he was killed. There had been warmth in his voice, but he hadn't needed to say it. There was a message in there, too. When he got back to the office, Dan thought, he would look out Ellen Chisholm's file.

Then he thought he might call Farhana McLean.

In the meantime, he said, 'I'm sorry I questioned Barber's integrity. You were right to trust him. You never wavered.'

Though he still couldn't see what he could have done differently, he was sorry he hadn't been able to save Barber, too. Perhaps if he hadn't dismissed him so roundly? If he had allowed Barber to hope, at least, offered him an alternative that made him less susceptible to Glen Starrett's lies, prevented him from being lured to the Gilchrists' house on the pretext of uncovering the truth.

'I wish I'd kept in better touch with him,' Ellen said.

They stood for a while, watching the digger at work.

'I wonder how many people went to Ralston with problems they wanted fixed,' Ellen said.

Dan shuddered. 'That's for someone else to find out. I really don't want to know.'

They turned away from the digger and began to walk slowly up the lane at the side of Ronald Gilchrist's old shop.

'They're going to have to rebrand,' Ellen said, nodding towards the bistro with its plants in old tins of masonry paint and the shelves made of scaffolding planks.

Dan barked out a laugh. 'How's Norna doing?'

Ellen had moved fast after Starrett's gun went off. She cuffed him to the radiator then pulled a cushion pad from the nearest chair and pushed it into Norna's side to staunch the bleeding, wrapping the woman's arm over it. 'Hug that into you, tight.' She retrieved her phone from where Starrett had pocketed it earlier, and called for help. Then she rang Calder.

'I'm already on my way,' he had said. 'Did you think I wouldn't work out what bloody stupid thing you were about to do?'

'Her brothers are trying to persuade her to have the surgery,' Ellen said now. 'She says she's terrified of ending up a vegetable. It was bad enough, the idea of wasting away. She says she'd rather go out with a bang. But she wasn't ready to go when Starrett shot her.'

By the time Calder arrived Norna had been as white as a ghost, her eyelids flickering. The cushion pad was already saturated with blood. 'Stay with me, Norna,' Ellen had been saying. 'Come on. Those brothers of yours need you.'

Norna's face had creased with pain. 'This isn't how I imagined going.'

'You're not going anywhere.' Ellen had looked Norna hard in the eyes. 'You wouldn't give that git, Finlay, the last word would you? He's telling everyone that tumour has made you crazy.'

'How did he ...?'

'You didn't tell him?'

Norna shook her head, weakly. She turned to where Starrett was slumped against the radiator. 'I told him.'

Ellen had looked at Dan, then back at Norna. 'We're going to need some help from you on this. You're going to have to stick around long enough to make a statement at least.'

'What would you do?' Dan asked.

Ellen shook her head. 'God forbid either of us ever has to face that decision.'

65

If I thought that I was nothing more than an NPC in this game, at least I can say that isn't true any more. For a short while at least, I played a part. I made a difference.

Al and Malcolm came to the hospital together to see me. There's still an awkwardness between them, but that static charge of antipathy has gone. And it isn't just because Al wasn't wearing that God-awful jacket.

Separately, they each confide in me. Al is afraid of facing Finlay in court because he says he is so angry he wants to kill him and he thinks everyone will be able to see that. He tells me he has nightmares in which Finlay, with all his charm and his clever words, makes everyone believe it was Al who did it, that he is led away in handcuffs and the last thing he sees is Finlay with his arm around Josh. He is seeing someone about the anger so he doesn't make the nightmare come true.

Malcolm doesn't even know now whether Connor ever genuinely liked him or whether he was just using him. Trying to get to the truth about where Franjo Horvat's body was buried, and how closely Dad was involved with the things Lawrence was doing. He needs to see a counsellor, too, but it's going to take time before he's even ready for that.

I miss Rob. It's a pain that isn't ever going to go away. The tumour doesn't even come close.

I close my eyes and breathe deep. The wooziness is not unpleasant. If I give into it I don't feel sick, just drowsy. Dreamy. The light plays on my eyelids, and the voices of the people around me gradually fade into the distance. I feel a warmth spread through me.

I turn my face up towards the sun. I listen for the sound of the waves breaking on the shore. I feel for the sand under my toes.

When I open my eyes again everything is silver-white and blue and golden. It is just as I remember it. And more. There are so many things I had forgotten. Look – the paw prints of a dog impressed in the concrete of the slipway. How I delighted in those. And the tiny pink shells that I called mermaids' fingernails. The mountains beyond Gairloch are sharp against the sky and I can see clearly across the bay to Port Henderson. Skye stretches away to the south west, and where the River Sand meets the shore, sea lettuce paints the rocks an emerald green.

I am running now, along the waterline, my feet kicking up light from the incoming waves.

Now I struggle up the dunes, using the footprints left by my brothers for leverage, with each step advancing and sliding back, advancing and sliding back.

There is grass under my feet. Now heather clawing at my shins. I am far above the water. Beneath me the cliffs drop away into a Prussian blue sea, laced with white. Fulmars wheel above the rocks.

And I can fly too.

I fly and I fall.

And where I meet the water, my brothers are waiting. Laughing and splashing, shouting and free. I am thrown into the air above the waves and caught. Again! Rob rides high on Malcolm's shoulders, until Al dives and takes Malcolm's legs from under him and they topple and plunge, all three of them emerging moments later, hollering and joyful.

Waves pluck at the rocks, push and tease at the shoreline.

Perhaps there is a man dangling a dog lead, strolling. The dog begins to bark at something in the distance.

Perhaps not.

Perhaps there are only fish.

Perhaps none of this is real at all.

66

Ellen thought about what Glen Starrett had said to her. It only takes one bad thing. To make you vulnerable. He was bluffing, she thought. But he knew enough. He was not the first and he would not be the last to suspect worse.

She knew when she applied to join the police that she could never hide what had happened, so she made it the reason for applying – which it was, she supposed. She spoke about how impressed she had been with the officers and the way they had handled the situation, the way they had dealt with her and Donna. She said it made her want to do what they did. To make a difference when something awful like that happened to someone. To be the person who knew what to do and could take control and be part of making it better. Making it right.

She never knew how seriously she was being treated as a witness, let alone a suspect, but the feeling of being under suspicion never quite went away. The mixture of anger and defiance and self-justification.

The impulse to strike first.

The guilt.

Though she knew she hadn't done it. She hadn't killed Donna's dad. She knew that because when they found his body his trousers were done up.

Still, she had always had the feeling that one day it was going to come back to bite her. And it would.

Just not today.

ACKNOWLEDGEMENT

The hardest part of writing a first book alongside a busy day job and the rest of life is keeping going. Having good friends who support the effort is enormously important. Thank you Jen and Helen for this.

The experience offered by the Arvon Foundation, which allows novices for a week at a time to prioritise writing and receive expert feedback and tuition, is hugely valuable and rewarding and I'd like to thank everyone at Lumb Bank, Mark Peterson and Claire McGowan for a brilliant week which really set me off on this path.

Mark Stanton at the The North Literary Agency, thank you for everything you've done. Not only the practical hard graft, your time, experience and notes, but the boost to feeling the whole thing was worthwhile.

Most of all, though, my thanks go to a very patient man without whose encouragement, love and support, I'd never have reached the end. Thank you, John.

ABOUT THE AUTHOR

Jude Forrest

Jude Forrest has worked as a museum curator, a media producer and lecturer. This is her first novel.

BOOKS IN THIS SERIES

Calder and Chisholm

Ghost Of A Chance

Coming Soon: Last Place Left To Look

BOOKS BY THIS AUTHOR

Ghost Of A Chance

How much are you willing to risk in order to uncover the truth?

When detective Sergeant Ellen Chisholm's former boss contacts her asking for help with an old case, she turns him down – she doesn't work cold cases. And apart from the fact that one of the key suspects from the time had recently tried to contact him, Barber doesn't seem to have much to go on.

But when Ellen and Detective Inspector Dan Calder are called out to a murder scene a couple of weeks later it begins to look as though Barber had stirred up more than any of them realised.

Returning to Edinburgh for her father's funeral, Norna Gilchrist has a devastating secret of her own. When a man is found dead in the garage of her parents' house she becomes convinced that her brothers know more than they are telling her.

The question she, Chisholm and Calder all want answered: is this death connected to the one twenty-six years previously? And if so, how?

As the investigation progresses each finds their trust and loyalty tested and for at least one of them there is more at stake than catching a killer.

Coming Soon: Last Place Left To Look

Some motives are years in the making.

With the birth of his first child imminent Adam has arrived on Skye in search of his biological father, Michael. But is he simply looking for answers, or does he have a darker motive?

In a bright suburban kitchen in Edinburgh, socially awkward Jason finds his mother, Maggie, bludgeoned to death. He tells DS Ellen Chisholm and DI Dan Calder that it had been him and her against the world. But they soon find that his mother had kept secrets from him.

Calder has learnt something about Chisholm's past, too, though not from her. He can't decide whether it matters. But when an old friend calls

Chisholm out of the blue it feels to her as though the past is creeping uncomfortably close.

As the trail leads Calder to Skye Chisholm becomes convinced that there is not one killer … but two.

GHOST OF A CHANCE

Printed in Great Britain
by Amazon